"Carrie Patel has conceived of a dark steampunk-esque yet futuristic world filled with anachronisms that, despite that, work well together. It's as if this world has been cobbled together from past cultures and times, which is not as unusual as it may sound, to make for an underground claustrophobic world that you can almost feel pressing down on your head and soul. And there's a library to die for – what bookaholic could resist? I know I couldn't and I hope you won't either."

Popcorn Reads

"Patel's voice is her own. I was impressed. [Her] debut novel is definitely worth reading."

Bookish

"While the story begins as a routine mystery, it quickly develops into something else entirely, and the tone drops more and more often into a darker mood...I think the worldbuilding was my favourite aspect of the book. The story sets up a promising storyline and an interesting world, and I'll be curious to see how the things develop in the city of Recoletta."

Bookaneer

"One of the best mystery novels I have ever read."

Avid Fantasy Reviews

"This is one of the fastest paced books I've read in a long time. Patel wastes no time with excessive description or extraneous scenes, but still manages to convey a full sense of the world and its underlying implications. The stakes are always clear, transitioning effortlessly from scene to scene, and I found the story impossible to put down. Fans of fast-paced narratives should definitely give this one a look. The ending is perfectly set up, but only in retrospect: I didn't see it coming, and the world is left completely upturned. In short, *The Buried Life* is a fantastic start to Carrie Patel's new series, and this one is going straight onto my 'Buy Sequel Immediately Upon Release' list."

Fantasy Book Critic

BY THE SAME AUTHOR

The Buried Life

CARRIE PATEL

Cities and Thrones

ANGRY ROBOT
An imprint of Watkins Media

Lace Market House,
54-56 High Pavement,
Nottingham,
NG1 1HW
UK

angryrobotbooks.com
twitter.com/angryrobotbooks
Deeper and down

An Angry Robot paperback original 2015
1

A catalogue record for this book is available
from the British Library.

ISBN 978 0 85766 552 2
EBook ISBN 978 0 85766 554 6

Set in Meridien by Epub Services.
Printed by 4edge Ltd.

For Richard and Lackie Lytle.
For Pravinchandra and Sonal Patel.

PROLOGUE

Jane Lin and Fredrick Anders had been on the run for two weeks when they reached Meyerston. They fled not only the revolt in Recoletta, but also the news that would surely follow it. It was a vague and amorphous thing, but Jane had seen well enough how it sowed panic, suspicion, and violence in its wake. She was not certain what form it would take in the communes, but she knew they would do well to stay ahead of it.

As difficult as it was to gauge the progress of an invisible and impersonal antagonist, in their journey between the communes, they'd encountered nothing more than courteous – if deliberate – remoteness. Footpaths and farmers guided them from one commune to the next, where they were received and dispatched with polite disinterest.

Until they reached Meyerston.

By then, Jane and Fredrick were over a hundred miles away from Recoletta, the only city they'd ever known. Untethered from this single fixed point, it felt as if they were floating through an alien and featureless landscape. They could have passed the same stretches of field and forest between the farming communes a dozen times and never known it. Counting the days had become a practice and a chore.

It hadn't started out that way. Reaching Shepherd's Hollow, the first commune they'd come across some two weeks ago, it had felt as if they'd emerged from the fire to gasp their first lungful of fresh air. They had been too focused on survival – on healing Fredrick's bullet wound and on knowing that they'd escaped Sato for the time being – to truly appreciate where they'd found themselves. Surrounded as they were by the glare of sunlight, the smell of evergreens, and the raw cold of winter, they only experienced these things on the periphery. Their focus was too narrow to encompass them.

But two weeks later, they had noticed this and more. Jane had grabbed a few changes of clothes for each of them before she'd left her apartment, but even all of them layered together was little match for winter aboveground. Their cotton shirts and trousers, and Jane's long skirts, had been made for the steadier subterranean temperatures. Here, the wind bit through the seams and the chill took hold of their bones.

The biggest shock, however, wasn't the brutality of the elements, nor was it the capricious and unpredictable motion of the surface world, stirred as it was by sudden breezes and unseen animals. It was the farming communes. Strange, small settlements that survived aboveground. That had, if legend was to be believed, existed in that way almost as long as Recoletta and the other underground cities had been inhabited.

Shepherd's Hollow, the first, had been a place of rest and recovery. A couple of the commune's trappers had found Jane and Fredrick on the outskirts of Recoletta and taken them in. Fredrick's bullet wound had been healed, and they had taken a week to recover and prepare for the journey ahead.

At the end of the week, once they were looking hearty enough to travel, their hosts had started to get nervous. Wondering, no doubt, why their guests had fled the city in such a hurry and whether the cause would find its way to their doorstep. Jane couldn't hold it against them. Goodwill only went so far.

Their scouts had guided them to their next destination, traveling north, they said, though neither Fredrick nor Jane would have known one way or the other. They avoided the railway where trains shuttled between the communes and the cities, and stuck to bridle paths through the woods. They were headed for a place called Logan's Valley, another commune on the way to Madina, the next city. It seemed to have been understood without saying that Jane and Fredrick were unable to stay in the communes. Jane had not had the luxury of selecting a destination when they'd first set out, but Madina seemed reasonable enough.

In Logan's Valley, their hosts, expressionless men and women who were said to oversee activity in the commune, had looked at them once and decided almost as quickly to send them further north at the earliest opportunity. That opportunity came, conveniently enough, the next morning, when a suspiciously underequipped hunting party gathered to venture into the woods.

It was easy to feel the welcome wearing thin, to sense the aftershocks of Sato's revolution in the shifting climate.

Still, the guides from Logan's Valley put on a polite enough fiction. The hunters didn't ask why the travelers were on the run, and neither Jane nor Fredrick asked why the hunters never ventured from the footpaths to follow the animal tracks that peppered the snow. Anyway, the hunters were gracious enough to provide the duo with rough spun but warm wool coats and trousers. Whether it was out of genuine kindness or out of a calculation that the unwelcome but mysterious visitors should not die on their watch, it didn't much matter. Jane was grateful. Even Fredrick, normally full of brotherly peevishness, seemed content.

But things were different when they reached Meyerston.

Their previous guides had needed to seek out the local authorities upon arriving in Shepherd's Hollow and Logan's Valley. Those men and women had been embroiled in the day-to-day tasks of operating acres of farmland, whatever that involved. Not so in Meyerston.

Upon their arrival, Jane and Fredrick found someone waiting at the edge of town. His arms were crossed and his expression grim behind his thick beard and hood. Jane realized that news of their journey, and of the revolt in Recoletta that had prompted it, must have finally outpaced them on their way through the communes.

She was beyond hoping that this would prove a good thing.

As they approached, the Meyerston man addressed not Jane and Fredrick, but their escorts from Logan's Valley, in the coarse pidgin that had become familiar to Jane over the last two weeks.

"Come along the way?" he asked. He had a thick, dark beard that hid his age.

"Just up from the Valley," said one of the hunters.

"These the ones've come up from the city?" the bearded man asked, jerking his chin at Jane and Fredrick.

"The same." It wasn't clear to Jane whether their interlocutors assumed she and Fredrick couldn't understand them or whether it was irrelevant. It didn't seem to matter, and she was too exhausted to care.

The farmers' impenetrable frowns seemed to bring them to some kind of mutually understood conclusion.

The bearded man nodded at the hunters. "There's pottage at the Sheaf and open beds, too."

The hunters nodded and grunted and continued toward town without a backwards glance, their heads down against the wind.

Alone with the grave, bearded stranger, Jane wondered what kind of news had filtered out from Recoletta and the other communes to leave him standing out in the cold like this, the tracks behind him almost filled in with snow. More importantly, she wondered whether it was the kind of news that painted her and Fredrick as liabilities to be disposed of, assets to be traded back to Sato, or something else entirely.

He turned to them. "Breeze tells you left Recoletta fourteen days past."

Fredrick was panting, his breath pluming in the cold. Even he had grown numb to their vulnerability. "Well, we were looking for a vacation. We'd heard the surface is lovely this time of year."

Jane couldn't tell if the bearded man was smiling beneath his thick whiskers, but she doubted it.

"And your leaving happened at the same time as another arriving," said the bearded man. "A great army moved into Recoletta, led by a man claiming to be kin of one of your councilors."

"Good news travels fast," Freddie said.

"We're not the only ones leaving," Jane said. "I'd bet you've seen exiles in the hundreds by now. Maybe more."

It was a gamble and a guess, but it seemed to be a good one.

This time, the bearded man did laugh. "Sure, but none of them were avoiding the trains."

Fredrick gave Jane a look. They'd debated hitching a ride from one of the communes. Fredrick had been in favor of it, but Jane had wanted to avoid any chance of running into one of Sato's enforcers, or into anyone else rounding up errant citizens. Besides, their hosts in the communes hadn't seemed willing to wait for a steam engine to roll through town.

However, it seemed as if their efforts at stealth had made them conspicuous. As a rule, Recoletta's city-dwellers generally only ventured to the surface to avoid underground traffic or when the surface otherwise provided a more convenient route. But visiting the communes, or any of the wilderness above and outside the city, was all but unheard of.

That they had run, and that they had taken special pains to do so quietly, was a dangerous thing to admit. And yet the bearded man was still smiling – broadly enough to spread his whiskers – and watching them with interest.

If nothing else, it reassured Jane that they would not be shot and left in the snow, at least not yet. That was comfort enough.

"Come on," he said. "You can trade your tale when we're someplace warm."

They trudged through the snow, quietly grateful for another

haven on the horizon, no matter how brief.

Their escort led them to a town that was much like the last two they'd visited: cobbled streets a little rougher than Recoletta's, but lined with trees and patches of grass; a thin dusting of snow, scraped bare by foot and horse traffic; and, most strikingly, houses, shops, and meeting halls, all built aboveground like piles of stones and timber. It still seemed beyond comprehension, to gather and lay materials, many of which had to be dug out of the soil anyway, when a space hollowed out of the earth offered better comfort and protection from the elements. But Jane was beyond worrying that the brick and wood buildings would collapse on her head with the slightest gust of a surface breeze, and she was well beyond seeing the men and women who built and dwelt in them as unskilled primitives.

As they passed through the town, the men and women stopped with their wagons of potatoes, bags of seed stock, and barrels of ferment to watch them. Even though Jane and Fredrick were now clad in the same warm, practical clothes as the farmers, they didn't quite blend in. And Jane could see in their curious and suspicious stares that news of their arrival had already reached these people.

They reached a cobblestone plaza and followed their host up a porch and into a long, narrow building. It was filled with long tables and benches, and while Freddie plopped himself onto the nearest of these, Jane was most grateful for the stove at the other end of the room. She crossed to it and warmed her numb hands, her ears still ringing from the wind outside.

A large cast iron pot sat atop the stove, and sweet, spicy aromas emanated from within. Jane was pleased to see their host appear at her side with three mugs, ladling the steaming liquid into each of them.

She followed him back to the table, where Fredrick had already perked up at the scent of the warm beverage. She sat next to him while the bearded man slid onto the bench across from them.

"Cider," he said, distributing three sturdy but chipped

earthenware mugs. He took a flask from his side and tipped a splash of amber liquid into his own beverage. He looked to Jane and Fredrick, his eyebrows raised.

Jane shook her head, but Fredrick slid his mug closer, nodding eagerly. When the bearded man had doctored Fredrick's drink, the three clinked their mugs together and sipped their steaming cider.

Jane was so lost to the sensation of the moment, the warming aches beneath her cold flesh, the sweetness of the apple and the spice of cinnamon and nutmeg, that she almost didn't hear the bearded man finally introducing himself.

"Salazar," he said. "Now that we're sharing a drink."

Fredrick hesitated, looking at Jane. They'd been careful to remain anonymous and to avoid giving out any more details about themselves than necessary, something their previous hosts had seemed perfectly content with. But this Salazar had already pieced together enough about them to know that they were at risk. Giving him a name couldn't make much more of a difference.

"Jane Lin," she said.

Fredrick shrugged. "Fredrick Anders."

"We've seen a lot of your people on the move," Salazar explained. "Traveling the railways, headed north toward Madina. We hear it's the same down towards South Haven, too. But these folk certainly haven't set foot on our hearths, and as for the men and women in the cargo section, taking our shipments and offloading supplies from Recoletta... well, we couldn't help but notice that a few of them are new to the job. And of the ones who'll talk, we get some colorful stories about what's going on down in that city of yours. But they're different stories. And seeing as you seem to know something about events down yonder, I was hoping you could clear up a few points of confusion for me."

Fredrick wrapped both hands around his mug. "Unfortunately, we've been out of the loop for a few weeks."

"Haven't we all?" Salazar said. "I'm not holding you to any special prescience. But among us, it's common for travelers to share the news on where they're coming from. Especially when they're relying on hospitality."

Jane remembered a story she'd been told weeks ago, at a party to which she never should have been invited by people who were, likely as not, dead by now. It had concerned Roman Arnault and his uncanny ability to survive by remaining relevant.

She was lucky to have made it this far on the goodwill of the farmers. But she needed something more. And on the other side of Salazar's threat, she perceived an opportunity – the ability to survive and, perhaps, thrive by remaining relevant.

If only she had something he needed.

And that was when she noticed it. She'd seen it many times, but she didn't recognize it at first because she'd only witnessed it obliquely, in interactions happening around but beyond her.

It was hunger. In the way Salazar pinched the handle of his mug, in the way his lips were slightly parted. He wanted, very badly, to know what had happened in Recoletta.

And then something else occurred to her for the first time.

She could use that hunger.

Jane was suddenly conscious of the way her own hands traced the irregularities in the mug, tiny craters where the bubbles in the glaze had burst, subtle ridges in the surface of hardened clay. Salazar seemed to feel them all, as if her clipped thumbnail scratched and picked at him while he waited for her to answer.

"Well," Jane said, hearing herself draw the syllable out. "I suppose it would help me if you could tell me what you already know."

His smile looked more like a wince. "As I said, Miss Lin, I've heard many stories but little context. A foreign army that's been executing the citizens, a returning savior who's restored the city's peace. Some say the problem began with murders among your whitenails, and others say that was merely a distraction. I am hoping you can sort this out."

"I suppose they're all true to a degree," Jane said. And she began with the story as she knew it, an incident that started as an increasingly alarming series of murders among Recoletta's allegedly untouchable whitenails. It had piqued first curiosity, then horror as the killings and their consequences began to shift and erase people's long-held notions of privilege and vulnerability in Recoletta.

Salazar listened without interruption, his breaths quiet and shallow.

Telling the story began to feel like a careful choreography, an exchange of phrased gestures and carefully modulated reflexes that was not unlike the silent dialogues she'd witnessed between the upper-class whitenails in Recoletta. She was beginning to see her unique situation – and her unique knowledge of what had happened in the city – as a kind of asset.

"And then they finally killed a councilor," she said. "After that, I suppose the bigger changes seemed inevitable. If even a councilor was vulnerable, then everything else was, too."

"Then this is where Sato shows up?" Salazar asked.

"Yes," she said, although in a way, he'd been there the whole time, directing events. Or perhaps it was truer to say that he'd already wound the pieces up and set them in motion, and he'd returned once they'd fallen into place. "Sato's people arranged for a catastrophe in the city. Once they'd set it off, they took advantage of the chaos to move into place. They isolated and overpowered the City Guard and took care of the remaining councilors."

Salazar's eyes widened. "They assassinated them? All of them?"

Jane paused, but she saw no reason not to tell him. "I didn't stick around long enough to find out. But I know at least one of them got away."

"Which?"

She wasn't sure whether or not it surprised her that this farmer would be familiar with Recoletta's leaders. The farmers were, after all, under the Council's thumb as much as any citizen. Or at least they had been.

"Does it matter?" she asked.

His mouth stretched into something that wasn't quite a smile. "It seemed to matter to somebody."

He was right, but perhaps not in the way he imagined.

Jane remembered letting Councilor Ruthers go, remembered the look of astonishment on the old man's face. It wasn't that she'd wanted him to live, rather that she hadn't seen the purpose of adding yet another death to the toll, particularly knowing what it would cost her, or Roman, had she allowed him to pull the trigger.

"Ruthers," she said.

His eyebrows telegraphed his surprise. Even if he'd only known the name of one member of the Council, it would have been Ruthers.

She looked at the mug between her hands. She'd drunk it down to the dregs, and now only a puddle remained, pale and flecked with cinnamon.

Salazar took her mug and Fredrick's. "Catch your breath. I'll fill these up."

As Salazar left for the cider pot, Jane turned to Fredrick. Neither said a word, but his half shrug and blank expression suggested that he was resigned to letting her tell as much of their story as she chose. That, or the whiskey was doing its work.

Salazar returned and added another splash from his flask to his mug and to Fredrick's. "So," he said, blowing at the steam wafting off his own cup. "It's a good story. It fits more or less what I'd pieced together from the whispers and insinuations coming from the train crews. But what I'm really itching to know is why Sato did it."

She hesitated. He was waiting for her to flake away the plaster of grand, visible events that had been smeared over Recoletta's final weeks. He wanted to see the schemes beneath them. And she balked because that knowledge was precisely what had forced her to leave.

He seemed to follow her thoughts. "You left because you were in danger, Miss Lin. The most likely explanation is that you know something. That also makes you dangerous." He was nudging her, trying to embolden her with suggestions of her own power.

It reminded her of an earlier conversation she'd had with Roman only two weeks ago, the same evening she and Fredrick had fled. Yet that discussion already felt much more distant. She remembered asking Roman Arnault many of these same questions about what had happened and why, hanging on his answers – and his sly glances and clever, quiet remarks – with bated breath.

She hadn't realized it at the time, but he'd had authority then. Even if her affection hadn't driven her to trust him wholly and irrationally, he had been the only source of answers for her. That had given his words power and lodged them in her heart in such a way that they would be very difficult to pry out even if they'd turned out to be untrue.

And here she and Fredrick sat, alone with a man asking her for an explanation. After she gave it to him, he would go on to give his own version – perhaps the same as hers, perhaps not – to his people.

He wanted reasons. Something to give meaning to an as-yet unfathomable series of changes.

Realizing that her fate might hinge on those very reasons, she gave him the ones she suspected he wanted to hear.

"Recoletta's weakening. Rotting from the inside. It was run by a few corrupt inbreds who have no particular skills to lay claim to except an incredible capacity for deceit and self-delusion." Something hot and turbulent sang in her blood. Even if she hadn't spared the matter much thought before, she knew everything she was saying was true. Whether she felt this good because her words seemed to have the desired effect or because she could finally speak them, she couldn't quite say.

He was leaning in, so she continued.

"Sato recognized that, which is why he stepped in. But what he doesn't recognize is that he's little better. Others are catching on fast, though. You've seen the numbers coming out of Recoletta. It's only a matter of time before his new city collapses on itself."

He'd listened, very still and very quiet. Now that she had finished, he nodded once and smiled. "Thank you, Miss Lin, you've been most helpful."

Silence descended, hemming them in. There was no noise from outside the building, no evidence that anyone was even nearby. Jane wondered whether Salazar had brought them to this room by themselves so that he could kill them now that he had his answers. It would certainly make things easier for him if he really did believe that they were dangerous, and it would preserve his version, whatever it might be, of what she'd just told him.

But he drained the last of his cider and looked out the window behind them. "You must be exhausted," he said. "You've certainly come a long way. Why don't you stay on as our guests for tonight and catch a train out? There's one due tomorrow morning, and I daresay you'll be less conspicuous hiding in the crowd. There will certainly be enough of one on the train if the last two weeks are any indication."

"Thank you," Jane said. Fredrick breathed a too-loud sigh of relief and looked at her.

She wasn't about to admit it to Fredrick, but she was secretly relieved at having a justification to take the train. Besides, as suspicious as she might be of Salazar's motives, he'd certainly have no reason to want them to get caught. Of that much she was sure.

Salazar left their mugs in a basin near the stove and led them back into the plaza. On the other side of the square was a three-story building marked by a sign that depicted a triumphant pig holding a bundle of wheat like a trophy. Jane supposed it was meant to be amusing, but mostly, it just reminded her that she was hungry.

"This is the inn," Salazar said. "Whenever you want to rest, Matthias can show you to your rooms. He should have stew on the stove, too."

Jane had to work very hard to listen to the rest of what he said.

"I've got to attend to other matters now, but you're welcome to stretch your legs around town. If you haven't had enough of exploring already, that is. If you need anything, just ask around. Someone will be able to find me." He nodded and left them.

Jane and Fredrick didn't have to discuss what to do next. They both turned into the inn for bowls of thick, hot stew. They ate quickly and silently. It could have been stringy beef and rehydrated vegetables and it would have satisfied Jane, but she was reasonably sure that she would have enjoyed this meal under any circumstances.

Fredrick finished first, shoving his bowl to the middle of the table. "Hot cider, beef stew, and the promise of a train ride. What else could go wrong?" He belched into his fist. "Besides twelve hours of blissful unconsciousness."

Jane ladled the last chunk of parsnip into her mouth. "We've still got a few hours of daylight left. Might be fun to explore."

"Oh, Jane." He groaned and folded his hands over his belly. "Haven't we seen enough farms and fields for a lifetime?"

"Look at it this way. When are we going to be out here again?"

He grumbled and pushed his chair back from the table, the legs screeching against the floorboards. "If that's a promise..."

They stepped out of the inn and back into the square. But, warmed and filled as they were, the cold didn't seem quite as daunting, and their thick coats seemed to hold their bodies' heat.

Jane led Fredrick at a brisk, deliberate pace, walking as if to see as much as possible in what time they had left. She followed the rough-paved streets past a tanner's shop, where skins hung from beams and scaffolds, and a butcher's shop next to it, with meats curing in the window. She supposed both shops got their raw materials from the same sources, and she turned to remark as much to Fredrick, but he wasn't paying attention. His gaze was fixed on something distant and, likely, only present in his mind's eye.

She left him to his thoughts and pressed on. Despite his inattention, he followed close behind.

As they walked on, Jane saw shops, storehouses, homes, and other buildings that she had to but peek inside to guess about. They were sturdy and practical, yet not without a certain savage charm. Theirs was the architecture of durability, something to withstand the relentless and unpredictable siege of the elements.

She was impressed by the size of everything, how the settlement seemed to exist like a city in miniature. Everything it needed – everything but the factories, anyway – lay in the miles connected by narrow but neat cobbled roads. And other things, which Recoletta needed as well, lay in fields and pastures just beyond the little town.

As they passed a storefront, Jane was struck by a whim. She jerked her head at Freddie, who followed her inside without a word.

The store's shelves were lined with all manner of goods: fruits in jars, pressed against the glass in colors that seemed brighter than real life; sacks of dry grains and beans; bags of flour and sugar; rolls of patterned fabrics; and a dozen little tools and implements made for improvised and autarkic industry.

She picked up the first thing that caught her eye – a knife with a folding blade – and took it to the counter.

"How much?"

The balding shopkeeper started. She felt that twinge of dread at what his answer might be and at how much higher it might be for the foreign rhythm of her accent.

"Which papers?" the man asked.

"Beg your pardon?"

"Papers." He tapped his fingertips together in a rapid pinching motion. "Your money."

"Oh!" Her hand involuntarily darted to the pouch where she'd stored most of her cash. The answer froze on her tongue, but only for a moment. For better or worse, she'd already thrown her lot in with Salazar. "Recolettan marks," she said.

He nodded. "Twenty."

She gasped. "You can't be serious. I could get the same thing for half as much in the city."

He shrugged, expressionless. "Well. You're not in the city."

At first, she thought it was a calculated statement, part of a price hike made in the spirit of vengeance or opportunism. But his tonelessness made it a statement of fact, and he busied himself with a ledger behind the counter so quickly and quietly that she knew he wasn't getting pleasure out of her disappointment. He wasn't watching her reaction at all.

There was only one explanation. The price was twenty marks.

"Excuse me," Jane said, drawing his attention from his book. "This knife. You sell it for twenty. How much do you pay for it?"

He picked at the corner of the ledger page with his thumbnail. "Eighteen." The price was almost too high to believe, but he spoke with so little emotion that, again, Jane couldn't help but take him at his word.

"You buy it from one of the craftsmen here?"

Finally, his face split in a thin, disbelieving smile. "No, from the city. All of my goods come from Recoletta."

"Except the foodstuff, of course. You grow most of that here, don't you?"

"We do. But Recoletta owns it. The city owns all our quotas."

Jane paused, her mouth slightly agape, waiting for him to reveal the joke. But he only folded his hands on the counter in front of him. "You- you're saying you grow this stuff, send it to Recoletta, and they send it back here to sell to you again?"

"Usually we just pay for a reserve of our production to avoid sending it back and forth. And some of the items here are consignment from other communes that produce crops and materials we do not. Also purchased through Recoletta, of course." His eyes suddenly narrowed and his mouth shrank to a small, firm line. Jane remembered the extra satchels her hunter-guides had carried, stuffed full of pumpkins and acorn squash. Perhaps there were some trades on the side, but nothing this shopkeeper wanted a potential representative of the city to know about.

In fact, he seemed eager to change the subject now. "If you'd rather pay with other papers – other currency – we take money from anywhere. Madina, South Haven, Underlake, wherever you like."

Jane slid twenty marks onto the counter. Who knew if it would have any value where she was headed, anyway.

The sight of the rumpled blue bills put the shopkeeper at ease, and he gave her the first genuine smile she'd seen since she'd stepped into the shop.

She kept her fingertips on the corner of the money. "Is there someplace around here I could exchange this for another currency? Whatever they use in Madina, perhaps?"

"Anyone here could do that for you. We've got a little of everything floating around."

Jane nodded, leaving the money on the counter. "I'll keep that in mind."

She slipped the knife into her pouch and left.

"That was interesting," she muttered through a plume of steam when she and Freddie were outside again.

"I know. Who makes anything out of tartan any more?"

"I'm not talking about the fabrics, Freddie. Did you listen to a word he said? They buy their own products back from the cities, and it sounds like they pay a fortune for them."

Fredrick shrugged and looked around. "Not much here to spend money on."

She threw her head back, staring into the flat white sky. "That's not the point." She looked back at him. "For people with nothing to buy, though, they have access to quite a few currencies."

He scratched the back of his neck. "Where do you suppose they get it?"

Where money flowed, so did information. She'd always

thought of the cities as isolated from one another, even while she'd marveled at foreign goods at the market. Yet she was beginning to see the shape of a thousand little official and unofficial channels where perhaps her information would have value. "That's what I'd like to find out."

As they toured the rest of Meyerston, Jane found herself looking for anything out of place. It was like watching for shoots of green in the snow, and now that she was paying attention, she was surprised at how much she noticed. Baskets that she'd specifically seen woven in Shepherd's Hollow. Apricots, dried for storage, which one local admitted came from a commune further north. Tools and manufactured goods that didn't bear the mark of any factory in Recoletta.

Fredrick only furrowed his brow when Jane pointed this out. "Of course some of them originate in other communes. Other cities, even. The shopkeeper told you they have to buy these things through Recoletta."

"Yes, but I don't think they buy all of through the city."

"Under-the-table deals, then."

"Of course," Jane said. "Demand meeting opportunity."

He sighed, looking back in the direction they'd come. "Does this give you a sudden desire for apricots?"

"No, it gives me an idea."

CHAPTER 1

ARBITRAGE

Jane owed much of her early success in Madina to her initial observations of the souk.

She and Fredrick reached Madina after almost three weeks of travel, blending in with the latest wave of Recolettan emigrants. Their slower journey had allowed them to adjust in ways the other expatriates had not; Jane found herself hearing her home city's accent like something foreign and seeing the shock and bewilderment that she hadn't had the luxury of experiencing when she'd left.

But Roman's final warning and the threat of Sato's retaliation had taught her caution that few of her fellow migrants had learned. Newcomers revealed their ignorance – and their vulnerability – as soon as they opened their mouths. Even though Recolettans and Madinans spoke the same language, the cities' relative isolation had incubated distinct patterns and connotations, and the subtleties were different enough to leave a wide margin for error. Recolettans asked for directions and assistance in the panicked tones that suggested they'd accept any answer. Whitenails demanded favors of locals who clearly saw no significance in their long, manicured fingernails. Some asked about prices while waving wads of money. In a way, she couldn't blame them. They'd never been anywhere else before.

When Jane arrived, she knew she needed to get her bearings. She needed to find the kind of meeting place where a variety of people crossed paths to exchange information and other things of value.

She needed a market. Fortunately, she knew how to find that.

She and Fredrick had pulled into town, fresh off the train from Meyerston, early in the morning. If Madina was anything like Recoletta, it was the time of day when merchants would be bustling to set up their stalls and others would be on their way to complete morning errands. So, dragging an exhausted Fredrick in her wake, she followed the tides of people.

In Recoletta, the market had been not only a place of commerce, but also a place to trade information. Neighbors greeted one another with fresh tidings on their lips, and the day's news wafted across the tiered levels and open stalls along with the scents of fish and the shouts of vendors. Aside from the Council chambers, of course, it was the best place to hear what had happened and what was on the horizon.

In this regard, the souk of Madina put Recoletta's market to shame. People were so familiar and talkative that Jane couldn't tell at first whether they all happened to know one another or whether social bonds in Madina were so flexible that total strangers simply happened to greet one another this way. This kind of quick and public intimacy would have been considered forward in Recoletta, particularly between people of such apparently varied social stations (which Jane could only guess at based on their apparently varied styles of dress). Yet here, people seemed to compete with one another in the sharing of news.

Unlike Recoletta, where information was exchanged in a tit-for-tat fashion, here, information was given out extravagantly and abundantly.

But information was only one thing Jane needed.

Next to her, Fredrick scratched the rough fabric of his shirt. "I'm hungry."

He sounded cranky and petulant, but Jane realized that she was, too.

Fredrick's head swiveled around the souk, suddenly sensitive to the suggestive aromas around them. "How much do you think those things are?" he asked, pointing to a stall a dozen feet away where a man was selling skewers of rounded fritters.

Jane led them closer. She couldn't tell what they were, but they smelled delicious – warm, savory, and heavy with the scent of frying oil. She watched a woman approaching the stall hand over a few jingling coins in exchange for a skewer.

Jane thought about the money in her pockets. A meal of fritters wouldn't be a problem. Nor would a few dozen after that. But lodgings – particularly something safer and more comfortable than the local equivalent of Recoletta's crowded, crime-ridden bunkhouses – would cost more. If Sato had sent someone to search for her, a public bunkhouse was the last place she wanted to be, particularly given how easily information seemed to circulate around here.

It was a paranoid thought but not, given their flight through the communes, an unreasonable one.

She would need to find a job, but she didn't know how long that would take. Seeing the number of refugees in her midst, she suspected the competition might be fiercer than she'd hoped.

So her thoughts returned to the money in her pockets. Booking passage on the train had, unfortunately, cost her more than she'd planned.

After her visit with the shopkeeper in Meyerston, she'd exchanged most of her Recolettan marks for Madinan dirrams before boarding the train. She'd suspected that, with so many Recolettans pouring into the city, the exchange rate in Madina might not favor her.

Before she could continue the thought, she was pushed from behind. Tumbling forward, she barely kept herself from falling into the knot of robed shoppers in front of her.

As she caught herself, she glanced over her shoulder and saw a woman in a Recolettan dress and petticoats. Her mind turned to Sato's henchmen, and she prepared to sprint, half-expecting to see a knife in the stranger's slender hand.

But she saw only fingernails, three inches long.

Without thinking, Jane composed her face into the sort of neutral apology that would have been required for a woman of her standing in Recoletta. The whitenail, however, quickly disappeared into the crowd, never having noticed Jane.

Jane was too relieved to resent the incident, but it set the gears in her mind spinning.

She nudged Fredrick, who was lost in the spectacle of an intricately latticed skylight overhead, and told him to keep quiet.

"Why?" he asked, looking absurdly wounded.

"Just trust me," she said. Fortunately, he was too tired and hungry to argue further.

Jane took several minutes to observe the scene around her. The first thing she noticed was that merchants and customers seemed to have lengthy and heated discussions with one another. When she listened in, she realized that they were arguing about prices. The escalation raised the hairs on the back of her neck – this wasn't the kind of thing that happened in Recoletta – yet just as she was certain a blow-up was imminent, the two parties would reach an agreement and complete the deal amicably. And then go off to repeat the process with someone else.

It wasn't long before she heard another angry discussion nearby, yet this time, she recognized the accent of Recoletta. She turned to see a man and a woman arguing.

"Preposterous," the Recolettan man said. "You can't possibly expect me to believe it's two-to-one."

The gray-haired woman stood in front of a stall strung with delicate gold chains. She shrugged. "Believe what you want. That's the rate." She looked over her shoulder as if bored. Her accent matched the local dialect.

The man sputtered and fumed, but seemed to realize he had no choice. He thrust a fistful of cash at her, one broken pinky nail wrapped over the wad, and she took it, briskly handing him a thinner stack of dirrams. He made a big show of counting them, his long-nailed fingers peeling the green bills back one by one.

That gave Jane an idea.

She eased her way through the crowd, Fredrick in tow. Her ears were tuned to Recolettan accents and her eyes watched for familiar dress and, most importantly, long fingernails.

It wasn't long before Jane found the petticoated whitenail who had pushed her. The woman stood in the midst of the crowd, looking about, consternation etched on her fine features.

Motioning for Fredrick to wait, Jane sidled up to the woman and greeted her with a bow. The whitenail watched Jane carefully, her eyes taking in her rugged, travel-worn attire and, predictably, her short-nailed fingers.

"It would seem we're both strangers here," Jane said. "An honor to make your acquaintance, my lady."

The whitenail gave her a stiff nod. Her expression had not changed.

Jane lowered her head in acknowledgment of her own low status. "I don't suppose you'd have Recolettan marks to trade, madam. I'm just on my way back, and I'd much rather do business with a fellow Recolettan. I'm sure you understand what I mean."

The whitenail laid a hand on her chest, taking a deep, gasping breath. "What a relief. I've been here two days and haven't dared trade a mark yet. Hard to trust anyone here, the way they scream and shout at one another. Anyway," she said, pulling back into her coolly genteel facade, "how much do you owe me for this?"

The preemptive remorse that had seeped into Jane's gut all but evaporated at the whitenail's sudden shift and the reminder that, even here and now, the older woman's trust had almost nothing to do with Jane's qualities and everything to do with her relative position. Which, apparently, still meant something to this whitenail on the verge of begging in a foreign city.

It was not hard for Jane to feign a demure and grateful smile. She thought back to the exchange she'd witnessed moments ago and doubled the rate. Four Recolettan marks for one Madinan dirram. Such was the whitenail's faith that she didn't hesitate to surrender her money to Jane. Jane took it, fighting harder now to hide her surprise and satisfaction even while something warm and sickly wormed its way back into her stomach.

The deal done, Jane made herself scarce as quickly as possible.

"I say, did you just do what I think you did?" Even Fredrick, who had suddenly lost interest in the patterned skylights, had caught the significance of what had just happened. He gawped at the money she hastily stuffed into her pockets, licking his lips. "Think we could get one of those fried thingies about now?"

Though Jane's appetite had suddenly deserted her, she recognized that Fredrick was about ten minutes away from a meltdown. She paid for their meal with most of her remaining Madinan coins, taking another opportunity to observe the souk.

Changing her money back at a reasonable rate would, she hoped, be a little easier.

Once the fritter had settled in her stomach, she approached another vendor, a man she'd seen sell half a dozen skewers of roasted meat. She smiled and said "Peaceful days," a greeting she'd heard exchanged among the locals.

He smiled, his eyebrows raised in surprise. "Peaceful days to you. Something I can get for you, miss?" He gestured at the slowly turning spit of meat with a grease-slathered knife.

"Actually, I was hoping to exchange some money." As she said it, she saw the shape of his wide, curious face slowly change, narrowing in calculation.

"Why, yes–"

"I couldn't help but notice," Jane said, eager to stop him before he got too far down that line of thought, "that you've seen quite a bit of business in the last several minutes."

He was quiet and smiling faintly, and Jane didn't know enough about local custom yet to know whether she'd been too forward. Based on what she'd observed, she thought not.

"I could exchange my marks uptown," she said, hoping her vague lie sounded credible, "but it's gotten rather busy, as I'm sure you've noticed. Besides, I'm certain you'll give me a fair rate."

He smiled and quoted a figure that was astonishingly close to the deal she'd witnessed between the whitenail man and the local woman.

Jane frowned slowly. "Is that the price you've heard?" She looked back at Fredrick. "Where did you trade your money? Back on the other side was it?"

Fredrick, still cognizant of her earlier cautions to silence, raised his sandy eyebrows and muttered something that could be interpreted as a vague agreement.

But the vendor was paying attention, and just as Jane turned away, he called back over her shoulder. She stopped, and when he beckoned her back, she only came slowly.

The rate he gave her wasn't much better, but given the exchange she'd made with the whitenail woman, she found that she now had twice the cash she'd had thirty minutes ago. The thought both thrilled and nauseated her.

And still, it was only a start. What she really needed was work. Ideally, something that not only paid a decent wage, but that also offered some kind of security. Or, failing that, the ability to see trouble coming. Her job in Recoletta had put her just close enough to the whitenails to get into their trouble without having access to any of their resources. She wouldn't put herself in that position again if she could help it.

But what options did that leave her in Madina, where she was unknown and unconnected?

Just as she was thinking about this, she felt someone else barrel into her. This time, the force knocked her to the ground. She pushed herself up, venom behind her lips, whitenail or no.

The culprit darted across the market. She saw him just long

enough to recognize him as the whitenail she'd seen changing money earlier, jagged fingernail and all. A gold-colored chain dangled from one clenched fist and as he ran, he jammed his prize into his pocket, the broken nail catching briefly on the fabric of his trousers. The crowd parted for him, though perhaps not as quickly as he would have liked. A delayed furor followed him, like a thunderclap after lightning, and Jane saw the vendor who'd changed his money, pointing after him and shouting.

As Fredrick pulled her up, the noise around them thickened. The crowd was developing a sense of purpose and a will of its own, and even Fredrick, scanning the crowd with hooded eyes while he bent down, seemed to realize that this was dangerous.

"We should go," he said, barely loud enough to be a whisper.

Jane agreed. But no sooner was she on her feet than the crowd around them had changed course, turning its focus inward, looking with new interest at the young foreigner dusting herself off and turning to go.

And just like that, the knot of people tightened, and she was trapped. The eyes around her carried a range of interested emotions – accusation, concern, curiosity, and suspicion – all of which were fixed intently on her.

It was then that the crowd parted again to admit a man dressed in dark, crisp trousers and a matching shirt. His presence cooled the mob, but he was also looking at Jane with interest.

"They say you saw the thief. You understand me, miss?" he asked.

"I saw a man running away. I didn't see what happened just before that," Jane said. As the crowd's attention settled back on her, she took a step away from Fredrick, hoping he might be forgotten in the middle of this mess.

The policeman – she hoped that's what he was, anyway – frowned and said, "I think you'd better come with me."

Jane obeyed, not daring to look back at Fredrick, but hoping he had the sense to follow at a distance.

Her escort guided her into a carriage. Unlike the carriages used by the Municipal Police in Recoletta, this one was mostly open. A gossamer canopy covered the top, and when she took her seat, she noticed that the doors and sides rose only as high as her upper arm. Were it not for the staring crowd, she almost felt as if she could have jumped out and run off.

She caught Fredrick in the middle of the crowd, fear etched plain on his face. She turned back toward the front of the carriage and took a deep breath, trying to settle her suddenly tempestuous stomach.

The nice thing about being carted away by the authorities – if there could be a nice thing – was that it gave her the chance to observe this new city. Her new city, perhaps, if she survived this ordeal.

The carriage clattered away from the market and into the open, leaving behind the curious onlookers. As it broke free of the crowd, Jane's pounding pulse subsided, and she finally allowed herself to look around without nervously scanning the crowd.

They rolled past the last of the shops, and the massive cavern seemed to widen in greeting. Jane was struck by how bright it was until, looking up, she lost herself in lacework of lights.

When the policeman at her side looked suddenly over, she realized she must have gasped aloud. Recoletta had skylights looking down on some of its larger thoroughfares, but this was something more. A steeply pitched roof came to a long, sharp edge some two hundred feet overhead. Yet the angled slabs that covered the tunnel were not solid stone, but rather a painstakingly carved grid of geometric patterns.

The flat winter light peeked into the tunnel between radiating and intersecting lines and through identical, star-shaped apertures. The tunnel seemed to curve away in the distance, but even there, it was suffused with a soft, pale glow.

Jane couldn't help herself. "It's like this the whole way down the tunnel?"

The policeman gave her an odd look, and for a moment, she feared she'd said something wrong. "How else do you keep it lit?"

Jane was silent the rest of the way, watching the ornate skylights and the locals in their loose trousers and fitted robes. As the tunnel they passed through widened, the sides of the tunnel sprouted suspended sidewalks that opened up on the balconies and porches of homes and shops, all seemingly marked by silk awnings or ornamental, carved doorways. Overhead, gangways and bridges connected the two sides of the tunnel, bearing the colorfully dressed residents and carts filled with stacked produce and other goods. As they continued, the walkways and balconies seemed to grow more numerous and more populous by the minute. In all of this, she felt echoes of Recoletta that vanished as quickly as they appeared. The two cities seemed like siblings snatched from the cradle and raised by different parents, with different manners, different rules.

Finally, they emerged onto a wide plaza, and the carriage stopped. Jane waited for her escort's signal to descend, and when she did, she stepped onto smooth gray stone that had been polished to a mirror finish. The plaza was large, easily broad enough to hold several dozen of the shops and buildings she'd passed on her journey through the farming communes, yet it was dwarfed by the wide steps leading up to a five-story stone facade.

The structure, whatever it was, wrapped around the stairs on three sides. From a distance, the flanking walls seemed as smooth as the polished floor, but as Jane got closer, she saw not only windows, oblong and pointed at the top and spaced in regular rows, but also embellishments and patterns that matched the style she'd seen on the skylights and elsewhere in the city.

"What is this place?" she asked the policeman.

He looked at her, his brow furrowed in surprise, before seeming to remember that Jane was not local. If Madina was anything like Recoletta, he probably hadn't met many foreigners before this sudden influx.

"This is the Majlis," he said, turning back to the looming stairs as if that simple answer explained everything.

They climbed the stairs, and Jane couldn't shake the notion that someone was watching them from behind the windows looming over them. They seemed to have been placed for just that purpose.

They approached a stone arch, tall and pointed at the very top, much like the windows. It stood in the middle of a short, trellised wall broken by smaller gates, and through this central arch, Jane saw a great doorway that echoed it in size and shape, as if the arch in the wall had been pulled from the front of the building.

Jane and the policeman passed under the arch and through the door.

She found herself in a hall that was every bit as busy as the plaza outside. Men and women, dressed in the practical and airy attire to which she was already becoming accustomed, swarmed and ebbed.

"This way," the policeman said, leading her across the hall.

A dome high overhead collected the sounds of shuffling feet and talking, whispering, laughing voices. Light streamed in from a ring of windows just below the curvature. Almost as soon as she registered them they disappeared, eclipsed by the long, arched hall through which she and the policeman now passed.

The new sights and sounds had, so far, distracted her enough to almost allow her to forget why she'd been brought here. No sooner had she remembered the thief in the market and her accidental role in the incident than the policeman guided her through one of the many horseshoe arches leading off of the central hall.

She paused in front of a long desk. The woman sitting behind it looked up at Jane's escort and motioned to another door. "They've caught him already," she said.

They entered a room that seemed small and dark, and all the more so for the tense company within it. Jane saw the whitenail thief with his arms folded tightly across his chest, his vendor victim, and two other people dressed in the same outfit as Jane's escort. There were flinty gazes and taut, snarling lips. Jane guessed that they'd just interrupted a heated discussion.

One of the other officers eyed Jane. "The witness?"

The whitenail and the vendor looked at Jane. His face was pale, but hers shriveled in resentment as she took in Jane's clothing. The suspicion was plain on her face.

Jane's escort returned a tight nod.

The third officer sighed. "She says he stole a gold necklace. Grabbed it from her stall and ran off."

The whitenail started forward, eyes wide and bulging, until the second officer laid a hand on his chest. "And he claims she's lying, that she sold him the necklace as part of a currency exchange." The officer glanced back at Jane with narrowed eyes. "And this woman saw something, yes?"

The vendor's eyes were fire beneath hooded lids. The whitenail's lips were pressed into a thin, prim line. As he met Jane's gaze, he gave a faint, almost imperceptible nod. A promise.

"What did you see?" her escort asked her.

Jane only hesitated a second. "When the trouble started, I was pushed to the ground," she said, looking at the whitenail, "and I saw him running through the crowd. He had a little chain of some kind that he was shoving into his pocket."

The whitenail's eyes flashed, the corners of his mouth twitching. "That means nothing," he said, gripping himself more tightly still with his folded arms, addressing the officers and ignoring Jane. "She didn't even see the face of whoever it was that pushed her. Or were you just looking for the first foreigner you could find?"

The whitenail didn't acknowledge her, but the officers looked at her.

"His fingernail," Jane said. "The right pinky. The rest are long, but that one's broken."

The whitenail, whose fists had been hidden under his arms, scowled. At a sharp glare from one of the officers, he displayed them for inspection. As Jane had said, the jagged pinky nail was the only irregularity in the otherwise perfect manicure. "That still doesn't mean I stole anything," he said. "Like I told you, it was part of our deal."

Jane cleared her throat. A sense of the whitenail's authority clung to her like a bad habit, but she forced the words out. "I remember seeing the trade, actually. She gave him a two-to-one exchange rate."

The second officer's eyebrows shot up. The third eyed the gray-haired merchant.

"He wasn't happy about the rate," Jane said, "but he took it anyway."

"She's lying!" the whitenail spat. "You found someone in the market who was willing to corroborate your version of events, and here she is." He cast Jane a withering glare, taking in her ragged clothing, her tangled hair, and her trimmed fingernails. "Testimony from the likes of her means nothing where we come from. There's a reason her kind can't–"

The vendor slapped him hard across the face. The sharp, staccato note of flesh on flesh rang in the suddenly silent room.

"Let her speak," Jane's officer escort said.

"I watched him count it," Jane said. "She gave him twenty-seven bills."

"You normally count money passed between strangers?" her escort asked.

"I wanted to know the price of a dirram," Jane said.

The other two officers looked at each other and then at Jane's escort. "That's exactly the number we took from him," one of them said. "In dirrams, anyway."

Jane's escort crossed his arms. "Then it seems the matter is settled." He raised his hand when the whitenail began to protest. "Get the two of them out of here, and see that the necklace is returned."

The two officers led the whitenail and the merchant away. Jane moved to follow.

"Not you," her escort said. "You'll come with me."

His voice was stern and serious. Jane felt her heart drop into the pit of her stomach. She had done what was asked. If more was required of her, it was likely not a good thing.

The officer led her deeper into the labyrinthine corridors of the Majlis. Jane caught glances – curious, perhaps apprehensive – from the men and women she passed. She looked down, only to find herself dizzied by the mosaics in the floor. The marble and wood-paneled walls hemmed her in on either side, and the policeman kept a gentle yet insistent grip on her arm.

She had only just arrived, and already, she was trapped again.

At last, Jane was brought to a room. It felt smaller and darker than the last. Candelabras branching from the walls cast dim, flickering light and threw shadows that jumped and shrank. Everything in the room seemed to move with a sinister, furtive energy.

The policemen led her to a hard-backed chair, and she sat stiffly, bracing herself. A table, small and low and scarred with use, stood inches from her knees. A man in dark robes entered the room from behind her, laid something on the table with a metallic clatter, and turned to face her.

His lips moved, silent against the rush of blood in her ears.

"Please," she said, her upper lip slick with cold sweat.

Expressionless, he turned back to the table. A noise, high and thin, jangled through the cotton in her ears.

He turned back to her, a cup of tea in his hands. He stood there for what felt like an eternity while her brain registered the tulip-shaped glass with its gilded rim, the dark and comfortingly familiar liquid within, and the forbearance on the man's face. Finally, she took the glass, less because she wanted tea and more because it seemed to be what was expected in this moment.

He retreated, and she noticed that the policeman had also left. So she sat alone in the strange, darkened room, and took a sip of her tea. It was sweet enough to make her cringe.

Something moved at the other end of the room. At first, she

thought it was a trick of the dim, guttering light – who lit a room only with candles, anyway? – but after several seconds, she saw movement again, stately and sweeping. Then someone glided across the room toward her, emerging from the wall where no door had been.

It was a woman, Jane realized, dressed in a brocaded but smooth-fitting robe that rose to her neck, wrapping under her jaw. What Jane first took to be a long curtain of hair was, she realized, a curtain of fabric that circled her draped head and rode across her shoulders. Something about her face seemed vague and hazy. It was only when she took the seat on the opposite side of the table that Jane could see that she wore a veil.

It didn't quite obscure her expression, but it made it harder to read, especially in the low lighting. It took Jane an extra second to parse that the brilliantly crimson lips beneath the veil were smiling. The woman raised a cup of tea beneath her veil and took a drink.

"Cakes will be arriving shortly," the woman said. "I trust you've been made comfortable?"

The question seemed almost comically absurd, but Jane didn't know what to say other than, "Yes." She sipped her tea again, fighting back a wince.

The other woman smiled. "You've come to Madina recently. Along with many others from Recoletta."

It didn't sound like a question, but Jane said, "Yes, ma'am," anyway, setting her half-empty glass on the tray.

"Understand that we have no intention of turning anyone away. We believe in hospitality," the woman said, refilling Jane's glass. "But welcoming so many newcomers at once presents certain challenges. My sources tell me you've witnessed one already."

Jane picked the tiny glass up by the rim, resolving to drink it more slowly. "There was a disagreement between a merchant and a whit… a man from Recoletta."

"And you chose the merchant's side," she said, her voice fluttering with amusement.

Something about this irked Jane. It made her decision sound

calculated and disingenuous. "Everything I said was true."

"I don't doubt it." The woman set her own cup on the gold tray and refilled it. "But there aren't many who would side with the foreigner in a matter like that."

After a beat, Jane realized that the woman was referring to the merchant, the local, as the foreigner. From Jane's perspective. "I'm the foreigner now," she said, thinking but not adding that returning to Recoletta wasn't exactly an option.

"That's clear-eyed of you," the woman said, pursing her lips. "And yet it would seem that not all of your peers are gifted with the same perspective."

Jane couldn't suppress a small smile at the idea of the whitenails being regarded as her peers.

It seemed as though the woman's full, painted lips quirked in response. "And, curiously, it seems that you did not share all of their advantages."

Jane felt tension creeping into her face, setting her grin into a rigid rictus.

"Ah, the cakes."

Jane sat there, her spine feeling numb against the hard chair, while the black-robed man swept into the room and deposited a platter of flaky pastries next to the tea service. The veiled woman took one and ate it, chewing slowly while the attendant departed.

The silence gnawed at Jane's nerves. "Am I a prisoner here?" The question felt uncomfortably blunt, but Jane was losing her patience for empty pleasantries.

The woman looked genuinely shocked, her expression quivering behind the veil. "I thought I made it clear. You're a guest. Now, have some cakes." She raised the plate to Jane.

Though her mouth felt too dry and her stomach too turbulent for any kind of food, Jane took a cake and dutifully popped it into her mouth. It was as sweet as the tea, layered with honey and ground nuts, but under the circumstances, it tasted as bland and mushy as a mouthful of porridge.

"Your countrymen have been pouring into Madina for over two weeks now. My counterparts in other cities have experienced similar influxes." The veiled woman wiped her fingertips on a crisp linen square folded on the tea tray. "It has not escaped my notice that you don't seem to match the dominant demographic."

Jane involuntarily glanced at her practical yet rumpled clothes, her short fingernails, and the stained canvas bag next to her chair.

Yes, she supposed she did strike a rather sharp contrast with the whitenail arrivals.

"I fear the trouble you witnessed will only become more common as my people get used to their new neighbors and as yours get used to their new... home. It would be useful for us to have the benefit of an honest broker. Someone who knows the customs of Recoletta and can help us settle matters equitably."

"Not that I don't appreciate the offer, but don't you already have people who do this? Men and women who know Recoletta?"

"In all your years in your home city, how often did you come across a Madinan?" The veiled lady smiled at Jane's silence. "Good intermediaries are rare, and few would have your perspective. Besides, there's something about a familiar accent that engenders trust, yes?" She tilted her head at Jane.

Feeling the heat rising in her face, Jane was suddenly grateful for the dim lighting.

"These are strange times. I need resourceful people, and I don't care where they come from."

Jane felt something like hope welling up in her chest.

The woman seemed to notice the change. "This is an offer, not a demand. But the manner of your arrival suggests you won't be returning to Recoletta any time soon. You will need some kind of employment here. And I can always make use of someone of your acumen."

Jane had to swallow twice before she could get the words out. "When do I start?"

"You already have."

CHAPTER 2

UNFAMILIAR TERRITORY

In the six months since Sato's revolution, Recoletta had become an underground archipelago. Pockets of civilization lay isolated by half-crumbled tunnels ravaged by Sato's bombs. Abandoned and half-ruined passages cut through the city like poisoned veins, allowing only the most toxic elements of society to pass between the dwindling havens of productivity and population.

Malone had prowled her ravaged city for six months, and still she barely knew it. It left her physically nauseated some days, just trying to keep up with it. The landscape changed daily as the ruin and corruption receded in one place only to bloom in another. The citizens that remained in Recoletta – and out of the shadows – shifted in their scattered pockets of civilization like nervous flocks, colonizing and abandoning new areas of the city each week. And yet even as they kept away from tumors of crime and neglect, their own movements only stirred the filth into new configurations, like sediment swirling at the bottom of a murky pond.

And yet it felt good to run through the city, even if it wasn't the one Malone remembered.

She turned down one passage, its mouth funneled by a heap of rubble. She had to slow her pace and light a lantern – the torches had all been stolen from the walls here. The approach didn't lend itself to speed or secrecy, but it was necessary nonetheless.

A mat of fungus had grown along one damp wall, and it filled the air with a musky perfume. Malone held back a sneeze.

She still didn't understand the politics of this new Recoletta. It didn't take more than common sense to know that things were bad and getting steadily worse, but she couldn't follow the minutiae of gestures, expressions, and inflections in the Cabinet meetings with Sato well enough to know whose fault it was from week to week (even if it was hers) or how promises and bargains were made over a raising of eyebrows and quirking of lips.

But this she knew and relished. Hunting her quarry through tunnels – even tunnels made unfamiliar by new layers of rubble and lichen – and becoming the hunted in a series of shifts and maneuvers every bit as sudden and deft as those that went on in the meetings. These subtleties differed in kind, not in degree.

She should have been thankful for the desk job. She could have easily set some hungry young underling like Inspector Angelo after the Bricklayer, let her earn her stripes (a memory of another hungry young underling rose to her mind, and she pushed it back as quickly as she could) while she turned in early and enjoyed the luxuries her position afforded. The opportunity for relaxation. She'd certainly seen enough action in the month leading up to Sato's coup – a month of murders and unrest in Recoletta – to have earned her rest.

But the wood-paneled walls of her new office only seemed claustrophobic. Johanssen's heavy oak desk – she still couldn't think of it as her own – felt like a weight pinning her in place.

Nor did the quiet of home offer any comfort. Recoletta had become an amorphous place of ragged flesh congealed around broken bones, and in the darkness of her apartment, she imagined she heard it contorting around her. The thought filled her with a kind of dread she was unable to admit even to herself. She closed her eyes each night, wondering what kind of city she'd wake up in.

Yet dashing and skulking through tunnels, she could feel the city under her feet, hear and smell the evidence of thousands of people still making their way in it. It reminded her that it was a real place of stone and metal and not merely an idea shaped by the debates between Sato and his cronies.

Her cronies now.

She got enough of a glimpse of the tunnel's progress ahead to douse her own lantern. If she could remember her reference points well enough to pick her way through the darkness, she could catch her opponent by surprise. It was simply a matter of navigating in temporary blindness.

She glimpsed a faint glow up ahead.

As disoriented as Sato's Cabinet meetings left her, the Bricklayer was someone she understood. A man – or woman – built by circumstances just as Recoletta was being undone by them. Where most people saw supply shortages, unkept passages, and broken gas lines, the Bricklayer saw opportunity. And in the last several months, he had constructed a niche for himself as the restorer of services, black-market provider, and rogue enforcer in the sections of the city where Sato's reach didn't extend.

And those sections grew with each new contortion and realignment.

Malone had heard many rumors about the Bricklayer, and not all of them seemed to refer to the same person. Some said he'd been hideously scarred in the night of fighting that heralded Sato's coup. Others said she was a deposed whitenail who'd found a new avenue to power after Recoletta's class structure had collapsed. Malone had been told that the Bricklayer was trying to rebuild Recoletta the only way he knew how, and she'd also been told that the Bricklayer would, in a few months more, be as rich as Councilor Ruthers had ever been.

At the end of the day, the Bricklayer's reasons didn't matter. He or she was a criminal for the catching, and that was all.

And the man she pursued now would lead her to the Bricklayer. Provided she could take him alive.

Malone hurried along, taking swift, silent steps through the dark ruin. The last glimpse she'd had of the tunnel before dousing her lantern was etched in her mind's eye, but she was reaching the end of the stretch she'd seen. Her toe struck a rock, sent it skidding ahead with a noise loud enough to raise the dead.

She reached the bend she'd seen earlier. Whatever lay ahead, she hadn't seen it yet. Water dripped from somewhere further down the passage while a stale draft kissed her left cheek. There was more than one direction her quarry could have gone, and judging from the relative silence and the dark, he was already far ahead.

The man she pursued had the advantage. He knew this area, the way the tunnels twisted and folded back on one another, where they led.

But he didn't know her.

She would have to take a risk if she wanted a chance at catching him here. Otherwise, there was nothing to stop him from fleeing or from doubling back and sneaking up on her.

Malone cracked the shutter on her lantern and brought the flame inside to life with a twist of the knob. She screwed off the top of the lantern so that the breeze just tickled the little flame. With one quick motion, she set the lantern just around the curve in the tunnel behind her, back the way she'd come, and felt her way into the branch on her left with gloved hands.

The lantern cast a dim, shivering glow from the depths of the tunnel. Not enough to illuminate her current position, she thought, but enough to get her fugitive's attention if he was still watching.

She would have to hope that he was still watching, that her ploy wasn't obvious to him, that a sign of her helplessness would draw him back and into the open. It was a risk. But eagerness, that mirage of hope when blood pounded into the brain, begat recklessness. It was a problem Malone had frequently observed in others but rarely suffered herself.

She drew her revolver and watched the blackness ahead of her, keeping her gaze from the light and the vulnerability it would bring. She waited for the barest hint of movement or shift in the air around her.

As she held her breath, she saw it. Darkness moving on darkness. Flickers of motion, formless but undeniable. He was circling back down the tunnel across from her. One hasty step echoed back toward her, telegraphing his impatience.

All she had to do was wait.

Tracking his progress back toward her, Malone held her breath and her position, conscious of the whispers of fabric, the squeak of leather, the unmistakable currents borne by any kind of movement.

That was when she heard a hammer click behind her.

She dropped to her knees just as the tunnels erupted with sound. Her back was, thankfully, to the muzzle flash, and for one brief instant it lit up the tunnel and the man across a dozen feet in front of her, his jaw locked in a grimace and one arm thrown over his eyes.

The half-blinding glimpse wasn't much of an advantage, but it put the other two men at a greater disadvantage. It was an imbalance she would have to seize.

She pointed her own gun at the spot where she'd last seen the other man and closed her eyes, firing into the darkness. A crash of thunder, but no cry of pain, no thud of meat falling to the floor. A miss.

And there was still someone behind her.

He had charted her quick evasion by now and, even blinded by the firing, could guess at where she was. Something hard and angular – the butt of his gun, perhaps – struck Malone in the back of the head. His aim was off, but even so, he was close enough for the blow to send bolts of red lancing through her vision.

She was lucky he hadn't fired. Lucky, perhaps, that his ally was still an indeterminate mass in the darkness ahead of her.

She fell to the ground and kicked, catching her assailant just above his ankles. He tumbled to the ground, and she used her momentum to pull herself around to face him. She heard a grunt and felt a tremor in the air as he swung his foot inches from her head.

She rolled to the side, and over the thrashing and struggling of the nearest man, heard the other thumping down the tunnel toward them, no longer mindful of stealth.

One thing at a time.

The man on the ground clicked his hammer back and fired again, still aiming at the spot where she'd first fallen. The man behind her yelped in surprise, not pain.

She had already pulled herself into a crouch and raised her revolver when the other man crashed into her from behind. Her gun fell, spinning away from her.

Malone still couldn't see, but she could picture her attacker's stance, right arm raised as a corner of his weight shifted off of her. Lips, no doubt, pulled back in a feral snarl.

She torqued her body and felt him tumble away.

The other man was getting impatient. Impatient enough to fire blindly into the dark. His qualms about hitting his own associate were rapidly diminishing.

And by now, they were all three equally dazed by muzzle flashes and choked with cordite.

She needed to find her gun.

She crawled deeper into the tunnel where she'd heard her revolver fall. The two men scrabbled behind her, no doubt trying to get their bearings and a bead on her.

A hand clamped down around her calf. She kicked and twisted, but he was ready for that this time. A heavy punch knocked the wind out of her, but she had to be thankful it wasn't a bullet.

Off to the side, the other man was getting to his feet.

Her nearest attacker launched himself onto her again. She resisted the urge to kick him off and instead waited, giving him enough time to land a ringing blow to her jaw. She turned her head and bit back a grunt of pain.

Next to and above her, a hammer clicked. She rolled, gripping her attacker by the front of his shirt. The gun fired, and his body went limp.

The man who had just fired the gun would only have heard the bullet hit tissue. He wouldn't yet know that he'd just killed his own associate.

And that delay between instance and realization was all the opportunity Malone needed.

She hurled the body still hanging over her into the remaining attacker. His feet skidded on the ground and he gasped in surprise, but his gun didn't clatter to the floor.

So Malone ignored the burning protest in her bones and leapt to her feet. The other man was still off balance, stirring up the air with flailing arms and grunting his frustration.

She raised her forearm to the level of his neck – what she estimated it to be, anyway, and charged. He slammed into the tunnel wall, coughing his emptied lungs into her face. But he still didn't drop the gun. Malone was starting to guess at how this would end.

To her left, the hammer clicked again.

She reached toward the sound and clamped her left hand around his wrist. Drove it toward the wall again. He didn't waste the shot and didn't drop the gun.

And her injuries, vague and indefinite, were starting to catch up with her, drawing reserves of strength from everywhere at once.

This time, he pushed back. Hard enough to get his arm away from the wall. Once he'd swung it forward, ahead of his body, it became an inexorably descending lever in Malone's hand. No matter how hard she pushed, her own arms were being forced down as he brought the gun toward her head.

These were not the options she'd planned for. A little tendon of resolve snapped within her.

Removing her right arm from his neck, Malone rammed her fist into the soft, yielding joint of his inner elbow. As she'd hoped, his outstretched arm bent inward, swiveling the gun back to his head.

Her left hand found his hot, sweat-slick trigger finger and pulled.

The report was loud and close enough that she heard nothing as he collapsed at her feet.

Even though the body didn't so much as twitch against her legs, she bent down and took the gun anyway. And, after several seconds of sweeping her hands along the floor, she found her own. Now blind and deaf, she had nothing but the feeling of her hands brushing stone, grit, mortar, and finally metal to guide her. The gunshot had been loud. Loud enough to attract attention several tunnels away. And if someone else – another of the Bricklayer's associates – came, running or creeping, she wouldn't hear him.

Malone reached down and felt for the pulses of the two men, ran her hands along their stiffening bodies, hoping for something salvageable.

There was nothing. She realized that she should be more grateful to have come out with her own life.

That had been too close. She turned to the man on the ground. The only difference between them was that he had been too slow to recognize the change that had occurred. She had taken advantage of it.

Malone rose stiffly and hobbled back toward the dim, sickly glow of her lantern. This was unfriendly territory. She would have to hurry out of it and hope that she could get someone at the station to come and collect the bodies for identification. She would have to hope they were still here by the time someone could be summoned.

She limped ahead, gasping silently at the pain in her bones.

Something was broken.

A few hours later, Malone was back at the station, her right wrist in a splint and the left side of her face swollen and purple. She was lucky, she'd been told, to have escaped with no fractures, breaks, or sprains, but her aching limbs and joints insisted otherwise. She would just as soon have skipped the hospital visit, with its endless prodding and long, disapproving frowns, but then she'd have never heard the end of it from Farrah. Vague, disapproving lectures were about the only words she seemed to get from the woman any more.

Malone trudged along the familiar route down a long hallway lit by trenches of flame, accompanied only by the echoes of her own footsteps. In the days before Sato's rebellion, when the station had bustled with inspectors and clerks and patrolmen – all comfortingly familiar faces, even if she'd never exchanged more than a word or two – the hall had seemed larger. Grander. Now, the place seemed as though it might collapse upon itself without the presence of so many people to prop it up. At last she reached the heavy, bullet-scarred door at the end.

She was still reminding herself that it was her office and not the late Chief Johanssen's.

And, as she swept through, there sat Farrah, ensconced in her nook between Malone's office and the hall outside. Another of Johanssen's relics and another aching reminder that this space would never really be hers.

As Malone passed through Farrah's office, she saw the other woman turn her head sharply, felt her censure blunted by surprise. Perhaps, Malone thought, it was at her own uncanny ability to seek out injury. Or perhaps it was merely that, this time, she'd gotten herself patched up right away. Either way, it was a small source of satisfaction in the middle of what was shaping up to be a long day.

And yet these occasions always brought Malone back to the real source of Farrah's disapproval. Sato and his allies were indirectly responsible for the deaths of Sundar – Malone's former partner – and Chief Johanssen. It was their revolution that had sparked the conflict that finally cost the lives of these two people Malone had cared about and a few hundred more. And even though Sato's cohorts had opposed the ones who had pulled the trigger, the City Guard and other supporters of the Council, it was tempting to blame someone who was still standing. Someone who could be taken down.

Even Malone had felt it. But she knew it for what it was – a futile tantrum of grief. Emotion cut off from the firm, reassuringly practical realities of the world.

What Recoletta needed was structure. Something to stave off the Bricklayer and his ilk, something to give form and meaning to the changing landscape.

She looked at her desk and sighed.

She would have gladly run back out the door and into the Bricklayer's tunnels if it would do any good. But the piles of papers on her desk were a problem that no amount of violence, force, or careful interrogation could solve.

She had never envied her late chief's job, and now that she found herself reluctantly installed at his desk, she wanted to burn it.

She sat down and began sorting through reports with a sinking feeling in her gut. Burglaries, looting, fraud, and much more. There was plenty of crime in Recoletta, but so far, most of the perpetrators had been devilishly hard to track down. The tangle of lawless tunnels seemed to absorb them just when her people got close, and even when they managed to nab somebody, a thief or counterfeiter or some other crook, two more sprang up the next week to take his place. Worse, half of her inspectors were new, pulled from Sato's ranks to fill the growing vacancies in the Municipal Police.

The revolution was over, but Malone still felt like she was under siege.

She'd been chief of the new Municipal Police in Recoletta for six months now, ever since Sato's coup, and she still felt like an impostor. The pleasantly musky smell of the office, the shape of the high-backed leather chair, even the coffee stains on the carpet all reminded Malone that this office should belong to Chief Johanssen.

And perhaps it still would, if she'd put the pieces together faster. The thought was as painful and familiar as an old wound.

The trickle of casework had started out slow after the coup. Mercifully so, as it had given her time to avoid this office, to get used to the other side of the desk in small doses. Of course, the calm hadn't lasted.

As Recoletta began to get used to the new state of affairs, concerns and reports had started to roll in. Immediate survival concerns evaporated and were replaced by complaints that were often calculated but no less frantic. Reports of stolen property, suspicious figures loitering in the neighborhood, and missing neighbors flooded her desk as Recolettans began to test the bounds of their new regime. Malone had to send the ragged and much-diminished staff of inspectors out to triage these various cases and accusations, but in many instances, they were complicated matters of hearsay. Tectonic shifts among the haves and have-nots. There wasn't a criminal to jail or a villain to blame, just multiple fundamentally irreconcilable sides to a story that grew more convoluted every day. Uncertainty, as thick and heavy as morning fog.

The only task that felt more futile than sifting through these never-ending grievances was sitting in on Sato's Cabinet meetings, where similar stories emerged on a larger scale.

Looking at the clock on the corner of her desk, she sighed and realized she was due at one in half an hour.

She grabbed her coat from a hook on the door and swept into the hall without a word to or from Farrah.

On her way out, she passed Inspector Velez and a trailing handful of hopeless-looking rookies. It was encouraging to see some activity, at any rate. Many of Malone's fellow officers had fallen during the coup, when confusion and suspicion put the City

Guard on the offensive at the station's doorstep. Bullet holes from the conflict still scarred the walls and cracked the corners of halls and doorways. The station was a burial ground, and those fresh reminders never failed to silence the survivors.

And now, many of them – like Malone and Velez – worked for Sato. The revolution had presented them with a common enemy in the Council and its minions. Sometimes, a common enemy was all it took to forge an alliance.

She headed to the surface streets and passed the shadows of verandas, the entrances to the city below. Most citizens opted for the convenience and comfort of underground travel, but the paved and cobbled roads aboveground seemed to have changed the least since the transition. Up here, in the relative quiet, Malone could pretend that nothing had changed, that she was still prowling her beat instead of shuffling from one stifling office to another.

Malone arrived at Dominari Hall, its great marble veranda still cracked and stained with blood, oil, and smoke, and the guardsmen nodded at her without a word. It had been the seat of the Council, Recoletta's former ruling body, for generations, and now Sato occupied it. He'd taken steps to make a few aesthetic changes, trying to distance himself from the Council he'd overthrown, no doubt. But even with the councilors' portraits removed, the place retained an unmistakable air of pomp and authority. And the wall hangings still smelled of gunpowder.

Yet as she navigated the lavish maze of offices and corridors, her mind was back in the Bricklayer's tunnels, charting a route and plotting her next move.

She followed the now-familiar path down lushly carpeted hallways and under gilded and marble-paneled archways until she reached the Council's old meeting chambers, where other members of the Cabinet were already assembling. A few pairs of eyes flickered in her direction, took in the bruises and the splint, and looked away again. It wasn't exactly politeness. Everyone simply had larger matters on their minds.

A wide, round table seemed to grow from the marble flooring, and the chairs surrounding it were all equally and obnoxiously ornate. Sato had changed much about the way Recoletta's government ran, but the gathering at the round table was one tradition he had kept. It was likely as much a matter of convenience as anything else. Malone couldn't imagine anyone moving the massive table from its place.

As Malone sat, Sato entered, flanked by two of his other advisors. Those who were already seated made a great show of coughing and shuffling their papers purposefully, but Sato didn't seem to notice. His snarl of red hair was wilder than usual, and dark circles dimmed his eyes. Malone remembered when she'd met him, like some vagabond prince, outside the Library of Congress. The scars and stains of travel had seemed glamorous on him, and the color in his cheeks had complemented his boyish vigor.

But after futile months in the city he'd fought and schemed to reclaim, an ashen pallor had settled over him like dust from Recoletta's crumbling streets. Looking at Sato was uncomfortably like looking into a mirror, Malone realized.

Sato and the other half dozen advisors chose seats around the table, and Malone felt rather than saw Roman Arnault sit directly across from her.

The mood was as tense as ever. Everyone sat ramrod straight, steeling themselves for another round of bad news. Only Sato leaned forward, his gaze fixed between his folded arms.

Mr Vaughn, Sato's secretary, cleared his throat and shuffled some papers. "This meeting is now called to order. We'll begin with status reports from all the departments and finish with remarks from President Sato. Going down the line, Mr Grenwahl with commerce."

Horace Grenwahl had a thick, lined face and the accent of a street sweeper. Malone couldn't help but wonder what the Council's generations of whitenails would have thought to hear Grenwahl's rough voice and working class slang echoing off the creamy marble walls of Dominari Hall.

But Grenwahl's deep-set eyes didn't miss much, and it showed in his reports. "Good news is, the decline's slowed since our last chitchat. The bad is, the south and east sides of town have all but shut down, and the market's down to a hundred or so stalls. Had roundabout nine hundred before."

Lines zagged across Sato's brow. "Last month, you told me we were stable at three hundred fifty."

"Last month, we were."

Sato's eyes narrowed. "At that rate, no one will be doing business in another two months."

Grenwahl cracked his knuckles and laughed. "They're doing plenty. Just not all legitimate-like."

Sato frowned, and Malone felt a spike of hope. If Grenwahl could shift Sato's focus from politics to the black market, she could use the opportunity to center his attention on the Bricklayer.

Three chairs to Malone's right, another voice broke in. "While I'm ever so pleased you find this amusing, we should focus on the reason our citizens are forgoing licit channels." The fluting accent and precise diction belonged to Nathan Tran-MacGregor, Sato's Minister of Finance. Malone had yet to figure out exactly why he'd joined Sato's revolution. Even though she wasn't familiar with his accent – he came from one of the many other cities Sato had traveled through before returning to Recoletta – his fastidious mannerisms and affected disdain all suggested privilege. Or aspirations to it.

Grenwahl uttered a contemptuous little laugh from the back of his throat. Even if Malone hadn't known Tran-MacGregor by his voice, she would have by Grenwahl's reaction. She wasn't sure if their mutual disgust had started from their seemingly different backgrounds or from their ministerial duties, which always seemed to put them at cross-purposes.

Grenwahl's generous lips curled. "It's a problem of confidence," he said, and Sato flinched. "The peddlers don't like opening their bags for swanky suits. So they sell where they don't have to."

Tran-MacGregor rolled his eyes. "If the merchants aren't willing to declare their goods to the appropriate authorities," he said, emphasizing his word choice, "perhaps we need to select our agents more carefully."

Grenwahl's wide smile broadened. "They can talk like me or lisp like you," he said. "The problem ain't with the agents, it's with the policy. You need to ease up or you'll choke the market."

It was a familiar argument and a more familiar feud.

Tran-MacGregor sniffed. "It would seem that we could do much better by choking one of our markets."

Grenwahl laughed harder, a rough sound. "Just let the markets right themselves. The only way to bury the black market'd be to fill every tunnel in this city with rubble."

It was an unpleasant reminder of the precarious state of affairs in Recoletta and of the lengths to which Sato had gone in order to topple the Council. A moment of fidgeting and silence followed, with everyone but Grenwahl finding something urgent to examine on the table.

Sato clasped his hands beneath his chin, his teeth seemingly clenched around some new contemplation.

Grenwahl chose that moment to lean forward, folding his thick-fingered hands on the table in front of him. The gesture almost looked spontaneous. "We need to ease up. On the borders, on the market. Let the merchants sell where they like. The most important thing is to keep up a healthy flow of goods and keep people from hoarding potatoes and trading stockings. As long as no one's gouging, we let this run its course for the time being. I've spoken with General Covas." He raised his eyebrows at the woman across the table. She met his gaze and nodded for the benefit of all. "And we're both of the opinion that our security depends on letting people feel comfortable, not backing 'em into a wall where their day-to-day business is concerned."

Tran-MacGregor adjusted his cuffs and glared holes into the table.

All eyes turned to Sato. His lips twitched. "Mr Vaughn, continue."

Malone shifted in her chair and made a conscious effort to keep her expression neutral. She wasn't sure whom she'd expected Sato to back, but his lack of attention to the matter disconcerted her.

It seemed as though his mind was fixed on other things.

Vaughn adjusted his spectacles, looking eager to move on. "Ambassador Chakrun, diplomacy."

The ambassador looked as if he hadn't slept in weeks. His olive skin was assuming a grayish hue, and new lines bracketed his eyes and mouth every day. "Nothing to report. Nobody's responding to our diplomatic overtures. The other city-states won't grant our envoys an audience or accept our goodwill gifts." He coughed into a hand. "I should, however, note that the... situation in the city, not the least of which is the current lack of control over the markets, does not inspire the confidence of our neighbors." He shared the quickest of glances with Tran-MacGregor. "Asserting our authority here would go a long way toward establishing a more secure reputation with these other city-states."

An uncertain silence followed. Sato sighed and made a rolling motion with his hand, and Vaughn moved to the next name on the list. "Mr Tran-MacGregor. Unless, ah, you've already covered it," he added hopefully.

Tran-MacGregor was leaning back in his seat, arms folded. "We need tax revenue, and we need to know what's coming into our city. My previous remarks conveyed the extent of finance's present concerns."

"Then we're on to General Covas. Military."

The general was a dark-skinned woman in her early forties. Malone had heard that she'd been a factory manager in her life before Sato. That surprised some because her smooth, steady voice always hovered just below conversational volume. But it had the effect of forcing everyone else to concentrate on what she said. "Nothing new. No unrest, no riots. Our first priority should be keeping things that way."

Sato nodded, his gaze distant and unfocused.

Vaughn shifted his papers and his eyes flickered to Malone. "Chief Malone with the police." The anticipatory quiver of his upper lip seemed to suggest that a second report with good news was too much to hope for.

She looked around the table and saw the others looking back at her. They already knew what she was going to say. She'd said it before and heard it lost in the myriad concerns of other departments. As she considered this, there was something calculating in their looks. She recognized it, knew it suggested an offer, an exchange of favors, but that nuance was a language she didn't speak.

Only Arnault looked back at her with contempt plain on his face. It was refreshing, really.

"Crime has continued to grow," Malone said. "My officers are reporting new burglaries and assaults every day, and we keep losing territory. There simply aren't enough of us to police the streets."

She turned to Sato, whose mouth was a thin, bloodless line.

"Give me more men. I need more people clearing out these tunnels. If we can spare soldiers..." Malone's gaze flickered to General Covas. The other woman's nostrils flared while her eyes narrowed to pinpricks. Malone knew she'd managed to step on her toes – again – but couldn't help pointing out the obvious. "We're all concerned about security. Black markets, too. If we can clean things up in the city–"

"With all due respect," Covas said, her voice calm but raised to a rare volume. Everyone snapped to attention. "Sending my soldiers to patrol Recoletta would be dangerous. People dislike being policed by their own military. It would invite comparisons to the old City Guard."

And the curfews and the period of mounting chaos during the Council's final days. Covas didn't need to say more.

But Malone had to make one more effort. "Sir, the Bricklayer. If we only–"

"The Bricklayer," Grenwahl said, managing to speak the name as if it were a playful moniker for something much less sinister, "is a boogeyman. Gives criminals something to fear and our dogged chief something to chase." His smile was as sickly sweet as treacle, and it was a slap in the face. "He doesn't exist. At best, he's an assortment of five or six different individuals operating independently of one another."

"If that's true," Malone said between her teeth, "those are five or six individuals we should eliminate."

"And when we do, five or six more will rise to take their place," Grenwahl said.

Malone opened her mouth to respond, but Sato spoke first. "Enough. Mr Vaughn, please continue."

"Er, next is Mr Arnault. Intelligence."

Arnault sighed in his usual languid manner, running a hand through his chin-length black hair. She couldn't believe herself – she'd set him up perfectly to join the others against her. As if Covas and Grenwahl weren't enough to deal with.

"Malone's right," Arnault said.

The other advisors turned to him, their eyes wide. For once, Malone did not feel that she was the only one left bewildered.

Arnault seemed to take his time in explaining himself. "My sources refer to the Bricklayer, too. But this isn't only a problem of crime. It's one of authority. The Bricklayer – whoever it is – cleans up tunnels. Gets rid of vandals. He's restored at least three ruined gas lines in the city, and he exercises his own form of vigilante justice. Executing criminals who prey on residents in his territories."

"He *is* a criminal," Malone said.

Arnault turned to Sato. "And he's undercutting you by addressing the very problems you should be handling." The rest of the table went quiet. Even though the advisors were quick to snipe at each other, they were all more cautious when it came to Sato. All of them but Arnault.

Sato gave Arnault a sober nod.

For one brief moment, Malone was certain Sato had finally been swayed. He was ready to give her hunt for the Bricklayer his full support.

"Mr Vaughn, is that everyone?" Sato asked, looking as if he'd just made up his mind about something.

"Just Mr Quillard," Vaughn said. "Library affairs."

Every head turned to a round, boyish figure with a timid smile. Nothing seemed to sway Sato's moods so quickly as news from Quillard.

And yet he seemed completely oblivious to this. Malone hadn't spent enough time with him to figure out whether it was incredible optimism, an extraordinary lack of social awareness, or a streak of cunning that ran deeper than any at the table could fathom.

He gave the rest of the advisors a timid smile, like a schoolboy called on to speak in front of the class. "Cataloguing operations continue to run smoothly. We're finding a great variety of literary, scientific, and historical texts. They've been organized as you requested, with the copies made available to the public. I think you'll be most pleased at our archives on antiquity – they've grown significantly since your last visit. I've arranged to have some of the records on ancient governance sent to you, as you requested."

Sato nodded and smiled over this news like an ill man over a bowl of hot broth. "Very good news, indeed."

Quillard continued. "We've had new visitors to the collection, too." Sato had opened the old Directorate of Preservation, the Council's formerly secret history archives, to the public, and he'd been moving copies and transcriptions there for people to read. Getting more Recolettans to visit the collection, to take an interest in the excavation of the Library of Congress, to embrace the history that had been off limits for so long – these were personal crusades for Sato and had been part of his original motivation for opposing the Council.

The other advisors frowned and shifted in their seats. Malone had quickly learned that, while many of his associates shared his vision for a more equitable and transparent government, few shared his zeal for history. Even those who did felt that, right now, his obsession was a distraction at best.

But something in Quillard's faltering smile gave Sato pause. "What exactly does that mean?"

Quillard wiped at his brow. "Well. The good news is, all of the books in the collection are copies, so this is more of an inconvenience than a real loss. But a few of our reading rooms were vandalized. About a hundred books, all told." He must have been one of the few people who wouldn't have tried to hide news like this. Perhaps that was why Sato had chosen him for the job.

Sato worked over something in his jaw. "I don't suppose we caught the persons responsible."

"No." Quillard inexplicably brightened. "But they did leave something behind."

He slid something – several somethings – across the table. Folded papers with garish block letters printed across them. Pamphlets.

Malone picked one up and flipped through it as she saw several of the other advisors doing. It was coated with a strange, waxy residue and filled with generic screeds against Sato, his foreign army, and all of the collaborators now propping up his regime: "Oppose the traitor Sato! Take back Recoletta, tunnel by tunnel!"

"Might help us track them down," Quillard said. He seemed to be the only person at the table who didn't acknowledge that this was bad news.

Everyone else was watching Sato and the rising color in his face. Malone felt she could tell exactly where he was in the pamphlet as he read, his lips working silently and his eyes narrowing.

"More than vandals. Insurgents," Sato muttered.

"Grumblers," Arnault said. "Nothing more." Only he seemed unconcerned by the pamphlets, but with him, it was always hard to tell.

Judging by the uncomfortable looks around the room, everyone else had made the uncomfortable connection between Sato's own rise to power and these seeming challengers.

Sato pulled his eyes from the page in his hand long enough to look at Arnault. "Black markets and petty crime are one thing. But this," he said, brandishing the pamphlet, "this is a call to arms. They're organized. And they've staged their stunt around the defacement of the books we've offered them, the very ones the Council always forbade. What is this if not a declaration of open rebellion?"

"They're acting out," Arnault said, as patiently as if he were explaining playroom bullies to a child. "As long as you allow them to, they'll come around to your position. They'll realize this tantrum is a freedom they never had under the Council."

"And yet they miss the Council," Sato said, assaulting one page of the pamphlet with a rigid finger.

"The devil you know," said Arnault, his expression unreadable.

Sato sighed. "It didn't start out this way. When the smoke cleared, everyone was happy."

"Because the smoke had cleared," Arnault said. "And because they hadn't yet confronted changes."

"That's the problem," Sato said. "They don't want to confront changes. They'd have happily let Ruthers and the rest of the Council bleed them for generations more as long as it was predictable."

"You just need to give them time."

"I need to give them a reason to see this government as legitimate. Once they acknowledge our administration, the rest will fall into place."

And while the others around the table shifted and made surreptitious eye contact with one another, Malone saw her opportunity.

"Sir," she said.

Sato looked up at her. So did the rest of the advisors.

Malone cleared her throat. "If you want the people to recognize your authority, you have to remove the clearest threat to it," she said, thinking of the Bricklayer and his shifting fiefdom. She remembered, vaguely, something another officer – she couldn't remember who – had said to her a lifetime ago. "Show them who keeps Recoletta clean."

Sato was watching her closely now. So was everyone else, and she knew from their expressions that what she had said had been the wrong thing, but she didn't yet know why.

"I just need leads. I have a department of reasonably capable inspectors. If even a few squads of Covas's soldiers could take over patrol duties, I could focus my efforts on stopping these people."

Arnault's eyes went wide with horror.

Sato nodded slowly. "The direct approach. That's what I've always liked about you, Malone." He opened his pamphlet wide. "Your first lead."

She stared at the creased paper, understanding of what she'd done only slowly dawning. "Sir, I was talking about the Bricklayer. His network–"

"Can wait for now. Locating these insurgents is your first priority."

How quickly they had evolved from simple pamphleteers. A wave of queasiness washed over her.

She watched the other advisors. Arnault seethed. Grenwahl and Covas eyed her coolly. The rest avoided her gaze completely. She would have to dig herself out of this on her own.

"I'm... not qualified for this kind of investigation." Malone gritted her teeth against her excuse. It tasted like bile, but it was better than a witch hunt. "And neither is my new department. I chase criminals. Smugglers, thieves, and killers. Tracking down political cells is not my area of expertise." If it had been, she thought with a grimace, she would have caught Sato long before he'd gotten this far.

"I know," Sato said, laying his pamphlet on the table. "That's why Roman will liaise with you on this."

The muscles in Malone's face went stiff. Across the table, she felt Arnault's rage boil over at her.

That was hardly fair, but it was beside the point.

Malone felt arguments and objections welling up inside her. Before she could give voice to any of them, Sato clacked his papers against the table and announced, "Dismissed."

The other advisors rose, making quick exits before they found their own burdens increased. She stayed in her place, knowing there was little else anyone could do at this point to actually make things worse for her. So she gathered her thoughts and waited until the room had emptied, and then she made her way to Sato's office as if pulled by its gravity.

She was annoyed, but not exactly surprised, to see Arnault already there. The two men looked up as she entered, and Malone read her own displeasure on Arnault's face.

"I was just about to call for you," Sato said, smooth and pleasant.

She squared her shoulders and planted her feet in the doorway. "I wanted to discuss these pamphleteers."

"Good. Because the two of you need a plan."

She felt the noose tightening.

"Have a seat," Sato said, lowering himself into a carved, high-backed chair. At a nod from Sato, Roman stiffly did likewise.

Malone sat, watching Sato's folded hands across the desk. Next to his elbow was a book – something with a thick cover and the shabby decadence typical of Quillard's archives. It was embossed with fading, gilded letters: *The Republic.* Plato.

Sato opened his mouth and took a quick breath, as if deciding how to begin. "Malone, I know the last few months have been rough on you. For several reasons. You lost many of your colleagues, and you're coping with a new position. One to which you are not, perhaps, well accustomed." He spoke slowly, looking away. He wouldn't acknowledge the parallel between them, but his sudden flush said clearly enough that he recognized it.

Malone's jaw muscles tightened. "This is not my usual method of investigation."

"Nor is sitting in an office and sorting reports. What you need is a culprit." Sato flashed a flat smile. "And I've found one for you."

She swallowed, preparing to barrel directly to the point. "Sir, it's the wrong culprit. We need–"

Sato's palm came down hard on the table. "We need to restore confidence, Malone." His lips were pressed together, and there was an edge in his voice she hadn't heard before. Even Arnault was motionless.

Sato continued. "We can't force the merchants back to their stalls or chase the black marketeers out of business. We can't even keep up with the thefts and assaults your people report every week. But we can handle this."

Arnault remained silent, still seated awkwardly at the corner of the desk, but a muscle in his cheek spasmed.

Sato folded his hands again and seemed to relax. Or slump. "We've all had to make compromises. But you'll do this work because it needs doing. Before it grows into something we can't handle."

A memory rose in her mind of the councilors Sato had executed, lined up and standing before their nooses. Only their faces shifted and changed until Malone wasn't sure whether they represented herself, or Sato, or the unknown pamphleteers.

She shivered, though at which possibility she couldn't tell. But one look at Sato's face confirmed that the matter was no longer up for discussion.

Malone steeled her nerves and swallowed the lump rising in her throat. "Understood. Although..." her eyes flickered to Arnault.

"You work better alone." He followed her gaze. "I've heard that speech already. But you're going to work together because you need his information and he needs your investigative skills." He looked back at Malone for a brief moment. "Now, unless there is anything else," he said in a tone that indicated there clearly wasn't, "I've got to get back to work. And so do you."

Malone made her exit as quickly as possible.

CHAPTER 3

UNEASY ALLIANCES

After that day in the souk, Jane made daily trips to the Majlis. She soon learned that the veiled woman who had hired her over tea and honey cakes was the Qadi, the elected judge and arbiter of Madina. Jane eventually came to understand that, while her closest counterpart in Recoletta would have been Councilor Ruthers, the two were actually quite different.

For starters, the Qadi, though powerful, could actually be voted out, was never known to have executed any of her rivals, and seemed to be genuinely admired by most of the people in Madina.

In the five and a half months since her hiring, Jane had not spoken with the Qadi again, but it still felt reassuring to have a patron in her position. And yet, remembering her own disastrous exile from Recoletta, she was careful not to place too much faith in the relationship.

For now, it was enough to enjoy the views of skylights and plazas and the simple luxury of a steady salary.

The job itself was less glamorous than the Qadi's invitation had suggested, but that was fine by Jane. Most days found her digging through archives and pulling files for more senior jurists, or sorting and storing records of more recent cases. On occasion – once she'd been in the Qadi's employ for over a month – she would be called upon to arbitrate a matter involving another Recolettan, sifting first through pages of allegations and then hearing long-winded speeches of the same.

She was a little baffled still to see that so much trust had been placed in her over the encounter with the whitenail and the merchant months ago, especially when the particulars of her new cases often seemed so vague. She told herself she was making the best decisions she could, but in practice, it often felt like she simply had to choose one name over another.

It made her grateful for the veil.

After she'd seen the Qadi wear one, she began to notice it elsewhere. At first, she couldn't figure it out – was it fashion, tradition, or a custom born of practicality? She saw it on men and women, and though the wearers most often dressed in the finer silks and woven wools that signified wealth, she noted this as a trend rather than a rule.

And then, five weeks into her tenure at the Majlis, when she was first called to sit in on a dispute, she was presented with a veil, and she understood.

The veil she wore was a shade of dark green that matched her robes. While it was sheerer than the one the Qadi had worn, and free of any ornamental embroidery, Jane was grateful for it as soon as she sat down to arbitrate and saw the angry gazes of the aggrieved and the accused turn on her.

That first time, she'd listened to the facts alongside two other jurists, men of experience who didn't pluck or scratch behind their veils the way Jane had been tempted to do. After they had heard the arguments from both sides – a Recolettan who claimed he'd been cheated out of a tidy investment and a Madinan who contended that the fool's expectations had been unreasonable – Jane and her senior counterparts had retired to confer.

Jane hadn't known what to think, except that the two adversaries in the hearing chamber should have kept a written record of their agreement to prevent controversies like this. But the two jurists with Jane had reached the conclusion that the

Recolettan had indeed embarked on a risky venture and now sought recompense where none was due.

"But these people, the ones who keep their nails so long, they're used to getting their way. Where they come from," one of the jurists had said, turning to Jane.

"We've tried to explain this, but they feel that we are being unfair. Favoring our own," said the other.

The first man had nodded to Jane. "But he hears this from you, and perhaps he'll understand. That our ways are not his, but they are fair. Especially when one of his own can rise to prominence, no?"

Jane had doubted that a whitenail would consider her "one of his own," but she'd heard the expectation clearly enough. And the implicit threat to her newfound position.

She'd felt the seconds tick by as she considered the directive. It had felt as though she'd swallowed something rancid, and her skin had suddenly chafed all over. Every instinct told her this was wrong, yet those same instincts told her that a refusal on her part was pointless. Their two votes would outweigh hers, and if she didn't serve her new masters, they'd find someone who would.

Anyway, hadn't she just been thinking that even she had no real way to tell the victim from the vulture?

It had always been a coin flip. And if the whitenail was too rash to learn the rules of his new city, it was no problem of hers.

Besides, her most providential job paid for her apartment, a quiet, safe place where Fredrick was holed up right now. If she didn't look after him, who would?

So she'd nodded at her superiors and said, "Yes, I understand." And when they'd returned to the hearing chamber, she'd cast her vote in favor of the Madinan, as had the first of the two jurists. The other had voted in favor of the Recolettan. For appearances' sake.

After that, she found herself summoned to adjudicate a few times a week. Not every hearing was so choreographed. But it was enough to remind her of the purpose and price of her position.

At least she had the veil.

It was privacy. It was authority. Even though the movements of her mouth and the direction of her eyes were still visible beneath the gauzy fabric, she could be anyone she needed to be behind it. It separated her from the individuals over whom she presided.

It was, she realized, a flimsy protection. But she took comfort in the pseudo-anonymity and in the supposition that no one, neither whitenail nor Madinan nor Sato, would be able to find her.

Not until the evening, almost six months into this new life, when she returned home and found someone waiting for her.

Jane turned the key in the lock and opened her door. She was surprised, not to see Freddie, but to hear him in conversation with someone.

"...no idea how good it is to see a familiar face," he was saying, tension edging his voice.

"I'm just grateful for a proper cup of tea." The second voice sounded familiar, but Jane couldn't place it until she pushed her way in the door and saw the regal woman seated at her shabby kitchen table, her hands folded neatly and patiently over the flaking varnish and bare pine. It was actually an old writing desk that she and Fredrick had picked up for the price of a week's bread and milk, and it looked too small even in their cramped apartment. Jane and Fredrick were forever alternating between sitting across from one another on the long ends, their knees knocking together and their dishes spread between them in a single crooked line, and sitting at the short ends, wedging their thighs around and between the table legs.

Yet Lady Lachesse had assumed her position at one of the long ends, her teacup and her clasped hands perched on the ruined surface as if it were made for her. Jane had previously met her through Fredrick at a gala in Recoletta, and the woman had looked no less commanding and composed there than she did here, in their understocked kitchen.

Something about the older woman had both fascinated and terrified Jane when they'd first met. Seeing her again, it wasn't hard to recall her gracefully predatory aspect.

Lady Lachesse turned her face up to nod at Jane as the younger woman entered, her hair swept up and silhouetted by the lamplight from the kitchen. Lady Lachesse still dressed in the fashion of Recoletta as if in defiance of local custom, the wide skirts of her taffeta dress trimmed with lace.

"Welcome home, Miss Lin," said Lady Lachesse. "Please. Do make yourself comfortable." She gestured graciously at the chair across from her.

It was too early to start a row. Jane bit back her indignation and concentrated on trying to make herself comfortable seated across from the venerable Lady Lachesse. The elderly dame's generous thighs had taken up most of the room under the table, and so Jane found herself sitting at an odd angle, one knee cocked under the table, and just close enough to reach the teacup that Fredrick placed in front of her.

Jane cleared her throat. "What a pleasant surprise to see a familiar face."

Lady Lachesse nodded, politely acknowledging this sentiment without actually returning it.

Fredrick shortly returned with the kettle, holding it high to pour a thin, corkscrewing stream of black tea into Lady Lachesse's cup. He crossed to Jane's side of the table, filling her cup with a utilitarian slosh.

Lady Lachesse raised her cup and took a long, deep drink from it, closing her eyes. "Such a luxury after the syrup these locals drink," she said, returning her cup to its chipped saucer.

"Happy we can oblige," Jane said, watching her over the rim of her cup.

"There comes a time," Lady Lachesse said, "when one takes great comfort in little familiarities. Perhaps you know what I mean."

Jane didn't, not yet, but "Yes ma'am" was the correct answer, so she gave it.

A Cheshire cat smile curled Lady Lachesse's lips as she contemplated Jane, running a finger around the rim of her saucer.

"It's hard to say whether our circumstances would have changed more in Recoletta than they have here," she said. Her eyes took in Jane's robes, simple but well tailored, and the rough texture of the rickety table. "Although I suppose these ghastly pajamas don't really leave much work for a laundress of your skill, do they?"

Jane felt a barb in the woman's words, but she knew better than to try to dig it out. And anyway, she had grown calluses after her years of work for whitenails like Lady Lachesse back in Recoletta.

Lady Lachesse smiled and, as if to emphasize her point, draped one arm across the table, tapping a four-inch fingernail on the shabby wood. She wore a small fortune in jewelry, another act of defiance, no doubt. Jane had seen other whitenails trade half as many trinkets for currency and the bread and comfort it promised.

And yet Lady Lachesse had invited herself to preside over Jane and Fredrick's tiny apartment as if any of her depreciating status still mattered. It was an elaborate and prideful bluff of a woman still clinging to the trappings of the city that had exiled her.

That, or Lady Lachesse had planned and prepared much better than anyone else. The older woman smiled, and suddenly, Jane wasn't so sure.

Lady Lachesse followed Jane's searching gaze. "I've managed to maintain a modicum of my status and a few of my favorite luxuries. But I hear you've done quite well for yourself."

Jane let her eyes linger on the shabby, mismatched furniture just long enough to make a point. "I've survived," she said.

"You've adapted, clever girl."

Jane took a sip of her tea. She suspected that this was merely the prelude to a larger point. And a request. Or, more likely, a demand.

Lady Lachesse continued. "Most of your former countrymen have not managed so well. As you've no doubt noticed behind that green veil of yours." She said it as though wearing it were somehow an act of cowardice.

Jane bristled despite herself. "You'll forgive my forwardness, but I'm certain you can appreciate the protection that certain resources provide. I've suddenly realized how nice it is to have them."

The elderly whitenail tsked. "There's no need for this petulance. Not when you and I are equals in this grand new city."

Heat flooded her face, but Jane stood fast against the rampant tide. "Is that why you've come? For the company of an equal?"

Lady Lachesse was silent for several seconds. Not angry, but thoughtful. "I came because you're too smart to squander your future for your pride. And because I also want to survive."

Fredrick, who had bustled about the tiny kitchen for about as long as he reasonably could, finally brought his own cup to the table, but there was barely room enough for Jane, let alone a third. He dragged his chair to the short end between the two women and sat beside the table rather than at it. He perched his cup and saucer where he found space.

"Recoletta is experiencing growing pains," Lady Lachesse continued. "It's not the city you or I knew, and it's not the city Sato expected, either. And we can't roll back the clock any more than he can prune and shape its growth. Do you understand?"

"Better than most," Jane said.

"You also understand," Lady Lachesse said slowly, "what vulnerability is like. That sinking feeling of finding yourself surrounded by more powerful forces, knowing that your advantages are few and your friends fewer still."

Jane felt the sting of the threat like a lash across her palms. She set her jaw against it. "And now, so do you."

Freddie's wobbly chair let out a timid squeak.

Lady Lachesse's prim smile curdled. "Ever the keen observer, Miss Lin. You may, however, find it advantageous to have a few allies in your corner."

"It seems I already do."

"You have employers, and by now, you should know the difference."

Jane swallowed a mouthful of tea and set her cup down carefully. Freddie scuttled off to get the pot, no doubt eager for an excuse to retreat. "If you're asking me to start deciding in favor of more whitenails..."

"Don't be crass. Any foolish enough to get themselves into trouble with the local authorities deserve the ordeal. I'm only suggesting that you use your considerable influence to help the rest of us."

Jane didn't want to sound eager, but she was curious. "I take it you have something specific in mind."

Freddie returned with the teapot, refilling the cups as quietly as possible. Even his eyes were glued to Lady Lachesse.

The older woman took her time, enjoying a long, slow sip of her tea. "Though they haven't done so openly, your new patrons are discussing Recoletta. Soon, they'll start sending messages. Receiving intelligence. They want to know more about what's going on in Recoletta even if they aren't yet willing to officially acknowledge Sato's government."

Jane balked, almost spilling her tea. "And you expect me to get my hands on this information?"

"You're good at that sort of thing, aren't you?" Lady Lachesse smiled sweetly.

"What use could it possibly be to you?"

"I want to know, Jane. There's a considerable advantage in foresight. One that you could, perhaps, use as well. You're comfortable now, but let's not forget how quickly one's position can crumble." She raised her teacup to her lips. "Speaking from experience."

Jane wrapped her fingertips carefully around the warm cup. "Perhaps you're right." She took a drink as well. "But why would I share anything with you?"

"As I've said, fortunes can change rather suddenly. It's wise to make friends where one can."

Jane set her cup back in her saucer. She could feel herself being forced into agreement. Yet she saw an opportunity to grab something for herself. "If I do this," she said, "I'll want something from you, too."

"An exchange? Do tell."

Jane suddenly realized she didn't have anything specific in mind. What could the whitenail offer? She had connections, it seemed, but Jane wasn't sure who they were or what use they would be. There was money, but the idea of taking wages from this woman nauseated her. She'd been a fixture of Recoletta's elite class for decades, but none of that could help either of them now.

And then she remembered. She thought back to her first meeting with Lady Lachesse, recalling the woman's uncanny mind for detail, her appetite for scandal. If anyone knew the details of an incident some twenty-five years old, it would be her.

"I want to know about my parents."

The surprise on Lady Lachesse's face gratified Jane. "I beg your pardon?"

Jane licked her lips. This was a gamble. It could be beyond even the whitenail's considerable knowledge. But she suspected not. "I want to know why they were killed." She kept her voice steady. She had to sound confident and resolute. Roman had told her that Councilor Ruthers was responsible, but he'd never explained why.

The thin smile returned. "How would you ever know I'm telling the truth?"

Jane mirrored the expression. "What reason would you have to lie?"

Lady Lachesse laughed, a surprisingly high and merry sound. "If you have to ask, you're in more trouble than I thought."

Jane felt her fingers tighten around her cup, realizing how relieved she'd been to actually leave behind whitenail presumption and whitenail privilege. She also realized that, on some level, Lady Lachesse was right.

Still, backing down would show just the kind of weakness that would whet the old woman's appetite. "I know part of the story already," she said, which was technically, if barely, true. "But if this is beyond you, then you can forget about it."

The older woman's laugh took on a dangerous edge. "I can manage, Miss Lin. I just wanted to make sure we had an understanding."

Jane felt a sharp pain under the table. She looked up at Lady Lachesse, but Fredrick's scowling face loomed in the corner of her vision.

"We do," Jane said.

The corners of the whitenail's mouth twitched upward. "I am so glad."

Lady Lachesse nodded on her way out the door, as if none of this were the least bit surprising. "I'll be sure to call on you, Miss Lin."

As the door snicked shut behind the older woman, Fredrick's raspy whisper floated over her shoulder. "Are you mad?" he asked. "Making a deal with her?"

Jane rounded on Freddie. "What choice did I really have? She'd found me."

He gave a hollow laugh and shook his head, watching her with mirthless green eyes. "Lady Lachesse has long claws, even here. You just showed her where to sink them."

"Then I've got you to thank for making the introduction." Jane carried her cup and saucer to the sink. She splashed water over it and began scrubbing at the ring stained in the ceramic.

"Don't blame me for this," Fredrick said, clearing the remaining cups. "You saw where things were headed and kept pushing. I watched you just now."

"And you kept us supplied with tea, let's not forget that." Jane scrubbed harder, her knuckles white beneath the suds. The ring wouldn't come out.

He sighed. "I didn't ask for any of this."

His words burned. Had he already forgotten that she'd sacrificed precious hours to come to his rescue before fleeing? Or did he think he could have stayed in Recoletta? "You regret leaving with me?" Her mouth felt dry. Whether from anger or fear, she didn't yet know.

He'd had no choice. "Of course not," he said. But in the pause, in the falling inflection, she heard something else. Perhaps it was merely exhaustion.

The water had turned her hands lobster red. She had forgotten how hot it was.

Fredrick set the cups on the counter. "She's a businesswoman, Jane. If she's made a bargain with you, she'll keep it."

Jane wasn't sure if he was trying to convince her or himself.

After the latest Cabinet meeting, Malone had decided to wait a day before getting started on her new investigation with Arnault. As much as she hated delaying the inevitable, she doubted that this ordeal would resolve itself quickly. Besides, she needed some time to think.

She arrived at Callum Station the next morning after a mostly sleepless night. She wasn't sure the supposed rest had actually left her any more clear-headed, so when she came to her office and looked at her waiting chair, big enough to swallow her and trapped behind a paper-cluttered desk, she decided she needed some tea first.

Besides, she knew already she'd have worse places to face today.

Thankfully, the kitchen, crowded between the halls and meeting rooms like a haphazard afterthought, was close enough to Johanssen's office. To *her* office.

Malone lit the stove and dug a bag of loose leaf out of a drawer powdered with the dusty sediment of tea leaves. She heard a rumbling in the cabinets next to her and looked over to see Farrah, her bright red hair blazing over her back as she dug for a teacup.

As Farrah turned, cup in hand, to wait for the kettle, Malone realized that this was the first time they'd been in this room together since the transition. The last time, Farrah had warned her that the City Guard was about to comb Callum Station for her.

"I never got a chance to thank you," Malone said.

Farrah looked up from the kettle. "What for?"

"For getting me out of the station," Malone said. "The day before the revolution." Six months late, the apology sounded paltry and contrived, even to Malone.

Farrah rolled her sleepy eyes back to the stove. It seemed premature, but she filled her cup nevertheless.

Malone looked at her own cup, empty but for a satchel of musky brown leaves. She should have been happy to let Farrah slip away, ending this uncomfortable moment, but her own guilt had built up like floodwaters behind a dam, and she could already feel it trickling through her resolve. "You were counting on me to fix things. So was Johanssen. And Sundar. I didn't make the connections fast enough."

"Forget it," Farrah said, concentrating on the hot water rising in her cup. "You've got enough to worry about right now. Reorganizing the Municipal Police, integrating some of the former City Guard, pulling in Sato's men, getting the city back in order." She set the kettle back on the burner. "Don't waste your time agonizing over what ended six months ago."

Malone lifted the kettle gingerly. There was just enough water left for half a cup. She set it aside. The room felt warm and her mouth dry. A dull kind of panic was entering her bloodstream, the same kind she felt whenever she thought back to Johanssen, Sundar, and the empty offices around the station. "None of this would have happened if I–"

Farrah looked back at Malone, her eyes bright. "You didn't kill Chief Johanssen. And neither did Sato. Captain Fouchet of the City Guard did, and he's dead, too."

Farrah's words brought back a similar memory of watching Sundar strolling into the Library, jaunty and unaware of the danger. A tightness settled over Malone's face.

"You can't save everyone, Malone," Farrah said, full of brisk sympathy. "Sundar wouldn't have blamed you, and you're certainly not doing the rest of us any favors by dwelling on this. You've got to focus on fixing the mess we're all in now."

She realized, too, that they wouldn't be stuck here, patching things up while Recoletta fell apart around them, were it not for her failure. "Johanssen could have handled this," she said. "I haven't been able to do the job he would have."

"So quit trying," Farrah said, blowing over the top of her cup and frowning at the exit. "You're not going to replace him, and neither is anyone else. You want to beat yourself up some more, then look at this as your penance. You've got to put things back together one way or another." She took a sip from the top of her cup and turned away. "If you'll excuse me, I've got work to do. And so do you."

Farrah disappeared around the corner, leaving Malone with her thoughts and a teacup empty but for dried leaves. Malone left it on the counter and shut off the burner.

She headed to Arnault's office. There was no putting it off any longer.

The corridor she followed wound away from the main hall and into the deeper recesses of Callum Station. Much to her dismay – and to Arnault's apparent displeasure – Sato had insisted on finding Arnault an office in the station. Even though they technically worked for the same side now, Malone didn't trust him, and she didn't like having him so close to her base of operations. She'd caught herself checking up on the kinds of details that she would normally have left to Farrah: the locations of files, the assignments of her investigators. Nothing out of the ordinary had happened, but that only increased Malone's fear that when it finally did, it would be subtle enough to escape her notice.

She continued, her boots loud in the quiet halls. Argument with Sato on the matter of Arnault's office had been pointless. There was plenty of space, and it wasn't as if she could point to a specific cause for suspicion or even a likely motive. And perhaps that was what bothered her most – she had no idea what Arnault wanted and thus no way to anticipate his moves.

As she neared his office, the sound of muted voices reached her ears. She stole closer, her footsteps soft and silent as she recognized Arnault's low voice and the singsong lilt of Olivia Saavedra.

If Arnault was Sato's eyes and ears, then it appeared that Olivia

Saavedra served as Arnault's. That was the most Malone could figure out, any way. All she could definitively conclude was that Olivia had a way of appearing everywhere at once, and whatever she observed seemed to make its way back to Arnault.

With hardly a second thought, Malone slid next to the cracked-open door, standing close enough to hear the conversation inside. The lack of activity in this wing of the station made it unlikely that anyone would chance by, but the risk energized her in a way that months of paperwork and bureaucratic reorganization had not.

"...No word from my contacts," Olivia was saying. "I think the most recent incident has made them more cautious."

"Do what you can in the meantime," Arnault said.

"Of course. I've been working on another pair of sources. I am expecting they will bear fruit for us in another couple of weeks." She emphasized the word "us."

"Then report to me when they do." Something about the volume of Arnault's voice suggested that he was looking down – at something on his desk, perhaps.

"I have it on good authority that the criminal networks will be ceding territory around Tanney Passage and establishing a presence closer to the Spine. Now would be the time to move a couple of these contacts."

"Then I trust you to handle it," Arnault said in his bored monotone.

As the silence stretched into awkwardness, Malone found her curiosity aroused not only by the covert operations the two were discussing, but also by their divergent tones: Arnault's chilly formality and Olivia's uncomfortable persistence. She hazarded a peek through the door. Through the narrow slit, she saw Arnault, bent over his desk and focused intently on it, and Olivia standing in front of it, her legs crossed at the ankles.

"I... thought you might have some suggestions. On how these contacts should be placed. I know you're a man who appreciates the importance of detail." Olivia took a few slow strides toward the desk, the roll in her step accentuating the roundness of her hips.

Malone ducked back around the corner as Arnault's head angled up.

"You have your recommendations outlined in your report?" he asked.

"Of course."

"Then I'll take a look at them when I go through it."

Malone heard another two steps followed by the fleshy slap of papers flopping onto wood. "I'd like to speak candidly," Olivia said.

"What's on your mind, Miss Saavedra." His words were flat, empty of the round inflection of a question.

"It's Olivia."

He said nothing, waiting.

Rustling fabric. Two slow, careful footsteps. A fingernail sliding across a hard surface. Malone couldn't resist the temptation any longer. She peered again through the crack in the door.

Olivia's back was to Malone, and she blocked all view of Arnault but for his protruding elbows.

"You're still thinking about her," Olivia finally said.

He turned away from her, back to the papers on his desk.

"It's touching, really," Olivia said. "The way you wait for her. Very affecting."

He sighed a short, staccato note of exasperation.

"But it's been six months. Do you even remember her face? Does she remember yours?"

After several seconds' pause, Arnault said, "You should go." He slapped a folder shut as she circled to the other side of his chair.

"What happened between you was important. I'm not saying it wasn't. But what else have you really got in common? You're different people. If you were to see each other now, would you really have anything between you?"

Roman said nothing.

"You belong to two different worlds," Olivia said. "All I'm saying is, you don't have to be lonely in this one."

Malone heard the shifting fabric and the squeak of soles on wood as Olivia turned back to the door. Malone ducked into an empty office just as the other woman's quick, soft footsteps approached the hallway. As Olivia passed the office where Malone waited, Malone felt rather than heard her sigh, something fragrant and sensual.

She waited just long enough to keep her timing from seeming deliberate before turning into Arnault's office.

He sat in a thick, high-backed leather chair much like her own. And, like her, he seemed thoroughly uncomfortable in it.

It was hard to tell if the scowl on his face was for her, for Olivia, or part of the normal landscape.

"So glad you knocked," he said.

"I thought we'd get straight to business," she said. "And you appreciate the direct approach."

He grunted.

"Sato implied that you'd know where to begin," she said. Not that she felt any better about investigating a bunch of ideologues, particularly when there were real criminals on the loose.

"He implied a lot of things," Arnault said. "Did you believe all of them?"

Was he drawing her out, baiting her into saying something that would get her into trouble? Or was he merely letting her know that he recognized her reluctance and the possibly treasonous tendencies at the heart of it?

"I'm sure he has his reasons," she said.

Arnault sneered. "And already you're going along with them, I see. Ever the faithful underling."

Coming from the man who had supported Sato's coup behind the scenes, the accusation surprised Malone. "Do you have a better idea?"

"You did," Arnault said. "When you suggested searching for the Bricklayer."

Malone didn't know what to say, but she was increasingly certain that Arnault was luring her into insubordination. "You saw how the idea was received," she said. "Are we supposed to ignore Sato's orders?"

He rolled his eyes as if she were being impossibly dense. "Has it occurred to you that the two could be related?"

Not for the first time, Malone wondered what exactly he and Olivia had been talking about.

She also realized that he had a good point.

Arnault continued. "If the dissenters needed a way to move something heavy, the Bricklayer's tunnels would be the safest way to avoid Sato's notice. Have you kept track of the printing presses in the city? There aren't many."

"Two have been reported missing," Malone said. "Although those are hardly the highest-value items to have disappeared."

"They're the only ones that could have generated the pamphlets we saw. And I'd bet you anything that at least one of them is somewhere in the Bricklayer's territory."

"Why so eager to find him?" Malone asked.

He gave her a scowl of disgust. "Is it so strange that someone would want to clean this place up?"

"You don't strike me as the crusading type."

"Merely practical," he said.

"Then I'll ask again. Where do we start?"

"Unfortunately, none of my networks have reported the sudden appearance of printing presses. So we'll have to work backwards, and you'll have to find out when those two went missing."

Malone had had enough foresight to review those files earlier that morning. "Four months ago," she said.

"That's quite a memory," he said, eyes narrowed.

"Like you said, it's not every day someone steals a printing press."

"Then we'll want to start looking in areas that have been Bricklayer territory for at least that long. I doubt anyone's been eager to move several hundred pounds of iron more than once."

"You have contacts that can give us some leads?"

"Correction," Arnault said. "I have contacts that can give me some leads."

The hairs on the back of Malone's neck bristled. "I don't like it any more than you do, but we're working together on this."

"That doesn't mean I'm going to reveal all of my sources. As I recall, your lack of discretion became problematic for some of your previous associates."

A hot wave of anger washed over her. "Coming from a man who overthrew his last government."

His eyes twinkled above a nasty grin. "Careful, Malone. You aren't questioning Sato's legitimacy, are you?"

"Of course not," she said between gritted teeth. "But plenty of people around the city are."

"A fact of which we are reminded at every Cabinet meeting. What's your point?"

"Only that we don't have time for your obstructionism." She swallowed her anger and redirected her mind to matters at hand. "Where are you hearing the most chatter?"

Arnault's shoulders straightened. "The city's quiet except for the factory districts."

"It's the hub of the black market," Malone said.

"That, and the *nouveau riche*. The Vineyard would be a better starting point for our purposes. It's been Bricklayer territory almost from the beginning."

Malone frowned. The Vineyard had been Recoletta's wealthiest district for generations. It should house the most fervent resistance to Sato, but it had been surprisingly quiet in her reports.

Arnault saw her bewilderment and laughed. "Perhaps if you spent more time behind your desk and less time chasing shadows, you'd know what I'm talking about, Chief."

"I've read the reports. There are hardly any coming out of the Vineyard."

"Is that really surprising?" He leaned forward on his desk. "Who exactly are they going to complain to? Sato's the one who brought the rabble in. Furthermore, it's not as... lively as it used to be."

"The whitenails are leaving," she said. Many of them had fled the city in the weeks just after Sato came to power. In the last couple of months, Sato had made it harder for people to leave, but Malone's information suggested that there was still a steady trickle out of the city. And if anyone had reason – and resources – to strike out, it was the whitenails.

And for all his invective, Sato had need of them, their capital, and their labor.

Arnault shrugged, seemingly remembering the same discussion. "We lose the lawyers, but we lose the doctors, too. So much for a lucky break."

"This doesn't make sense. Half of the whitenails have left, and you're telling me the rest have taken up organized dissent? I can't picture a bunch of whitenails moving a cast iron printing press."

"Desperation brings out the best in us all."

She didn't have a good argument, much less a stronger suggestion as to where to begin. Still, his focus on the Vineyard left a sour taste in her mouth. "And how do you suggest we begin?"

"Armed with pistols and lanterns, I'd expect. I didn't think you'd have any qualms about diving right in."

There was something he wasn't telling her. She was sure of it. "I prefer a little direction," she said.

"A three thousand-pound printing press shouldn't be too easy to miss."

Despite Arnault's seeming willingness – eagerness, even – to rush into the Vineyard, they agreed to take the rest of the day to gather leads. Malone was unable to find anything in her backlog of reports to suggest a definitive direction. Her subordinates, mumbling and averting their eyes, all but admitted that the network of tunnels in the Vineyard had gone unpatrolled for months. It felt like a losing battle against the Bricklayer's cronies, they said.

As irritated as she was, she was careful to keep her tone steady with them. She couldn't afford to lose the few reliable officers she had. Besides, they were right.

Arnault had cautioned against starting too early in the morning, saying that they'd draw less attention if they made their move later, when more people were out and about.

She left from Callum Station after lunch, dressed inconspicuously but with her weapon visible, at Arnault's insistence.

As strongly as she disagreed with him in most matters, she didn't object to this.

Not surprisingly, Arnault had other business, and so she met him just outside the Vineyard rather than at the station.

He shifted on his feet and looked around as if embarrassed to be seen with her. "Do you have to be so conspicuous?"

She held out her arms and looked at her black clothes. "I'm not even in uniform."

He rolled his eyes as if she were being deliberately obtuse. "Forget it."

There wasn't so much a border between the lawless tunnels – Bricklayer territory – and the rest of Recoletta as there was a vague and shifting no-man's land. As Malone followed Arnault past an abandoned patisserie and a row of shops with boarded-up windows, she could almost feel a change in the air pressure.

They turned a corner onto a street where rubble, shattered glass, and other detritus littered the ground. The remains of a battle, looting, riot, flight – Malone couldn't tell. These things had happened all over Recoletta, and in the Vineyard more than anywhere else.

"Do you have a plan?" Malone asked.

"I have a few contacts. We may run into one," he said after a pause.

The thought brought her little comfort.

They followed a ramp down to a plaza below. Malone wouldn't have even realized she was in the Vineyard, once the most opulent district in the city, were it not for the precise maps and diagrams filed away in her head. And even these were starting to change, along with the political and physical topography of her city.

The wide tunnels were choked with debris, and the walls were chalked, painted, and scarred with slogans and symbols. None of them looked familiar to Malone from her smuggler-hunting days, but she was beyond surprise at that.

Arnault led them through what must have once been a storefront. The sign outside the door had been burnt black, and the ornamental reliefs had been torn from the walls, but the smell of fine spirits and malts hung in the air, a faint perfume over the sweat, smoke, and gunpowder.

Just the kind of place Arnault would meet a contact.

The contact in question waited on the other side of a narrow labyrinth of smashed shelves and overturned tables. He had a beard like a tangle of cobwebs and wrinkles outlined in soot and dirt. He could have been as young as fifty or as old as seventy – it was impossible to tell how much of his apparent age had accumulated with years and how much came from the cosmetics of ruin.

He looked up, neither surprised nor startled to see them. "Mr Arnault," he said. "What'll it be?"

"Just information. We're looking for a few people."

"We're still civilized around here." The man reached under the counter in front of him and set three short glasses on top of it. "And this is no proper talk without a dram." He reached under the counter again and pulled out a bottle half-full of amber liquid. The label had been peeled off, leaving only streaks of white like trailing clouds, but the man held the bottle with pride and reverence. "The twenty-year?"

"You are too kind," Arnault said.

The man only grunted. The stopper gave a wet squeak as he pulled it out.

"None for me," Malone said.

Arnault looked at her as if she'd just committed the gravest of social sins, but their host nodded and removed one of the glasses. When the other had been filled, he and Arnault raised one each.

"To Recoletta," the host said.

"To Recoletta," Arnault echoed.

"Wherever she may be."

With that, each man drank. This was not the reckless and unrestrained toss of the head with the extravagantly impatient gulp, but rather a slow, savoring sip. Arnault closed his eyes, lost in an instant of careless bliss that Malone had not thought him capable of.

And after a handful of seconds that passed at the pace of warm honey, his eyes snapped open, and he was back to business.

"Now," their host said, surfacing from his own glass, "who exactly are you looking for?"

Arnault pulled something out of his jacket and placed it atop the counter. "The people who made this."

The whiskey merchant unfolded it, sliding something from between its pages and under the counter. He scanned it, turned it over, rubbed his narrow fingertips together, and Malone remembered the waxy residue on the pamphlets. "I see."

"And that's about all we know about them at this point," Arnault said.

The merchant scratched his cobweb beard and made a thoughtful rumble deep in his chest. "You understand that I have no... personal connection," he said. "I've heard rumors, but nothing more, I'm afraid."

"Are they connected to the Bricklayer?" Malone asked when the old man's pause had stretched on too long.

And while Arnault looked up again as if she'd again said something unbelievably crass, the old man startled, gazing back at her with apprehension. He set his glass on the counter. "I'm afraid I wouldn't know much about that, either. I make it a point to stay out of the Bricklayer's affairs." She could see him clamming up, withdrawing, his hands retreating from the glass into frail fists.

"I understand completely," Arnault said. "We both do." This with a significant glance back at her. He turned back to the merchant. "We appreciate whatever you are able to share." He gave the older man a slow nod.

"Of course." The merchant mopped his face with a ragged silk handkerchief. "The Twilight Exchange has been set up at Maxwell Street Station for the last three days. Should be there a couple more before it moves again. I've heard word that the people you're looking for have a contact there. A cheesemonger."

Malone bit her tongue. Arnault was no fool in his dealings, but it was all she could do not to say something that would inevitably earn her another barbed look.

Arnault slipped the pamphlet back into his jacket. "We'll head to the exchange, and we'll see that your name stays out of it."

"Please, stay as long as you'd like."

"One of these days, I'll take you up on that." Arnault raised his glass to the wan lamplight and inspected it before finishing it in another long, slow sip. He set his empty glass back on the counter, and Malone followed him back to the street.

They were a dozen paces back into the rubble and shadow of the streets before Malone spoke. "That man. He knew something."

"And he told us," Arnault said, not deigning to look at her. "Which is why we're headed to Maxwell Street Station now."

"No. About the Bricklayer."

"That's not who we've come to find tonight."

Malone half considered jumping in front of him, but she was certain he'd barrel right past her anyway. "Convenient for you to point that out now." Particularly when he'd been the one to bait her with a possible connection in the first place. "Especially after your transaction back there."

He shook his head. "What conspiracy are you onto now?"

They passed the line of shops and into a narrower tunnel with a vaulted ceiling that tapered to a fine point. Most of the gas lamps had been smashed or ripped from the walls, but every third or so burned steadily. It was just enough to navigate by. "You paid him. I saw."

The corners of Arnault's mouth twitched with cruel satisfaction. She could barely see it in the low light. "Like you've never paid a contact."

"You slipped it into the pamphlet. Hoping I wouldn't notice."

He placed one hand over his heart. "I was only trying to protect your delicate sensibilities. And look where that got me."

Flippancy to hide deceit, like hasty sweepings over tracks. Arguing with him was useless, but it felt good.

His grin returned. "You might not be so uptight if you'd just had a glass of the single malt."

The passage seemed to narrow up ahead. Or was it just the tunnel vision of her anger? "We all need limits. I draw the line at sharing the spoils of looters and profiteers."

Arnault was silent for several seconds before Malone heard his dry chuckle. "Francis Petrosian has owned that shop for thirty-five years. He's survived, no thanks to us, by selling information and whatever else he's able to get his hands on these days. Used to sell the finest spirits in Recoletta. You saw about all he was able to salvage."

Malone said nothing as they emerged from the passage and into another plaza. It opened to the streets one level up, where tall, arched windows looked down on them. Smashed, draped with ragged towels, and strung with clotheslines, they had once been some of the most coveted apartments in Recoletta.

But as she looked up and around, Malone noticed something else, which was that she could actually see the plaza clearly. Gas lamps, mismatched but functional, protruded from the walls, and though the paving stones were cracked, they were clear of rubble and litter.

Arnault seemed to have noticed the same thing. "Careful," he said, his voice low. "We're in Bricklayer territory now."

The thought silenced her questions and padded her steps. And yet with the apprehension came a kind of reckless delight.

As they passed through lit and swept streets, Malone saw men and women conducting seemingly ordinary business – carrying bags of groceries, walking hand in hand, and bearing satchels and briefcases, thin-lipped with purpose. If they lived in fear of a mysterious criminal overlord, they seemed to have forgotten it for now. The gas was on, and the storefronts had been sanded and chiseled smooth.

By all appearances, they had walked into a functional neighborhood, and yet it bore no resemblance to the Vineyard.

Something was unmistakably different, even if Malone had a difficult time pinpointing it. Perhaps it was an inevitable side effect of the infliction and repair of so much damage; maybe, when the spurs and spars in the stone were ground smooth, when the streets were swept clean and the floor tiles polished, maybe some essential part of the Vineyard had been scoured away.

Or maybe it was the people. Dressed in simple yet clean slacks, blouses, and skirts, their nails trimmed short, they didn't look like whitenails. But, then again, neither had the whiskey merchant.

Before Malone could ponder the matter further, her attention shifted to the rising sound of activity up ahead.

Before the revolution, Maxwell Street Station had been the transportation hub of the Vineyard. A stop for the railcar and suspended trolley lines that ran through the district, it had borne whitenails across Recoletta. Jet-black coaches, polished daily, had waited along the adjacent avenues and tunnels.

Transportation service to and from Maxwell Street Station had stopped about a month after Sato's takeover. But as Malone and Arnault approached around the curve of Blackstone Street, the place seemed to rumble with the thunder of wheels and the steam hiss of brakes.

Yet they passed under a wide, basket handle arch and entered the station, and the railcars were still, slumbering metal snakes, and the suspended trolleys nested in the eaves on the upper level of the station. All around them, however, were people bartering, arguing, and parleying in the quick, hushed tones that Malone knew for black market patois.

While the black market wasn't confined to a single location, most people had come to associate it with the Twilight Exchange.

What had started as haphazard and spontaneous meetings between a handful of desperate and resourceful traders had grown into a massive and deceptively organized marketplace – even Malone had been unable to pinpoint it before. It was said that the Twilight Exchange was now the largest and most lucrative market in Recoletta. Seeing it for the first time, Malone had no doubt this was true.

She and Arnault passed between makeshift stalls and blankets spread with goods, from everyday soaps and oils to fine jewelry.

Yet they'd been directed toward someone specific.

"A... cheesemonger?" Malone asked.

"Someone who sells cheese."

"I know that. I'm asking if you know who we're looking for."

"Whoever it is, I'm sure we'll smell him when we're close."

They willed themselves invisible, which wasn't too difficult when everyone else around them was obviously doing the same.

The merchants were crowded close together, but each looked as if he or she could pack up and disappear with the folding of a blanket or a sweep into a basket. What had enabled the Twilight Exchange to survive long enough to grow was its mobility – when it first formed, it had appeared at a new street corner every night. Contrary to popular belief, it was named not for the times of day at which it appeared and disbanded, but for its transient nature – it was said to vanish as quickly as the last light of day.

Malone had heard that in its first month, it never popped up the same place twice, and merchants and buyers alike relied on word of mouth to find it. These days, it still supposedly dissipated and reformed around a network of those in the know, but that network had grown large enough to leak. And the Twilight Exchange would, at least, generally stay in one place for a few days at a time. The sheer number of merchants required it.

Which could make finding their cheesemonger difficult, Malone thought as she looked through the throngs.

Across the station, she caught sight of a stack of exotic-looking pastries. "We should at least head for the foodstuffs," Malone muttered. "Those sellers are likely to group together."

"That's what we're doing," Arnault said.

She looked back at the pastry stand and then at their parallel path. "The shortest distance between two points is a straight line, Arnault."

"Only if you don't mind scaring them off. Now, relax and try to enjoy the scenery."

But, now that she knew where they were headed, all she could pay attention to was their leisurely pace toward the goal.

At long last, they found a man selling strips of salt-packed fish from a barrel, and a thrill quickened in Malone's gut.

Arnault scowled as if he'd read her thoughts. "Just keep your head down and follow my lead."

So she did, eyeing flour-dusted rolls, sticky buns, berry preserves, and thin sheets of cured ham, and realizing again how ridiculous this all was.

Until a tangy, pungent odor hit her nostrils and she saw the woman sitting cross-legged on a spotless blanket, ringed with wheels and blocks wrapped in parchment paper or cased in red or yellow wax.

She glanced up at Arnault, who had already stopped to examine the wares. They were stacked and bunched with a system of organization that seemed to defy any obvious logic.

"What are you looking for?" the woman asked. Her graying hair was coiled in a tight chignon, and she looked up at Arnault over gold wire-rimmed spectacles. Her plain dress was an inch too short in the sleeves, but her shoulders were draped with a finely embroidered shawl.

"What do you have?" he asked.

She smiled, but her expression wasn't friendly. "Sharp cheddars. Blocks of hard sheep's cheese. A few rounds of creamed goat cheese. And some ripe blue."

Arnault was silent for several seconds. "Is that all?"

She gave him a second, thoughtful look.

"We were sent to you on a personal recommendation," he said. "I was hoping you'd have some special stock."

The woman adjusted the spectacles on the bridge of her nose and looked away, as though she'd written him off as an idling browser. "All of my wares are of the finest quality, sir. If anything I've mentioned interests you, let me know."

Arnault pulled the folded pamphlet out of his jacket and held it out to her. "I'm looking for something like this."

The cheesemonger recoiled from it too quickly, her eyes white with surprise. "I don't know what that is, but you seem to have made a mistake."

He shook the creased pages inches from her spectacles. "You haven't even given this a good look."

She sniffed and turned away from him again with the affronted dignity of someone fleeing an unsuitable dinner conversation. "You're obviously at the wrong stall. I suggest you take your business – whatever it might be – elsewhere."

She unstacked and restacked her parchment-wrapped cheeses, something to occupy her attention while she waited for this awkwardness to pass, no doubt. She sorted haphazardly through the piles in front of her, yet in the middle of her chore, she reached behind herself to touch several blocks covered in red wax. It seemed like an unconscious movement, and it gave Malone an idea.

"I'll take one of those," she said, pointing at the red blocks.

The woman looked back at Malone, her eyes widening as she must have realized what she'd just done. "Those aren't for sale," she said, her voice flat.

Malone pulled her wallet out of her pocket and paged through the crisp bills. "How much?"

"They're not for sale," she repeated with more conviction. "Those are on reserve. Special order."

Malone paused, her fingers astride a pair of ten-mark notes.

She glanced over at Arnault, whose teeth were just slightly bared.

Malone reached into her other pocket and removed her badge, a silver shield that fit easily in the palm of her hand. It was the same one she'd been issued when she'd first joined the Municipal Police years ago, even though her position as chief had come with a larger and more ornate badge.

But the small size came in handy now, and she knelt to show it to the cheesemonger. "It would be easiest if you let me take a look now."

The vendor raised her head one more time, her resolve melting as she looked around the market and saw no source of aid or relief. She grabbed one of the blocks behind her and slapped it between Malone's knees with a sullen frown.

A knife sunk into the center of the block. Malone looked at Arnault in irritation as he wedged a cleft in the wax, but even she'd heard the crumple and squeak of paper. Arnault stripped the wax and the thin parchment layer beneath it away, revealing a stack of pamphlets like the one he'd brought.

"Where did you get these?" Malone asked the cheesemonger.

The woman smirked. "You said we had mutual friends."

"You can tell me, or you can tell Sato himself."

The cheesemonger's smile fell. "They come about once a week. They drop these off, and I see that they get distributed to a few regular buyers."

"Names," Arnault demanded.

"We don't exchange those," she said, scowling. "For obvious reasons. The man who normally drops these off goes by 'Marcus,' but that's all I know."

"Where would we find them?" Malone asked.

She scoffed. "You think they'd tell me something like that?"

"You seem to be a tight-knit network. And I think you'd rather tell me than Sato."

She licked her lips and glanced around again. "It's some place on the south side. Outside the factory districts."

"That's a big area."

The cheesemonger rolled her eyes. "It was in one of the neighborhoods that vacated early. Not far from Turnbull Square. They needed some place they could move a printing press."

It sounded right. Malone's skin prickled with caution. "How do I know you aren't just getting rid of us?"

"Because I'm not eager to see the two of you again. Besides," she said around a spreading grin, "those fellows will do a much better job than I can." She nodded over Malone's shoulder.

Malone turned, feeling Arnault shift beside her. Coming toward them were a man and a woman, dressed to blend in but plowing through market stalls as they made a beeline in their direction.

As the woman saw Malone and Arnault turn, she reached into a gray duster and pulled out a pistol.

"Run," Malone said, but Arnault was already on his feet.

She leaped after him. Out of the corner of her eye, she saw their pursuers break into a run. She could only hope they wouldn't open fire in the middle of the crowd.

There was no time to ask Arnault where they were going. He ran ahead, clearing a path between the merchants and shoppers, and she followed in his broad wake. Everyone here seemed on their guard, as if this kind of thing was not unexpected.

She found herself leaping over fallen pots and crates, casualties of the marketgoers' haste to duck out of the way.

The wide arch of an exit loomed ahead, separated from them by a couple dozen stalls that glinted with gold and silver. And then she saw another pair – two men – running along the opposite wall at full speed, on a collision course with them.

She didn't dare waste a breath shouting to Arnault, but he broke into a sprint – he must have seen them. Despite his limp, he was fast. She matched his pace.

The last throng of marketgoers seemed to recognize the situation. They dove out of the way.

Malone heard a cry of surprise in front of her. Arnault was

falling, and her panicked brain was struggling to make sense of the copper pot skidding across the ground, the blank stares from the onlookers.

At least he went down behind the cover of a plywood display.

She grabbed him by the collar and levered his feet, her still-tender wrist ablaze with pain. It was all she could do for him.

Before she could take off again in the direction of the arch, a hand seized the back of her coat, reeled her in. She turned to see Arnault snarling back at her and fought the instinct to strike out at him.

"Too late," he said.

Their adversaries had closed the distance to the arch and now spun, picking a path toward them through the stalls.

Behind her, gasps and shouts announced the approach of their first two pursuers.

And around them, the onlookers had formed a wide circle. Most were backing away, eager to be clear of the imminent collision. But a few eyed Malone and Arnault with predatory glares, their hands twitching at hip level.

"We've gotta move," she said.

He sprang to his feet and darted to their right. Toward the pair approaching from the arch.

"Wait!" Malone called.

But either he didn't hear her or didn't care. After a split second of internal debate, she cursed and chased after him.

His instincts for self-preservation were keen enough that he must have a plan in mind.

And as she tore after him, trailing a dozen feet behind, she saw it. A service tunnel stood to the side, its wooden door hanging open.

Close.

Yet Arnault wasn't exactly running toward it. His path – and hers – carried them down a broad avenue between the stalls, a few degrees off from their goal.

The two men they'd seen near the arch had spun and were dashing to close the distance between them.

Malone heard a deafening crack behind her, and the wall ahead sneezed a plume of dust.

She pushed her legs to catch up to Arnault, but she was at her limit, and her lungs were burning.

Suddenly, he pivoted, picking up speed as he sprinted for the door.

Malone cried out when she realized what he'd done.

The men from the arch were only a few yards away now, and she was directly in their path. Their bird-of-prey expressions locked on to her.

She turned two rows behind where Arnault had changed course, pushing aside a pair of unfortunate merchants. She didn't have the luxury of his wake now, and she shouted in hopes of clearing a new path.

She ducked and dodged between the few too slow – or too dumbfounded – to move, hearing snarls of frustration as the pursuers closed behind her.

They couldn't be more than a few feet away. Only a few stands of kettles and glassware stood between her and the door.

She saw a stand stacked high with tin pots and cups. A plan formed in her mind in the split seconds as it loomed closer, something formed of impulse and desperation. She had no words for it, just the dull realization that it would either trip her up or foil her pursuers, who couldn't be more than a bound behind her.

She grabbed a support pole as she ran by. It came away in her hand.

The entire stand toppled with the clatter of wooden planks and the crash of metal.

Malone could not look back to observe her handiwork, but she saw its effects reflected in the dumbfounded stares of the men and women who gazed on behind her, open-mouthed with shock or delight.

She turned her attention back to the door just in time to see Arnault disappear behind it.

An instant later, it began to close.

She shouted, fury and dismay boiling out of her in something that wasn't so much a word as pure atavistic expression.

Her mind divided the seconds, then divided them again. No matter how slowly the door seemed to close, her strides felt slower still.

Moments earlier, her legs had refused to chase faster after Arnault, had kept something in reserve that even the force of her will could not tap.

They held nothing back now. She drew on the last of her strength and threw herself toward the door in a final, desperate push.

Pain split her shoulder, and darkness hovered on the other side of her closed eyelids. Something heavy slammed shut.

It wasn't until she heard her own heavy breathing echoed a few feet away and heard the muffled sounds of commotion that she realized she'd made it through.

A clunking noise sounded, reassuring in its weight.

"Get up," Arnault said, moving away from the door. "We've got to go."

Her breaths were still coming in deep, heavy gasps. Prying words from between them felt like snatching flesh from a hound's jaws. "What. The hell."

"We can argue about this later. That lock won't hold them."

Her eyes were adjusting to the relative darkness. "You..."

He stood over her, holding out an open hand.

She slapped it away and crawled to her feet. He was already walking down the hall, and she had to move in a limping trot to keep up.

Arnault half-turned. "They'll have to double back a few times to catch up to us. That, or break through the door. Either way, if we move fast, we can get out of here first."

Malone stuck closer, determined not to give him any opportunity to slip away again.

After a couple minutes of following the winding tunnels lit with the dying stars of undercharged radiance stones, her breath had returned to an even swell, and the quivering meat of her legs felt stable enough. Still, her own voice came out of her chest like something that had been run over jagged stones.

"What was that?" she asked, sounding calmer than she felt.

"An escape," he said. "And a narrow one."

"You know what I mean."

He finally looked over at her. "I reached the door first. I had no idea whether you would make it in time, and so I made a decision."

"You were going to shut me out."

His laugh was shallow and humorless. "When I glanced back, you were still a ways behind. And then I heard a crash. Tell me, would you have waited? Held the door open for me with armed attackers just steps behind?"

She knew the answer in a heartbeat, but it seemed beside the point. "I wouldn't have led you into them."

"If only I were so cunning."

She didn't believe him. She saw him register this. He didn't care.

Malone was quiet for several seconds, following him as he followed the angles of the service tunnel. Wherever they were, they were well past Maxwell Street Station by now. "Who were they?" she asked.

"How should I know?" he said. "The Bricklayer's enforcers, if I had to guess. They certainly didn't look like station security."

She looked at him again, and he looked back and shrugged. It was possible that he really didn't know.

"We're almost out," he said.

They finally exited into a wider tunnel, just a few blocks away from the whiskey merchant. The streets were clear, and they hurried back to safer territory before that could change.

"We can follow up on the factory district lead in a few days," Arnault said as they stepped into the Spine, the half-mile wide tunnel that stretched across Recoletta.

"I work better on my own, Arnault."

"As much as I'd love to oblige– "

"You seriously think I'm trusting you again after this?"

"Trust has nothing to do with it," he said. "You need my information, my networks. You need someone who knows the factory districts."

"I know them just fine," she said.

"Not like I do."

Malone was about to argue, but she said nothing. As much as she hated to admit it, he was probably right.

"What I don't need," she said between clenched teeth, "is a knife in the back."

He closed his eyes. "And here I thought you were a professional." They snapped open again, and he glared. "You don't trust me. I get it. The feeling is mutual." He took a step forward, one hand resting on a stone balustrade. "And if you can honestly tell me that, under the same circumstances, you wouldn't have shut that door, I'll resign today."

"That isn't the point," she said.

"You're right. The point is, you need me if you want to find these people."

"And why are you so eager to help me do it?"

He only turned and grimaced at the expanse beyond the railing.

"Fine," she said. "Then tell me when I'll have the pleasure of your company again."

His voice softened. "Like I said, it'll be a few days. Sato's given me another chore as of this morning that shall require immediate attention."

"I don't suppose you'd care to share what that is."

He gave her an unreadable look and turned to walk back to Callum Station.

CHAPTER 4

DIPLOMACY BY OTHER MEANS

As much as Jane wanted to reject Lady Lachesse and everything she stood for, she knew the older woman was right. About her vulnerability, about Recoletta's vulnerability, about her own need to find leverage. In the days that followed, she found herself hearing the hidden threat in conversations with her superiors and noticing how easily her colleagues and neighbors could become captors and informants.

And yet here she was, more secure and, in many ways, more comfortable than she'd ever been in Recoletta. She had risen by her own resourcefulness and by the unaffected practicality of her new city.

At least, that's what she'd told herself. But thinking back, peeling away the layers of this story slice by painful slice, she realized there could be more to it. Fragments and motives that it had been all too convenient for her to ignore.

Why had the Qadi herself needed to meet Jane if she were only being hired as a jurist? Jane had initially thought the position one of great prestige – still did, she told herself, setting her lips in a grim frown – but the cases Jane handled were almost exclusively mundane affairs that concerned relatively small amounts of money. And she had not seen the Qadi since that mysterious meeting over tea and candlelight.

For that matter, why had she been hired in the first place? Because she had unique insights into Recolettan culture and society? Because she had the right accent for breaking hard realities to embittered whitenails?

Her value was that of a convenient middleman and an insightful insider. This was a story she'd been told, that she'd reinforced and fleshed out herself, that was now a perilous and widening blind spot. She could almost hear Lady Lachesse tut-tutting her, her red lips a ribbon-thin smirk.

The idea made her face burn with anger and shame.

She made her way to the Majlis, as exposed in the broad, open plaza as a mouse in a field. She climbed the stairs, engulfed by the two surrounding wings and feeling the presence of their tiny, high windows like roosting owls.

Jane was so enveloped in her own thoughts as she entered the Majlis that she didn't initially recognize the crackle of tension in the air: furtive glances over veils, careful whispers shielded by raised hands. She didn't notice that everyone else was moving carefully and quietly until one of the guards stopped her, raising a hand to bar her passage.

A sudden flare of irritation burned through her blood despite the man's politeness. "Sayideh, your pardons, but it will only be a moment."

A question, indignant and inquisitive, rose to her lips, but years of quiet deference held it down. Nevertheless, she followed the guard's quick glance over his shoulder and saw the procession that must have been the cause of the fuss.

Two men argued, trailed by a train of attendants that followed in respectful – or purposeful – silence. The men themselves were notable in that they did not wear the veil or dress of the locals, and they seemed heedless of the quiet that their squabble broke. One, stern and bearded, wore slacks and a close-fitted jacket that might almost have passed for local dress in Recoletta. The other, slender and smooth-faced, with a dark, clean-shaven head, wore a long-sleeved, tailored robe that accentuated his own narrow build. It was black like the servants' robes in Madina, but it seemed to be made of a starchier material, with a row of buttons from the short, stiff collar to the bottom hem. As Jane looked on, the two men turned to a spot where the latticework bordering the hall was broken by a curtain and disappeared behind it. A couple of their attendants followed, and the rest dispersed as if they'd been bound for other destinations all along.

The guard standing in front of Jane nodded and melted back into his post by the wall. Jane continued on and passed the spot where the two foreigners had vanished, glancing at the half-hidden hallway out of the corner of her eye. She remembered seeing the Qadi emerge from a similar passage, and in the succeeding months, she'd noticed them all over the Majlis, snaking along and between other corridors and rooms.

In that time, she'd come to understand that they served a similar function to the veils she and others wore, allowing various functionaries to conduct their business and move between meetings with a degree of privacy. Not that she had ever used the latticed halls herself – whenever anyone gave her directions around the Majlis or assigned her to visit a particular person or meeting room, they pointed her through the wider main halls. It was yet another sharp contrast from Recoletta, where back entrances and quiet corridors were used to allow people of Jane's station to pass without disturbing their superiors.

But, like the locals, Jane had developed the habit of averting her gaze from those private corridors, aware nevertheless of intermittent, flickering movement.

Yet even while she looked away from the hidden corridor, she began listening to the whispers and murmurs around her. They were vague and guarded now, but she knew of one place where she might count on freer gossip. She considered the time and decided that she might excuse a few minutes' lateness with the fuss surrounding the two foreigners.

Her decision made, she turned down an adjacent corridor and ducked into the women's restroom. There were a few things that remained constant between Madina and Recoletta.

She entered just as a trio of women were making their exit, and she took advantage of the commotion to slide around the bank of mirrors in the middle of the room. The high-walled stalls provided ample cover.

Yet before she could retreat into one, she heard two women on the other side of the sinks, whispering in the urgent singsong of friendly conspirators.

"A beast of a man, that one," said the first, scandalized and delighted.

"Which?"

"The chancellor, of course. Who else?"

"How should I know? All these foreigners seem the same."

Jane held her breath, trying to listen while she clutched the fabric of her robe.

"Well, he's the worst, from what I hear. A taste for drink."

"I could say the same of more than one of our illustrious leaders."

"Yes, but could you say that they keep a bottle stashed in the bottom of their desk drawers? And that a good half of it empties every day?"

"No! Where did you hear that?"

"From Rahim. He has a taste for serving boys, too."

Feet pattered, and Jane took an unconscious step backward. It was past the point where getting caught would be awkward.

"But what is he doing here, anyway?" the second woman asked.

"The same thing as Father Isse, I'm sure."

"Oh, clever you. I suppose that's all you can say when you don't actually know."

"I do, too. Only..."

Jane heard the whispers and backed into a stall, fighting the urge to ease the door shut. Hesitant, clattering motion followed around the corner.

"See? There's no one here."

"Are you sure?"

"Of course I'm sure. So spit it out before someone joins us."

Jane heard a swish of fabric as one of the women looked from side to side.

"They say it's about that city to the south. Recoletta."

"And the warlord who's torched half the districts? Everyone knows about this."

"No, that's a silly rumor. But I have it on good authority that he lives half the time in Old World ruins outside the city."

"Anyway, what does this have to do with the chancellor?"

"That's the whole reason he's here, of course. To oversee the takeover of Recoletta."

"What? That can't be right."

"Tsk! You've heard the way the Qadi's attendants talk about her black looks and the long, loud meetings between her and the other two, yes? They won't let this continue."

The footsteps drew closer.

"I really think there's someone here."

"You're imagining it," the other woman said, but still they got closer.

Suddenly, a door opened at the other end of the bathroom. The two women collected themselves in a flurry of whispers and rustling fabric and fluttered away like two birds startled from a bush.

Grateful for the timely interruption, Jane gave the newcomers an innocuous smile as she made her way back to the sinks to time her exit.

When she arrived at the office she shared with a dozen other low-level jurists, several pairs of eyes swiveled in her direction. Her heart sped up as she mentally ticked through the possible causes. Was this about her lateness? Had someone caught her eavesdropping?

Her breath caught in her chest. Had Lady Lachesse given her name?

Just then, something stirred in the far corner of the room. She turned.

A man with a pleasant face and a curling mane of blond hair smiled at her. "Miss Lin? I'm Farouk Bailey. If you'd be so kind as to come with me?" He gestured at the door politely enough, but Jane knew a command when she heard one. She obliged, hiding her fear behind a tight smile.

In the hall, Bailey drew up next to her and pointed their way further down it, away from the front door and the areas of the Majlis Jane knew best. He straightened the immaculate sleeve of his ivory robe. "I understand that you're from Recoletta." He said it with the characteristic stiffness of a man who had no interest in small talk but who'd realized that it was sometimes necessary.

"Yes," Jane said.

"Mm." They continued in silence for several seconds, passing rooms with ornately carved wooden doors, all closed. Jane had never been this way before.

He finally spoke again. "And... how are you liking Madina?"

"It's lovely," she said, trying to keep the edge out of her own voice. She wished he would stop attempting something that was clearly so awkward for him and, under the circumstances, trying for her.

"Wonderful to hear. Hospitality is a virtue here." Coming from him, the statement was almost comical. "The Qadi in particular wanted to ensure that you were having a pleasant transition."

Something in his careful, rehearsed tone suggested that he'd been specifically instructed to say that. And Jane suddenly realized that he would not spare her the courtesy, perfunctory as it was, if she were in trouble.

She risked a glance at him and saw the calculation in his expressionless brown eyes.

She wondered what he saw in hers.

"Yes, well, it's nice to be someplace a little more... stable," she said. "If you know what I mean."

Jane looked into his eyes and saw that he did, indeed.

He grinned. "As I said. We do pride ourselves on our hospitality."

She knew enough not to say more.

They continued the rest of their walk in a comfortable silence.

They reached the end of the hall, and Bailey stopped in front of her to ceremoniously push the door open. Jane smelled the sweet vapors from the tea before she saw the setting on the other side.

The carved door swung open, and Jane saw the Qadi, veiled and robed, seated in front of a tea service. The jolt of recognition she felt told her that she'd correctly foreseen this tableau at some point during the walk.

"Miss Lin," the Qadi said. "Please, make yourself comfortable."

The Qadi was one of the only people in Madina who referred to her as "miss" instead of "sayideh." Jane circled around to a chair that had been conveniently pushed away from the table, watching her for some sign of what she was looking for.

Behind the tinted veil, the Qadi's eyes darted somewhere over Jane's shoulder. "Ah, the biscuits."

The tray slid onto the table with barely a sound. Bailey had taken a seat between her and the Qadi in the intervening moments.

The older woman took the pot and filled three glasses. Jane raised hers and swallowed a scalding mouthful.

The Qadi had not touched hers, but she smiled at Jane, her lips a sharp line behind her veil.

"Miss Lin seems to have settled in quite nicely," Bailey said. He sounded rehearsed again.

"One must not presume," the Qadi told him, then turned to Jane. "And how have you settled in?"

"Very well," Jane said.

Bailey's shoulders relaxed, but the Qadi sat as tall and regal as ever.

Even behind the veil, Jane knew the calculating look in the Qadi's eye. She'd seen it in her former employers' eyes back in Recoletta. And in the eyes of the other two jurists that day, months ago, when she was first told how to cast her vote. She was being evaluated. For what, she wasn't sure, and she reckoned she had a handful of minutes to figure it out.

Bailey's fingers pressed along a fold in his garment.

"I've been made very welcome here," Jane said. "The job, the city, the hospitality of the locals – it's all made for a pleasant adjustment."

A brief dilation of the Qadi's pupils, nothing more. "That's good to hear."

A silence followed. "Has there been any concern about the quality of my work?"

This time, the Qadi's eyes widened in surprise, and a little sliver of teeth showed through her smile. "Your efforts have been more than satisfactory. We have few among us who understand Recolettans as well as you."

And there, in that pause, in the minute tilt of the Qadi's head, was the invitation.

Jane had to speak slowly, pausing herself to pretend that she did not see it. "Indeed," she said. "It's just nice to be away from there. And to be someplace I can make a difference."

"In that case, I have another job for you." The Qadi's lips widened in another grin, her chin tilted back, and Jane saw what the Qadi had perhaps seen in her.

Grievance.

"Mr Bailey is overseeing certain meetings with representatives of Recoletta. He needs someone who can take notes and who can observe the proceedings with discretion." So, the Qadi was interested not only in her habitual prudence, but also in her apparent isolation from the rest of the Recolettan expatriate community.

And the willingness she'd exemplified to turn against it when it served Madina's interests.

The Qadi continued, reaching for her tea. Bailey hadn't yet touched his. "Your unique insights into the mannerisms and inclinations of your former fellows would also prove useful. If you would see fit to employ them again on our behalf."

Even if she hadn't, the correct answer would have been clear enough. "Of course. When do I begin?"

The Qadi looked at Bailey.

"The coach is ready and waiting," he said. He began to rise, his glass still untouched on the table, but a swift look from the Qadi seemed to drain the strength from his knees, and he sat back into his chair.

"You'll want to be off. After you've finished your tea, of course."

"Of course." he said, picking up his glass, his face reddening. He took two quick gulps so that the level in his glass was even with Jane's. "As soon as Sayideh Lin is ready."

Jane looked from Bailey to the Qadi, both of whom watched her with anticipation and varying levels of patience. She drained the rest of her tea, and Bailey did the same.

The Qadi nodded. "It gives me pleasure to share my table with you both."

Bailey rose and gave her a quick bow. "The honor is mine."

Both sets of eyes swiveled to Jane, and she followed with a quick nod. "An honor, Qadi." She'd seen too little of the woman to have grasped what was expected in situations like these.

Nevertheless, Bailey was satisfied enough to signal her with raised eyebrows and a brisk walk toward the door. She followed, exiting with him back into the hall.

When they'd passed a dozen feet from the meeting room, Bailey whispered to her between clenched teeth. "Don't ever do that to me again."

Jane was on the cusp of asking what she'd done, but the furious set of his brow told her that anything further would only insult him. So she murmured her apology and followed him the rest of the way.

Despite the Qadi's apparent assurance about her flexible loyalties, it seemed odd that she'd been chosen for a job of such seeming urgency.

After several tense seconds, Jane risked a question. "May I ask where we're headed?"

"To the carriage," he said in the same tone as before. Jane suspected he was being deliberately obtuse, but in either case, her inquiry didn't seem to bear repeating. The rest would become clear soon enough.

Bailey led out her to an exit she'd never seen before. They passed through a narrow and altogether forgettable door and into a cobbled alley where a featureless black carriage waited. This wasn't like the open coaches or thinly curtained litters she'd seen elsewhere in the city, nor was it like the rumbling, rolling boxes of Recoletta, by turns stately and forbidding. This was a vehicle that was meant to be forgotten, and something about it made her shiver.

She must have stopped, because Bailey stopped beside her and leaned in. "I told you we were going to the carriage, yes?"

She nodded and followed him inside. The space was small and cramped, with two benches facing opposite one another. Bailey took the forward-facing bench, comfortably occupying the middle of it, and so she slid into the seat opposite him, her knees almost knocking against his.

He finally smiled. "Frightfully sorry about all this cloak and dagger business. I just wanted to get away with a minimum of fuss. I'm sure you understand," he said, inflection rising. He seemed to expect an answer.

"Of course," Jane said, though she still didn't. Some unseen figure outside the carriage closed the door.

"Ever so glad to hear it." He gave her a smile that was just deep enough to rise above contemptuous. "Here, you'll need this." He took a black leather satchel from beneath his bench and placed it on hers. Inside, Jane found several sheaves of paper and a couple of pens.

She regarded Bailey as their carriage slid into motion. Something about him had changed. Away from the Qadi, he seemed on a more comfortable footing. And he was also sizing her up, a fact that should have made her more uncomfortable.

"So, this is about the envoy from Recoletta?" Jane asked. Perhaps that was why they needed her – to deliver more bad news in the proper accent.

Bailey tilted his head downward in a motion so slight she wasn't sure it counted as a nod until he spoke again. "We're just going to hear what he has to say."

As if she had suggested anything different.

"So much upheaval in Recoletta. You must be anxious for your home city."

It was such an obvious baiting, especially after their chat with the Qadi, that she almost didn't respond. But he continued watching her with those brown eyes and that nearly contemptuous smile.

"Not really my concern these days," she said a little too emphatically.

"No need to get upset," he said. "I was merely wondering how you're handling everything."

It occurred to Jane that Bailey might not have been in favor of her inclusion in this errand. The thought didn't surprise her, though she wasn't sure what the source of his objection might be. Did he think her an untrustworthy foreigner, unsuitably low-caste, or, laughably, a competitor for the Qadi's favor? She'd known types in Recoletta that would have objected on all of these grounds, but she didn't yet know what kind of man Bailey was.

Regardless, she would have to play her part carefully around him.

If only the curtains had been tied back, she could at least have distracted herself with the scenery. Instead, she listened to the muffled rumble and creak of the carriage wheels.

She might have dozed off. When they stopped, she looked around with a start, waiting to see what Bailey did. He got out of the carriage without a word or look in her direction. She followed.

They emerged in front of a heavy wooden door, the lone

feature of note in a short, rough-hewn tunnel. There was none of the delicate patterning found elsewhere in the city, no elaborate carvings, no skylights. Only a row of stalactites silhouetted against the far end of the tunnel, grinning back at her like jagged teeth.

"Whenever you're ready," Bailey said. She looked over to see him holding the door open, a thick and splintering monstrosity. She passed through it, and it slammed closed with a thick thump that made her jump. "Nerves, sayideh," Bailey said again. She could hear the smile in his voice.

She passed into a parlor, surprisingly well appointed for the derelict tunnel outside. It was scattered with an assortment of short-legged, mismatched tables and low, cushion-strewn seats. Pictures hung on the walls, stylized representations of horses, fish, and unfamiliar birds with long, fan-like tails.

There appeared to be other rooms further back, but Bailey made a move toward the seating area.

"This doesn't look much like a meeting space," Jane said, examining a low table inlaid with some opalescent material. Several chips of the stuff were missing. It certainly looked like the right kind of place for bad news.

"It's not, officially," said Bailey. "But we do hold certain informal tête-à-têtes here when needed." He ran a hand along the curved wooden back of a chair. "It's quiet and removed."

A sudden wild fancy occurred to Jane. "Do you mean to murder the envoy?"

He laughed loudly, bending forward and thumping the back of the chair. "Heavens, woman, of course not," he said, yet there was something in that laughter she didn't trust. He collected himself, dabbing under one eye with a sleeve. "The Qadi didn't tell me you were so ruthless. In all seriousness, we've got more to gain by talking to the envoy than by killing him. One death would hardly change the equation in Recoletta."

This she believed. And she believed just as readily that, were it worth the bullet, the man coming to meet them would be executed.

"This isn't an official meeting," Bailey said. "We'd like to keep our discussions with the envoy quiet for now. We still don't recognize Sato's bloodbath as the means for establishing a proper government, and so we can't receive this envoy as a representative of one."

"I understand," Jane said.

"Then, please, take your seat. I expect he should arrive any minute now. And don't forget this." He pressed the satchel she'd left in the carriage into her hands.

Jane selected an upholstered seat near the wall, shifting and squirming until she'd made herself relatively comfortable in the legless seat, and pulled a pen and pad out of the satchel. She took a box of matches from the side table next to her and lit a thick-wicked oil lamp, adjusting the knob until the flame burned steady and bright. As much as she was at a loss for what to do about Bailey, Lady Lachesse, and the as-yet unknown envoy, it felt good to busy her hands with something.

There was movement outside. A tremor rose through her legs, and she had to still herself, reminding herself that this was almost certainly their envoy.

Boots stamped up to the door which, despite its formidable size, did a poor job of muffling sound. It groaned open, revealing three figures in a square of dull light before it slammed shut behind them.

Bailey blinked in cool vexation.

The first two figures to cross into the room, a man and a woman dressed in the simple garb of Madinan guards, bowed to Bailey and stepped aside. Jane's breath caught in her chest.

Between them limped Roman Arnault.

Roman looked almost exactly as she remembered him, if a little gaunter and a little better groomed. His uneven gait reminded her of their parting months ago, an impression that was not diminished by his careful, prowling aspect. His face was a mask of studied nonchalance, his eyes taking in the dimensions of the neglected parlor and its mismatched furniture. He looked bored and calculating.

Until his eyes fell on her.

They flickered wide, the whites glowing like twin moons in the darkness, the pupils cold, unreadable pinpricks. The expression lasted only a second before he again wrapped himself in that deliberate look of apathy, like a man burrowing into a heavy coat.

But it was just long enough that Jane's anxious gaze darted to Bailey.

He was dividing his attention between Roman and the pocket watch in his gloved hand. He snapped it shut. "Right on time, Mister..."

"Arnault."

"Arnault. Of course." Bailey stood motionless for two ticks, with Roman a sullen mirror image. Neither man extended a hand. "Please," Bailey said, waving Roman to the chairs.

He limped to one not quite across from Jane, but near enough that they could see each other clearly. He lowered himself slowly enough for Jane to detect the strain in his movements.

While Jane did her best to keep her rate of breathing, her grip on the pen, the angle of her head all perfectly normal, Bailey sat down a few seats over.

"Don't worry about her," Bailey said, nodding at Jane. "She's just here to take notes." His bland expression brightened with an imitation of a friendly smile.

Roman's eyes rolled from Bailey back to Jane, but he said nothing.

Now that he was close, Jane was able to get a better look at him. She drank in the vision, soaking in details that she hadn't expected to see ever again, searching for something that might betray some clue as to his state in the months since she'd seen him. His dark suit looked clean and well kept, and it actually seemed to fit him. His hair was pulled back into a low, neat ponytail. But his eyes looked sunken and shadowed, and his face was leaner than she remembered.

He was also looking at her with perplexing urgency.

"Jane. Jane," Bailey said, looking and leaning in her direction. Ice shot through her veins.

She snapped her gaze toward Bailey.

"I was just introducing you."

"Yes. Of course." Jane nodded at Roman. "How do you do." She focused on focusing, on keeping her attention on the pad in front of her and filling it with words.

Roman nodded back before returning his attention to Bailey. "I assume you've brought me here to discuss rapprochement?"

Bailey pushed his lower lip into a frown. "I'd like to think there's been no disharmony between us. We only wish to understand your situation. Much has happened in Recoletta these past few months, and all of it behind closed doors."

Jane's head snapped up of its own accord. Coming from a Madinan, a citizen of a city whose official buildings and high houses were riddled with hidden passages and secret entrances, it was an odd statement to make.

Roman's brow likewise creased. Madina had likely had little regular contact with Recoletta, outside of routine trade, in the months before Sato's revolution, just as Recoletta had not had much contact with other cities – outside of South Haven, she recalled – in the same timeframe. But, of course, politics was about selective memory. City-states tended to keep to themselves as a matter of both convenience and preference.

Which made the presence of the chancellor and Father Isse all the more interesting. She wondered if Roman knew about this.

Roman spoke. "We understand that there's been some concern about recent changes in Recoletta. Sato wants it understood that these changes have no bearing on Madina or any other city-state, that they were completely internal. Nothing in our cities' long-standing peaceful relationship needs to change."

Jane scribbled in her clean shorthand, racing to get the words down.

Bailey raised his eyebrows and nodded once.

"On that front," Roman said, "we would like to restore trade. Our warehouses have stored the quantities of finished steel that would normally have been shipped here." He paused. "And your glass is the finest in production."

Bailey's eyebrows arched even higher. "Glass, Sayidh Arnault? An interesting choice under your present circumstances."

Roman's flat expression did not change. "As I said, conditions in Recoletta are stable. And as you said, there is no disharmony between our cities."

Bailey's lips puckered into a smile. "Disharmony, no. But caution... that is another matter. And while I trust you completely, sayidh..." He leaned forward, the flexed fingers of one hand splayed against his chest. "It is the Qadi and the rest of her advisors who I must convince. And this Sato is unknown to us."

Roman stretched one arm along the back of his settee. "What kind of reassurances do you want?"

Bailey winced. "Think of them as goodwill."

"If you say so."

The diplomat placed his hand on his chest again. "Sayidh Arnault, it is our sincerest desire that peaceful and productive relations prevail between our two cities. However, surely Sato can appreciate the position we're in." He paused. "And even if he can't, I'd imagine you can. Ideas are contagious. We must be careful about our contact, lest they spread."

"You're afraid of an idea."

"Oh, yes. As your Sato should be. What ever made him think he could hold fire?"

"I imagine he simply saw this as the natural progression of things." It was impossible to tell what Roman thought of this notion.

"Most idealistic, to be sure. But make no mistake: stir up the depths, and it's filth that rises to the surface."

"How colorful."

Bailey clasped his hands. "I've no wish to antagonize. Only to be prudent. If you're clever, you'll try to see where I'm coming from."

Roman said nothing, but the dull burn of irritation wafted off of him. Jane found that it was catching with her, too.

Bailey shifted in his seat and rolled his shoulders, warming up to his main point. "We are looking forward, Sayidh Arnault. Sato had his revolution," Bailey waved his hand, stumbling over the word. "And now we would like to see that we maintain a strong friendship."

"Then it seems we are in agreement," Roman said in the same flat monotone. Nevertheless, he was still comfortably stretched out in his seat.

"Indeed." Bailey seemed to genuinely brighten at this. "I knew a reasonable man like you would understand our requirements."

A heavy pause hovered in the air between the three, slowly stretching into something uncomfortable. Bailey, watching Roman with a fixed and expectant stare, finally blinked. "The requirements, sayidh. As I told you, I need to bring certain reassurances to the people who make these decisions."

A thin sigh hissed out of Roman's nose. "I don't suppose my journey here counts as reassurance enough."

Bailey laughed, then seemed to realize that Roman was not making a joke. "Why, no. I was looking for data. Numbers that can be taken back and digested at will by my superiors."

Roman pulled out a pen and a small sheet of paper.

"Taking notes, Mr Arnault?"

"Writing my grocery list."

Bailey chuckled uncertainly. "You Recolettans are funny people."

"Hilarious."

"Anyhow," Bailey said, his eyes lingering on the pen and paper in Roman's moving hands, "as I said, the purpose is merely to understand Recoletta's health. That we may know how to be good neighbors ourselves." He cleared his throat.

Roman said nothing, watching back with his disinterested gaze.

"First. We would like to send one of our own advisors to Recoletta's Counci... I mean, Cabinet." He smiled slowly at his own correction. Jane couldn't help but notice the sudden shift in tone.

"Also. We would like to see Recoletta's own trade data, crime reports, and population figures. The better to help us organize our own assistance, of course."

Despite concentrating on the notes in front of her, Jane couldn't help glancing at Roman, looking for some sign of his reaction.

As usual, there was none.

Bailey must have been looking for it, too. "I am sure none of this sounds too burdensome. But perhaps there is some particular matter you would like to discuss?"

Roman was still writing, his nose pointed at his notes. If Jane knew anything about him, he was trying to get a rise out of Bailey.

"Well, Mr Arnault?" Bailey said after a pause. "How do those terms sound to you?"

Roman finally looked up, giving Bailey a thin smile. "The decision does not rest with me."

"Then I will trust you to take them back to Sato for his consideration." A touch of irritation edged his voice. Right on schedule.

"Yes. After my grocery shopping."

Bailey laughed again, but this time, he just sounded like he didn't want to be left out of the joke, whatever it might be. "Well, it sounds like we've each said our part."

"Such as it is."

"And you sound like you have other places to be."

Roman rose and shook Bailey's hand. "Thank you for your hospitality."

"Our door is always open."

Roman turned to Jane, his hand extended, and her heart skipped a beat in thrilled nervousness. She couldn't imagine he would do anything so reckless, but if anyone would, it would be him.

Bailey looked on in quiet patience.

Roman took her hand and kissed it. His eyes met hers for the first time since the meeting had begun, but what caught her attention was the feeling of something smooth and dry sliding into her palm.

He gave her the slightest of nods.

Roman swept out, followed by the two guards, and Jane clutched at her satchel, careful to keep whatever Roman had given her carefully tucked into her palm. As Bailey consulted his watch, frowning, she took the opportunity to tuck it further into her sleeve.

"Let's go," Bailey finally said. Roman's carriage was already clattering away, and Bailey was no longer making any effort to hide the annoyance in his voice.

Climbing into the carriage, situating herself across from Bailey, Jane became uncomfortably aware of her right arm. How it was angled, where it rested in her lap, if Bailey was looking at it or if he was simply letting his eyes go into soft focus in the direction of her bench. The mysterious paper prickled her skin, and she resisted the urge to pat it down.

Bailey's hands were clasped in front of him, and she realized that he was staring not so much at Jane as at some transparent focal point in her vicinity. His jaw worked from side to side, and he finally looked up at her with the quiet concentration of a man who was working something loose from between his teeth.

"Well. The Qadi sent you along for your expert opinion," he said. "What is it?"

Jane frowned and folded her arms more tightly about her stomach. "He seemed frustrated. I'm not sure the meeting went as well as he'd hoped, either."

Bailey gave her a look as quick and sharp as a needle jab. "Focus on what's important," he said, as if she should know what that meant. "Did he seem convinced? Enough to furnish the information we requested, that is."

Jane blinked, studying Bailey. She'd had enough employers to know that some wanted the sudden, cold dousing of an honest answer whereas others wanted to ease into it slowly with convenient and placating suggestions.

"It sounded as though he'd have to speak with Sato first," Jane said. "And I'm not sure he knew what to expect, either."

"That is the question," Bailey said, running his fingers through the unoiled ringlets at the back of his neck. "How much he trusts Sato. Whether he could be swayed into nudging Sato himself."

Jane felt the same question uncoil within her mind. It slow-dripped into her system, a numb, spreading unease. She'd been a fool not to consider it earlier.

She looked up to see Bailey staring back at her in some private exasperation. He shook his head.

"These Recolettans are impossible to understand."

Jane returned to the Majlis and felt eyes on her. She busied herself with her work and resisted the temptation to check the note in her sleeve until she knew she was alone, keeping it secret and close like so much else. When she finally retired to the washroom for a break and the chance to check her hidden prize, it was warm with the heat of her skin and smelled faintly of clove cigarettes. She unfolded it, her heart racing and palpitating.

It was a grocery list.

Cabbage, peppers, rice, turnips, onions. Jane scrutinized the list, turned it upside down, held it to the light. She was still trying to puzzle out a hidden meaning when the door began to creak open. She shoved the list into her robes and hurried to the sink as a pair of clerks scurried in.

As she kneaded her hands under the water, she realized that the hidden meaning might be even simpler than she'd expected. After all, hadn't Roman said he planned to go grocery shopping before he left town?

She idled through the rest of the afternoon, reserving just

enough attention for her duties to avoid suspicion. Her neighbors at the other desks said nothing about her errand that morning, but whenever she chanced to look up, she could swear she saw one or two heads quickly turn away.

When her shift ended, it took a concentrated effort to keep from rushing out the door. The deliberation gave her another chance to consider her own uncertainty about what her upcoming meeting held.

As she made her way out of the Majlis, she let tides of the crowd wash her toward the marketplace, already packed with the early evening shoppers.

Looking around, Jane realized that it would be almost impossible to pick Roman out of this crowd, which was possibly the point. She would have to trust that he would find her. She fished the grocery list out of her pocket and dutifully headed to the produce stalls and the vegetables that Roman had specified. As she sorted through the turnips, she felt someone draw near and heard Roman's familiar obsidian voice.

"We're not alone."

She started to turn. "It's seven o'clock at the market, what did you–"

"Don't look back. I'm not talking about the crowds, I'm talking about the scouts. I was followed. Keep sorting through the turnips and meet me at the cabbages in two."

Jane spent another thirty seconds looking for the perfect pair of turnips, and then she meandered over to the cabbages, where Roman was rolling one of his clove cigarettes.

She sidled up next to him. "I thought you were giving up your nasty habits."

"It's a distraction," he said. "And don't pretend that you don't find it just a little charming."

Jane dug a shriveled and browned cabbage from the bottom of the stack. "Oh, look, it's one of your lungs."

"Listen. I'm going to draw off my pursuers, and you're going to make your way to the Jeweled Pheasant on Al-Maktoum. Find a quiet corner and wait for me there. Trust me, it won't be hard to find you," he added when Jane opened her mouth to speak. "Move along to the carrots and get going when you see the signal."

"What's the signal?"

"You'll know it when you see it." Before Jane could protest, Roman had faded back into the crowd, his cigarette burning between his fingertips. She scanned the crowds as she picked through the carrots, but she'd already lost Roman. She was hoping she'd be able to spot his signal when gasps and shouts of panic caught her attention. She followed the sound to a thin plume of smoke rising from a stall canopy one level below her. Two or three bright tongues of flame licked around the plume, and a tight ring of onlookers formed around the rising fire as those closest to the burning stall pushed back while those on the fringe pressed forward to get a better view.

A chorus of voices rose in alarm, instruction, and speculation, but beneath the mingled notes of panic and excitement, Jane heard another of urgency.

"Move, you! Out of my way!"

At the far side of the crowd, a man wearing nondescript dark clothing was attempting to shoulder his way through the circle of people plugging the market walkway. His eyes met Jane's and he looked away, but not fast enough. As Jane backed away from the carrot stall, her gaze fell on another pair of eyes on the other side of the commotion. Roman stared back at her, mouthing silent commands, and Jane turned on her heels and walked as quickly as she could towards the exit.

There were steady streams of people leaving the market with curious and anxious glances over their shoulders, and Jane was easily able to slip among them. She was almost clear of the market and the thwarted scouts when a gloved hand fell on her arm.

"Not so fast," said the hand's owner, a fiercely lean man with five-day stubble and ash-blond hair peeking out from under his skullcap. Something about his voice was strange.

"Let me go."

"In a moment." Whatever his accent was, it wasn't Madinan, and it certainly wasn't Recolettan.

Jane couldn't wrest her arm from his grip, and even if she could, she'd never lose him on her own. The crowds parted around them like a river around a stone, but no one had stopped to see why the gaunt man and the small woman had stopped in the middle of foot traffic. Not yet, at least.

Jane filled her lungs and yelled. "Thief! Thief!"

A few of the people around them walked faster, but more stopped and turned. "Now wait a minute..."

Jane glanced at the watching faces. If not quite irate, they were eager for a bit of theater, and she intended to give them some. "I felt you grab it. Just now," she said, patting her waist and affecting the local lilt. "What did you do with it?" She let an expression of dismay and outrage creep into her face. "That watch was a gift from my grandfather!"

An angry murmur rippled through the crowd behind them. Disbelief dawned in the scout's eyes, then horror. "Don't be ridiculous–" Even his coarse growl didn't disguise the unusual way he rolled his r's and lengthened his vowels.

Jane couldn't let him say too much. Doubt showed its fraying edges in the onlookers' expressions. She needed to get them invested before one of the guards intervened. Something that would raise their temperatures. "We showed you hospitality," Jane said. "Welcomed you into our city. And this is how you repay us?"

Murmurs of indignation and disgust rippled through the crowd.

"This is enough," the scout said. "We're going."

"Not just yet," said a burly youth in a saffron robe that looked two sizes too large. The dirt-darkened hem of his outfit scraped the ground as he strode over. "Seems you've got something to return to sayideh before you go anywhere." The scout tried to push past him, but two of the youth's friends stepped forward to block his path.

"This is ridiculous!" the scout said. "On my honor, I've taken nothing." He pointed at her, his hand trembling with fury. "She's not even–"

"Then you won't mind if we search, will you?" asked one of the youths. Jane backed away to let her protectors close on the scout. The crowd's attention was momentarily focused on the scout and the vigilantes, and as the circle of onlookers tightened around them, Jane slipped away and left the scene at a fast walk.

Jane felt her nervous breaths finally slow when she came within sight of the Jeweled Pheasant. The flowing calligraphy on the sign was mottled and dull where the original gilding had worn off, but the painted bird next to the letters was unmistakable. When she pushed the door beneath the sign open, a sour odor assailed her nostrils, and she reconsidered the relief she was just starting to feel.

It occurred to Jane as she crossed the Pheasant's mysteriously stained threshold that she would have more trouble looking inconspicuous here than she had in the streets outside. A dozen pairs of eyes, most of them yellowed or bloodshot, followed every tentative step that she took. Their owners nursed tumblers filled with amber liquid, or greasy glasses brimming with beer the color of sickly urine, and many held either a cigarette or the hose of a water pipe. The crowd was thick enough to fill the tables but thin enough that everyone seemed comfortably ensconced in a seat. Regulars, she suspected.

That was one way to get used to the smell.

In the far corner of the room, Jane spotted a rickety stairwell that seemed to lead up to another floor. It might not be any pleasanter up there, but it might at least get her away from the other patrons' curious stares. She then saw the bartender, who stood in front of a row of casks cobbled together with rusting rings and rotten wood. He followed her gaze and plunked a heavy mug onto the bar, looking back at her.

Jane approached the bar, casting quick glances at the other

patrons' glasses. "What do you have?"

The bartender seemed to chew on something before answering. "This barrel and that barrel," he said, pointing to two casks behind him.

"What's the difference?"

The bartender shrugged and pointed to two different patrons across the room. One looked comatose while the other was guardedly sipping his drink and peering about the room.

"What he's having," Jane said, nodding to the conscious patron.

The bartender poured Jane a draught that settled a good inch below the rim of her glass. She slapped a couple of coins on the bar and continued upstairs.

The upstairs room was quiet and musty, with a few ancient but sturdy chairs gathered around scarred and stained tables. Guttering candles burned just brightly enough to cast long, furniture-shaped shadows across the uneven floor and walls. It looked like just the sort of place that Roman would suggest for a clandestine meeting. She hoped he would arrive soon.

Not ten minutes had passed when Jane heard a soft but heavy step on the stair and, more disconcertingly, felt it in the creak of the boards below her feet. Roman's face appeared at the landing followed by a full mug of the same stuff that she had ordered. He slid into the chair across from hers without once looking at it.

Jane's thumbnail picked at a rough spot in the glass. How did you greet someone when you'd seen them just hours ago but hadn't really spoken with them in months? When you'd fully and reasonably expected that you probably wouldn't again?

"Glad you made it here safely," he said, setting his own glass down as if afraid of the noise it might make.

She laughed at the unexpectedness of it all. "Me too. Feels like ages."

"Didn't mean to keep you waiting," he said, turning the glass in one hand. He rushed ahead before she could clarify her meaning. "Matters on the way over required careful attention."

"You mean the fireworks?"

His eyebrows inched together. "I told you. It was a distraction."

"For a spy, you're not very subtle."

"I'm incredibly subtle. Distractions, by definition, are not."

She remembered her own diversion back in the market, the roaring crowd, the scout's hand on her wrist. "Who were they?"

"Qadi's eyes, I suspect." He raised his glass and sniffed the pale yellow liquid. Finally, he took a sip and smacked his lips, shrugging.

But Jane was still thinking back to the scout's accent. "They didn't sound local."

He held the glass motionless in midair. The thin meniscus of beer moved not an inch. "You heard them."

"Just one of them. Latched onto me instead of your distraction."

He muttered something that had the shape and timbre of a curse. His head whipped over his shoulder, gaze locking onto the stairs from the first floor.

"He didn't follow me here," Jane said, irritation rising like bile in her throat. "I made certain of that. But he didn't sound local."

Roman's gaze swiveled back to her, wary and curious.

"I didn't recognize the accent at all," Jane said.

"Could be a foreigner in the Qadi's employ," Roman said. Jane strove to identify the look in his eye. Suspicion? Accusation?

Or something else seen through the veil of her own warring emotions?

"Could be," she said. But she wasn't convinced. And he didn't look it, either.

Silence followed, scratching at the back of her throat like the smoky air downstairs. Jane had already swallowed a mouthful of the flat lager before she realized she'd raised the glass.

"On that subject." Roman frowned at some distant corner as he followed some private train of thought. "What exactly are you doing here?"

The question felt like an echo from her own thoughts. Several answers rose to her mind. "Surviving," she finally said.

"Seems you've put yourself in the line of fire," he said.

"Trying to stay out of it last time didn't much help." She took another drink, as if to wash down some of the frustrations and objections on the tip of her tongue. "Besides, I could say the same to you."

He grimaced. "Despite my best efforts." He set his glass on the table in front of him, anchoring it there with a broad hand. "The transition in Recoletta has been difficult. This back-room welcome today, it's more than we've received anywhere else so far."

Jane's elbows rested on the table, two pivot points as she leaned forward.

He noticed her posture and hesitated. "I don't suppose you're in a position to help," he said.

A tingle of foreboding ran along the back of her neck. "Help how?"

"Information," he said. "Some hint as to how the rest of the gears are moving, where the pieces are assembling against us." His fingers twitched around his glass, a moment of indecision. "This is survival."

A queasy feeling rolled in her stomach, the notion that she'd been naive, tossed and shaken by uncertainty.

Yet she knew his position and could easily believe it wasn't so different from her own. "This morning was the first I'd seen of any plans to make contact with Recoletta in an official capacity." She mentioned her surprise meeting with the Qadi and Bailey's cagey prodding.

She knew the question before Roman asked it. "What do they want?"

Her hands, resting on the table, turned in the smallest of shrugs. "I think they want information, too."

He grunted. "But what for?"

Jane returned her hands to the slowly draining anchor of her glass. "I thought that was your area of expertise."

Roman gave her a half smile and snorted into his glass as he took another drink. "Should be. But Sato's got me playing politics."

"You've always played politics. Just behind the scenes."

He winced as he brought his glass back down, and Jane wondered exactly what she'd said wrong. "Whose side are you on this time?" she asked.

"The same one I've always been on," he said. "Mine." Something seemed to close up inside him, mirrored by his hunching shoulders and guarded gaze.

She remembered something Lady Lachesse had said about allies, and she realized she hadn't yet mentioned the woman to Roman. She looked around the upper floor, alert to listening ears, but the only other person was an old man at the end of the room, too far away to hear, surely, keeping his glass warm with one hand and spinning a coin with the other. A Recolettan mark, she thought. No, wrong currency. A Madinan dirram.

As she watched the coin spin, too far away to know its value, Lady Lachesse's name was on her lips, something cold and metallic. It was currency, and it occurred to her that she didn't yet know what she would get for it, how Roman would use it, or even what it was worth.

And she was not in a position to squander resources.

She closed her mouth and swallowed the words as if stuffing a coin back into her pocket.

He inclined his head. "You were going to say something."

She sighed, shaking her head.

His chin dropped nearly to his chest. "It wasn't supposed to be like this."

"I suppose not," Jane said. Something tasted sour, and she didn't think it was her drink. "With what you and Sato knew about the Council, I'm sure anything must have seemed like an improvement."

Roman set his glass down with a hard thunk. "That's not what I'm talking about."

"Then what are you talking about?"

He waved a hand around the rickety room, and the candles cast monstrous shadows across the walls. "This. Running and scheming like a pair of criminals. Playing information like poker cards." He reached his hands across the table, as if to take hers, but they stopped in the middle, palms up and curved, as helpless as two insects on their backs. "I'm just glad you're safe, Jane."

Her heart burned like a stitch in her chest. "This isn't safety for either of us," she said. "Not yet."

"I know," he said, looking at the shallow pool in his glass as if it were a marker of time. "We should go."

Words welled up in her chest, things she hadn't said, things there'd been no time or opportunity to say.

"I suspect we'll meet again under similar circumstances," he said. "Until then, keep your ears open. And be careful."

"As always."

He smiled. Not the careless, mocking grin he'd worn in Recoletta, but something too raw and exhausted to be fake. "You go first," he said.

She slid the remaining half of her drink to him and rose. She stopped just long enough to kiss his cheek, a surface as rough and cold as metal filings.

She left, keeping her head down as she walked down the stairs and out of the bar. She did not look back.

CHAPTER 5

THE REVISIONISTS

Arnault had surfaced from his mysterious errand only that morning, but it wasn't a moment too soon for Malone. Working with him made her want a hot shower, but at least she had him where she could see him.

She gave her revolver's cylinder a quick spin, checking the chambers. "I know Sato believes they're dangerous, but try to take them in one piece. For questioning." She peered at him as she snapped the cylinder back into place.

Arnault said nothing. It was impossible to tell what that meant.

They set off, returning to the rubble-strewn neighborhood around Turnbull Square and branching into an abandoned network of warrens. As they passed the last of the guttering gas lamps, Malone reached for her own lantern, uncomfortably conscious of Arnault's proximity in the shadows. They were in a part of the city where a stray bullet was a convenient explanation for many things.

She glanced over her shoulder. Arnault didn't look any happier about the arrangement than she did. Not that he ever looked happy about anything.

However, he had drawn on his shadowy network of informants and insisted that this was the place that they would find their pamphleteers. The passage twisted ahead of them, the glow from

Malone's lantern glistening on the condensation-slick rock. While the factory districts themselves had been strongly pro-Sato after the revolution – the denizens had been among Recoletta's poorest and had taken quickly to Sato's message of a classless society – the surrounding neighborhoods were a patchwork of loyalties.

And this, clearly, was one of the contested areas. Street signs hung askew. Most of the lamps out here had been smashed or liberated entirely from their fastenings. She made a mental note to send a pair of groundskeepers out here to check the gas connections, already aware that, even if she remembered, it would probably be months before anyone had the time or inclination to get around to it.

The streets were deserted, and the refuse that littered them had settled into the landscape like some sort of invasive plant species. Almost anything of discernible value, from the sturdy wood of storefront signs to the copper fastenings of torch brackets, had been stripped. None but the most desperate, probably fugitives from other parts of town, would have stayed here. On the bright side, that should make finding their quarry easier.

On the other hand, it gave Arnault ample opportunity to attempt to dispose of her without any witnesses. If that was his intention. After all, he'd been the one to insist that they continue their search in this neighborhood.

Arnault shoved his hand in front of her, and Malone's darted to her gun.

"Tracks here," he said, pointing to a pair of deep grooves in the stone.

She relaxed, letting her hand fall from her side and shining her lamplight at the disturbance. She could just make out a pattern of hard edges and ridges in the dirt.

"Went that way," she said, pointing down a narrower tunnel on their left. But Arnault was already heading in that direction with his rolling, strangely graceful gait.

The passage widened into a moss-rimed cavern littered

with rubble. Chunks of the walls and ceiling had fallen away, presumably dislodged by one of the bombs Sato's men had placed on the night of the coup. Through the gaps, she glimpsed the darkened corners of abandoned rooms and halls.

She scanned the rubble littering the cavern, jagged chunks of rock strewn and precariously stacked. If any of these places had maintained structural integrity, it could be an ideal place for a hideout. Or an ambush.

She looked for Roman, only to see a shadow disappear around a boulder. She followed, aware of the crunch of pebbles under her feet.

Rounding the boulder, she found a dead end of piled debris.

A voice whispered over her shoulder. "This way."

She spun, catching her breath between her teeth. Arnault beckoned her with one curling finger.

She followed him around another curve of wreckage to a cleft in the cavern, barely perceptible until she almost stepped into it.

She glanced at Arnault, who stood a few paces behind her, wondering how he'd found it. "Ladies first," he said, gesturing at the entrance. As much as she disliked having him at her back, she liked less the idea of letting him know it.

The cleft led to a narrow hall that stretched into darkness. Malone lowered the filter on her lantern, dimming the light to a matte glow. Pressing on, she soon heard voices echo down the hall. She stole a brief backward glance at Arnault, who loomed behind her like a portentous shadow.

Still the voices continued unchanged and unabated. She couldn't catch what they were saying, but their dull monotone bored cadence suggested that the speakers had not heard them enter the hall. Which is why Malone believed she and Arnault had the drop on the dissenters and why she was surprised when a heavy hand shoved her to the ground.

She cursed herself for not properly anticipating this.

Malone twisted onto her back and drew her revolver, but she

had already heard two shots. Her sights zeroed in on Arnault, and her finger was tickling the trigger when she realized that he wasn't even facing her. She followed his aim further down the passage, the way they had come, and saw a silhouette standing against the gray light of the tunnel mouth. Arnault fired another shot, and the figure collapsed.

Arnault looked down at Malone, and his eyes flickered to her gun, which remained pointed at him. "I'm good at covering my ass. You should be thankful," he said, lowering his gun.

She heaved herself to her feet and brushed at her coat. "I'll be more thankful if you haven't just killed one of our witnesses."

"Maybe next time I'll push you in front, and then you can deal with him yourself," he whispered between his teeth.

"Don't get snide with me. This is your job, too."

"And he walked in behind us, and I made a judgment call. I know what it looks like when someone means to kill."

I'll bet you do, she thought.

Yet Arnault was right, and Malone was rapidly readjusting her estimation of the people Sato had sent them after.

At the end of the tunnel, their downed adversary groaned in pain.

"So much for the element of surprise," Malone said.

"Twenty seconds ago you wanted him alive."

Malone shouldered past Arnault to the fallen man. He lay gripping his thigh, his breath a high, sharp wheeze. The ground beneath his leg was slick with blood, but not enough to worry her.

Arnault loomed over her. "Take his gun and give him a handkerchief. We've got–"

He ducked as a bullet whistled over his head.

"Too late for that." Malone turned to face the other end of the hall, drawing her revolver. A shadow of movement flickered, and two more shots chipped the tunnel ceiling over her head.

The straight, narrow walls offered no cover. She glanced over her shoulder. Dragging the wounded man out of the tunnel under fire was going to be a challenge. And if the attackers followed them to the rubble-strewn cavern and picked them off from the cover of the boulders...

Beside her, Arnault fired another shot down the hall. The echoes rang in Malone's ears, but she still heard him bellow over the gunfire.

"Enough! You're going to drop your weapons and come out with your hands up or I'm going to shoot him. Again."

There was a pause and the buzz of fervent whispers from down the hall. At least they seemed to be considering it. Malone hoped they wouldn't call their bluff.

Arnault thumbed the hammer. "I'm going to count to ten. One. Two."

The pace and pitch of the whispers rose.

"Three. Four."

More hisses of argument from down the hall.

"Five. Six."

The wounded man coughed and forced a grim snarl. "Go on and kill me. We're not telling you shit." His voice was hoarse with pain and affected bravery.

Arnault barely glanced at the man. "Seven. Eight."

Still whispering, and no sign of movement.

Arnault shrugged. "Ten." He pointed his barrel at the end of the injured man's foot and fired.

The toe of his boot bloomed crimson. The victim screamed, all traces of courage suddenly forgotten.

Malone turned to Arnault, but her objections caught in her throat when she heard them voiced by their assailants down the hall.

"You said you were counting to ten!"

"I did," Arnault said. "And next, I'm going to count to five."

Malone cursed under her breath. This was supposed to be simple. Then again, these people were supposed to be toothless ideologues.

"We'll kill you!" one of them shouted.

"Not before I get to five." The man below him screamed. "Either way, you're going to have to step into the hall."

Silence. This was rapidly getting out of hand.

He thumbed back the hammer again. "One."

Before Malone could decide whether it was wise to stop Arnault, there was another shout from down the hall. "Fine! We're coming!"

There was a clatter of metal on stone, and three splayed shadows stepped into the hall ahead.

Their wounded captive moaned with relief. Malone felt her own shoulders relax.

Arnault moved the barrel of his gun to the man's neck.

The three figures stopped. One cried out, "Wait, what are you doing?"

"Resting my arm," Arnault said. "Keep moving."

They shuffled forward again, slow and steady, each careful not to get ahead of the others.

As they stepped closer, Malone raised the shade on her lamp and turned it toward them. Two men and a woman blinked back at them, their hands up and their expressions as bleary and bewildered as if they'd just woken.

"That's all of you?" Malone asked.

A man with a sharp nose and a lantern jaw gritted his teeth at her. "Go back and check if you want."

Malone knew a troublemaker when she saw one.

"I will." She got to her feet. "And you'll come with me." She motioned for him to turn and walk ahead of her. She gave Arnault a parting glance.

"Don't mind me," he said. "I'm perfectly comfortable."

Malone's hostage hazarded a quick glance at her.

"Two more big steps ahead," she said.

He complied, but she saw his cheek dimple in a grin as he did.

"I should probably introduce myself," he said after a pause. "Marcus Dalton."

"Save it."

"I'm just trying to be polite." When she said nothing, Dalton continued. "Wouldn't you rather get the story now, while we're out of earshot of that thug?"

She felt a twitch at the corner of her eye. "Keep moving. Don't slow down."

"I'm only saying–"

"I know exactly what you're saying. Quiet." At least she'd had the presence of mind not to leave him with Arnault.

He shrugged. They reached a bend in the hall where the smell of gunpowder stung her nose. Shivering gaslight lapped at the walls.

Malone gasped when she saw the room on the other side.

It looked like one half of a whitenail's private salon. Elegant, claw-toed desks, their polished surfaces laid out with solid bronze ink pots and crystal brandy decanters, sat in front of velvet-cushioned chairs. Neat stacks of papers lined the carpeted floor, and oil paintings of stern, venerable old Recolettans and torchlit cavescapes hung on the remaining walls, overlooking the remaining half of the room.

The other half of the room was collapsed beneath tumbled walls and a half-caved ceiling.

But Malone was fixed on the whole and furnished half of the room, which was still large enough to accommodate a couple dozen people. Or a printing press.

"Quite a place you've found for yourselves," Malone said.

"Yes." Dalton stood several paces in front of her, his back still to her.

Malone had thought it a coincidence that she and Arnault had been chased through the Twilight Exchange the other day. But now, looking at this lavish hideout and considering the seeming extent of their network, she was reevaluating that assessment, too.

"Turn around," Malone said.

He did, his face composed and serene.

"Where is it?" Malone asked.

A shiver ran through his face. It would have been too quick and too subtle to notice had she not been looking for it. "Where is what?"

She nudged at a stack with the toe of her boot. Pamphlets – the same that she and Arnault had gotten from Sato, the same they'd found in the cheesemonger's possession – spilled across the floor.

Dalton gave her an intolerable grin.

It never ceased to amaze her, the way a suspect would lie even when caught and confronted with evidence. She was half-convinced that, if only she could have them stare at a mirror instead of her, they'd realize how ridiculous they looked and give up the farce.

"Really, Inspector. I hope you've marched in here with more than just a suspicion and a handgun. Or do you people even bother with warrants anymore?"

"Where did these come from?"

He shrugged. "Came with the place. Must've belonged to the previous owner. We threw out the dirty picture books, but I guess we missed these."

She sighed. "There's a printing press."

"I'm sure there is." His grin widened as he watched her. "Perhaps you should have sent that partner of yours with me, after all."

Malone aimed her revolver at the carpet next to his polished leather loafer and fired.

He jumped back, yelping. "What the hell?"

"I'll ask you again. Where is your printing press?"

"Is pamphleteering somehow illegal now?"

"Fomenting unrest is. I can count just as well as my partner, you know."

He shook his head, the panic tide rising in his face. "I don't actually know where the pamphlets came from." But something in his eyes was composed, controlled. He had chosen his words carefully.

"One."

"You're making a mistake." His fear of her was catching up to his fear of what he was hiding. But not fast enough.

She thumbed her cylinder, checked the chambers. Spun it carefully. "Two."

"I don't know where the printing press is. I swear it." His voice was high and sharp, but there was something deliberate and purposeful about his words.

The trick was chipping away whatever armor of half-truth he'd constructed around the lie.

"But someone here does," Malone said.

"No! None of us," he said, full of panic and earnestness.

Not quite it. Malone thumbed back the hammer. "But you know who does."

She saw the fear in his eyes again just before he closed them. Not fear of her, but fear of his secret. "I can't..."

She fired, pointing the gun at him. He screamed as the hammer came down on the empty chamber.

He stood, trembling, his hands over his ears and she pulled the hammer back again. "I will ask you one more time. Who prints the pamphlets?"

"A whitenail. From one of the old, powerful families."

The thought struck Malone with both dread and exhilaration. It explained Dalton's resources. And it gave her someone to chase. "Give me a name," Malone said.

He laughed bitterly. "Those names mean nothing now."

"Not to me."

He looked at her revolver and sighed. "Clothoe. Lucinda Clothoe."

The name sounded distantly familiar, but Malone pushed the search to the back of her mind. "Where can I find her?"

"You don't. That's not the way this works."

"There's no use in protecting her, Dalton."

The smug grin crept back to his face. His courage was returning all too fast. "You think that's what I'm doing?"

Malone tilted her head in the direction of the door. "I think you're keeping your friend from medical attention."

His smile melted away. "And Sato's mercies, yes? His chances are better out here."

Malone considered Dalton, his sudden despondency, the way his fingers clenched into a fist at his side. She also considered the slow unraveling she'd seen in Sato, the hollowing of his cheeks and the darkening of his eyes. The man had a taste for political theatre that had been apparent in his execution of the remaining councilors shortly after his takeover.

Perhaps Dalton was right to worry.

"What if I could keep you at Callum Station under my own guard? No word to Sato."

Dalton snorted. "So instead of answering questions for Sato's goons, we answer for you and yours. Is that supposed to be an improvement?"

She cocked her head. "You think it is."

He hesitated.

"You're still going to have to give me something. A way to contact Clothoe. But you can either deal with Sato or you and I can handle this like..." She looked around the room. "Civilized folk."

His eyes slowly rolled to the door behind her. "And what about your pet?" His voice was barely louder than a whisper.

She thought. "Let me figure that out."

Malone marched Dalton back down the hall to where Arnault waited with the other three. The downed man still lay on his back, moaning softly.

Arnault barely looked up as she and Dalton came into view. "I heard shots," he said.

"I'm fine."

He shrugged.

"No printing press," she said. She was irrationally irritated that he hadn't even asked about it. "But there's a room back there full of pamphlets and stolen furniture."

The other man standing near Arnault, an older man with a neat gray beard and neat gray clothes, grimaced and bit his lip but said nothing. Arnault caught it, too.

"Not stolen," Arnault said.

The older man hesitated for a second before nodding. He looked relieved to be acquitted of that much, at least.

"We're not thieves," the woman said.

"Just violent insurgents, is that it?" Arnault asked.

"We call ourselves the Revisionists," Dalton said.

Arnault rolled his eyes.

Prickling hairs on the back of her neck reminded Malone that she was vulnerable here, stuck between Arnault and their bickering prisoners.

"We can sort this out in the city," she said. The peculiarity of the word choice only occurred to her after she'd spoken – as if Recoletta's borders had shifted with the rubble, and they'd found themselves in an indefinable no-man's land.

That didn't seem far from the truth.

"You're arresting us? But we haven't done anything," the woman said.

"Except open fire on the chief of police and her deputy," Malone said.

Arnault shot her a dangerous look.

"That was Parsons and me," Dalton said, nodding at the injured man. "The rest of them are clean."

Malone pulled a set of handcuffs from her belt. "Then we can discuss this back at Callum Station."

The older man and the woman gnawed their lips and looked back at Dalton. So that was the way it was. He gave them a tiny nod, and while they still looked just as concerned, they seemed to swallow whatever protest had been on their lips.

"You'll have to carry him until we can pick up a carriage," Arnault said, nodding at Parsons. The woman and the gray-bearded man knelt to hoist him up. Parsons gasped and groaned, but Arnault had bandaged him. She suspected, from the glassy look in the wounded man's eyes, that Arnault had also given him something for the pain. It made her wonder at the kinds of supplies he carried with him on a regular basis.

While Arnault oversaw Parsons' arrangement over the shoulders of the other two captives, Malone motioned for Dalton to approach. He obliged, obedient as a schoolboy, his hands held out in front of himself.

She fastened the cuffs around his wrists, and even though he didn't lean toward her – that would have been a fatal mistake – there was something intimate in his velvet-soft whisper.

"When are you going to do it?" he murmured, his voice lowered and pleasantly burred.

A series of treble clicks announced her success. "Do what?" she asked, but even so, she took his meaning well enough that she kept her own voice quiet.

"You know." He glanced at Arnault and raised his eyebrows in theatric suggestion.

Malone followed his gaze, but some part of her already knew what he was talking about. She was surprised at her own lack of surprise, and she told herself that this wasn't because the idea had already been circulating in her own head.

Or because of Arnault's episode at the Twilight Exchange. Or his mysterious meetings with Saavedra, his spy around Callum Station. Or his closeness with Sato.

The more she tried to talk herself out of it, the more she realized she couldn't trust him.

She tested the cuffs with a quick tug. Secure.

Ahead of them, Arnault was already marching the other three along the corridor toward the boulder-strewn cavern. He hadn't bothered to cuff them, but he seemed to be keeping a close eye on them, leaving his back, as broad as the side of a carriage, to Malone.

It was almost too perfect.

"After you," Dalton muttered. She heard the grin in his voice.

"Start walking," she told him, not daring to meet his eye.

And as she followed Dalton along the tunnel, her revolver felt like a warm presence at her hip. It would be easy. She could do it. She was certain enough that Dalton would see that the other three supported her story if it became necessary – easy enough in Parsons' case, at least.

Besides, allowing Arnault to deliver these agitators to Sato would not only mean their end, but the end of any investigation into their networks and sponsors. Sato was plainly losing patience with slow, careful solutions.

She thought all of these things, saw the scene play out before her, and yet her hand felt like lead at her side.

They were just breaking into the cavern when Malone heard her own name from the head of the procession.

"Over here," Arnault said.

She approached, feeling guilty already.

He glanced at the four captives, who stood just out of earshot. Dalton looked studiously away.

"Been thinking," Arnault said. "Maybe it's best we keep things quiet about their detainment. For now. We'll need time to get our questions answered. And Sato can be impulsive. Not what we need right now." He looked to her, careful and calculating and watching for her reaction.

Malone felt the warm, adrenaline-edged wash of relief. "Fine," she said. She could barely hear her voice over the nervous thunder in her chest.

He nodded and returned to lead his group, showing his back again as if on a dare. Malone moved back to Dalton, who looked at her with a question in his eye.

"Keep moving," she said as Arnault led the other three captives into the wrecked cavern. She gratefully took up her position at the back of the procession where none could observe her trembling hands or clumsy steps.

CHAPTER 6

SUBPLOTS

Fredrick had complained about the smell of smoke and cheap liquor for days after Jane had returned from her secret meeting with Roman. She'd been on the verge of telling him about Bailey and the Qadi, the whispers of the foreign strangers in the Majlis, her two meetings with Roman, all of it. But she'd remembered his exhausted melancholy after Lady Lachesse's surprise visit, and she realized she couldn't add to his worry.

Or perhaps, she considered, she merely couldn't bear to see that beaten look on his face and wonder whether the friend who had gone into exile with her had come to regret it.

Besides, it wasn't like nosy Freddie not to ask questions. The fact that he'd asked her nothing about where she'd been told her that he really didn't want to know.

So instead, she'd asked him about his job search, about the newspapers and ad agencies he'd been inquiring with, and she'd gotten a pained frown in response.

"I gave up on those last week," he'd said, swirling the sediment in a mostly empty teacup. "Had to lower my standards a bit. If one of these big houses would have me, I'd even take a job as a butler." He'd thrown back his head and drained the rest of his cup.

He'd obviously been too worn down to realize the vague insult in his remark, and she hadn't had the heart to point it out to him.

So for the two days following her clandestine meetings, she'd been careful to give Fredrick his space and thankful that he'd grown too prudent to keep his regular stock of gin and brandy.

On the morning of the third day, Jane left her apartment block while the lamps in the halls were still dim with the early-morning burn. She passed into the streets, cool and quiet in the absence of bodies and activity. This much she was used to, part of her daily journey to the Majlis.

What she did not expect was the carriage waiting at the intersection, as dark and imposing as a hearse.

It stood directly in Jane's path, astride the very street she walked. She knew with a dizzy feeling of apprehension that it was there for her, and there was no one else out anyway to dissuade her from this notion.

It was the Qadi's men, she'd decided. Maybe Bailey himself. They'd kept closer tabs on her than she'd expected. Maybe they'd even caught Roman and forced him to talk (he wouldn't have given her up quickly, she thought with a wave of nausea). Or maybe these were the same scouts who'd pursued her and Roman to the market.

She ran through the possibilities as she let her steady, even steps carry her forward. She couldn't run – if someone had planned to find her here, doubtless they'd planned for that, too – and even if she did escape, where would she go?

She wouldn't act guilty. She wouldn't give them reason to suspect more than they already did.

Jane kept her head down and her gait steady, all the while eyeing the carriage door to see who would emerge.

When she was barely a dozen feet from it, the door swung open, pushed by a pale, long-clawed hand.

Jane stopped, overcome by a rush of relief. It was not an emotion she'd ever expected to associate with Lady Lachesse.

The hand withdrew, and Jane quickened her pace to climb into the carriage.

The seats inside were upholstered in red velvet – much more comfortable than the hard, practical benches she'd sat on when traveling with Bailey. Lady Lachesse had taken the backward-facing seat, and so Jane sank into the opposite seat. The whitenail pulled the door closed.

"For just a moment, I was sure you were going to bolt," Lady Lachesse said. Jane's eyes were still adjusting to the pale light that filtered in through the gauzy curtains, but the other woman's voice was colored plainly enough with amusement.

"I'm not used to being received in this fashion," Jane said.

The whitenail gave a low chuckle. "You are too modest, Miss Lin. As I understand it, you're keeping ever more fashionable company these days."

A surge of panic surged in Jane's stomach. Was she referring to Roman or merely to her latest meeting with the Qadi? There was no way the whitenail could have known about her secret meeting at the Jeweled Pheasant, she told herself. Then again, there was no way she should have known about any of it.

And sitting there, trying to guess what exactly Lady Lachesse knew and how she might use it, Jane understood what Freddie had warned her about.

The carriage rumbled into motion.

Lady Lachesse smiled. "I do hope you don't mean to be so coy for the entire ride. It is charming, but it makes for a rather tedious journey."

Jane sat up straight, her back pulling away from the cushion as if from flame. "Where are we going?" Her gaze shot to the street outside the window, all but featureless through the diaphanous curtains.

"Patience, girl, I know you have to get to work. We must keep up appearances."

The queasy feeling in her stomach settled, but she had to fight the urge to twitch the curtain aside, just to check.

It was moot anyway. Wherever they were going, she would be

in the carriage until Lady Lachesse decided they'd arrived.

"Now," Lady Lachesse said, leaning forward. "Tell me everything."

Jane swallowed, tasting a dozen different versions on the tip of her tongue. She chose the one that began with her reaching the Majlis three days ago to find the place turned upside down by the presence of two men from outside the city. Lady Lachesse's posture angled forward even further, and on a whim, Jane let her story trail off.

"Well?" Lady Lachesse said. "Go on."

"Oh." Jane shrugged. "I didn't catch much about those two."

"Their names? You must have heard something."

Jane's thumbs hooked together as she pretended to concentrate. "People seemed rather careful when talking about them. I'm not sure I heard names, only..." She sighed. "One wore a long black garment, like a stiff robe with buttons up the front."

"Father Isse," Lady Lachesse said.

"Yes, that's him." She paused again. "And the other..."

She looked at Lady Lachesse again and saw the other woman eyeing her like a snake considering a morsel. She couldn't ham this one up too much.

"The chancellor," Jane said.

Lady Lachesse sat back as if coiling up to spring again.

"These men," Jane said. "Do you know what they're here for?"

The whitenail smiled. "I'd rather hear the rest of your story before I begin mine."

Jane nodded. Even through the luxurious padding, it felt as if the carriage driver were finding every rut and ridge in the road.

"I was met by a man named Bailey," Jane said. She mentioned her conversation with the strange man and their tea with the Qadi, careful to include every detail she could remember, hoping to make up for her rather transparent prying a moment ago.

"And then," she said, "we went to see the envoy." There was little to tell of the journey in the flagrantly anonymous carriage.

But when she reached the part in her story when Roman walked into the meeting house, the words again died on her tongue as she wondered again about what the older woman already knew.

Jane took the split second of hesitation to study the whitenail's face for some sign of awareness or suspense. It was studiously blank.

Either way, Jane took a risk, either that Lady Lachesse already knew of Roman's role and would note his absence from her story, or that Lady Lachesse did not yet know about him and would find leverage once she mentioned him.

Jane coughed before the pause could seem significant. "That's when the envoy arrived," she said.

Lady Lachesse nodded with what looked tantalizingly like satisfaction.

Jane continued, recounting the careful dance of words and intentions between the two men, careful all the while to refer to Roman as nothing more than "the envoy."

"And what did Chakrun want?" Lady Lachesse asked.

Jane blinked at her, dumbfounded but knowing better than to ask the question in her mind.

The whitenail made an impatient winding motion with one hand. "Ambassador Chakrun. What did he want from Bailey?"

Jane realized suddenly that Lady Lachesse had already cast the envoy in her mind, luckily enough. She didn't dare ask more about Chakrun, but she could only assume that he was someone who'd come to Recoletta with Sato.

"Normal, peaceful relations with Madina," Jane said. "Specifically, he asked about restoring trade."

"And what did Bailey say?"

"A lot of nothing, if you'll pardon my saying so."

The whitenail chuckled again. "You are quick to learn. But surely he wanted something."

Jane thought back to the musty old parlor, the air thickening with dust and tension as Bailey laid out his requests. "He called them reassurances," she said. "He wanted information about Recoletta's current operations – trade data, census information, the like. And he wanted to put a so-called advisor in Recoletta's Cabinet."

Lady Lachesse laughed again, deep and hearty. "I'm sure Chakrun loved that."

Jane felt an uncertain smile on her lips. "If Sato will never agree to those terms, then what was the point of suggesting them?"

The whitenail paused, pursing her lips. "Sometimes, the purpose of a question lies not in the answer, but in the asking. Questions can communicate intent. Reveal gaps in knowledge."

The world was momentarily silent but for the squeaking and rumbling of the carriage. "What do you think the Qadi intends?"

The older woman angled her chin. "That's only one part of the question. We must also ask what Chancellor O'Brien and Father Isse intend."

"But who are they?"

"Leaders of other cities – the Hollow and Underlake. That they've made this rare effort at cooperation should tell you something about the common threat they perceive."

Jane waited.

"Our current and former Recolettans are not the only ones having trouble with the new way of things. The changes in Recoletta have been even more distressing for some in power out here." It was clear enough that "out here" referred to the wide world of cities that were not Recoletta.

"More so because they still have much to lose," Jane said.

"Precisely." Lady Lachesse was leading her through a careful dance.

"So what do the three of them – Father Isse, the Qadi, Chancellor O'Brien – what do they want?"

The older woman smiled again. "If I know them, they all want something different." She took a deep, slow breath, her eyes searching the dark roof of the carriage as if for answers. "In most regards, the chancellor is a direct man. He'll prefer the direct solution. By his reckoning, that likely means another battle on

Recoletta's doorstep." She shifted on the luxurious cushions. "Father Isse, on the other hand, is careful. He'll want to see all the angles and look for leverage between them. No doubt it was his idea to probe Sato with these impossible requests."

"And the Qadi?" It was odd that Lady Lachesse would volunteer so much information, but Jane was not one to waste a good opportunity.

Lady Lachesse's eyes dropped back to Jane like swooping hawks. "That's what you need to find out."

"Me?"

"I don't talk for my health, Jane. Why do you think I've shared so much? I want you to know what to look for."

Of course. "And just where would I look for that?"

"Oh, Jane, I wouldn't presume to tell you your business. Rubbish bins, desk drawers, the mouths of domestics? And that's assuming you can't find your way into any more secret meetings." Her smiling lips just barely covered her teeth. "I'm sure you'll find a way."

Left unsaid were the words "you'd better." But Jane felt them clearly enough, tiny hooks sinking into all of the places where Jane was making herself vulnerable to the old woman. With each new meeting, it felt as if she were tilting her head back, showing Lady Lachesse a new patch of tender flesh.

She thought back to Fredrick's warning. To Fredrick, adrift in this city that he hadn't actually chosen. And as loath as she was to put herself in Lady Lachesse's pocket, it occurred to her that there was another boon she could ask. "I'll need something else first," Jane said.

Lady Lachesse's eyebrows arched in inquiry.

"You're asking me to find considerably more than my position will allow. You know what this will require of me. So I'll need another..." she shied away from the word "favor." "Another resource from you."

"Ask."

"Fredrick needs a job. It doesn't have to pay especially well," she said. The last thing she wanted was for Lady Lachesse to think this was some clever way of asking for money. "But it needs to make use of his skills."

"How fortunate he is to have a friend like you." In the low light, it was impossible to tell what kind of smile Lady Lachesse wore.

Jane shivered.

"I'll find something for him. But let us not get sidetracked. You had your meeting, heard Bailey and the ambassador trade terms. Was there anything else?"

And here was the moment of truth. Did Lady Lachesse know that she'd snuck off for a private meeting after the official one had concluded? It was possible, even, that the spies, the scouts she and Roman had diverted, were connected to her.

But she wagered not. The man who had stopped her hadn't been Recolettan, and Lady Lachesse seemed to be under the impression that Bailey had met with this Chakrun, not with Roman.

Besides, if sharing information with Lady Lachesse up to this point constituted showing her jugular, then telling her that she was having secret one-on-ones with Recoletta's spymaster would be the same as putting her head on the chopping block.

So Jane pretended to think back. "No," she finally said.

Lady Lachesse nodded. Sitting back in her cushioned bench with a glassy-eyed expression, she had the look of someone digesting a large meal.

After the silence had stretched on long enough, Jane cleared her throat. "You were going to tell me about my parents."

Lady Lachesse's eyes slowly swiveled back to her. "I wasn't certain if you still wanted to hear it."

"Why–" Jane forced herself to take a breath. "Yes, I want to hear it."

The whitenail cocked her head and ran a long, pointed fingernail over a cheek that looked as crinkled and delicate as crepe. Jane began to wonder if the older woman was waiting for her to say "please."

"Your parents were acquainted with Augustus Ruthers." Lady Lachesse was the only person Jane had ever heard refrain from calling him "Councilor Ruthers."

Of more immediate concern, however, was the fact that Jane had already known of their acquaintance on some level. "I know Ruthers had them killed," she said before she could stop herself. Belatedly, she wondered if she'd given away too much, but she hadn't wanted to spend her credit with Lady Lachesse on old news.

"Oh?" The whitenail's voice rose with polite interest. "And how did you know that?"

Jane considered lying. Or saying nothing. But the slow lowering of Lady Lachesse's head and the too-casual tone of her voice suggested that she'd have none of it.

Besides, this was ancient history. She had nothing to lose by telling the truth. "Roman told me," she said.

Lady Lachesse responded with a careful nod. "Did he tell you that, for a time, they were political allies?"

It was all Jane could do to shake her head.

"Your parents were ambitious, but they didn't have the social or financial capital they needed. And so they sought it from Ruthers."

"What do you mean?"

"They were rising stars in the Bureau of Architecture." Most of Recoletta was run by various bureaus, agencies, and directorates. The Bureau of Architecture was responsible for approving any new construction and excavation in the city. Each such agency operated under the auspices of a particular councilor.

Ruthers had headed the Bureau of Architecture.

"But as they learned, there's a wide gulf between resourceful middle managers and executives with real power. And on the other side, your parents saw wealth. Authority. Prestige. All the things that come from – and return to – the Vineyard."

Jane felt as though the air had been sucked from her lungs. This wasn't the story she'd expected, and she wasn't sure she wanted to hear the rest. But she knew she needed to.

Besides, she didn't dare show her discomfort to Lady Lachesse.

"Your parents were clever enough to realize they needed a patron. And they found one in Ruthers for a time. But with such an asymmetry of advantages... well. When a man like Ruthers racks up favors, the interest is steep. I think your parents realized that too late."

"What kinds of favors?"

Lady Lachesse almost blushed. Almost. "I don't relish indelicacy. And it's all perfectly mundane, to be honest. Promotions, disregard for certain rules and procedures, introductions to others who offered certain opportunities. You get the idea."

Jane's mouth felt dry, her tongue numb. "But what got them into trouble with Ruthers?"

Lady Lachesse peeled the curtain away from the window with a long fingernail. "I'm afraid we've reached your stop."

Jane looked out on an empty, unfamiliar street. "You must be mistaken."

The older woman stiffened. With so many other concerns prominent in her mind, Jane did not immediately register that she'd indiscreetly contradicted a whitenail.

"Appearances, Jane," the other woman said. "Just keep going in this direction, toward the larger shops. It would not do for us to be seen together so close to the Majlis."

"But the rest about my parents–"

"A story for another time."

Heat rose in Jane's face. "You promised me answers. You've told me almost nothing."

"Your expression says otherwise. Besides, you still owe me more information."

The carriage door popped open, likely at the hand of the unseen driver who had borne them this far.

"Don't worry," Lady Lachesse said. "I'm sure there will be future opportunities for me to finish the story. In the meantime, be a resourceful girl and figure out which way the Qadi's leaning and what her coalition is planning. You have three days."

"You expect me to find something in three days?"

"Events are moving fast, Jane. You'd better keep up."

Jane climbed from the carriage onto the even cobblestones. It felt good to have something solid beneath her feet even if she was being dismissed like a serving girl.

"Oh, and Jane," the whitenail called from her perch. "Do be careful around the Qadi. She seems to have taken you under her wing, in a manner of speaking, but favors like hers don't come for free. And you can see the danger of crossing someone like her."

Jane turned away to follow the row of shuttered shops to the Majlis. The blood pounding in her ears barely muffled the sound of rolling wheels and clattering hooves as the carriage turned and pulled away behind her.

CHAPTER 7

ANOTHER VERSION

By the time Malone had summoned a doctor for Parsons and tucked Dalton and his other two compatriots – Cabral, the woman, and Macmillan, the older man – into a quiet holding cell in Callum Station, it was well into evening. Nevertheless, Farrah had still been at her desk, and when Malone had explained that she'd brought in detainees who needed to be monitored quietly, Farrah had agreed without question.

"I'll see that they're comfortable," Farrah had said, already on her way out. "Message on your desk."

And, as indicated, Malone had found an envelope on her desk. It was blank, but the single piece of paper inside had been signed by Sato, and it instructed Malone to meet him at his office as soon as possible.

She'd glanced at the clock with its spiderleg-thin arms pointing to eight o'clock. Knowing Sato, he'd still be ensconced behind his desk, and he'd expect her to meet him there.

She'd set off for Dominari Hall, considering what she would tell him about her progress with the pamphleteers.

She hadn't mentioned anything to him about their episode in Maxwell Street Station, and she and Arnault had agreed that it would be best to say nothing about their capture of Dalton and his fellows. And as grateful as she was that Arnault was of one mind with her on this, she didn't yet know why, and they hadn't decided what they would tell Sato when he asked about their progress. Which, invariably, he would.

She'd arrived at Sato's office to find him poring over reports, assessments, and dog-eared books with the focus of an accountant scouring a balance sheet. He hadn't abandoned his conviction that fixing Recoletta was simply a matter of finding the missing information, lining up the proper facts, and building an argument that everyone could agree upon.

While Malone had waited for him to pull himself from his reports, she worked on lining up her own facts.

Still hunched over his desk, Sato had turned his face up to her. She'd noticed the change then – his eyes seemed to have sunken into his skull, and what little fat had once graced his cheeks had since been shorn off by sleepless nights and gnawing worry.

She'd shivered and wondered what could have aged him in the few days since their last meeting.

"Sit, please," he'd said.

She'd sat.

He'd swept the papers aside and seemed to clear his mind in the same impatient motion. "I have something rather unorthodox to ask of you, Malone."

She'd bitten the humorless grin from her lips.

He'd pulled a yellowing envelope from his desk drawer, pinching the edges. "As if our problems from our neighbors, our own citizens, weren't enough." He'd handed it to her.

The envelope had felt coarse, and pulling back the torn flap had released a flurry of strange yet familiar smells: woodsmoke, grass, and the mingled musk of man and beast. Smells of the surface.

She'd pulled out the letter and read:

To President Sato:

We wish to congratulate you on your recent ascent in Recoletta. The story of your departure and return, and of your mission for justice in the city, has made the rounds among our communes.

In fact, your story has become an inspiration to us all. We were heartened to hear of your commitment to establishing better conditions for your citizens and encouraged by your dedication to a more peaceful, equitable order.

It is with these principles in mind that we extend our enthusiasm for your changes as well as our hopes that they will extend to us. We have tried to offer these sentiments on previous occasions, but we understand that our congratulations have likely been eclipsed by your other responsibilities.

However, we are confident that you will understand our position.

Our provision of certain foodstuffs and materials to Recoletta has become unduly burdensome. And while we would like nothing more than to continue supplying the city, we would require certain assistance to compensate for the time we spend in forest and field.

Specifically, we need the regular services of doctors, educators, and engineers to afford our people the time and opportunity to continue feeding your city.

Again, we are assured of your reasonableness in all things, and we're grateful that you have set such a promising model of the future to come. We are confident that you will be quick to include us in it.

We are happy to host you to discuss the details in person, and we will await your response with hope and patience.

Yours,
Meyerston
Shepherd's Hollow
Woodsey
Fairview
Wheatton
Logan's Valley

Sato had looked back at her, his arms hanging loosely from slumped shoulders.

"They sent this along with half of the normal food production. We can't have this. Not in addition to everything else."

Everything else – black markets, rising crime, political instability, and the ceaseless hemorrhaging of capital and skilled labor. Malone's shapeless, malformed city was at risk of collapsing upon itself.

Sato had leaned forward, spreading his hands across his desk as if it were the only thing holding him up. "Do you know what makes the cities so different, Malone? Why you might travel to South Haven or Underlake or Ciudad del Mar only to find the accents so strange, the food intolerable, the customs so bizarre?"

She must have shrugged, or nodded, or blinked, because he'd continued.

"It's because we all grew up differently. After the Catastrophe… yes, I see you squirming, you don't like hearing about it any more than anyone else, but this is a history lesson you need to hear. After the Catastrophe, the cities kept their doors locked and their tunnels sealed. Probably didn't even have the skylights that allow for those gardens we all love. And they stayed that way for decades. Over a century, in some cases." He'd raised his hands, warming to his subject.

"Imagine that you and your inspectors lived in Callum Station on one side of town and Arnault and I lived here, in Dominari Hall, on the other. Imagine we never talked, never wrote, never heard news of one another. Can you imagine how different we'd be after fifty years? After a hundred?

"That's how it happened with the cities. And when they finally threw their doors wide and crawled blinking out into the sunlight, it wasn't a yearning for contact that drove them to it. No, it was hunger."

His eyes had glittered within their shadowed sockets.

"For all our differences, Malone, that's what all the cities have in common. We depend on the farming communes. Won't survive without them. And that's why we have to nip this in the bud."

Malone had stared at the letter then, wondering how ink could be filled with so much poison.

"There's a train leaving tomorrow that'll pass through Meyerston," Sato had said. "I need you to deal with them."

Her stomach had plunged. That would mean leaving the

detainees for at least a full day. And while she trusted Farrah to take care of them in that time, she still had her doubts about Arnault. "Sir, have you considered sending Ambassador Chakrun?" Even as she'd made the suggestion, it had felt feeble. Once Sato made up his mind about something, little could change it.

He'd dismissed the idea with a wave of his hand. "He's reached five new shades of gray since our last Cabinet meeting. I can't trust him to handle much more than official relations with the other cities at this point. Besides," he'd said, lowering his voice. "I need someone who can make an impression."

She'd watched his eyes, two pinpoints of darkness. "Not a deal."

"Not a deal," he'd agreed. "I didn't liberate Recoletta from the Council only to be chained down by the communes." Sato had curled his hands into claws and scraped them back across his scalp. "We still need them, and they still need us. That second part is what I want you to go and remind them of."

What he wanted was a blunt instrument, and he meant to use her like one. As much as she'd wanted to point this out – the way she might have to Johanssen, had the old chief ever given her cause to – the gauntness of Sato's cheeks and the grim contrast between his pale brow and his darkened eyes advised against this. "I see."

"Good. Because with everything that's already going on in the city, I can't have it known that there's a threat of food shortages. Contain the problem, Malone. And if they aren't amenable to suggestion..." He'd slid a paper packet across the table.

The gulf in her stomach had grown. "What's this?"

"You know exactly what it is."

She'd picked it up, felt the way the powder whispered under the paper as it shifted. "And who exactly do you want poisoned?"

"The leader, obviously."

In Malone's experience as an inspector, questions, rather than arguments, had a way of wearing down a flimsy story. She'd phrased her next one carefully. "And they're supposed to let me go my way when this leader mysteriously dies during my visit?"

"I'm nothing if not discreet, Malone. It'll take twenty-four hours for that powder to kick in, and when it does, it'll look like a bad cold. I wouldn't discard you so easily."

It had brought Malone both a strange comfort and a buzzing sense of distress to think that that he still had use for her.

"Another thing." She'd tapped the letter with the corner of the packet. "This came from six different communes. What makes you think there's one leader?"

He'd laughed. "There's always a leader, Malone. You don't set this many people in motion without a unified vision. It may not be an official designation, but someone is setting their course. Get rid of him and the rest will fall easily."

She'd traced the hard edges of the packet as she framed her question. "That would mean that you've got a plan to deal with the entire group."

"As you said, there are six communes, and it's taken them this long to act decisively. They can't be all of one mind. We can nudge them to a better course of action." Again, he'd smiled. "But let me handle that. For now, just worry about the task in front of you."

There had been lazy comfort in that directive, and it had scared her. But she'd needed time to think, and there was nothing to do but take the poison packet with her.

She'd risen and left the office, slipping the poison into her pocket like a bribe. While Sato's momentary lack of interest in the pamphleteers had seemed like a relief, his new preoccupation changed that equation considerably.

There had at least been one thing to be thankful for: an excuse to sleep before her journey.

But first, Callum Station.

By the time Malone returned, Farrah had already finished getting the detainees settled in.

"They've got cots, blankets, and enough food and water to last the night," Farrah had said as soon as Malone had walked into the other woman's office. "And a bottle of merlot to share."

Malone had stopped on her way to her own office, looking back at Farrah.

The redhead had shrugged. "You said they weren't prisoners, strictly speaking. And you want them to talk."

"How did they seem?"

"Nervous. Quiet. If you were thinking of going down to have a chat, I don't think this is the time for it. They're still rattled, and I didn't give them nearly enough to get them drunk."

Malone had, in fact, been considering some preliminary questions. But Farrah had a sense for moods and inclinations where Malone only saw motives and facts. She'd learned to trust the other woman's judgment.

"Parsons'll be fine, by the way," Farrah had finally said, frowning. Disappointment, likely, that Malone hadn't already asked. "Arnault only managed to clip off his two small toes.

"That's great." She'd cleared her throat. "Listen, I've got to run an errand for Sato. I'll probably be out a day, maybe two."

"Good, because I'm not waiting around like this tomorrow night."

"Just keep an eye on our guests. I don't want anyone else going to see them. Someone asks, say they're suspected looters getting the silent treatment."

"And Arnault?"

She'd sighed as she considered it. "Let him see them. But tell me if he does."

Malone had finally returned to her apartment to see that the hours had evaporated like cheap liquor on the tongue. She'd have to leave for the train station in little more than six hours.

At any rate, it had given her less time to dwell on the sorry state of upkeep at home.

Many Recolettans – even some of her own inspectors, she was sure – had taken advantage of the sudden shifts in real estate to upgrade themselves to nicer, larger units. Or, at least, to avail themselves of the luxuries left behind in abandoned homes – real silver, fine china, marble busts, and portraits done in oil.

The idea left a bitter taste in Malone's mouth, and besides, the time and hassle involved seemed like unnecessary burdens. She'd barely kept up with her own minimalist accommodations as it was.

And as she'd stepped over the threshold, a glance at the wall clock and a faint tingling of unease had reminded her that she hadn't been home before midnight in over two months. The rumpled bedsheets, the stacks of unwashed coffee cups, the brim-full trash bin – these had all reminded her of what her tasks had been keeping her away from.

Then again, perhaps it wasn't that simple.

The only thing that wasn't layered with dust was the cello sitting in the far corner of her bedroom. Malone had bought it after Sundar's death, and she still hadn't worked up the nerve or the energy to play it, but she polished it once a week before collapsing into bed. She'd stopped and considered it, as she did every time she found herself alone and home, but she couldn't stand the thought of her inexperienced fingers wringing sour notes from the instrument. Instead, she'd packed a valise and collapsed into bed for a few hours of fitful sleep, her dreams plagued by crumpling cities and faceless councilors standing before their nooses.

She arose early the next morning, thankful as ever for an excuse to flee the silent apartment.

The walk to the train station was too quiet. Every footstep echoed in empty streets. Recoletta felt like a ghost town. The problem was, there was plenty going on. It was just happening in rogue districts and out of sight.

The train station itself was surrounded by a contingent of guards. Sato had begun looking for ways to stem the flow of emigrants, and it was telling that this had perhaps only halved the rate of egress. Assuming there was any truth to Sato's numbers.

Even as the guards saw and recognized Malone's black uniform, they didn't step aside until she showed them her seal.

She settled into a nearly empty compartment with an odd sense of relief, squeezing her valise into the overhead rack. The train rumbled beneath her, steam flooded the tunnel, and with a lurch, they were off. Malone was removing her long cloak by the time they reached the surface and the soft glow of morning light. The sun played hide-and-seek between rows of sober pines and bursts of wide-open sky, and just as Malone would start to nod off, the sun would flash, brilliant and red against her eyelids.

As the train pulled farther from Recoletta, it shed something of the city's atmosphere, too. The air felt lighter. Malone wasn't sure what she was really looking forward to more: the reprieve from Recoletta or the chance to explore what she'd only glimpsed before.

The train stopped in a handful of communes along the way. Men and women loaded and unloaded crates to and from the cars in the back of the train, and yet there was more fuss than activity. More than once, she saw the train's cargo handlers point at the cars, their bodies leaning forward and their faces reddened with the force of argument. The farmers' responses were shrugs, folded arms, and shaking heads.

By the time the train slid to a stop in Meyerston, it was late in the afternoon. Of the handful of passengers in the car, Malone was the only one who rose. Few people traveled outside their cities, and fewer still made stops in the communes. Malone descended from the train, the wild agoraphobia that had gripped her the last time she'd been out in the open like this little more than a tingle at the base of her skull.

Commune laborers bunched around the train. Their ruddy arms gripped sacks and cart handles, and they spoke among themselves in low, conspiratorial tones. As Malone passed, their heads turned and their eyes narrowed – whether at her or at the glaring sun, she couldn't tell, but whispers and mutters rose in her wake.

She followed a dirt path across a tree-specked field and into town. Recolettans talked about farmers as if they lived in one-room shacks and mud-thatched huts. But many of the communes were only a few hundred years younger than the cities, and each was large enough to provide food and goods for several thousand city dwellers.

Meyerston stretched out as far as Malone could see, swallowed by a copse of dark trees in one direction and rolling hills in the other. Looking at the expanse of stone, brick, and timber construction rising from the earth, she thought she could see where the town had started and how it had expanded, each new layer radiating outward like rings in a tree.

Carving space from stone and hollowing caverns under the earth – this made sense to Malone. But wrangling form from the void, taming and ordering empty space – this was an enigma.

She reached a paved plaza with roads continuing in four directions. It brought a smirk of surprise to her lips to see horse-drawn carriages not unlike the ones that plied their way along Recoletta's subterranean streets.

Smoke curled from chimneys and dissipated in the cooling air. Malone heard all the sounds of a busy day's final activities: neighbors and friends shouting snatches of conversation out windows and across streets, laden carts rolling by, the squeak and gush of a water pump, and a hammer cracking in a yard. And for all their familiarity, there was something perilous about them – they rose and died in the open air when they should have echoed along tunnels and caverns.

And as she continued, she caught curious, suspicious glances from the farmers, who recognized her as an outsider. Whether it was her pallor, her dark clothes unbleached by the sun, or simply something foreign in her gait, they knew. There was always a tell.

With that thought in her mind, she followed the aging buildings toward the center of town, hoping that the protest movement's organizers would make themselves obvious.

As Malone continued, she picked up on the current of the foot traffic – the purposeful energy of people headed toward something and the backwards glances and lowered voices of those headed away. She followed the former and proceeded down cobbled streets, straight and narrow, between the buildings, to a din of voices.

The crowd thickened, and Malone emerged into a wide plaza framed by the brick and timber faces of some of the oldest buildings she'd seen yet. The town square was packed despite its size, and when Malone felt her pulse rise, she had to check herself and remember that she hadn't seen many gatherings this large in several months.

And when she did, it was usually a bad sign.

The onlookers faced a two-story building with a long, raised porch. Ten men and women stood on it, looking back at the crowd. The eldest of the group lingered at the front of the porch, his rounded paunch brushing the railing as he leaned against it.

Yet as he talked, his fingers drummed the railing and smoothed back his cotton-white hair. He had been pushed to the forefront by circumstance, necessity, or his fellow communers. But he clearly had not chosen the position at the front of the railing.

Malone paid attention to his words.

"You said you wanted a change. You wanted our grievances brought before the cities. I remember – I counted the votes thrice. And so that's what we've done. We've sent a letter to Recoletta, and now it falls on the city to respond."

A voice from the middle of the crowd called back. "I can tell you how they'll respond, Callo."

An agitated murmur rippled through the crowd, and Callo raised his hands for silence. It took several seconds, and while the whispers and grumbles slowly faded, one of the men behind Callo shifted, his arms crossed.

Malone continued to watch the shifting man while Callo spoke.

"That was a risk we all discussed and agreed upon when we voted. There are no guarantees. But we said we wanted better lives for ourselves and better opportunities for our children."

The shifting man had a thick, nearly black beard, but behind it she could see his mouth pull into a tight frown of agreement. He was straining to keep from nodding along with Callo.

"But how do we know about the rest of the communes?" another voice called. "It's all well and good for us to take this step, but if they don't follow through, we'll be left high and dry."

The din of voices rose, drowning out Callo as he raised his

hands and shouted for order and silence.

The angry, bearded man finally stepped to the railing. "Enough." His voice cut through the roar. The arguments subsided and, one by one, heads turned toward him. "You think the other communes aren't having the same conversation? Questioning whether we can be trusted, whether the others can be trusted? This," he said and pointed an accusing finger at them all, "this is the fastest way to prove them right. The fastest way to turn against one another. And when Sato's eye is already on us, we don't need more enemies."

Malone remembered Sato's assurance that the movement had a leader.

Another voice piped up from the crowd. "Sato ignored our first three letters. How do we know we even got his attention?"

Just then, the speaker turned his searchlight gaze to Malone. "Trust me when I say he's listening." His look was brief but intense. Only Callo seemed to pick up on it, and then he, too, saw Malone, taking in her pallor and her perfectly black attire in a single moment of anticipation and dread.

Callo took advantage of the lull. He cleared his throat. "Friends, I think it's clear from this meeting that we've all got a lot of work to do." He spoke to the crowd, but his eyes kept darting back to Malone. "We've taken the first step. Now, we wait and see how Recoletta responds."

The crowd dispersed in that grudging, deliberate way of grumbling schoolchildren. Malone stayed in place while the crowd parted around her, a stone in the stream. When most of the assembly had left the square, she approached the porch. The group standing there watched her with a mixture of hope and trepidation.

She counted six men and four women including Callo and the firebrand. Callo stepped forward. "You've come from the city."

Malone nodded.

He looked back toward the square, where the remaining onlookers had turned their curious attention back to the porch.

"Let's get inside where we can speak with more privacy."

Malone and the rest of the contingent followed Callo into the building. It looked like a meeting house of some kind, with long wooden tables and a line of windows spattered with grit. The air felt stuffy and close, baked by the sun overhead. There was a stairway at each end of the room, one leading up and the other leading down. Malone instinctively headed for the latter.

The firebrand called out. "That's for potatoes and emergencies, city dweller. This way."

She followed the rest of the group up the stairs. Sweat beads popped along her arms as the wooden steps creaked underfoot. She realized her fear was probably irrational, but she also didn't see the point in building rooms so far above solid ground.

The upper floor was even more stifling than the lower room. The firebrand eyed her as she removed her coat. She kept herself from undoing the top button of her shirt and rolling up her sleeves, but she was sorely tempted.

"Let's open some windows," the man said. "I don't think our guest is accustomed to the climate."

Now that they were all gathered, she got a better look at him. He seemed younger than she'd first guessed – probably in his mid-thirties. The lines on his brow were sun and sternness, not age. The face underneath the coal-black beard was probably even considered handsome.

The eyes of the other leaders darted between Callo and this younger man. There were questions on their lips, but the bearded man was in no hurry.

"A drink, Miss..."

"Malone. And yes, at the risk of sounding clichéd, I'll have what you're having."

A woman wearing a blue cotton blouse disappeared down the stairs while the firebrand pulled a mismatched pair of glasses from a cabinet against the wall. Next to them, she caught a glimpse of earthenware jugs, tin cups, and copper mugs. A pair of windows slid open. The dry breeze brought relief.

"Please," Callo said, gesturing at the chairs around a large oak table.

Malone took her seat, and she took the stemmed glass that Callo's bearded counterpart set in front of her. She recognized the mark of a Recolettan glassmaker on the foot, but the thick bowl and gaudily spiraled stem had been out of fashion in the city for at least a decade.

As the firebrand finished distributing the assorted stemware, the woman in blue returned, her steps thudding and creaking across the downstairs floor and finally up the staircase. She handed one long-necked bottle to him and uncorked the other herself, and between the two of them, they began filling the glasses around the table.

The liquid that sloshed into Malone's glass was an almost colorless wine that glowed with the last rays of the setting sun. She drew it closer, surprised by the faint chill in the glass. She wanted nothing more than to hold it to her neck.

Callo raised his glass in a silent toast while the firebrand finished serving the rest of the gathering. No two glasses were alike.

Malone raised her own glass in response.

"Now that we're sharing a drink, we should get to know one another," the young man said as he took his own seat.

Starting with Callo, the others introduced themselves, and she sipped her wine, as crisp and tart as a green apple. She concealed a grimace. The introductions made a full circle around the table, ending with the bearded firebrand.

"Benjie Salazar," he said.

"Nice to meet you all," Malone said. Watching the conviction in their eyes, and knowing she was about to twist it against them, she made an effort of will to meet their gazes.

"So," Callo said. "What exactly did Sato send you here for?"

The walls popped and cracked, and she suppressed a wince. "Talking terms," she said. The words stuck to her tongue like the sharp wine.

Expectation flickered again in the eyes of most of the farmers' representatives. Callo merely looked weary.

"Your terms or ours?" Salazar asked. His face betrayed guarded amusement.

Salazar would be hard to sway, but the others were still holding onto hope. And with hope came recklessness.

"A little of both," Malone said. "If you're willing to work with me." She reminded herself that, technically, that was true.

Excitement rippled through the other eight delegates as Malone dangled the bait and they rose to snatch at it.

Only Salazar looked thoroughly unconvinced.

Callo spoke next, cautious optimism creeping into his voice. "And what kind of compromise does Sato suggest?"

Malone folded her hands behind her glass, pretended to consider the question. She was more conscious of Salazar's steady gaze. "Sato's sympathetic to your aims. I think he'd be willing to work toward most of the boons you've requested in another six months."

Callo nodded, and the other delegates breathed sighs of relief.

Except for Salazar. "Horseshit," he said. "You're here to stall us." Something about his earnestness seemed suddenly familiar.

The others looked from Salazar back to her, and she could feel the temperature in the room shift again. The poison packet seemed to radiate her accumulated body heat. She was beginning to see the elegance of Sato's logic.

The thought turned her stomach again.

"I'm here to convince you to wait," she said. "That's not the same thing as stalling."

A nasty grin crossed Salazar's face. "If Sato's so genuinely interested in helping us, then why didn't he respond to our first three letters? Wasn't until we cut the grain quota that you lot took notice."

Not for the first time, Malone missed Sundar and his easy way of smoothing over tensions. She forced a thin smile. "This comes at a difficult time for us. We're reestablishing peace with our neighbors–"

"We're your neighbors," Salazar said.

"Which means that, if the other cities turn on us, you'll be caught in the middle."

A man in a worn flannel shirt bit his lip, looking grimly convinced.

But Salazar hadn't given up yet. "A delay isn't a compromise. If Sato wants to show his good faith, have him send something we asked for. A dozen doctors, teachers, and engineers. That would mean something."

Malone blinked back at him. "You want professionals. Sato isn't going to compel his own citizens to go anywhere. So why would they choose to come here?"

It wasn't until she saw Salazar's lowered eyebrows and bared teeth that she heard the insult in her words, and by then it was too late. "If this is an undesirable place to live," he said, "it's only because you city dwellers have kept it that way."

Malone cleared her throat. "As I said, Sato will work with you in his own time. But the combined leadership of the surrounding cities will not."

Salazar cocked his head. "It sounds like you're telling us that Sato's desperate."

The sharp edges of the packet poked at her belly. "I'm telling you that he could be your ally if you'll be patient."

"Sato had his revolution," Salazar said. "Why should we have to wait for ours?"

"He waited fourteen years."

Salazar glowered at her under furrowed brows, but she could see the logic seizing the others, smoothing their grimaces into sober, thoughtful frowns. She knew the look – they were grateful for a way out of the corner they'd blocked themselves into. Without Salazar's influence, they'd be easy to convince.

It was getting harder to forget that packet that Sato had given her. It seemed to rattle and shift with her every movement in a way that reminded her of crumbling bricks and toppling walls.

"So I'll ask again," Malone said, wetting her mouth with another sip from her glass. "Are you willing to be patient for another six months?"

The delegate next to Callo looked ready to burst. "If there were a guarantee, perhaps," he said. "We could get the other signatory communes to agree."

Callo tried to mask his disappointment. Salazar did not. "You fool," he said, shaking his head.

"Relax," Malone said, trying to salvage the situation. "It was clear enough from the meeting in the square that the protest hasn't been popular with everyone." She wanted to remind them of that.

Salazar attempted to take the reins again. "I can see what you're doing here, Miss Malone. It may work on them, but it doesn't work on me." He looked at her, not quite glaring, but watching for a reaction, no matter how small. Malone was again struck by a resemblance that she couldn't quite put her finger on.

The other delegates looked at the two of them, drifting back into a center of uncertainty. Salazar continued. "We'll ally with one of the other cities before we compromise with that hypocrite."

"You think I'm stonewalling? You'd get no concessions from them," Malone said.

Salazar grinned, again looking like someone else. "Doesn't matter. Sato'd have to listen to us once he's under siege and we're feeding his rivals."

"He'd let you run straight into their arms," Malone said. "And if your new patrons didn't break you to keep you in line, Sato would stomp you into the ground as an example, and no one would lift a finger to stop him." Malone held up the glass, cloudy with years of use. "The cities give you their castoffs at best. You think they're going to tolerate a list of demands from you?"

Callo folded his hands and closed his eyes. Salazar crossed his arms and looked away. The rest of the delegates glanced at one another anxiously.

Salazar turned back to her. "It appears Sato isn't convinced that we'll go through with this. I suppose we'll have to show him how serious we are."

"Maybe you will," Malone said. "But your allies may not follow you."

Salazar's look of brutal satisfaction evaporated.

"In fact, I think you're pretty certain some of them won't," she said. "Or could be persuaded not to. Many of your own citizens in the square sounded rather anxious about this. How hard would it be to convince your co-conspirators in Wheatton or Woodsey to accept amnesty and, say, reduced quotas in exchange for abandoning this pact?"

"You just told us Sato wouldn't compromise with us," Salazar said. "But he'd compromise with our confederates?"

Malone should have heard the danger in his tone, but she only heard the gravely edge of anger and dulled certitude. "I couldn't say what he'll do," Malone said. "All I know is that he only deals on his own terms. And he'll do what's necessary, whatever the cost."

"When he finds out about our schism," Salazar said, glaring.

Malone suddenly realized that she had gone too far.

Callo coughed. "I suppose you'll be wanting to get on the next train back to the city." His voice trembled as he glanced between Salazar and Malone.

Salazar took a long swig of his wine. "Doesn't come until tomorrow morning. I'm afraid you're stuck with our castoff hospitality for the night."

Malone kept her face a mask of neutrality, but she was calculating, coasting on the frantic energy of panic. Salazar's emptying glass was all the way across the table. Even if she got the chance to use the poison, it wasn't supposed to kick in for a full day. Where would she go in the meantime? Had the other delegates already been pushed beyond the point of reason?

Callo was quiet again, and the others kept their eyes on their wine glasses. It was the between-courses silence of an overlong dinner party.

Malone looked at her own half-empty glass, feeling her stomach drop.

"The inn's just off the main square," Callo finally said. "They'll have extra beds for the night."

"Surprised we've got one of those?" Salazar asked.

"Much obliged," Malone said, ignoring Salazar. Beads of sweat popped out on her forehead. From heat, panic, or poison, she couldn't say.

The other delegates waited for Salazar and Callo to push back from the table before rising. When they did, they rushed out, and it was Callo who hung back. He touched Malone's arm lightly. "This didn't quite go the way I was hoping," he said. "We don't want to add to Recoletta's burden. We're just looking for better opportunities here." He spoke with the falling inflection of someone who already knew he'd lost.

Even as Malone listened to Callo, her gaze flickered to Salazar, who stalked out with the rest of the delegates. Was Callo really that naive about the younger man, or was he trying to lure her into a false sense of security? Either way, it was a moot point.

"I appreciate your good faith," she said, turning back to Callo. "Understand that I'm just the messenger."

Callo grunted. "You'll be wanting to get settled in, I expect." He didn't meet her eyes. "The inn's just off the square. Green door with a sign overhead. I can show you if you'd like."

"I'll manage," Malone said. "Thank you for your hospitality." She hurried out of the building, taking just enough time to maintain the facade of civility.

When she got outside, the square was already full of people. Crowd camouflage was normally an advantage, but she didn't have her bearings here, didn't know how to blend her step and her profile with those of the people surging around her. She needed cover while she figured out how to escape. Lamps winked and flickered at the corners of buildings, and she quickly found the green door under a hanging sign that announced the Sheaf and Sow inn, displaying a picture of an absurdly feminine pig holding stalks of wheat like a bouquet of flowers.

Malone shouldered her way inside, keeping her head down. The building, like the rest in town, she supposed, felt rickety and musky with the myriad odors and temperature fluctuations that seemed to be the norm on the surface. The innkeeper looked up from a long, wooden counter. Malone read suspicion in his gaze, but she told herself it was merely the surprise of seeing a new face – he couldn't know who she was or where she was from.

Or if he did, she was in greater danger than she'd supposed.

"A room, please," she said, approaching the counter.

"How many nights?" He spoke slowly, taking in her outfit.

"Just one."

He turned to the wall and pulled a key from a row of hooks. He jerked his thumb at a stairway in the corner. "Upstairs, second-to-last door on the left. You, uh, want me to show you?" Too hopeful.

She gave him a tight smile. "I can manage." She took her valise and went up the stairs, half expecting the floor to give way beneath her at every step.

Malone found her room and locked the door behind her as soon as she was inside. She kept her pistol in hand as she checked under the lumpy bed, in the closet, behind the moth-eaten curtains that brushed the floor. But there was barely any place for anyone to hide, and really, she supposed it was too obvious. Salazar would come for her when she wasn't expecting it. She had to get out before that could happen, even if it meant walking through the night to the next commune. She'd be safer on the train tracks than here.

But she couldn't leave through the front door. Salazar would be watching.

She crossed to the window. It looked out over an alley between the inn and an adjacent building. A glow from the revelries in the town square spilled into one end, and she could see the unobstructed ground below.

Malone looked back at the room. The alley was her best chance, really. Both ends were open, and no one appeared to be paying attention to it. She had to move while that was still the case.

She tested the curtain. Probably sturdier than the bedsheets. And quicker, too, if she could avoid putting her full weight on it. She pulled out a knife and made two quick slashes to triple the fabric's length and a third to separate the new sections from the rings. She glanced into the alley a final time to make sure it was clear, and then she dropped her valise out the window.

Malone climbed onto the sill. The first-floor windowsill about ten feet below her would allow her to take her weight off of the curtain. As long as she could get there before it ripped.

She began her descent, bracing her feet against the brick wall and trying to take some of her weight off of the curtain. Her feet scraping against the masonry sounded too loud, her movements too clumsy. She grunted. She'd been stuck behind a desk too long.

The fabric began to tear, and she quickened her pace, trying to keep her feet steady against the wall even while she felt for the windowsill beneath her. She lost her purchase against the wall as the ripping curtain suddenly dropped her another foot. Searching and scrabbling, her boot smacked glass. She slid another half foot and found the sill beneath her, narrow but sturdy. She steadied herself against it, leaning into the wall just as the rest of the curtain came free overhead and fell into a coil in the dirt.

Malone hopped to the ground and picked up her valise.

She turned left, away from the square, and headed toward the darkness. She could only hope that no one had decided to watch for her there.

Malone kept her head down. As she neared the mouth of the alley, she looked up again to check the way ahead. What she saw stopped her in her tracks.

She could have sworn it was Sundar, her dead partner, standing in the shadows, a gleeful smirk on his face.

It took a split second for her to realize that she was gaping at Salazar, but by then, it was too late to run.

He glanced at the window. "Out here, we typically just use the stairs."

Malone felt absurdly embarrassed.

Salazar turned his gaze back to her, a half smile creeping across his face. "You know, it looks almost like you were trying to skip town. But I think I understand why."

She drew her revolver and trained it on Salazar. "I'm glad we see eye to eye on one thing."

He looked at her gun. "You've misunderstood me. Not that I can't appreciate your concerns."

"Glad to hear it."

"Allow me to make an observation," he said, holding his hands up. "You shoot me in this alley, and that party in the square will turn hostile rather quickly." He pointed carefully down the alley.

"It's a calculated risk."

He almost laughed, flashing his strong, appealingly crooked teeth in the darkness. "So is trusting in my goodwill. And, if I may say so, your odds are better with me."

"Says the man lurking outside my window."

"What, you think I was going to knife you?" His smile vanished in an instant. "I absolutely would if I thought it'd do a lick of good. Though it would send an irrevocable message to your boss, my cohorts are nervous enough as it is. They're on the verge of giving in, something you've already figured out." He inclined his head toward her, not quite a nod. "Actually, I wanted to invite you to join the festivities."

There it was again, that smirk and that glimpse of Sundar just behind his beard.

She wasn't quite ready to lower her gun. "And why would you do that?"

"Because I've got old-fashioned notions of hospitality. And because I'm hoping to show you something that may change your mind."

She was curious, if nothing else. Curious and almost convinced.

She felt something else, too. A quaking at her core that she hadn't had the luxury of attending to earlier. "I hope you've got something to eat at this gathering," she said, holstering her gun.

His grin spread. "And now you see my strategy."

They turned back toward the main square. As they passed her window, Salazar looked up again. "Hospitality aside, I expect Jeffries is going to add that to your bill. Unfortunately, it isn't some Recolettan castoff."

Shame bloomed inside her, along with wonder that she could feel guilt at such a dispassionate observation.

But he was already looking toward the square. As she followed him to it, she was startled at all of the scents and sounds that she hadn't noticed from her place in the shadows: meat, savory and crackling on a row of spits in the middle of the square, and crowds laughing and dancing to the music of some stringed instrument that Sundar would have recognized.

She turned to Salazar, but her escort had disappeared. Before she could look twice, he was back at her elbow, a tin mug in each hand.

"Is every evening like this?" Malone asked.

He laughed. "You cave folk have funny ideas about us." He took a drink from the mug in his hand. "Here," he said, passing her the other cup. "Try this. Better than the stuff you had at the meeting house."

She only hesitated a moment. It was beer, strong and hoppy, but refreshing. Malone drank gratefully.

"We do this when we have guests," Salazar said, stretching his hand to encompass the fire pits and the clusters of people. "But that doesn't mean it's really for you." True enough, everyone seemed to be focused on the roasting meat and cheery music.

"Do you get many guests?"

"No. That's why we do this. Here, try the venison."

Malone found herself accepting a steaming hunk of meat with her free hand. The grease running into her sleeve would normally have bothered her, but she was famished, and the flavor was unlike anything she'd ever tasted.

"You seem to have a good life here," she heard herself say as she reached the bottom of her mug. She was starting to notice the symmetry of the streets and the structure of the plain, sturdy buildings. She didn't know how she'd missed it before. "What do you really want from Sato?"

"You see this," Salazar said, waving a rib-bone at the scene, "but you didn't see the pox that took a child from every other home last year. You don't see papers because only a few of us know letters. And you don't see how damn hard life out here can be when we're busy filling our quotas. We want safety and comfort, Malone. And we want opportunities in the city."

Malone ate the rest of the suddenly flavorless venison.

"You have much experience negotiating?" he asked.

"Not the way you mean it." She pulled the poison packet out of her pocket and showed it to him. "Sato conquered a city overnight. What do you think he'll do to you?"

He looked at the tiny envelope for several seconds. "He ambushed Recoletta, and he spent months bringing his friends in first. You're overestimating him. Especially if he needs to resort to this."

She shook her head. "There are, what, five thousand of you? And how many guns? You can beat your ploughshares into swords, but not into rifles." The flickering firelight painted the festivities in shades of chaos and violence.

"If your President Sato wipes us out, who's going to till his fields?"

"Are that many of you really willing to see your families dead?"

"Better than slaves. Funny how a person's got plenty to say about injustice when he's looking at the man on top of him. Not so much when it comes to the one below him."

"Recoletta's reorganizing," Malone said. "Give us another year and I'll try again with Sato."

He laughed again, this time without joy. "And in a year's time, you'll say to wait another year. Sato's dug himself a hole that'll take a generation to get out of."

"These things don't change overnight," Malone said. She realized her mistake as soon as the words escaped her lips.

"Oh, but they do," Salazar said. "They do for you cave dwellers. Your whole city changed overnight. It's changing so much, you people don't know what to do with yourselves. Now it's full of books that your too-fine citizens don't even want to read. But it's good to have some things that stay the same, isn't it?"

Malone's lips tightened. "We've been operating under the feudal system for centuries. Sato hasn't added one ounce to your burden."

"Nor has he eased it. Not when he was too busy grabbing himself a city." Salazar took another gulp from his mug.

"That's because it's still a fair deal. Your communes supply us with food and raw materials, and we provide protection and emergency relief."

"Protection from what? The only ones have ever threatened us are you cave dwellers. I'm asking for schools, doctors, and professionals."

The moon was a sliver behind the trees. "You're asking for cities," Malone said.

"Why shouldn't we have what you folks have?"

"Who's going to grow your food?"

"I'm not saying we're all going to leave the fields. I just want us to have the same opportunities as you."

"The same opportunities," Malone said. "They're not what you think these days."

"I know," Salazar said.

Malone looked back at him.

"You think we hear nothing? This railway is a conductor for many things, Miss Malone. Tap it on one end and the reverb will carry all the way to the next city." Something in Malone's look must have given her away. "And that's part of the problem, isn't it? Recoletta's problems aren't a secret."

"And neither are developments in the other cities, are they?"

A slow smile spread across Salazar's lips. "You're quick, Miss Malone."

"It's Inspector Malone."

"So, Inspector. This comes down to one question: is your loyalty to Sato, or is it to Recoletta?"

"You already know or you wouldn't ask." She gulped the warming beer in her mug. "But defending a city calls for difficult choices."

"Don't I know it." Salazar raised his mug to her. "That's one thing we have in common."

She lifted hers, metal clinking on metal. "So. We both recognize that Sato isn't going to give. And if you push him, you'll wind up with a confrontation. Where does this leave us?"

"I suppose that depends on what you plan to tell him. Are you going to give him the information to crush us?"

"I don't think it matters what I tell him," Malone said.

Salazar grinned, looking again like Sundar. "It's not a question of what, but of how. You said yourself that it takes tough decisions to defend a city. You willing to betray your boss to do it?"

She said nothing. Again, they both knew the answer.

Finally, she spoke over the rim of her mug. "There will be a cost for you, too. An army at your doorstep. Blood in your streets."

"I'm ready to make the hard decisions, Malone. That's why I'm standing behind Callo."

Malone took a long, slow drink, tasting every barb and bite of bitterness.

"Stop your shipments altogether. Do it now, together, before the rest of your allies have a chance to rethink it. Force Sato's hand."

Salazar stared into the flames. He gave no sign of acknowledgment.

The next morning, Malone boarded the train headed back to Recoletta. As it pulled away, she looked back at the commune to see the farmers standing shoulder to shoulder, a wall in the morning mist. Their hands were empty and at that distance, their faces were blank and anonymous.

CHAPTER 8

THE FATHER AND THE CHANCELLOR

After her meeting in Lady Lachesse's carriage, Jane put her ear to the ground. She needed something she could use, something that would illuminate the inscrutable backroom politics of the Majlis.

Something that would placate her newest patron.

The Majlis seemed to sprout new windows every day. It wasn't possible, Jane knew, but the increasingly complicated plots in which she was finding herself – and the paranoia that was beginning to crowd the edges of her vision – drew her attention ever more toward windows with high vantage points, flickers of movement in the shadows, the rasping tones of whispers.

And so when one of the Qadi's messengers came to fetch her the afternoon after her meeting with Lachesse, she assumed the worst. But with the messenger's cool brown eyes on her, she had no choice but to follow and try to hide her trembling knees in a swift gait.

She walked with the man down familiar corridors – the same, she thought, that she'd walked with Bailey a few days ago – but just when she thought she knew what lay around the next corner, they'd turn in a different direction or find a wall where she'd remembered a door.

When the disorientation became maddening, she turned her gaze to the floors and watched the mosaics unroll at her feet.

Finally, the light from incandescents and fractal-patterned

windows overhead dimmed to the discreet glow of candlelight, and Jane knew they must be near their destination. As the messenger guided Jane to a massive, carved-oak door, the sound of voices on the other side was little more than a melodic hum.

The messenger pushed the door open to reveal the Qadi, Chancellor O'Brien, and Father Isse reclined on settees and perched on long, angling chairs, all the while seated around – what else? – a low wooden table laden with tea.

"Jane," the Qadi said. "So good of you to join us. Come, there's a seat for you here."

Jane accepted the Qadi's invitation to join her on the small, low-backed sofa as the sliver of light from the door behind her disappeared. She wasn't sure how she was supposed to sit, or if perhaps she was expected to recline, and so she settled on an awkward position in one corner of the strange chair, the short back curving against her tailbone. It was a small comfort, however, to see that the chancellor looked even more uncomfortable, propped on his elbows in a sloping settee.

"Glad you could make it," the Qadi said, as if she'd had a choice.

Nevertheless, Jane smiled. "Thank you for the invitation."

"You haven't met my companions here, but this is Father Isse of Underlake and Chancellor O'Brien of the Hollow."

Both men nodded in turn, the chancellor with a tense grimace.

"A pleasure to meet you both," she said.

"And this is Jane Lin, our resident Recolettan," the Qadi said, a little more slowly than seemed natural. The others murmured polite and indistinct greetings.

Marshaling a bland grin, Jane gazed at the intricate latticework across from her and over the two men's heads as the awkward seconds ticked by.

"Jane, we were just discussing the meeting that you and Bailey shared with that Mister... what was his name?"

A nervous twitch shivered through her calf. "Arnault."

"Yes, that's it," the Qadi said. "Quite an enigma, at least

according to Bailey. We were hoping that you could provide us with your own perspective. The three of us seem to be at a crossroads." Out of the corner of her eye, Jane saw the Qadi turn her veiled head to Chancellor O'Brien and Father Isse.

Jane should have felt more nervous, but the raw edges of her fear were blunted by a careless sort of joy at the convenience of it all – here the Qadi and her companions were about to unload their suspicions and inclinations, if only she could draw them out.

"I'm happy to help however I can," Jane said.

Chancellor O'Brien glanced to Jane's side, probably at the Qadi, but Father Isse kept his steady gaze fixed on Jane.

"You see, we were perplexed by Mr Arnault's response," the Qadi said. "Bailey described the man as on edge. Dare we say... unpleasant? I think this is merely the way of Recolettans, if you'll forgive the generalization. Formal, uptight, particularly in unfamiliar settings. But the good chancellor here, he sees Arnault's reaction as evidence of hostility."

"As he sees everything," Father Isse said, almost too quietly to hear.

The chancellor scowled, although to Jane it looked like the exasperation of a man who simply did not like hearing his opinions trotted out for examination and dissection.

And as Jane studied his expression, she thought she saw a flicker of movement just above and beyond his frowning head.

"But if any of us would know how to read a man like Arnault," the Qadi said, "it's you. How did he seem to you, Jane?"

She had to snap her attention from the shadows and back to the conversation in front of her. "Definitely uneasy," she said. "But I think it was like you said – he didn't know what to expect. Or how the meeting would progress."

"What we need to know is what he's after," Chancellor O'Brien said. "Bailey said the man didn't like his terms."

Father Isse rolled his eyes behind rimless spectacles. "And who would have?"

Chancellor O'Brien glared at the other man. "Then what did he want? Is he even interested in rapprochement?"

Jane felt the full force of the chancellor's anger even though she abstractly knew that it wasn't directed at her. "I- I think so," she said.

Father Isse smiled, and Jane studied his placid features as long as she could without seeming rude.

And then she saw it again. Shifting shadows in the darkness behind the tracery. She was certain of it this time.

The Qadi pressed something into her hand. "Jane, you must have tea. What kind of gathering is this otherwise?"

She accepted it absently, peeling her eyes away from the wooden scrollwork at the other end of the small parlor. "If I may ask, what exactly are you trying to figure out?" She blew over the top of her cup, hoping to hide the tremor in her hands. "Perhaps that would help me better answer your questions."

The three city leaders exchanged a quick look.

"We are simply trying to discern Recoletta's intentions," the Qadi said.

"How much of a threat Sato currently poses," said Chancellor O'Brien.

Father Isse tilted his head forward, as if about to agree, but he only raised his curving glass to his lips.

Jane took a sip of tea, wincing as the sweet, hot liquid burned her tongue. "He's hundreds of miles away. And he's dealing with his own problems. Or so the rumors say, anyhow. How could he be a threat here?"

"He's an unknown quantity," the Qadi said. "After all, I'm sure your whitenails would have asked the same about him a year ago. It pays to be cautious."

Stretched across a chaise longue, Chancellor O'Brien leaned forward on one elbow. The chair was too steeply angled for him to sit upright, and so he lay on his side, his body extended like a mermaid's on a rock in some fanciful drawing. He wore a grimace of barely salvaged dignity, and yet the more she observed of the

Qadi's carefully opaque manners and Father Isse's contemptuous eye rolls, the easier it was to imagine the two of them sliding into the more comfortable seats – and reserving the one next to the Qadi for Jane –forcing the chancellor into the awkwardly reclined chaise.

"These problems." Chancellor O'Brien propped his head against his hand, frowned, and shifted again to rest his arm on the chaise. "Arnault give you any indication of what they are? Or how severe?" He spoke between clenched teeth.

"He did mention that he was interested in restoring trade." Jane spoke slowly as she mentally separated her two meetings with Roman. "So I'd imagine their commerce has suffered. But I'm sure Bailey would have told you that."

"Never mind Bailey for the moment," the Qadi purred. "We're interested in your assessments."

Something clattered to the ground behind the lattice. The noise pierced the silence like a needle – the Qadi flinched, and the cords of Chancellor O'Brien's neck popped and strained as he resisted the urge to turn his head. Only Father Isse seemed unruffled, his smooth, egg-round head dipping as he bent to refill his tea glass.

"You were saying?" the Qadi asked around a pained smile.

"Only that I think Recoletta is looking for trade." It didn't seem to Jane as though she were giving anything away that the three leaders hadn't already surmised. "And nervous about encroachment by other cities. It seems that Sato's revolution hasn't been popular with his neighbors, so while he may genuinely want reconciliation, I think he's concerned about what form that would take."

"Would he accept food aid?" Father Isse raised his newly filled glass, his arms long and spindly beneath the fitted sleeves of his cassock. This was the first time Jane had heard him speak above a whisper, and his accent seemed vaguely familiar.

"I don't understand," Jane said.

"Recoletta's intercity trade has vanished in the last six months, and rumor has it that the city's own farmers have gone on strike," Father Isse said. "I am asking if you think Sato would be inclined to accept an emergency shipment of dried grains and other non-perishables. As a token of our goodwill."

Wisps of recognition floated just on the periphery of her mind. "I don't see why not," she said.

"Then it's settled," the Qadi said as, across from her, Chancellor O'Brien grumbled something indistinct. "You and Bailey will raise this with Mr Arnault at your next meeting."

The chancellor shifted again, assaulting the chaise longue with his elbows as he struggled for a more comfortable position. "You want to war–" He scowled at Jane. "Notify him?"

"You send chocolates as a surprise," the Qadi said over the rim of her glass. "Not a trainload of comestibles."

Father Isse nodded slowly, his spectacles flashing in the candlelight. The three city heads were aligning themselves, and the order was becoming clear enough to Jane.

"What I mean," Chancellor O'Brien said, "is that I'm not certain the Hollow's goods can wait."

The Qadi inclined her veiled face. "Another two weeks at most."

Chancellor O'Brien leaned on his crossed arms, looking like a sullen child. "I shall trust the judgment of my learned peers."

Father Isse set his cup in the glass saucer on the table. "There's no benefit in cornering Sato. A desperate man is a dangerous man."

The man's rolling r's knocked loose a memory in Jane's mind of a stranger in the market and a hand on her arm. She knew suddenly where she'd heard Father Isse's unusual accent – from the mouth of the scout who had accosted her on her way to meet Roman.

Jane sat stock still, paralyzed and surprised by fear. The leaders seemed too caught up in their own discussion to notice a change in her, but she felt her eyes drawn again to the carved screen, though she knew not by what.

"Jane, you've been most helpful," the Qadi said, laying a silk-gloved hand on her arm. "But we shouldn't keep you from your other duties."

"Of course," Jane said. She felt as if she were speaking around a mouthful of sand, but the three leaders turned their attention back to one another quickly enough once she had stood. As she reached the door, an attendant on the other side pulled it open. Another waited, laden tea tray at the ready, to supply the meeting with further refreshment after her departure. Even as Jane exited and the door smacked shut behind her, she couldn't help but feel eyes on her.

But the walk back to her desk, the motion of her legs, and the air outside the tea parlor energized her and cleared her head. She let the tension drain from her and began to work out a plan as she followed the attendant back to familiar territory.

By the time she reached her desk, she had an idea.

Her schedule was clear for the rest of the afternoon – no hearings, and no other meetings that she knew about – and her grumbling stomach reminded her that she hadn't yet stopped for lunch.

Jane looked at the wall clock hanging over the door. It was almost two. A little late, but not too late for lunch. Besides, she had a reasonable enough excuse for taking her break later – she had, after all, been called into a meeting with the Qadi. She had time.

In the Majlis, even servants and attendants were afforded a leisurely hour, sometimes an hour and a half, for lunch. It had seemed like an unbelievable luxury at first, and out of habit, she still wolfed her meals in fifteen minutes, but she was thankful for the time now.

The details of the meeting came back into focus as she thought through the steps of her plan. It appeared that Father Isse had gained ascendancy. Jane recalled what Lady Lachesse had told her about Isse being the subtler of the Qadi's two allies. He also seemed like the most dangerous.

As Jane's mind worked, so did her hands, gathering up her scarf and veil and stuffing them into her robes. She headed once more out of the office.

Food aid. Father Isse had proposed sending a shipment of food to Recoletta. Chancellor O'Brien had grumbled – what exactly had he said? Something about notifying Sato. But he'd corrected himself.

He'd almost asked why they wanted to warn Sato.

About what? That was the question. Whatever it was, it should be enough to satisfy Lady Lachesse for the indefinite future. She'd also need to warn Roman when they next met.

But how would she fill in the gaps in the city leaders' plans?

As she found herself alone in the women's powder room, her hand already clutching the veil and scarf, she suddenly realized what she had to do. What she was already planning to do.

Her pulse was thudding again.

She slipped the veil over her head and fastened the scarf over her hair and under her chin. The contours of her face, the shape and color of her eyes, and the set of her mouth were still recognizable enough to anyone who knew her – or anyone paying close enough attention – but there were few enough people who would. She was counting on that.

She was also counting on the fresh tea tray to keep the Qadi and her partners occupied a little while longer.

Jane swept out of the powder room, her face more or less obscured.

Something was brewing between the three city heads. And while Father Isse appeared to have spearheaded the plan, it was clear enough that all were in on it. Now, Jane had to figure out where she could most easily get some clue as to what that was.

The Qadi's quarters and offices would be the most extensive, the most well guarded, and the hardest to search. But the two men were only visiting – they'd be living and working in suites. Still several times larger than the apartment she and Freddie shared, no doubt, but it narrowed her search considerably.

And whose rooms to check?

Father Isse didn't seem like the kind of person who left so much as his spare change out in the open. Except to catch someone like her, perhaps. And if he truly was connected to the spy in the market, she'd do well to stay as far from him as possible.

That left Chancellor O'Brien.

Lady Lachesse had called him "direct." To Jane, he'd seemed downright reckless. Perhaps enough so to make her search easier.

There was something he'd said in the meeting, too. Something about "the Hollow's goods" waiting until the next meeting with Roman.

Gooseflesh rose along Jane's arms. Whatever these "goods" were, she had a strong suspicion they'd explain much of the plot against Recoletta.

To the chancellor's quarters, then.

There was just one problem.

The Majlis comprised almost ten acres. Jane only knew a quarter of it. She knew the offices where scribes, administrators, and other city officials worked. She knew the meeting rooms, paneled with lacquered wood in weaving scrollwork patterns, and she knew the office suites of the Qadi and other key bureaucrats.

But she was unacquainted with the extensive private quarters, lush apartments and suites where resident and visiting dignitaries stayed.

The irony was that in her present capacity, she had little cause to visit those quarters. In her past life as a laundress, she could have come and gone without note.

Jane needed an excuse. Barring that, she needed a better disguise.

At that moment, she nearly ran into one.

A man in plain black robes, his arms filled with a basket of linens, spun out of Jane's way just as she almost collided with him. She gasped, stopping in her tracks and stumbling over an awkward apology, but he was already gone.

She had hardly seen him. And it gave her an idea.

The attendants, bearing trays of tea and snacks, went almost anywhere they pleased in the Majlis. And, in their head-to-toe black robes and veils, they were almost indistinguishable from one another as long as no one looked too closely.

More importantly, they were treated as if they were invisible, a social phenomenon Jane was quite familiar with.

She could imitate the posture: a quiet but purposeful stride, head down and shoulders back, eyes focused on the task at hand. She just needed to get her hands on some of those robes.

She turned on her heels and followed the man she'd nearly run into, keeping an innocuous distance.

Shortly enough, he disappeared behind a curtain. She would have missed his exit had she not been watching him so closely – heavy with embroidered arabesque patterns, the curtain hung flat against the wall, seemingly more decorative than functional.

No hesitation. She had to look natural.

Jane followed him behind the curtain.

She found herself in the middle of a long passage. Though plain and narrow compared to the hall on the other side of the curtain, it ran parallel to the other as far as she could tell.

Jane wondered how much else she'd missed.

As she lingered, taking in the scope of the corridor, another black-robed attendant brushed past, giving her a curious glance.

So much for avoiding attention. The linen-laden attendant turned at a bend in the corridor up ahead, and she followed again.

These corridors lacked the latticework that gave the other "secret" passages a view of the main hallway, and every person Jane passed wore the same black robes. The attendants would notice her own veil and look away politely enough, but even that gesture bore the stuttering hesitation of inquisitiveness.

She needed to find a better disguise before she attracted too much attention.

Fortunately, the man carrying the basket didn't lead her much further.

He went down a steep flight of stairs and into a spacious room that was warm and humid with the steam of washbasins and scents of lavender and detergent that Jane knew well. When he turned to dump the items in his basket, she slipped in behind him and ducked into a partitioned nook stacked with towels and bedsheets. She counted out the seconds and, after twenty, heard his quick stride head back around the corner and out the door. She stepped out.

The other end of the room was full of men and women at washbasins, all too busy to notice her at the moment. Shelves and cabinets lined her side of the room, and she peered into them one by one, passing over crisp linens, towels, bright uniforms, and bolts of folded fabric as she searched for attendants' outfits.

At last, she opened a cabinet to find stacks of black robes, and, sneaking another glance over her shoulder, she grabbed the one on top.

It was a little large, but that made it easy to slip on over her own dark green outfit. She removed her veil and pinned the hood under her chin so that it followed the contours of her head and the back of her neck. The hem of the outfit just brushed her toes, but by the time she noticed, it was too late to change.

She looked again at the washbasins on the other end of the room, where a row of men and women were still busy soaking and scrubbing. The man she'd followed had deposited his basket somewhere and was on his way out the door. He didn't give her so much as a passing glance.

So far, she had managed to avoid attracting attention. Good.

Steam hissed behind Jane. "Excuse me," someone said.

Jane turned. Standing behind her was a woman, wrapped in a cowled black cloak like the one Jane now wore. She stood over an ironing board and next to a rack hung with freshly pressed robes – she'd been behind it when Jane had first entered the laundry room. She looked to be about nineteen, with a smooth, open face and wide eyes that seemed to look right through Jane.

"Yes?" Jane asked.

"You must be new," the younger woman said. "I thought so." An impish grin crossed her face. "What is your name, sayideh?"

"Lucy," Jane said. It was the first name that popped into her head.

The other woman's eyes brightened, still pointed at something just over Jane's shoulder. "What a lovely and unusual name," she said. "I'm Amina." Her brow creased. "Your accent," she said. "You don't sound like you're from Madina. But I've heard others who sound like you – Recolettans, yes?"

Jane coughed. She needed an excuse to end this conversation as quickly as possible. "You're very perceptive, Amina."

The young woman laughed. Even as she faced Jane, her hands danced over the stiff cotton tunic on the ironing board, turning it with little plucking motions. When her hands finally found a wrinkle, she traced it with her fingertips before pressing it with an iron waiting at her elbow.

All this without once looking at the fabric before her.

Jane shifted her body to one side, testing her theory. The woman's eyes did not follow her.

She was blind.

"I'm curious," Jane said, pacing closer. "How did you know I was new? Before we spoke, I mean."

"It just sounded like it was taking you a while to find the robes. And you don't seem to know where the changing room is," she said, her voice dropping to a coy whisper.

"I see."

"A thousand pardons, sayideh – I meant no offense. The Majlis is a big place."

"Very," Jane said.

The young woman's expression shifted from chagrin to eagerness. "Perhaps there's something I can help you find?"

Jane swallowed the "no" inches from her lips. "Actually," she said, "I was looking for Chancellor O'Brien's quarters."

Amina's eyes and mouth rounded into little o's of surprise. "He's staying in the east wing. Upper floor. Where he's less likely to be disturbed." She paused, something dancing on the tip of her tongue. "I hear he's a... strict man."

Jane knew the look. She also knew that nothing whetted the appetite for gossip like a morsel of scandal. "So do I," Jane said. "I also hear he has a taste for drink. And serving boys."

Amina leaned forward, gleefully conspiratorial. "You hear much, Sayideh Lucy. But don't let Sayideh Khorlev hear you talk like this. Rahim returned with the scent of the chancellor's gin on his breath last week, and she's had him scrubbing toilets ever since."

"I'll be sure not to," she told Amina.

The young woman nodded. "Now, the quickest way to the east wing is up these stairs and back to the tunnel." Amina gave her specific but clear instructions along the service corridor. "After you've passed the kitchens, you'll find a curtained exit about twenty paces ahead on your right. That'll leave you in the courtyard of the east wing. The second set of stairs clockwise from the service corridor will take you to the chancellor's apartment."

"Thank you, Amina. You've been very helpful."

Amina's face brightened with a kind of joy that Jane rarely saw others express. Perhaps she'd simply never learned to mask and mute her expressions, never having seen them on her face or any other.

So Jane followed Amina's instructions, stopping, on a whim, at the kitchens for a pot of tea. Balancing the engraved silver tray with a tall, four-legged pot and pair of glass cups and saucers, she took long, careful steps along the hall, trying to pretend as if she'd done this before. The high, curving spout seemed to give her a haughty sniff as she maneuvered around the curtain, as thick and stiff as a horse blanket, and into the east wing courtyard.

A twelve-pointed star radiated from the middle of the floor, the tiles that formed its outline weaving and crisscrossing with a dozen other iterations and variations of the same pattern. Daylight streamed in from the domed skylight overhead and bounced off of the smooth floor tiles, polished even now by another black-robed attendant.

Jane turned toward the staircase Amina had described, holding her tea tray high as an obvious excuse. The floor shiner seemed too intent on the tiles to notice. Just as well.

The staircase was shallow and wide, and the door that waited at the top might as well have guarded a bank vault. Its broad edges were banded with black iron, and the massive keyhole formed the mouth of a great roaring cat.

Jane's heart sank as it occurred to her that she did not have the appropriately massive key that was surely required to pass this epically proportioned portal. But she gave it a push anyway, and it swung open more easily than she would have imagined.

The apartment on the other side was more luxurious than she would have expected for a man like the chancellor – thick-woven rugs scattered around the floor protected the feet from the pitiless depredations of travertine. A silk-upholstered sofa was fortified with tasseled cushions and throw pillows. The incandescent lights around the room were diffused to an inoffensive glow by shields of frosted glass.

And yet, as Jane looked around, it became more obvious where Chancellor O'Brien had actually nested, fashioning a little haven of utility from the fluff of luxury – he'd thrown the drifts of blankets from the canopied bed and swept away all but one battered pillow. The nightstand had been denuded of all but a pitcher and tumbler, seemingly fugitive bric-a-brac crowded onto the mantel above the fireplace. The desk against the opposite wall was piled and stacked with papers, any frippery abandoned to other, less useful surfaces.

Jane slid the tea tray to a spare corner of the desk and began sorting through the papers atop it. She didn't know yet exactly what she needed – some hint or artifact of the plot the city leaders were working through – but she hoped that evidence would be obvious and copious enough to make her task quick and easy.

Unfortunately, the intelligence at hand didn't offer much – at least, not much that Jane could discern. She came across receipts and bills, inventories of items as mundane as rice and lumber, and notes transcribed in an infuriatingly obscure shorthand. If there was a story to be told in these tedious details, it would take more time than she had to piece it together.

She shuffled through the desk drawers with waning hope,

thanking whatever meticulous craftsman had so carefully oiled the slides and padded the panels. She found blank sheets of paper, spare ink pots, a letter-opener shaped like a dagger, and the infamous bottle of gin, but nothing useful. Even a man like the chancellor wasn't likely to leave something truly important in the open.

She'd need to look elsewhere for the blueprint of whatever plan he'd coauthored.

Then, a soft pop sounded from outside the door. Or Jane thought one had. She froze, hovering near the tea tray and listening with all the still focus of a doe in the woods.

After five long, uneventful seconds passed, she returned her attention to the room. She needed to work fast.

The chancellor's relentless colonization of the room made Jane's job considerably easier, and her eyes quickly fell on a dilapidated old trunk that sat like a tumor on the pale travertine. It must have been something the chancellor had brought with him. Surfaced with mottled, rust-colored leather and reinforced with metal bands, it looked like the kind of thing the Qadi's people would long since have discarded.

Jane tugged at the lid, hoping for the same kind of luck she'd had with the door. It didn't budge, didn't even give her a stubborn click to acknowledge her efforts. It was solidly locked, and the numerous scratches and scuffs around the keyhole corroborated Jane's suspicion that she'd need something more.

Straightening her back, she scanned the rest of the room, her eyes passing over the crowded shelves, bare nightstand, and even the closet stuffed with robes for all seasons and occasions. The key could be in any of these locations (or none of them), but without knowing more about the chancellor's habits, they all seemed equally improbable.

On a hunch, she padded over to the bed and checked under the pillow. Nothing. She lifted the corner of the floor mat. Still nothing.

She should have known, of course. The chancellor would keep something like this on his person, almost certainly.

She was just rising to her feet when she heard a heavy plodding outside the door. Growing nearer and louder. There was no mistaking it now, and there was no time to flee.

So, she rushed back to the desk, the luxurious carpets swallowing the sound of her footsteps. She stopped in front of the tea tray, turning her back to the door just as it sighed open.

Jane felt a minute swoosh of incoming air and a hard stare of disapproval on the back of her neck. The pressure and the temperature in the apartment rose precipitously.

"Just what are you doing in here?" Even without turning, she recognized the chancellor's voice from the brief meeting an hour or so ago.

"Tea, sayidh." At the last moment, she kept herself from saying "sir." She began pouring a glass. She hoped it lent credence to her story, and more than that, it allowed her to keep her back turned to him a little longer.

He growled. "I didn't order any tea."

"I can take it if you wish," she said. It was as good an excuse as any to leave.

"Leave it." He gave another feral grumble, as if this pointless exchange had somehow been forced on him. "Just empty the waste bins while you're here."

"Of course, sayidh." Jane picked up a wastebasket at her feet, noticing a few crumpled balls of paper within. Something useful, perhaps? Out of the corner of her eye, the chancellor was shrugging out of his jacket and aligning himself with the coat rack by the door. Jane turned from him and into the bathroom, dumping a few cotton swabs and wadded tissues from the little trashcan there into the wastebasket from the desk.

By the time she turned back to the main room, he was seated at his desk, his back to her.

She forced a deep, slow breath. Almost free. All she had to do was make it to the door.

Jane swallowed and pressed on. The walk to the door seemed

to stretch out, like an ever-lengthening hall from a nightmare, but she imagined the colorful carpets underfoot as an offering of flowers at a parade. She bore the wastebasket aloft in front of her like the head of a fallen foe.

The door, and the sanctuary beyond, was only three paces away when the chancellor coughed and sputtered behind her.

"What exactly is the meaning of this?"

Jane turned slowly, holding the wastebasket between them as if it might ward off his attention. But he wasn't even looking at her – he was glaring at a half-empty tea glass between a curled thumb and forefinger. And he seemed to address it when he spoke:

"How many times have I told you people to serve mine black? This is like drinking honey straight." Another noise of animal disgust issued from his throat. "Hand-holding and coddling. It's as if you people think no one can be bothered to lift a spoon on their own."

"I'll... take it away, sayidh," she said.

His gaze snapped to her. "And bring me more. Prepared properly," said the man who, moments ago, had not even wanted tea.

"Of course." She edged toward him. He was still staring, more or less, at her, but he seemed to see nothing through his veil of rage. She took the tray as carefully as she'd take a food dish from a rabid dog. Balancing it in one hand and the wastebasket in the other, she slipped out the door while the chancellor directed his burning attention to the matters on his desk.

The wadded papers rattled around in the bottom of the basket as she padded down the steps. Her fear of the chancellor above – or another prowling attendant below – was just barely greater than her anticipation. The other attendant was still polishing the floor when she finally made her way back to the courtyard. Jane kept her head down as she retreated to the safety of the service corridor.

However, the corridor scarcely felt safer than the main hall. Attendants bustled to and fro – just as one person cleared the short branch where Jane waited, a new set of footsteps would approach from the other end. And even though the gazes of the passing men and women tended to remain politely pointed at nothing, Jane knew better than to take that for a lack of attention.

The bigger question, she realized as she continued back to the kitchen, was whether she should even risk going back to the chancellor's office. If he recognized her, it was all over.

Then again, if she didn't placate Lady Lachesse, she might not be any better off. Maybe the old woman was full of bluff and bluster. But Fredrick didn't seem to think so, and Jane would rather endure another finite ordeal than the worry of wondering how and whether Lady Lachesse was going to bring the hammer down on her.

Besides, there was still Roman to think about. Roman and the rest of Recoletta.

She picked up her pace. She'd already made her decision. Now, she was just going through the motions of explaining why to herself.

And as for the risks, well. She'd likely overestimated the man. In the few minutes they'd shared the room, he'd only looked at her once, and even then, it had been with the unseeing stare of a man who'd turned his focus inward.

She almost laughed. There was such power in anonymity, in subtlety, and men like Chancellor O'Brien had no idea.

Besides, sudden flight bore its own risks, too. Suppose the chancellor, spurred to a fit of petty malice (which Jane wouldn't put past him), decided to punish this serving girl who'd abandoned both his tea and his wastebasket. If the right questions were posed to the right people and word got around that Amina had given directions to his office to a nonexistent Recolettan woman named "Lucy" who'd been fumbling around the laundry room, it would be a question of when, not if, suspicion fell on her. There weren't many (perhaps any) other Recolettans working at the Majlis.

A rush of aromatic steam heralded the entrance to the kitchens, prying her pores open one by one. Cooks and attendants rushed about, shouting orders and questions over the clanging of pans and the shouts of other orders and questions. Jane found a capable-looking woman wielding a ladle and a calm sense of authority.

"I need a pot of tea, no sugar," Jane said. "For the chancellor."

The woman's eyes widened in solemn understanding. She pointed to a bare section of countertop. "Leave the tray there. You'll have another ready in three minutes." She glanced at the wastebasket in Jane's other hand. "Trash is around the corner."

Jane shouted her thanks, but the cook had already turned her focus back to the kitchen. Jane headed back to the hall to find the garbage room the other woman had mentioned.

It was a quiet little nook of a room sectioned off by a thin curtain. A long, dark chute led off to some unknown depth. For now, the room was empty enough for Jane to risk pulling the crumpled papers out of the basket.

The first was a short list of numbers, squiggling currency symbols, and a few mundane items: pomade, bath powder, and, of course, gin.

Jane dropped the receipt back into the basket.

The other page was harder to decipher.

The numbers were arranged in neatly delineated columns. She kept trying to make sense of the senselessly abbreviated headings when finally her eyes fell on the note scribbled below the figures:

Total forces mustered. Can move with three days' notice.
– Sergeant Mussola

Time slowed to a halt as she read and reread the page, searching for another interpretation. Troops in Recoletta. War in the streets again. Something ached in her, as dull and distant as a phantom limb.

Quick, shuffling feet on the other side of the curtain reminded her of where she was and what she still had to do. She shoved the balled-up paper into one of the robe's voluminous pockets and dumped everything else into the chute.

The tea tray was waiting as promised, a little trickle of steam rising from the pot, when Jane returned to the kitchen. The matriarch with the ladle gave her a quick nod, and Jane took the tray, retracing the path back to the chancellor's apartment.

When she nudged the thick door open, the chancellor was still at his desk, scribbling away, his lips pressed tightly together.

Across the room, the battered old trunk, the same one she'd tried to open not ten minutes ago, lay open.

She must have stopped, because the chancellor looked up at her. "You may leave it on the desk," he said, his tone almost conciliatory, as if he'd decided that his myriad frustrations might not actually be her fault. She circled around to his side of the desk, keeping her eyes on the page before him and her pace just slow enough that he'd mistake her deliberation for respect.

She set the tray on a corner that had been left bare for her purposes.

But when she saw what he was writing, she brought her hand down on the corner of the tray, upending the pot all over the chancellor and his desk.

Even then, as a wave of dark liquid crested over white pages, as the chancellor's head turned to face hers, the movement as slow and unnatural as an owl's, she wasn't sure if it was something she'd done on purpose or if her hands had spasmed in fear or out of some manic sense of fatalism. But by the time Chancellor O'Brien turned his burning gaze on her, the reasons no longer mattered.

She remembered her bare face and couldn't believe now that she'd taken so much risk just to possibly peek at a few notes. She turned her face down but felt the heat of his stare on her forehead like the noonday sun.

The first bead of sweat slid down her temple.

"Make yourself useful, girl," he said.

It seemed to take forever for his words to congeal into practical meaning in her ears. When they did, she bobbed her head once and turned toward the bathroom for a towel.

"Where do you think you're going?"

She froze, turned back, and looked at the mess. Her eyes darted from side to side, but of course there was nothing. That was the point. Not daring to lift her head, she knelt and sopped up the spilled tea with the front of her robe. She felt the chancellor's gaze on her the whole time.

And yet, stronger than the fear watering her blood was her anger at this humiliation. She would make this count.

So when she'd dabbed the last of the mess from the travertine, she rose, careful to tuck her head behind her shoulder in a gesture that the chancellor would surely mistake for shame.

Let him.

While he reveled in her cowed posture – back hunched, shoulders drawn together, hands slowly mopping at the pool of tea – she scanned his desk and found exactly what she was looking for.

The ink was already blurring and bleeding, but the chancellor's response to Sergeant Mussola was still clear enough:

Ready transport in eight days. Madina will send one of its own trains for your purposes.

She was dimly aware of her hand, clutching a wad of her black robe, repeatedly buffing the same spot as she read, reread, and memorized the line.

The chancellor's snort reminded Jane that she wasn't alone.

"I've always wondered what you people wear under those robes," he said. "Figures."

She looked down at herself to see the green of her regular robes showing beneath her knees. She dropped the wad of soiled robe, and the heavy fabric fell like a stage curtain. But the chancellor laughed in a way that told her he'd clearly mistaken the reason for her discomfort.

But only because he didn't recognize her face. She needed to get out before he did.

"Hurry up," he growled.

Her toe bumped against the tea tray, and on a sudden impulse, she lifted it and swept the stained and sodden papers into it. Let the chancellor tell her otherwise.

A noise of protest rattled and died in his throat.

She grabbed the corner of her black robe and gave the surface of the desk a final sweep. "A thousand pardons, sayidh," she said, thickening her consonants after the local fashion.

"I don't care how many, just get out of here."

She bobbed her head and hurried out, the tray rattling with the faint shaking of her hand.

The passage down the stairs, the radiant rotunda with its assiduous attendant, the dim passage back to the kitchen – everything passed in a blur, her ears ringing. She set the tray on a bare patch of counter, taking the dripping papers before anyone could say a word.

She ducked back into the alcove with the garbage chute where her breathing, loud and ragged, echoed in the tiny space. She fought for control, squeezing her eyes shut and counting each rapid lungful.

Finally, she opened her eyes again and peeled the soiled pages from one another. Receipts, news reports, and hopelessly obscure communiqués. The only page that meant anything was the one she'd already seen, the response to Mussola. She salvaged the wadded troop numbers from her pocket, tore off the black robe, balled the other soggy pages into it, and dumped the whole mess down the chute.

Thus unburdened, she at last brought her breathing under control.

CHAPTER 9

THE UPPER HAND

Jane sat on the pilfered messages a full three days before meeting with Lady Lachesse again. It felt good in a way she hadn't expected. Like polishing a wealthier woman's pearls and pretending, just for a while, that they're yours.

Nevertheless, another surprise had been waiting for her when she returned home from her extraordinary day.

Fredrick had retreated into one of the low, pillow-crowded seats, which was usual, and he held a glass of wine, which was not.

Rather, it had not been since their escape from Recoletta – that was one change for the better for him since settling in Madina.

When Jane walked in the door, he waved at her as if they were on opposite sides of a street. Her heart crumbled in her chest. Barely an inch sloshed around as he beckoned her. Knowing Freddie, that only meant he'd filled his glass to the brim and drunk the rest already.

"Come," he said, slapping the pillow next to him. "Sit, sit." That's when she saw the other glass, resting on the floor near her seat. By some miracle, he hadn't knocked it over yet – it was as full as his must have been minutes ago.

She sat next to him, slow and steady, lest a sudden error on her part send him, her, the wine, and his thankfully high spirits careening in some unknown direction.

"Not my usual drop," he said, regarding his own glass as if someone had filled it while his back was turned, "but I wanted you to have some, as well. You always did prefer a nice red to the harder stuff." Looking up at her through his eyelashes, he sounded like he was reminding her of this.

Jane picked up her glass, which he was watching intently. It wasn't a proper wine glass, but rather a tall, narrow water tumbler, thick as an old man's eyeglasses. Under his hungry, hopeful gaze, she took a sip, forcing her lips into a smile as she swallowed.

If she'd just demonstrated that the wine wasn't poison, he couldn't have looked more relieved. "Feels so nice to have a good time again," he said, leaning back against his pillows.

The only thing worse than letting him continue would be bringing him down too hard. She remembered rough nights that had turned to rougher weeks, back in Recoletta when their respective situations had felt less dire.

So she laid her hand on his arm and spoke in the low, soothing voice one might use to coax a frightened animal. "Tell me what happened today, Freddie. We can talk it out." She was already eyeing the wine bottle, wondering how she could sneak it away from him and whether he was still sober enough to note its absence.

"Don't sound so serious," he said. "I got this so we can celebrate." He grinned like a fool before she could prod him further. "I got a job," he said, whispering as if at the most monumental of secrets.

Jane had already forgotten about that element of her morning carriage ride with Lady Lachesse. In fact, most of the day prior to her meeting with the Qadi had slipped from her mind, but in all fairness, she couldn't have imagined that Lady Lachesse could respond so quickly.

The thought gave her pause.

But Fredrick evidently mistook her hesitation. "I did so. And it's a perfectly good job." He turned away from her, cradling his glass against his chest as if to save it, and his dignity, from her disbelief and disapproval.

"That's wonderful news," she said, hoping he couldn't hear the anxiety she felt. "What is it?"

His pout slowly puckered into a smile. "You won't believe it." He was clearly counting on her to. "I'm going to write. For the local paper."

"Freddie, that's fantastic."

He winced and held up his hands. "It's not like what I had back in Recoletta. It'll mostly just be bulletins – the kind of thing they print and post around town to warn you about a tunnel closure or a market day or something." The glow returned. "But it'll be decent money. And I'll have my ear close to the beating heart of the city – a city, anyway."

"I'm so proud of you." For the first time in a long while, Jane smiled in earnest.

He wriggled deeper into his pillows. "Anyway, that's why I wanted us to share this." He raised his glass and topped it off.

Jane took another sip, tasting it for the first time. "Mmm." It was good. Better than either of them had any need to buy. "Where did you get this?"

"That's the thing." He slapped his knee. "It was waiting on the doorstep when I got home. A little congratulatory gift from the new bosses."

Her throat tightened mid-swallow. Fredrick was a clever man but easily distracted.

Looking at the half-empty bottle and the ten-year-old vintage, Jane had no doubt that the gift had come from someone who knew him well enough to know his distractions.

They finished the bottle together, and Fredrick, thankfully, did not acquire any more over the next few days. And he seemed to settle in well enough at his new job, coming home full of gossip and energy.

Jane was glad for it, but not quite glad enough to let her guard down.

When Lady Lachesse's dark carriage stopped for her again, she was halfway home from a day of work at the Majlis. She was crossing one of the winding, high-ceilinged tunnels that twisted around the market. Tea stalls and sweet shops were catching their second wind while the last light of day filtered in from the great arched skylights. A row of carriages idled along the passage, but Jane felt eyes watching her from within one of them even before the door popped open.

Jane climbed in, shutting the door behind her, and waited for her eyes to adjust to the dimness while the street moved beneath her.

"If you're going to pick me up not a stone's throw from the market, the curtains probably aren't necessary," Jane said, blinking.

"Now, Jane. It pays to take precautions where one can. You of all people should appreciate this by now."

Her gentle chiding reminded Jane of the wine she'd left for Fredrick, and her gut twisted.

"Speaking of," Lady Lachesse said, "how is our dear friend Fredrick enjoying his new job?"

"We both appreciate that he's happy and working," Jane said, swallowing a hot lump of anger. "And that he's still sober, no thanks to you."

Lady Lachesse feigned hurt. "Whatever do you mean?"

"You know exactly what I mean."

"That bottle was a gift."

Jane couldn't remember if everyone in Recoletta had acted so innocuously oblivious or if this had just been a tactic of the whitenails. "A gift for a borderline alcoholic?"

"No, it was a gift for you." Lady Lachesse's voice sank to a low, quiet purr. "A reminder that an advantage can quickly become an affliction."

The hairs along the back of Jane's neck prickled in agreement.

"Now," Lady Lachesse said. "Tell me what you've had the chance to learn."

Jane told her about the meeting she'd sat in on between the

Qadi, Chancellor O'Brien, and Father Isse. She described the chancellor's stewing perturbation and the understanding that had bound the Qadi and Father Isse.

"A lovely start," Lady Lachesse said. "I do hope you were able to find more."

"They're sending a trainload of soldiers from the Hollow into Recoletta."

"When? And how many? I need details, child."

Jane had read over the pages enough times to have memorized even the deployment numbers by category. Still, Lady Lachesse wanted proof, and that was why she'd kept the papers she'd salvaged from the chancellor's office tucked in her robes all day.

She wanted to demand something first, but she sensed that Lady Lachesse wasn't ready to concede anything, and Jane wouldn't win a standoff – especially not after what the older woman had just said. So she produced the two stolen pages – the deployment numbers as well as the chancellor's drafted reply. Lady Lachesse held the pages, as soft with wrinkles as crepe paper, pinched between her fingernails.

"Nicely done indeed," Lady Lachesse said after her eyes had crawled over the pages.

And even though Jane knew that the woman's opinion didn't really matter, that this was, in fact, high praise from Lady Lachesse, she gritted her teeth at such a cool appraisal of her efforts.

But as Lady Lachesse appraised the intelligence with the same cool eye, Jane came to suspect that the woman's composure came from more than whitenail habit.

"You knew this was going to happen, didn't you?"

"It was just a question of when and how. So I needed details."

"But you're here. In Madina," Jane said. "What does any of this have to do with you?"

Lady Lachesse finally peeled her eyes from the pages. "I told you, Jane. It's about adapting."

"So in five days, the chancellor's forces take the city or they don't." She said it as casually as if they were discussing the possible outcomes of a handball match, but her gut lurched. "Why do you care about what happens in Recoletta?"

The whitenail laughed. "I don't. I'm interested in the Library."

Jane felt a response form, fall still, and die in her mouth half a dozen times. "But I thought–"

"That all whitenails opposed the excavation? That we'd sooner bury the whole mess again?" She clucked. "Then again, I suppose you worked below us for too long to give us more credit."

"When the Qadi and her allies take Recoletta, they'll bury the Library for sure."

"When they take Recoletta, they'll realize they can't. The only thing worse than digging it up is destroying it." She held up one clawed hand, her nails as sharp as little daggers. "Destroy it," she said, drawing her hand into a perilous fist, "and you show people that it was worthy of their fear. And then they begin to wonder what you've stolen from them."

"Then what happens to it?"

"What the Qadi doesn't yet realize is that the Library is an advantage as well as a burden." She leaned forward, her hands clutched in her lap. "Jane, it's one of the greatest repositories of information in the world. And information is a valuable resource."

Jane kept her face still as she listened.

"But like any resource, information must be managed. Maintained. Access must be controlled, in certain cases. It must be organized and distributed in a competent fashion. And the Qadi and her allies will want to entrust that responsibility to someone they trust. Whose pedigree they know."

Jane blinked. "A whitenail in exile. Someone with no commitment to Sato's other changes."

Lady Lachesse sat back in her bench. "Don't sound so surprised. I was a railway baroness before the revolution, and I know how to maintain connections."

"Why are you telling me?"

Lady Lachesse sighed and smiled sadly. “I keep hoping you'll learn.”

Jane sat in silence, listening to the rattle and squeak of the carriage wheels. Finally, she said, “There was something else you were going to tell me.”

Lady Lachesse looked up from the pages resting in her lap with her clawed hands. “About your parents.”

“You said that they were allied with Ruthers. Until he asked something of them that was too much.”

“They had outlived their usefulness for Ruthers. And I think they had realized – finally – that he had no real intention of advancing someone of their station. Their ambition had made them convenient tools, but he would never see them as allies.”

As equals, Jane thought.

“But your parents weren't to be dissuaded. They made one last gambit, hoping to convince Ruthers that they were too resourceful to be pushed aside.” Lady Lachesse inclined her head. “And in a way, they succeeded.

“In their dealings with Ruthers, they'd accumulated certain details about his business proceedings.” She waved a hand. “Evidence of bribes paid and received, competitors threatened, that sort of thing. They'd been prescient – or perhaps foolish – enough to keep evidence of these occurrences, so when they finally pressed Sato about their advancement and got the expected rebuff, they threatened to go public.”

“They wanted to publish their evidence?”

“So they claimed. Of course, the paper wasn't willing to risk a councilor's wrath to assist in the political maneuverings of two nobodies.” She shrugged an apology.

“So Ruthers killed them?”

She barked with short, staccato laughter. “Ruthers isn't one to waste a resource. He laughed in their faces and threw them out. See, Ruthers had certain rivals in the Council. And that's the thing about pawns. They're easy to sacrifice.”

The muscles of Jane's jaw clenched.

"Ruthers was in the on-phase of an on-and-off feud with Councilor Sato, the late father of Recoletta's current autocrat, and he needed someone to send a message. So it was convenient, in a way, that your parents made their stand when they did.

"Ruthers had come into possession of certain missives from Councilor Sato that proved his involvement in some rather unscrupulous dealings. Dealings that ran contrary to Ruthers's interests. So he arranged for your parents to pass them on to an interested third party. In one move, he managed to thwart Councilor Sato's plans and step out of the line of fire himself. When Sato's deal went sour, questions were asked, and the fatal leak was traced back to your parents." She folded her hands in her lap and went quiet as if that explained everything.

The color seemed to drain out of the carriage. It could have just been the darkness from the curtains. "You're saying that Councilor Sato killed my parents?"

"Had them killed. But I suppose it's a fine enough distinction."

"But Councilor Sato..."

"Was the most beloved of all of Recoletta's councilors? Was a shining beacon of goodness and light in a corrupt institution? Don't believe everything you read in the papers, Jane." She settled further into her seat, the padded leather squeaking and sighing as she pressed her shoulders into it. "Councilor Sato was, without a doubt, the tamest of a bloodthirsty bunch. And people did love him. But not because he was all purr and no claws. He got things done, and he generally did focus on the goals that would most benefit the people of Recoletta. And he was comfortable with the cost that these ends entailed."

"I..." Jane swallowed. "I was told that Councilor Ruthers killed my parents." There was a dangerous tremor in her voice, and she wasn't sure whether it had come from anger at Ruthers, the long-dead Councilor Sato, her own foolish parents, or Roman Arnault.

"In a way, he did. He knew perfectly well what the consequences would be." She opened her long-nailed hands. "I'm sure that whoever gave you that version had a perfectly good reason for doing so." A smile crept up on Lady Lachesse's face, as slow and deliberate as a bad lie. "You seem distressed."

Jane looked away as her pulse filled her ears. She felt anger – at Roman for his convenient lie, at herself for believing it. At her parents, even, gone because of their own foolishness. She waited for the wave of shock with its undertow of grief, but what sorrow was there in a memory that had never been hers? She breathed the stale, overly perfumed air of the carriage and felt her lungs filled. If the past was a line stretching back to some indiscernible origin and ahead to a fixed but indeterminate point, it had just been twisted and severed. There was no blueprint behind her and no map ahead of her. She was free.

The carriage had slowed to a halt. "Your stop, Miss Lin. Don't forget it."

The needles in Lady Lachesse's words seemed to slide off of her skin. Even as she descended from the carriage, her limbs weak and wobbly, she felt the strange enervation of adrenaline. Whatever had just been sucked from her had been replaced with something else, and as it filled and flowed within her, she would discover a strange new strength.

As she picked her way along the darkening streets, each cobblestone felt solid and firm beneath her.

The restless night and the morning after Jane's meeting with Lady Lachesse gave her anger at Roman more than enough time to simmer. It also gave her time to soak up this new feeling unfolding within her, this complacency bordering on relief that her own parents had not died martyrs, but rather as conspirators in their own scheme.

By the time the messenger came to summon her for her meeting with Bailey, she felt as though ire and sweat had sloughed off some old, fragile layer of herself.

She followed the messenger along a route that was beginning to grow familiar. Even though the Qadi had told her that she and Bailey would have a new message to deliver to Roman Arnault, the memory of her theft from the chancellor's office hung about her like an odor. She couldn't shake the fear that someone would have sniffed out her guilt.

By the time they reached the back exit and its bay of carriages, Jane was thoroughly mired in the many concerns racing around in her head. Were it not for the attendant in the corner of her eye, she would have run into the man gliding toward them. As it was, she saw the attendant gracefully dodge to one side as the doors to the alley swung open, and she was just quick enough to follow him.

She looked up in time to see Father Isse, his dark eyes shining behind his spectacles and his cassock wrapping his slender body like a funeral shroud. He seemed to be looking at her, but he passed as quickly as a morning fog. Seconds later, she and the attendant were in the alley where Bailey waited. The air was heavy with the fumes and fury of an unfinished argument.

Jane's stomach turned to ice. She didn't dare ask Bailey what he and Father Isse had been discussing, but the question quickly began gnawing at her.

Before she could wonder further, Bailey waved at the carriage behind him. "Let's go," he said. "It wouldn't be hospitable of us to keep Sayidh Arnault waiting."

They climbed into the carriage, which rattled and bounced on the way to the main streets.

"I understand that you met with the Qadi and her associates recently," he said. Gone was his usual veneer of politeness.

"Yes."

He grunted. "Then you know what we're to offer this time. Not that it needs to be said, but we won't mention the presence of the chancellor or Father Isse. All Mr Arnault needs to know is what we're offering. Understood?"

She nodded.

"Excellent." His piece said, Bailey settled into his seat and did an admirable job of pretending that Jane did not exist.

When they arrived at the meeting house, another carriage was already waiting. Jane followed Bailey into the house to find Roman in the same seat he'd taken last time, his back to them.

"Mr Arnault," Bailey said, working his way around the clunky consonants with surgical precision. "So good to see you."

Roman rose, giving Bailey a small nod. He only glanced at Jane. "Good as always of you to extend your hospitality."

Jane followed Bailey around to their seats. Strangely, as she looked at Roman, she felt only a dull echo of the rage she'd experienced earlier.

"Please," Bailey said, gesturing at Roman's chair as he sat. "You have had the chance to discuss our previous terms with Sato?"

Jane pulled out her notepad and pen and began writing.

Roman shifted his bad leg. "You mean the suggestions that we allow one of your people to sit in on all of our internal meetings and compile comprehensive statistics on the inner workings of Recoletta? I mentioned them to Sato, and he reacted about like you would imagine."

"Well, if he should change his mind, the offer still stands."

"How gracious of you. And now, perhaps you could tell me what the Qadi thought of our trade proposals."

Bailey smiled, tapping the arm of his chair. "On that front, I've got something that, I think, you'll like even better. Something for nothing." Jane felt his eyes on her but kept her head down.

Roman said nothing but looked on dubiously.

"We're offering biweekly food shipments. Nothing particularly lavish, mind you – dry grains, a portion of our winter squash surplus, some cured ham now and then. But it should be enough to sustain you through this business with your farmers."

Roman's eyes were searching Bailey, roving and scanning as if the angle of his body or the tilt of his head might give something away. "That's generous of you."

"Nonsense. It's in our best interests to see that Recoletta comes out on top of this. We may have our differences regarding the governance of cities, but we are absolutely united when it comes to preserving a productive relationship with the farming communes."

"I don't suppose that's an offer Sato can refuse," Roman said. He looked briefly to Jane.

Bailey grinned. "Not unless he wants another wave of riots on his hands."

"You are persuasive, Sayidh Bailey. When could we expect the first shipment?"

"Why, as early as tomorrow. We were confident you would receive this suggestion with enthusiasm, so we saw no cause for delay. And the sooner we move, the sooner we send a strong message to the farmers about the solidarity between cities."

"And what is it you expect from us?" Roman asked.

Jane peered over the edge of her writing pad in time to see Bailey shrug. "Simply your assistance in offloading the shipments once they arrive. As I said, we've no wish to see Recoletta fall to its farmers."

"But you wouldn't mind seeing us fall to someone else, is that it?"

Bailey's thin smile looked exasperated even to Jane. "Recoletta already fell, Mr Arnault. We've no wish to see it happen again. If you can survive the farmers, we'll have plenty of time to work out the rest of this."

"Fair enough." Roman looked around at the hodgepodge and dilapidated furnishings. "I don't suppose you brought me all the way here just to discuss food shipments."

"And why not? One sends chocolates as a surprise. Not a trainload of comestibles."

The hairs on the back of Jane's neck rose. These were almost the exact words the Qadi had used, and hearing them come from Bailey unnerved her for reasons she couldn't define.

"Besides," Bailey said, "as I recall, you like to do your grocery shopping here, don't you? I don't suppose there's much of that to be done in Recoletta at the moment."

Jane heard mischief and sudden merriment in Bailey's voice, but was there also something else? The low, cool tenor of a threat?

If Arnault heard it, he gave no sign. "I'd be remiss to pass up the opportunity." He smiled for the first time, showing his teeth.

Bailey rose. "Then I won't keep you. As always, Miss Lin and I appreciate your visit." He turned toward the door, giving Jane a look that could have meant anything.

Jane returned to the Majlis with Bailey, doing her part to avoid eye contact the whole way back. At her desk, the remaining hours trickled by. The meeting, the curious glances from Arnault, Bailey's strange reticence, and most of all, Father Isse's unexpected apparition, set her nerves on edge, and she found herself recycling the same paranoid questions for the remainder of the day.

Regardless, she would have to meet with Roman again. To find out what he knew and to confront him with what she'd learned – about both the Qadi's plans and her parents.

By the time Jane reached the market, the place was already bustling. She headed straight for the vegetable stalls that she had visited last time. She hadn't caught sight of Roman yet, but she was sure he was near, waiting and watching.

The thought of him lingering nearby, looking on, and plotting his approach suddenly infuriated her.

She was just passing a crate of bright orange peppers when she felt a presence over her shoulder.

"Make your way to the onions," a voice – Roman's – murmured. Warm breath tickled her ear and prickled the hairs along her neck. She pretended not to have heard him but headed in that direction all the same. When she reached the bin, he was already there, sorting through white and yellow bulbs.

She saw him out of the corner of her eye, a bulky, nondescript figure in dark robes and a loose head wrap. She examined a medium-sized, tight-layered specimen while she waited for him to begin.

"Same place," he finally said. "Wait five. I'll draw them off first."

"Hmm," she said, picking up another onion while he skulked away. She worked her thumb under the loose, dry outer layer and inspected the shiny skin beneath until she was certain he'd gone.

When she'd counted off a minute in her head, she turned back to observe the souk.

The crowd ebbed back and forth, a mass of talking, haggling, browsing people. None spared her so much as a passing glance. It should have brought her comfort, but she remembered the fleeting, impenetrable look she'd gotten from Father Isse, and she shivered.

At two minutes, she wound her way from the produce to the copper and pewter goods.

Thirty seconds later, she saw him.

She caught him looking away too quickly. And as he turned his head to an unnatural angle and flashed her a view of graying mutton chop sideburns and overlarge, reddish ears, she knew he wasn't the same man who'd accosted her before. Seeing him might have been a relief. The thought of multiple pursuers, organized enough perhaps, to keep the man she'd seen out of her sight, chilled her gut.

Jane backed behind a rack of hanging pots before he could look again.

When he did, his roving, searching gaze was unmistakable. She backed further away, careful to keep an eye on him.

Three minutes had passed by the time she turned past cases of rings and pegs hung with bracelets.

She had almost lost sight of her pursuer when a hand clamped on her wrist.

Jane heard her own startled, strangled cry as she looked down and into her challenger's face.

The woman was short, even shorter than Jane, and there was

something familiar about her sincere, age-crinkled face that took Jane several seconds to recall.

"I must apologize," the woman said, her grip still firm on Jane's arm.

It wasn't until Jane had tugged her arm free of the older woman's grasp that she recognized her as the gold merchant she'd encountered on her first day in Madina.

"I did not trust you, sayideh. I insulted you." The woman looked down at her now-empty hand as if Jane's arm had vanished from thin air.

"It's really fine," Jane said, already looking again for her pursuer.

"It was a grave thing. Words can't dismiss it so easily."

Jane began backing away again. Where, she didn't know. "Honestly, we can forget about it."

"No!" The older woman looked up, her face smooth in its seriousness. "Maybe this is easy for you. But not here, not for me."

Every flicker of movement seemed to conceal a runner headed for her, and every turning gaze seemed to rake her where she stood. But she forced herself to look at the older woman.

"I understand," Jane said.

The merchant sighed. "In Madina, it is deeds, not words, that heal a past hurt. If there is ever anything – anything – I can do, you must let me know."

The crowds had already blended and mingled again, each individual as indistinguishable as a fish in a school.

"Actually, there is something you could do."

The older woman smiled. "Tell me."

Jane explained that she was being followed by a man with long, gray sideburns. She suspected there were others with him, though she didn't know how many. All she knew was that she'd heard of more than a few cases at the Majlis of attacks against assimilated Recolettans, like her.

And when the merchant nodded, patting Jane's arm, Jane buttressed her conscience by reminding herself that the important parts of her story were true.

They waited until the man with the sideburns wandered into view again. When Jane pointed him out, the merchant grinned.

"Leave this to me," she said.

Jane had no choice but to trust the woman. Yet as she backed into the crowd, she saw the merchant turn to her neighbors and whisper a few quick words. Those two men did likewise, and within seconds, there was a shift in the crowd, as subtle and decisive as a changing wind.

It was no assurance, but it was the closest thing she could hope for. She hurried back to the Jeweled Pheasant as the crowd hardened into a barrier behind her.

As she entered the smoky pub, she took a deep breath and brushed her clamming palms against the edge of her robe. She walked up to the bar, slammed a handful of damp coins onto the dented wood, and accepted a short glass of semi-clear liquor from the bartender.

Up the rickety stairs again, where Roman already waited, worrying a splinter out of the dilapidated table. He seemed about to rise, but he gripped the edges of the table instead.

"You all right?" he asked when Jane sat.

"Just had to lose a scout," she said.

His grip on the table relaxed. "That's not what I meant."

She took a drink and shuddered, to her embarrassment. Still, it wasn't as bad as she'd expected. "I thought you were taking care of our followers."

"So did I. I didn't realize they had such a close eye on you." He raised his own glass, tilting his head at a curious angle.

She took another drink from hers just to occupy herself. She drank too deeply and just barely kept herself from coughing it out. "Well. I get the feeling Father Isse's been keeping a close eye on a lot of things."

Roman froze, and his own glass nearly slipped from his hand. "Father Isse?"

"He's head of–"

"Underlake. I know. You didn't tell me he was here."

She swallowed her annoyance. "I didn't realize what this meant when we last met."

He set his glass on the table with an unnecessarily loud thunk. "You mean he was already here then?"

Her grip tightened around the smudged glass. "Obviously that's what I mean."

The words came out more sharply than she'd intended, but Roman didn't seem to notice. "Jane, this is an extremely delicate time. You need to trust me to know what's important."

"Do I?" She took another gulp of the searing liquor and barely tasted it.

"Is there anyone else – anything else – unusual that you've noticed?"

Her mouth had begun to feel unnaturally dry. Surprisingly, it wasn't an unpleasant feeling. "Let me think," she said, turning her glass and watching the remaining half of her drink lap at the sides. "Another foreign gentleman known as Chancellor O'Brien. Showed up around the same time as Father Isse as far as I could tell."

"Shit." He leaned closer. "Jane, this is important."

"So you keep telling me."

"I need to find out what's going on in there." He raised his head and looked around the deserted upstairs, as if the answer sat at one of the empty tables around them.

"I'll tell you what's going on," Jane said. "The Qadi has convinced you to accept trainloads of food from Madina. Meanwhile, Chancellor O'Brien is maneuvering twenty-six hundred soldiers, including three hundred infantry, into Recoletta. And thanks to Father Isse's plan of food aid, you'll let the advance guard into the middle of Recoletta four days from now. By the time your people roll back the cargo doors and see what's waiting, it'll be too late."

Roman was momentarily speechless. The sight was even more satisfying than Jane had expected.

A lump bobbed in his throat. "How did you put all of this together?"

"I paid attention to the right details." She took another drink. Only a thimbleful remained when she set the glass down again. "I told you, Roman. I wasn't keeping anything from you on purpose. But that's more than we could say for you, isn't it?"

"What's that supposed to mean?"

"My parents. You told me Ruthers murdered them. But that wasn't the whole story."

"Jane, I…" He waved a feeble hand. "I wasn't trying to mislead you. It just seemed like a simpler explanation at the time."

"Simpler for whom? For you, so that I'd help you and your new boss get rid of Ruthers?"

His hand fell back to the table with a hard slap. "I couldn't have known you'd go after him like that. Besides, you let Ruthers go. Please." He ran his hands over his dark mane. "If you want to split hairs about it, Ruthers maneuvered your parents into the line of fire. Is he any less guilty for not pulling the trigger himself?"

"Don't try to reframe the argument. You knew full well what I'd believe."

He sighed. "I thought it would be easier for you. I was just trying to protect you."

"No." She threw her head back and drained the last of her glass. The burn of the liquor was exquisite. As it trickled into her gut, something else inside her snapped shut like a blossom at dusk, and she saw the man across the table in a vision of hard lines and stark, washed-out colors. "You wanted to protect your idea of me."

She heard the feeble tone of his protest even while his words garbled and jumbled in her ears. When she rose, he did not follow. She made her way downstairs, feeling as though she'd been released, though she was not certain from what.

And she had not yet begun to ask herself what notions of him she harbored in the secret recesses of her heart.

She stepped into the street. He had brought her little but trouble. Even the ways he'd tried to help, the little measures he'd taken to protect her, had merely been half measures to mitigate some of the trouble that his acquaintance had brought her. She told herself that this was the wiser course of action even while she worried that she was already too entrenched to be independent from his help.

Still, if she was going to find herself in trouble, at least it would be trouble of her own making.

She took a final look at the door of the bar just before she passed out of view. He was not following her.

CHAPTER 10

HIDING

In the days since her return to Recoletta, Malone had walked its streets feeling like a traitor. As best as she could tell, the food shipments from the farms had stopped coming. Every hollow-eyed stranger, every empty shop, every shattered window dug a ragged scar across her conscience.

She even began to hope that the Bricklayer, whoever and whatever he or she was, had started to bring in more foodstuffs through back channels.

Her debriefing with Sato had been shorter and less arduous than she'd expected. She'd arrived at his office just as Arnault was leaving, his face disfigured by his customary scowl. Sato had seemed distracted, but some of the color and shape had returned to his cheeks. He'd cleared the clutter from his desk and seemed organized. Collected.

None of the usual shipments from the farming communes had accompanied her to the city, but he hadn't asked about that. Instead, he'd listened quietly as she'd relayed a sanitized version of her meeting with the commune leaders, in which they were dogged and determined and she'd been all but chucked onto the next train back to Recoletta.

He'd nodded, tenting his fingers and looking for all the world like he was thinking about something else entirely. She should have been relieved that he'd given her own story so little scrutiny, but not knowing what preoccupied him worried her all the more.

She wasn't surprised, then, when Sato called a last-minute Cabinet meeting late in the afternoon.

Somewhere along the line, the Cabinet meetings had transitioned from planning and strategy to cataloguing the impossible problems facing Recoletta. Malone and the other advisors gathered like storm clouds, and the atmosphere in the meeting chambers thickened accordingly. They looked around at each other like crumbling, cracking things, each wondering which of the others would break first.

Arnault, however, looked at no one.

Sato joined them last of all, still seeming strangely restored. Everyone else – everyone but Arnault, she noted – seemed too wrapped up in their own concerns and calculations to notice.

After the requisite settling and fussing, Sato lifted his head and smiled. "Nathan Tran-MacGregor. Finance."

Tran-MacGregor tugged at his collar and squeezed the grimace between his lips into an obliging smile. "As our illustrious president has informed us, all is not well in Recoletta, and most of you are familiar with finance's continued difficulties. Chief among these challenges is my ministry's almost complete lack of income." He shot Grenwahl a long, steadied stare. "It is impossible to fund public works, defense, reconstruction, and city services without steady income. Income which usually comes from taxes and tariffs."

"Begging your pardons, Mr Minister," Grenwahl said, doffing an imaginary hat. "I didn't realize I was supposed to be doing your job, too."

Tran-MacGregor rolled his eyes and sighed, more loudly than necessary. "Since basic verbal comprehension also seems to be beyond you, let me restate myself. I am only asking that you produce the tax revenue that is your ministry's responsibility. Nothing more, nothing less."

"Then let me help you with your math," Grenwahl said. "I've seen your budget. It looks like rich folks' holiday dinner. Learn to make do with less."

Tran-MacGregor blanched, then curled his lips in disgust. "We have to invest in Recoletta's infrastructure and human capital in order to rebuild."

"And like I've told you, you're asking too much of a rebuilding economy. Lower the tax rates and offer more perks for good business. You're about to strangle the market," Grenwahl said.

Tran-MacGregor looked like he wanted to strangle Grenwahl.

Sato folded his hands and looked patiently between the two men. "As always, thank you for your contributions, Nathan. Horace, do you have anything further to add?"

Grenwahl blinked, registering surprise on his ruddy features. "Just that our coffers are the emptiest they've ever been. What few shopkeepers there were are closing up and moving further underground. So to speak." He crossed his arms and leaned back in his chair. "And there's been talk of food riots. Seems there's a rumor abroad about farm strikes."

Just as the a murmur began to rise around the table, Sato said, "Thank you, Mr Grenwahl," and motioned to Vaughn.

"Yes, ah, next we have General Covas... and the military." He looked up anxiously.

Covas, straight-backed even now, rested her elbows on the table. "We had a spike in desertions last month. We're still enough to form a strong perimeter around the city, but flagging morale's showing up in disciplinary problems, too. We're lucky the unrest hasn't been more organized. There've been a few incidents involving unruly crowds and rotten fruits." She hesitated, glancing down between her thumbs for a quick moment. "If the citizens weren't holding onto their food so tightly, I think we'd be hearing more of that. Point is, the general sentiment among the troops is that it's getting hard to tell who the real enemy is."

"Just hold them together a little longer, General," Sato said.

"Yes, sir."

Vaughn returned to the agenda. "Mr Quillard, the Library."

As usual, Quillard seemed to be the only one unaffected by the general atmosphere of gloom and desperation. "I'm pleased to say that we're making good progress on our catalogue of the Library's stores. We've managed to archive and copy an additional five hundred sources in the last week alone. At our current rate of progress, it would take at least a few hundred years to get through the entire collection, so we're obviously setting priorities." He said it as if this were a minor obstacle to understanding the Library.

"Only a few hundred years?" Grenwahl said.

Quillard was the only person at the table who didn't catch the sarcasm. In fact, he seemed to be delighted that someone was taking an interest in his department's work. "Actually, Mr Grenwahl, the building that we're calling the Library is only part of the picture. Research suggests that there are at least two other major buildings. There's no telling what waits for us there!"

Malone had to admire Quillard's boundless enthusiasm even if she couldn't share it. The rest of the advisors looked at him as if he were a simpleton, but he weathered his thankless job better than the rest of them. The long hours, glacial progress, and lack of popular support hadn't dented his cheery disposition as far as she could tell. It was more than Malone could note for the rest of them.

"And the special references I asked you to locate?" Sato asked.

Quillard's smile fell. "Have been set aside for study, sir. As I understand it, there's been some progress duplicating the results, but it's not really my area–"

"That'll be all," Sato said.

"Anything else, Mr Quillard?" Vaughn asked.

"No." The librarian's eyes were glazed over and fixed on the table.

Vaughn cleared his throat. "Very well, then. Moving along to... Ambassador Chakrun."

The ambassador mopped his forehead. "More of the same. I thought we were making inroads with South Haven, but that's fallen through."

"Next, Mr Vaughn," Sato said, making a rolling motion with his finger. Malone hadn't seen Sato looking this confident in weeks. But there was something about his unnatural calm that she didn't trust. It reminded her of a mirror-smooth surface over a turbulent current.

Arnault was looking at Sato the same way.

"Mr Arnault, intelligence," Vaughn said.

With a start, Malone realized that she hadn't spoken to Arnault about their detainees in days. He'd suggested keeping the secret from Sato in the first place, but with all eyes on him now, Malone wondered if she'd been foolish to trust him.

"I've been meeting with sources in Madina to assess our neighbors' intentions," Arnault said. "The Qadi has gathered the leadership of both the Hollow and Underlake to discuss our situation." He paused and glanced briefly at Sato.

"And tell us what you've learned," Sato said carefully.

"They're preparing an offensive. The details are unclear at this point, but it's believed to involve a force of soldiers from the Hollow."

Covas frowned. "How many?"

"Unknown. Presumably, enough to take the city, with the right maneuver."

It sounded ambitious but not impossible, especially with Covas's own forces dwindling. Malone watched Arnault's expression for some sign of anything else he might know – or suspect. But he hadn't looked at her yet.

"Who are our sources?" Chakrun asked. The talk of even qualified diplomatic progress seemed to revive him.

Emotion shivered across Arnault's face. Malone doubted that anyone else, except possibly Sato, could have noticed. "I've been meeting with a Recolettan exile in Madina."

Chakrun squinted. "If he's an exile, can we trust him?"

Arnault's eyes flickered to Chakrun. His furrowed brow relaxed. "I do. And he's well placed to find this kind of information."

Sato nodded. "Any other intelligence to report?"

Malone held her breath. Arnault scanned the table, his gaze resting briefly on her.

"No."

She hadn't realized her hands had balled into fists, but she unclenched her fingers and let out a slow breath. She looked at Arnault, sitting on the other side of the table with his mouth clamped shut and his arms folded tightly on the table in front of him, knowing he was keeping something – perhaps many somethings – back. But for the first time, it occurred to Malone that he might not be keeping it from her.

"Chief Malone? Are you alright?" Vaughn was frowning at her, and the rest of the Cabinet members were waiting. "Your report, Chief."

Malone cleared her throat. "Crime rates are roughly the same as the last meeting and the meeting before that. We haven't gained any new ground in the contested districts, but we haven't lost any, either."

Vaughn glanced back at his agenda. "Any progress on the dissidents?"

She kept herself from looking at Arnault. "We're following leads," Malone said. "Nothing to report."

"That's all, Chief?"

Malone looked over at Sato. He nodded.

"I recently paid a visit to one of our farming communes," she said. "We discussed their reduced contributions. I tried to reason with them, but they're determined." She glanced at the faces around the table, by turns stern, anxious, and disbelieving. "They've declared that they're ceasing all contributions until their demands, which would afford them the rights and status of citizens, are met."

The rest of the table erupted. Questions, protests, and exclamations – directed at no one in particular – rose to the chamber's high ceiling.

In a way, it was refreshing. Malone hadn't seen their gathering become this animated in almost three months.

Vaughn banged his gavel against the table – something he'd never had to do before. It took a few seconds for the assembly to quiet down, but when it did, he cleared his throat, frowning. "This concludes the Cabinet's reports."

Sato's smile was a little too steady, and it broadened. "We've all heard them today. Problems. Conflicts. We've heard them from the beginning. And we've been trying to resolve them the wrong way."

Sato pushed back his chair and began pacing a slow circle around the table. The advisors began looking at one another with increased apprehension. Even Vaughn was twisting the gavel in his thin hands. Only Covas remained impassive.

"I came to Recoletta talking about history," Sato said, still circling. "Yet I forgot the history of this place. We live in a city defined by centuries of repression and oppression. Power is the only language people understand, and it is the vocabulary we will have to employ."

"Sir," Covas said. Her tone was cool, but the rest of the advisors looked at her as if she'd just leapt atop the table. "The Hollow's soldiers outnumber us and are better trained. If you're suggesting we take the battle to them–"

"The soldiers of the City Guard were more numerous and better trained than our forces," Sato said. "Yet our own casualties were minimal. Power isn't numbers or strategy. It's a force of will. The element of surprise. It's the ability to determine and do what is necessary."

Malone's stomach turned. She felt as if she were watching a collision in slow motion, seeing every angle of the disaster and powerless to stop it.

"President Sato," Arnault said. His voice crackled like a static charge in the cold. "People accepted certain excesses from Ruthers and his lot. They won't take them from you."

Sato leveled his gaze at Arnault. "By the time I'm finished, they will."

The room was silent for several seconds.

"Many of you have chided me at one point or another for my frivolous obsession with the past." Sato smiled, mocking their dismissiveness with a flapping hand. "You see stories and legends where I see lessons. Examples.

"We're adopting new measures, effective immediately," Sato said, still pacing around the table. "First, Recolettans belong in Recoletta. No one leaves the city without authorization. Second, anyone in possession of dissident writing will be jailed and duly investigated. Malone, you'll handle this."

Malone kept her expression steady, but she felt trawling eyes on her. Especially Arnault's.

"Third, we're going to impose strict rations until this nonsense with the communes is sorted out. But we can use that to our advantage, too. Any citizens who identify dissidents, vandals, or black marketeers will receive an additional portion."

There was a long silence as Sato finished his slow march around the table, at last anchoring himself to the back of his own chair with a sturdy grip.

Vaughn spoke up. "Will that be all, sir?"

Sato blinked. "For now. I'm going to visit the Library to check on a certain work in progress." Sato smiled, and Quillard blanched, still avoiding the man's gaze. "Keep Recoletta under control for the next few days. When I return, I'll show you the true value of antiquity. Dismissed, everyone. Except General Covas."

Malone followed the other advisors out of the room, trying to shake her sense of foreboding. No one risked a backward glance.

She'd left the other fleeing advisors and turned toward Callum Station when she heard a voice behind her.

"So," Arnault said. "He still doesn't know."

She glanced back. "About our mutual friends? I'm not sure why you think I'd tell him."

"You've been occupied elsewhere," he said. Malone could feel him watching her curiously, carefully.

"I've been busy," she said.

"Sato's kept you busy."

She lengthened her stride. "I could say the same about you."

He matched her pace. "Relax. It's not an accusation. I'm merely observing."

"Then do it on your own time. Like you said, I'm busy."

"I'm not asking you to slow down for me, Chief. But we need to do something about our guests in Callum Station," Arnault said. "Sato's new ultimatums make their detention a riskier endeavor."

The same thought had occurred to Malone, but she hadn't yet figured out what to do. "What are you suggesting?"

"That we move them. Obviously."

"Where? The entire city will be looking for them."

"Nobody knows who they are. They'll only draw more attention locked in the station," he said.

She stopped and faced him, keeping her voice low. "Where else could we even move them, Arnault?"

He watched her face for a few seconds. "I know an abandoned home in the Vineyard. Wouldn't take much to turn it into a reliable safe house."

She turned away and marched on. "You can't be serious. That district is bedlam."

He caught up with her. "The place I'm talking about is on the outskirts. Not far from Petrosian's whiskey shop. Things are still quiet there."

"And they'll practically be neighbors with the Bricklayer's people. Their allies, as best we can tell," she said between her teeth.

"Only a problem if someone finds out. And after Sato's announcement about extra rations, I don't think they're going to be so sure about their allies."

Malone pressed her lips together and sighed. As crazy as the idea seemed, Arnault's logic was beginning to work on her. "But Callum Station's a known quantity. I know who comes and goes. The men and women there report to me."

"Don't be so certain," Arnault said.

She looked at him again, slowing. The rigid lines of his face suggested resignation, desperation, exhaustion. Not malice. "Saavedra?" she asked.

"Always been Sato's."

Arnault's concern began to resolve itself into a problem with dimensions, substance, and weight. Probing at its boundaries, Malone finally understood the reason for his urgency. Olivia Saavedra had a way of finding herself behind locked doors and in closed rooms to a degree that rivaled even Farrah's own considerable abilities.

And as Arnault had become more and more of a fixture at Callum Station, Malone had noticed Saavedra swiveling her spotlight focus accordingly.

They were out of Dominari Hall and in deserted streets before Arnault spoke again, and Malone realized how long she'd been quiet.

"You know I'm right about this," he said. "What's your hesitation?"

She frowned, mostly because he'd read her accurately. "There's always an angle with you."

He opened his mouth to say something and closed it almost as quickly. He snorted. "How's this for an angle – if Sato finds them in Callum Station, I'll be sure that you take the fall for this on your own. Think what you'd like, but you've got no choice but to go with me on this. I'm offering us both a way out."

Malone grimaced even though she couldn't really blame him. "Fine, but we do this on my terms. We're going to need help."

He turned his head to look at her. "Your desertion rate's almost as bad as Covas's. Someone in the station you think you can trust?"

She smirked. "Helps that I haven't made a career out of burning my bridges, Arnault."

His smile raised the hairs on her arms. "Still plenty of time for that."

Malone looked quickly away. "Get your place ready. We'll move tomorrow."

"Good. I wasn't going to give you any more time."

When Malone described the plan to Farrah the next morning, the redhead accepted her role with the matter-of-fact professionalism that Malone had long known her for.

"The best time would be after midnight when everyone's cleared out of the station," Farrah said.

"Hard to guarantee," Malone said. "Besides, it would raise more questions if anyone saw us at that hour. What about first thing in the morning, just before everyone shows up?"

Farrah shook her head. "That'll look even stranger. Besides, she gets in earlier every day."

"Saavedra?"

Farrah nodded.

"Maybe we can keep her busy."

"She'd figure it out. And even if she didn't, someone else might. I see her talking to new people every day. Too many of them are faces I don't even recognize."

A thought occurred to Malone. "Is she Arnault's or Sato's?"

Farrah flashed a knowing smile. "She'd like to be Arnault's. But the way she comes and goes, I think she's reporting to Sato."

"Tell me about her," Malone said.

It wasn't hard for Farrah to think of something. Malone had found that it rarely was difficult for a person to think of something to say about someone he or she spent so much energy loathing.

Saavedra showed up every day, sometimes first thing in the morning through the wee hours, sometimes only for fifteen minutes. But she was never alone. Eyes followed her as she sashayed to the records room or perched on her desk, one languorous leg attenuated over a chair as she read through stacks of files. A pinky fingernail, slowly exploring the terrain between her perfect, white teeth, commanded attention. When she bent over, rummaging through stacks and files or retrieving fallen pages, she didn't seem to notice the way an ever-present audience followed her movements. But Farrah did.

Malone checked to see that the hall outside the office was still clear. "So she's charming her way into confidences around here."

Farrah waved a hand. "That's only half of it. She makes herself visible so you think you know what she's up to. And so you think she's gorgeous and empty headed. But she's got people all over the station, and she's got an ear to the ground. Even when she's got her ass in the air."

Malone thought for a moment. "We can at least keep her accounted for when we move the dissenters out."

Farrah shook her head. "I told you, she'll figure it out. She's clever."

"Everybody has a weakness."

Farrah blinked at Malone for a moment. Suspicion clouded her eyes. "You don't mean..."

"You said she has a soft spot for him. And it's believable."

"But do you trust him?"

Malone sighed. "We don't have a choice."

"Still. Good luck getting him to agree."

It was one of the last parts of the plan that needed to be mapped. Fortunately, Arnault was brooding in his office when Malone went to look for him. As she began explaining the problem of Saavedra's unpredictable hours and her growing net of contacts, Arnault began to redden. As amusing as his discomfort was, it only confirmed the value of the plan for Malone.

"I'd intended to help you get them out of the station and into the Vineyard," he said, already sounding defeated.

"Farrah can do that. She can't distract Saavedra."

Arnault made a noncommittal growl and tugged at the button on his collar.

"Meet us in the Vineyard after your date. Surely it can't take you that long." With that, she turned and left.

Malone went next to see the Revisionists. She'd considered explaining the situation when she and Farrah finally came for them that night. But goodwill was still a rare and precious commodity between them, and she saw an opportunity to win a few points with them by being forthright.

Anyway, it was the kind of thing Sundar would have done.

She shook the thought from her mind as she reached the holding cell.

The Revisionists, including Parsons, his injured toes now a smooth nub, were seated around the cell with stiff backs and tight frowns. Malone had given them the most private, comfortable space at her disposal, but no amount of comfort could wash the oily suggestion of captivity from the place. The cell was about the size of a cozy uptown apartment, some seven yards by ten yards, not including a private bathroom. Although it was really intended for one or two people, Malone had reasoned that the four Revisionists would be most comfortable if kept together. Another trick she'd learned from Sundar.

The room had four individual cots piled with all of the blankets and pillows the Revisionists could want; spotless, polished floors covered with soft, if worn, rugs; shelves stacked with reading materials; and even a homey layer of powder-blue paint along the walls, a rare decorative touch in the utilitarian Callum Station. All in all, it was barely smaller than the hideout where she and Arnault had discovered them.

Yet the only one of the group who seemed to have made himself at home was Dalton. He was reclining in a stuffed, high-backed chair, his hands clasped behind his head and one ankle crossed over a knee. "The good Chief Malone. What a pleasant surprise."

"We need to talk," Malone said.

Dalton stretched and gave a languorous yawn, as extravagantly relaxed as a guest who'd long overstayed his welcome. "As much as I've enjoyed my stay here, I really need a bit more time to unwind first."

"We're out of time," Malone said.

Parsons, Cabral, and Macmillan looked at her with the wide, wary eyes of hunted animals. Dalton only shrugged.

"The farmers are striking," Malone said. "The city's under strict rations. Sato's issuing an ultimatum."

"Oh, another?" Dalton yawned again.

She ignored him and looked at the other three. "Double rations for any who identify looters, organized dissenters, or other enemies of Recoletta."

Dalton snickered. "Six months ago, that would have included Sato and his collaborators, wouldn't it?"

"What does this mean?" Cabral asked, looking between Parsons and Macmillan.

"It means we can't keep up this pretense of detaining you as suspected vandals. We've got to move you some place less conspicuous." She looked to Dalton. "And you've got to give me something on the rest of your collaborators."

"Or what?" He laughed. "You'll turn us in to Sato? You'll tell him that you've been keeping us here under his nose, waiting for us to spill our intelligence exclusively to you?"

"Marcus," Cabral hissed.

He looked over his shoulder at her. "Don't be a pushover." His head turned back to Malone. "The chief knows I'm right."

"What I know," Malone said, "is that you're running out of options, and you're about to run out of allies. Now. I'll be back after midnight to move you to a more secure location. In the meantime, get some rest, and consider who you want to take your chances with – me or Sato."

Dalton finally leaned forward, his feet sliding from their elevated perch and onto the ground. "Where are you taking us, Inspector?"

Malone backed toward the door, ignoring Dalton's deepening scowl and instead watching the thoughtful frowns his three companions wore.

"Answer me, Malone," Dalton said.

She turned and left, locking the door against his indignant curses.

Malone left Callum Station late in the afternoon. She didn't want to give anyone reason to suspect she was staying late. Besides, a little time and space to clear her head seemed like just the thing.

She wandered deserted streets, heading vaguely in the direction of Turnbull Square. After a while, it became difficult to tell whether she was moving in circles or whether the passages had all begun to look the same.

Her options weren't looking much better. The farmers had found Recoletta's weak spot, and they were using what little means they had to dig in. Sato, in response, was tightening his chokehold on Recoletta. As for the Revisionists, Malone suspected they'd happily see their city torn apart and patched together a dozen times more before it resembled something they would deign to call "Recoletta." The coalition forming in Madina was a greater mystery still, but its members wouldn't be content, it seemed, until Recoletta was utterly broken.

And for her allies, Malone had Farrah, who was reliable if barely civil, and Arnault, who was neither. Malone sighed.

Before she knew it, the skylights were darkening, and she was, unsurprisingly, no closer to solving any of her riddles than she'd been at the start of her walk. And, she finally had to admit, she had no idea where she'd wandered.

By the time she got her bearings and returned to Callum Station, it was close to ten, and the place had all but cleared out. The surrounding streets, too, were as silent and still as usual. Farrah was in her office, cool and opaque behind her usual demeanor of merciless professionalism.

Farrah gave Malone the address and key to their eventual destination, which she'd gotten earlier from Arnault. "We're going to stand out, traveling like this," she said.

Malone privately agreed, but there was nothing to be done about it. "Once we get a half mile or so away from the station, it won't matter. We'll look like anyone else as long as we keep our heads down," she said. The one convenience of Recoletta's turbulent political situation was that everyone did their best to avoid notice.

Farrah didn't look convinced. "Or they could bolt."

It was a risk they had to take. "Right now, we're the most reliable allies they've got."

Farrah frowned, buttoning her jacket. "If they believe that, then what's with the arsenal?"

Malone was checking the placement and fastenings of various holsters, belts, and accoutrements. A collapsible crowbar hung by her left thigh, not far from a lock pick set. Her trusty revolver was in place on her right hip, and a snub-nosed pistol was fastened around her calf just inside her right boot.

Malone fastened her overcoat down the front. "I like to leave my options open."

"At least the knife around your thigh is inconspicuous. If anyone were to stop you, you'd look like you were up to something."

"Anyone who knows me knows I'm always equipped. And anyone who actually tries to see what's under my coat has bigger problems."

Farrah shrugged and held up her hands. "Just remember it's my head, too, Chief."

Malone didn't say anything, but her mind turned to Sundar. Farrah's must have, too, because she didn't say anything further.

Farrah and Malone proceeded quietly to the Revisionists' cell. So far, the route was clear, and they could only hope it would stay that way for their return trip. Malone unlocked the door to the detention area in the east wing. The Revisionists' cell was the only occupied unit in the area, so the corridor was silent. But when Malone unlocked and pushed open the door, the quick, furtive looks that passed between the Revisionists suggested that she had just interrupted a conversation.

Cabral stood as Malone and Farrah entered. "Time to go?"

Malone nodded, but Dalton shot them both a defiant glare. "She still hasn't answered my question."

Cabral rounded on him, exasperated and fearful. "For heaven's sake, not now!"

"I want to know where the good inspector is taking us. How do we know it's not to Sato?"

Time was ticking away. Arnault had structured his outing with Saavedra to give them a comfortable window to move, but Malone didn't dare count on either of them – Arnault or Saavedra – being predictable. "If I were sending you to Sato, it wouldn't be like this," Malone said. "And I certainly wouldn't have bothered to warn you this morning."

Dalton pushed himself out of his chair and walked over to Malone in long, deliberate strides. "That's a great story. Especially if you want to keep us talking."

Parsons flashed Dalton an angry look. "We can talk about this later."

"Are you all soft? She's Sato's chief of police. She's already told us that her boss is doubling down on his hunt for our co-conspirators. Now, she's making a big show of smuggling us to safety so that we'll hand over the same information. What's to say she won't turn around and give it to Sato as soon as we cave?"

Malone had been afraid of something like that. She looked at the rest of them. "I don't have time for this. You all know your chances. If you want to come, then circle up. Otherwise, stay here."

Cabral stood up. "No. We stay together."

Malone had been afraid of that, too. "Then get your friend moving." Malone turned to Dalton again. He was standing six feet away, but it felt closer. "You may not believe that I want to help you, but I know you believe that I'm not going to tolerate any nonsense." She flicked aside her cloak, showing him her revolver. "I'll leave you dead in the street before I let you run out on me. A body is easy enough to explain these days."

Dalton raised an eyebrow, calmly amused. "You'd gun down an innocent man, Inspector?"

"From where I'm standing, you're not innocent."

He smiled, showing teeth. "I was getting tired of this place, anyway."

Malone was beginning to regret the plan, knowing how a man like Dalton could erode the group's trust in her. Still, she couldn't leave him, and for all she knew, Cabral would drown him out as the voice of reason. Sundar would have known how to handle him, and he would have been horrified to know that Malone was secretly hoping Dalton would give her an excuse to shoot him.

In any case, she didn't have any more choice now than the Revisionists did.

Malone took a bundle of heavy coats and hats and tossed them to the Revisionists while Farrah briefed them on the need for secrecy and stealth. "Put these on, too." Malone pulled two pairs of cuffs from her belt. "Parsons and Macmillan, you're together. Dalton, you'll be with Cabral." A brief look of apprehension passed over Cabral's face, but Malone could only hope that being cuffed to Cabral would keep Dalton in line.

"You're the chief," Dalton said. "You mean to tell me we can't just walk out of here?"

"People would ask questions. And if any of them report to Sato, or if any of them talk to someone who reports to Sato, we'll have problems."

"That's funny. I thought this was your station."

Malone ignored the comment as she unlocked the cuffs. "Wrists out."

She didn't have to look at Dalton to hear the mischievous grin in his voice. "Not much of a promotion, was it?"

Malone cuffed their wrists together, hiding the metal bracelets under the long coat sleeves. Dalton rattled his chain peevishly, swinging Cabral's arm with it. "You missed a spot, Inspector."

"Hold her hand," Malone said.

Dalton left his arm hanging, but Cabral obediently grabbed his hand, folding the chain into it. Parsons and Macmillan were, with some awkwardness, concentrating on keeping their hands close together without clasping them. They looked a little odd, but as focused as they were on keeping their hands together and staying in step, Malone couldn't imagine them bolting. "You two in front," she said to them. "Dalton, you and Cabral will walk behind them."

Cabral stepped into position with Dalton trailing just beside her. Farrah had already moved out, motioning Parsons and Macmillan to follow. They filed out of the east wing's detention hall, and Malone locked the door behind them. She could hear the steady, soft patter of Farrah's footsteps ahead. So far, the coast was clear.

Unfortunately, she realized that she could also hear the rattle of chains ahead. Parsons and Macmillan were falling into a strange, faltering rhythm as they attempted to keep the chain between them steady. "Hold hands," Malone whispered, her breath sharp against her throat. The two men didn't acknowledge her, but they gave each other a probing, resigned look and clasped hands, tucking them as far up their sleeves as possible.

The clanking had stopped, but so had Farrah's footsteps. The Revisionists were oblivious, and Malone darted ahead of them, holding her hand up for them to stop.

Up ahead, Farrah called out in an unnaturally loud voice, "Well, aren't you here late, Inspector Gupta."

Malone could just hear Gupta's footsteps approaching. "Keeping busy, Farrah. What about you?"

Gupta was one of the dwindling holdovers from the Municipal Police in the days before Sato's revolution. He'd been a competent enough larceny investigator in the old days, and Malone hadn't found any reason since to doubt his loyalties or his aptitudes.

Still, she was increasingly leery of trusting anyone, and the fact that Gupta was here so late only raised her suspicions about him.

Malone waved the Revisionists back. The hall they were in continued straight for several yards, and Malone couldn't unlock the detention area quietly enough. She urged them farther back and was pleased to see that they were at least all holding their chains to keep them quiet.

Up ahead, Farrah laughed. Coming from anyone else, it would have sounded nervous and artificial under the circumstances, but Farrah managed a mirthful, full-throated chuckle. "You know I practically live here."

Malone and the others were backing away as quickly as they could without making noise, but the first bend in the tunnel was still a dozen yards away, and Gupta would hear them if he got much closer. She motioned for them to stop, hoping that Farrah could turn him around.

Around the corner at the other end of the hall, Gupta was proving receptive to Farrah's merriment. "If we're out this late on a Friday night, we might as well get some fun out of it. I'm just finishing up. What do you say we wrap up here and grab a drink?"

"I may be a while," Farrah said. "But you should get out of here. While you can."

Gupta laughed, and Malone turned the Revisionists so that they were huddled together with their backs to the end of the hall. Malone stood facing them and ready to intercept Gupta if he passed their hall.

"You know, I've still got a few other things I can work on, and I might as well since I'm here," Gupta said. "Why don't you, ah, come get me when you're done? No sense in walking home by yourself at a time like this. To your real home, I mean."

"It's your Friday night," Farrah said. "If you really want to spend it in your office, I won't stop you."

"Excellent! Then it's a date."

Before Malone could breathe a sigh of relief, the sudden clopping of Gupta's boots drew nearer. Farrah took a swift, skidding step to intercept him.

"Isn't your office the other way?" she asked. "I won't know where to find you if you go wandering off."

"Oh, just following up on some records. Older stuff, to be honest." Gupta's careful, deliberate tone made Malone suspect that he was making it up as he went along.

"Olivia Saavedra's office is closer. Why don't you try that office first?"

"I beg your pardon?"

"She's practically pulled half of the records into her office. I told her she can't expect me to keep anyone out if she's using the place for public storage." Farrah crossed her arms, rocking back on her hips. "Not that she hasn't made enough of a spectacle of the place."

"I, ah, have no idea what you mean."

Farrah sighed. "Don't be coy. Everyone knows what I mean."

Gupta sputtered and bridled. "Miss Sullivan, I assure you, I've been far too busy to stand around gawking at Miss Saavedra."

The edge between condescension and reassurance in Farrah's voice was so fine that even Malone couldn't tell the difference. "Of course you have, but you're about the only one. Frankly, I've heard more than enough about it."

"Ha, I know what you mean," he said quickly. "Shameful, really. The way everyone talks about it, you'd think we've got nothing but time on our hands. But what can you do?"

"Anyway, don't let me keep you," Farrah said.

"Right. You'd best get back to work, I expect. Then I'll see you later." Gupta's final inflection left it somewhere between a question and a statement.

"Yeah."

He walked away, and a few seconds later, Farrah appeared around the corner, wafting them toward her with swift, urgent motions.

They set off again, following Farrah at a distance. Reaching a staircase near the east wing exit, Malone and the Revisionists waited while Farrah climbed the stairs to see how things looked ahead. She returned less than a minute later, shaking her head. "There's a guard rotation right outside the door. There's no room to hide, and I don't know those guys. We'll have to try the main surface exit."

Dalton opened his mouth, ready to protest, but Cabral yanked him along with a little more zest than Malone would have expected from the woman.

The corridors around them yawned, wide and tempting. It would have been easy to bolt ahead, but Malone didn't dare take the risk. She kept the Revisionists moving at a normal, steady pace so that if anyone did stumble upon them, the situation wouldn't look any more suspicious than it already did.

They finally reached the main hall, lit from above by trenches of flame set high in the walls. Farrah hurried ahead to check the entrance and the probable guards, but Malone held up a hand to kept the Revisionists steady.

"Come on," Parsons said. "Let's just run for it."

"Easy," Malone said. "We're not rushing anything." Yet caught between two long rows of offices in the wide and straight hall, it was tempting.

Farrah disappeared into the entry lobby several dozen yards away. As they continued, their brisk footsteps seemed to echo all the way down the passage ahead of them, an unwelcome but inevitable herald.

They were just passing Farrah's and Malone's conjoined offices when the wooden double doors swung open. It was impossible to say who looked more startled – Gupta or the Revisionists.

Gupta, however, had fixed his guilty, wide-eyed stare on her, seemingly ignoring the four strangers in long coats. "Chief Malone. Have you, uh, seen Miss Sullivan?"

"She's not in her office."

"Right. I was just looking for her." Gupta kneaded his hands together and turned his shame-stricken face to the floor.

"With the door closed?" Malone asked.

He laughed awkwardly. "A habit, Chief. I didn't even realize I'd done it."

She searched his reddening face, his sweat-slick hands squirming against one another, the unbuttoned overcoat that swayed as he shifted. He looked mortified rather than panicked – enough, thankfully, that he'd only given the Revisionists a passing glance. Still, she would have to ask Farrah to keep a closer eye on him. "I suggest you continue your search elsewhere."

Gupta was already edging away from Malone with quick, shuffling steps and furtive glances. "Of course, Chief." But his gaze shifted, and he did a quick double take at the four strangers.

"I'll be sure to tell Miss Sullivan you were looking for her."

His eyes snapped back to her. "I greatly appreciate it." When they wandered again, it was to eye the broad clearing of the hall. He looked like a cornered animal ready to bolt.

"Don't let me keep you," Malone said.

He laughed nervously. "On my way, Chief." Turning, he cast a final confused glance at Malone and her four guests.

As Gupta disappeared down the hall and around a corner, Malone turned back to the Revisionists. All of them heaved deep sighs of relief except for Dalton, who looked wickedly amused. "Glad to see you've got things under control, Chief."

They reached the rotunda where winding flights of stairs and an elevator rose to the surface. They didn't see Farrah, but they didn't see any guards, either. Malone prodded the Revisionists up the stairs. Dalton looked longingly at the elevator, but even he didn't say anything. When they reached the surface exit at the top, they could hear Farrah's voice as she spoke to the guards.

"I was sure I saw someone leave this way," she said. "You haven't seen anyone?"

"It's been quiet, ma'am. Anyone who's out to cause trouble is doing it somewhere more interesting," one of the guards said.

Malone peeked out of the stairway and saw Farrah holding the attention of two guards. They were clear enough in the abundant lamplight. Farrah had their backs to the stairs where Malone waited, but she could see the undefended exit between their broad shoulders. She gave Malone the slightest of nods.

Malone had chased her share of criminals through the nooks and alleys between the verandas that jutted to the surface. Now, she had to look for her own escape route through the jumble of aboveground structures.

The Revisionists were huddled in the stairway, awaiting Malone's directions. She beckoned them up and pointed them around a corner, one that would get them out of sight as quickly as possible. Farrah didn't react, but Malone knew she had seen them.

She sent Parsons and Macmillan first. They were clear of the station's veranda and halfway across the open street when the two guards began to turn. The cuffed men froze in a patch of moonlight.

"We should be getting back, miss," one of the guards said.

"Not yet!" Farrah said it with such quick authority that both guards paused mid-turn. "Something else I need to discuss with you two."

Parsons and Macmillan glanced back at her, and Malone urged them forward with rapid buffeting motions, her jaw rigid with silent fury. She grabbed Cabral's wrist and guided her onward as the other two resumed their cautious progress.

Out of the corner of her eye, Malone saw Farrah making wild, attention-grabbing hand gestures as she spoke. "...people coming and going at odd hours? Chief's been especially concerned about it lately. She wants to make sure the station's secure, especially in this climate." Farrah spoke slowly and deliberately, and Malone had almost gotten her last two charges to the safety of the corner as Farrah finished.

One of the guards coughed and spoke up again, his voice slow and cautious. "Now, I wouldn't know anything about that. You and the chief are here as long as anybody. If there's anything to notice, I'm sure you two would have picked up on it."

Malone had just made it to shadows and safety when he finished.

"I guess you're right. Keep up the good work," Farrah said. The guards' heavy footsteps crunched in the grit as they retreated to their posts. Malone waved the Revisionists up the next street, and Farrah met them at the intersection.

"Took you long enough," Farrah murmured.

"We ran into Gupta."

Her brow creased. "What did you tell him?"

"Nothing. He was too busy explaining what he was doing in your office. Keep an eye on that one."

Farrah shook her red mane but said nothing.

The six of them continued through the surface streets, gradually leaving the radius of Callum Station and, with it, the chances of being seen by anyone who might recognize them.

"These roads are a mess," Dalton said, picking his way over drifts of litter and ridges of broken and uneven cobblestones. "Any chance of taking a railcar?"

"Not with those bracelets," Farrah said.

It was several minutes more before they began to hear signs of life. A rumbling din of voices and feet came from somewhere ahead, rising over the tops of verandas like the slow swell of an avalanche.

Farrah cocked an ear. "Sounds like a big crowd."

"They going to cross our path?" Malone asked.

"I'll check it out." Farrah raced ahead with long, agile strides.

Dalton and Cabral had stopped ahead, and Macmillan and Parsons waited behind them. "We're still moving," Malone said, laying a firm hand on Macmillan's shoulder. The four Revisionists continued toward the noise, Malone following behind.

The sound rose to a growling, grating cacophony. Shuffling,

stomping boots echoed along the streets, and Malone found herself doubling her initial estimate of the size of the crowd. By the time Farrah jogged back, the crowd had grown loud enough that it couldn't be more than a couple of streets away.

"Hard to say if it's a party or a protest, but whatever it is, it's headed toward the factory districts," Farrah said. "We'll have to go right through them."

The warm night air prickled Malone's scalp. "What about going around them?"

"No use. We'd have to double back to Callum Station. That, or swing wide enough to cross Sato's neighborhood."

Parsons was rubbing at his wrist. Macmillan spoke up, his voice high but even. "There's a passage back to the underground not far from here."

Farrah shook her head. "The tunnels are packed even tighter. We'd never get through."

The front line of the horde appeared, flickering between verandas like flames between logs.

Malone leaned toward Farrah, raising her voice over the crowd's low thunder. "Hostile?"

Farrah shrugged. "Mostly drunk."

The Revisionists huddled together, following the conversation and the advancing multitude with wide, haunted eyes. Parsons shot Malone a pleading gaze.

"Lead the way," she said to Farrah.

They pressed on, and the throng oozed into their street from various alleys and cross-streets. Farrah took Cabral's hand and guided her forward, and they knifed through the crowd, Dalton trailing behind. Parsons and Macmillan tightened their grips on one another and followed, pulling one another through the crowd. Malone urged them on, keeping Farrah and her two charges just in her line of sight.

Farrah's bright red hair made an easy visual target, but Malone's eyes kept darting to Cabral and Dalton. He wasn't walking any faster than he had to, but Malone couldn't get close enough to prod him forward without passing Parsons and Macmillan. It wouldn't take more than a quick surge in the crowd to push the two of them off course or under a procession of trampling feet. Still, she glanced ahead to make sure that Dalton and Cabral were still moving forward.

Dividing her attention between the two pairs, it took a few angry whispers and a bony shoulder sideswiping hers before she realized that she was attracting unfriendly looks from the crowd. She kept her head down and angled her body forward.

The crowd thickened and spread. Malone could no longer see the end of it, and its glacial pace made it an even worse mess to get through. The air grew sour with the heavy stench of mingled breath and alcohol.

People became bolder as more of them clogged the street. A man passing by Malone muttered about corruption and Callum Station. Another gave her a glare that dared her to try something, anything, worthy of a fight.

Malone's uniform had once been enough to part crowds, but here she felt the group constrict around her, emboldening and emboldened by their mutual audacity. Malone avoided eye contact and fixed her gaze on Farrah and the other two with her.

The crowd converged and parted again, and when Malone caught her next glimpse of Cabral, the woman was rigid with shock. A gasping shriek escaped her lips that Malone could hear even above the din of the crowd. Dalton was pushing through a knot of people, and he was now too far and moving too fast to be cuffed to Cabral anymore.

Farrah looked back at Malone, the whites of her eyes flashing. "Go!" She gripped Cabral's arm in one hand and was already reaching for Parsons with her other. He seemed only too happy to comply, especially as the people around them stirred and growled in response to the commotion.

Malone took off, shoving past people and moving upstream

against the throng. Some cried out in anger, others in confusion, but Malone was focused on the ripple moving through the crowd ahead of her as Dalton pushed ahead. Between Malone's cloak and fitted black clothes and the two lines moving through the crowd, some of the spectators got the gist of what was happening. Shouts and jeers surrounded her.

"Arrest me, good Inspector!"

"Two days past my rent!"

Malone ignored them, but as she elbowed her way further into the mass, the taunts grew angry and aggressive. Dalton was making headway, but the onlookers were squeezing in around Malone.

A voice rose over the turned heads. "Watch where you're going! That uniform means nothing here."

As Malone's progress slowed, she got a better look at the men and women around her. They were ragged with that look of people who have grated and rubbed against one another all night, exposing the rough burs of temper and raw, long-nursed grievances.

But there was something else about them that didn't match her previous experiences with disorderly crowds and riots. Malone felt it in the smooth fabrics that brushed up against her and saw it in the wrinkles and rips marring silk blouses and woolen jackets. She heard it, too, in the crisp diction and unimpeachable grammar of the mob's insults and catcalls.

"You can't lock us in here!"

"We won't be left to drown in the dregs, understand?"

Suddenly, Farrah's comment about the horde's march toward the factory districts surfaced in her mind. As did Sato's announcement of his plans to ration the food stores and lock down the border. He must have gone public while she'd been enmeshed in matters at the station.

Watching the way the angry throng eyed her – looking down their noses and curling their lips in distaste – Malone thought of the one person that a crowd of aggrieved whitenails would hate even more.

"Looter! Thief!" she shouted, pointing toward Dalton.

Uncertainty flickered in the eyes nearest her. But the crowd began to shift, as steadily and inexorably as a turning tide. The heat of the whitenails' combined attention and anger shifted to Dalton.

The only people worse than the cops, soldiers, and politicians who'd stripped them of their privilege and locked them in this decaying city were the looters and opportunists who had robbed them of their dignity and wealth in the midst of the chaos.

Sure enough, Dalton's tumbling progress slowed and finally stopped as the murmurs, growls, and shouts caught up with him. The mob relinquished its grip on Malone, and she shoved her way to the front.

Dalton squared off with a broad-shouldered man in a patched and faded tuxedo jacket. Other whitenails formed a ring around the pair.

"A rather fine shirt under your ratty old coat," Dalton's challenger said. "Where'd a louse like you get it?"

"It's mine, you idiot," Dalton said.

"Don't take that tone with me, boy." The man in the tuxedo clenched his long-nailed fingers into a capable-looking fist. "Around here, we enforce certain standards of decency and dignity."

Either Dalton hadn't heard the accusations or he didn't care. "Clean out your ears. I don't repeat myself."

Malone pushed her way to the front just in time to see the man in the tuxedo coat deck Dalton.

"Wearing it doesn't make it yours," the tuxedo man said. "I asked where you got it."

Dalton spat blood upon the cobblestones and looked at the tuxedo man with disgust. "From someone I duly compensated."

The man in the tuxedo kicked Dalton in the stomach with expensive but scuffed leather shoes. "You've got a lot of nerve for a man on his knees. I know a lot of families who were duly compensated by people like you. Maybe it's time to pay you back."

A sinister murmur of agreement rose from the crowd, and Malone shoved through the final barrier of people.

She shared a tight circle with a coughing, grimacing Dalton and his seething assailant. Dalton hadn't caught his breath yet, but Malone didn't want to give him the chance to bait his attacker further or explain who he really was. Of course, at this point, it was just as likely that none in the mob would believe him.

Malone stepped between Dalton and the tuxedoed man. "You've made your point," she said. "It's time for me to make mine." She hoisted Dalton up by one arm and pulled him to the edge of the circle.

None of the onlookers budged, and the man in the tuxedo folded his arms over his broad chest. "We're not finished yet. Maybe you should leave this one with us."

Malone knew better than to reach for her gun, but she glanced at the waists and hands of the men and women around her. Few of them were armed with anything more than their bare fists, meaning that they hadn't come looking for a fight. She saw a few pistol-shaped bulges, but they were all tucked in belts and pockets for now. "I can't question a bloody pulp."

"For all the questioning you Municipals are doing, there are a lot of these types still running around with impunity. I'm not letting this one get away."

"Neither am I," Malone said.

For once, Dalton had the sense to keep quiet.

"That's peculiar," the man in the tuxedo said, "because you're headed away from the station." He nodded once, pointing his chiseled nose toward Malone's rough trajectory. "The only establishments of note in that direction are the Barracks and Sato's headquarters." Sato's motley army and Cabinet had not endeared him to the aggrieved whitenails, and his failure to punish the looting and violence that had ensued on the eve of his invasion had not improved his standing.

Malone tightened her grip on Dalton's arm. Suddenly, she also wondered about Farrah and the three other Revisionists. As far as she could see and hear, the crowd was a churning, roiling sea of humanity, and she couldn't distinguish anything else beyond the contracting knot of people around her. She had to hope that the others were making their way through the distracted mass.

"You're wasting my time," Malone said. "You can march on the factory districts if you've got nothing better to do, but I'm finding the rest of this guy's accomplices."

The tuxedoed man took a step closer. "I've seen the kind of justice you Municipals mete out to them. This one won't get off so easily."

Blood surged in Malone's head. She'd see to him all right. "No, he won't. But you'll leave that to me."

"According to whom, Madam Inspector? We have you at a disadvantage, and you know it." His eyes flickered toward her holstered gun.

He was right. She had no chance of overcoming their numbers. And, as the snarling, scowling faces closed, she wondered if it wasn't already too late. Even if she left Dalton to the mob – and the temptation to do just that grew by the second – mobs maintained a narrow, binary delineation of loyalty, and she'd already put herself on Dalton's side.

Besides, these people wanted blood. Even Dalton's might not be enough.

Dalton found his voice. "This is absurd. I'm–"

Malone brought her elbow down on the small of his back, dropping him to his knees again and sending a ripple of surprise through the whitenails. They were still glancing and muttering among themselves when she drew her gun and leveled it at Dalton's head. "I will make him pay," Malone said, "after I've gotten what I need from him. But if anyone gets any closer, I'm executing him right here. Then everyone loses. Except him."

The whitenails began to back away, holding out their open palms. They didn't look any happier with Malone, but they seemed grimly convinced that she might be capable of the kind of violence she was promising.

Again, the man in the tuxedo spoke for the others. "It's a shame there weren't more brave fools like you in the Vineyard when scum like him came for us." The sudden gleam in his eye jolted realization into Malone.

"You've found other protectors since then."

He grinned. "The Bricklayer's been doing your job for you lately. And if he finds out that you're doing favors for this one," he said, jerking his chin at Dalton, "I'm afraid you'll regret it very much."

Malone dragged a stumbling Dalton forward, and the crowd parted around them, still watching warily. The mob was already loosening ahead of her, its invisible connective tissue stretching and warping as people gave up on the spectacle and resumed their march to the factory districts. Malone didn't slow and didn't look back until she heard the dull thud of hundreds of footsteps receding into the distance. Dalton was either too bruised, stunned, or scared to speak.

They rounded a corner, and Malone pushed Dalton face-first against a veranda wall, grabbing an extra set of cuffs from her belt as he groaned. She twisted his arms behind his back and cuffed his wrists together. "If I don't see Farrah and the others when we get to the safe house, I really may hand you over to the mob."

He said nothing as she yanked him after her. The idea that she should send for help to deal with the mob vexed her like an unreachable itch. Even if she hadn't had Dalton to deal with, there weren't enough police to keep a night shift, and Sato had Covas's forces stationed around the borders. By the time she rousted help, the rampaging whitenails would have finished their work, anyway. And so the factory districts would burn tonight, and there was nothing she could do about it.

The thought hollowed her out. She chewed on it, turning it over in her mind. She was so distracted at first that she didn't notice the trail of leaflets that papered the street, trampled and mottled so that in the near-darkness, they almost blended in with the cobblestones. She picked one up, examined it, and tucked it into her coat.

As they reached the quiet outskirts of the Vineyard, Malone tied a plain black blindfold around Dalton's head and pulled his hat low. She kept a firm grip on his arm, steering him around rubble and over rough, broken paving stones. The longer they walked, the more unnecessary the blindfold seemed – between the gates torn from their hinges and the crude fortifications piled around other verandas, the place was almost unrecognizable. The fine marble verandas looked as if they'd been plopped into the dark, deserted streets of the factory districts.

To Malone's surprise, she found Arnault's address easily enough. She circled and backtracked a few times, watching for signs of anyone lurking nearby and enjoying Dalton's obvious confusion. Besides, something about the meticulousness of the ritual calmed her nerves and slowed her breathing after the ordeal with the mob.

When she was satisfied, she rang the bell at the veranda gate. She didn't have to wait long for Arnault to appear.

A door creaked open somewhere below them, and Arnault ascended the stairs from the residence to the veranda in long, smooth strides. His face was motionless, but the upper lip gleamed with sweat in the glow of his lantern.

"They're fine," he called down the stairs, opening the gate of the sleek black veranda. He fastened four different latches once they were through and leaned a scuffed slab of plywood against the gate.

"The most important defense," he said, catching Malone's gaze.

"What's that?"

"Camouflage."

Dalton snickered.

"You first," Arnault said, holding the lantern aloft at the head of the steep staircase.

They proceeded down the stairs. The door was open, and the other three Revisionists huddled in a circle of chairs in the drawing room, looking like children awaiting punishment.

"About time." Farrah swept in from another room, her cheeks puffed with relief. She glared at Dalton while Arnault engaged the door with a noisy and extensive combination of bolts and keys. "I hope you're worth the trouble," she said.

"I hope you don't make more," Arnault said. He slid a bolt with an emphatic thump.

Parsons, Macmillan, and Cabral hid their faces behind cups of tea. Dalton looked on at their meek pleasure for several seconds. But none of his comrades spoke up, either to offer him a cup or any word of commiseration, and he finally dropped into an armchair just outside of their orbit.

Malone surveyed the domicile. Someone – Arnault or one of the infamous looters – had stripped the place of all but the minimum comforts. The beds in the rooms along the hall, the rugs spread across the tile floors, the deeply cushioned chairs on which the Revisionists now perched – all were variously torn, stained, or worn thin. The teacups the Revisionists cradled were chipped, and the scattered furnishings – a ripped oil portrait, a broken vase, a frozen clock, and splintering dressers – wouldn't have been worth the effort to carry into an adjacent room, let alone another domicile.

Arnault and Farrah had seated themselves in the living room by the time Malone finished her circuit. She pulled up a chair across from the Revisionists.

"Where should we start?" Farrah asked.

"Or when," Malone said. She watched the four agitators avoid her gaze and one another's. All save Dalton seemed to understand their changing circumstances, but none wanted to turn traitor to their cause. Whatever, exactly, it might be. "Tell me what brought you together," Malone said, feeling strangely as if she were repeating someone else's words.

Dalton remained silent, and Cabral and Parsons nuzzled their teacups, but Macmillan spoke up.

"For me, it was the chaos. Sato's invasion took us all by surprise. Most of us locked our doors and waited for the madness to end. But some people... they caught the scent of what was going on outside and it made them hungry. Doesn't take much with some folks." He nodded at the surface. "You saw that lot outside."

"I remember," Farrah said. Her voice was quiet but firm, and Malone remembered the secondhand account she'd heard of Farrah's long vigil just outside Chief Johanssen's office – now her office. "The City Guard thought that the police were trying to overthrow the Council, and we thought they were just looking for an excuse to round us up and shoot us." She paused. "But the fighting ended that night."

Cabral looked up and scowled. "Maybe for you."

"The soldiers stopped fighting," Macmillan said. "The Municipals were decimated, and the City Guard had lost to a foe they'd never even seen. Sato's army had officially won, but what were the thousands Sato had brought in supposed to do?"

"Sato called his lieutenants almost as soon as he arrived in Recoletta. They were to order their squads to stand down." Even as she said it, Malone heard the hollowness in that statement.

"I'm sure he did," Cabral sneered. "But they weren't soldiers. Not in the conventional sense. He couldn't have expected to control that many people turned loose in the city they'd just conquered."

Macmillan set his cup back on the table at his knees. It leaned under the added weight. "The bigger problem was the rest of Recoletta. Chaos breeds anarchy, and anarchy breeds opportunism. Even once the shape and weight of Sato's leadership began to fill the void, he couldn't police the entire city. Not the way his dramatic entrance had left it."

Malone knew that all too well.

"Besides, some groups saw Sato's victory as their victory."

Farrah folded her arms. "Let's be clear. By 'some groups,' you mean the ones that came from the factory districts, right?"

Macmillan nodded. "Primarily. At first. But those lines began to blur after a while."

Parsons cleared his throat and refilled his teacup while the table pitched and yawed. "They marched into the Vineyard first. Most were from the factory districts, but plenty weren't. I don't think they even knew what they wanted when they arrived, but they figured it out quickly enough. Money. Valuables. Violence for its own sake. Entire homes, in some cases." He scratched an ear, and for the first time, Malone saw the burn mark that rippled the flesh of his lobe. "Some of us fought back. Some of us fled."

Even though Malone had always seen her involvement in Sato's regime as mainly circumstantial, the four Revisionists were looking at her – and at Farrah and Arnault – as if they were somehow the avatars of this blundering injustice.

Farrah crossed her ankles. "There were proclamations against that kind of thing. We issued them. So did Sato." Malone heard something of her own defensiveness in Farrah's tone.

"And who was around to enforce them?" Cabral asked. "Besides, not much credibility in telling people to leave their neighbors alone when Sato swooped in and invaded an entire city the same way."

"Sato didn't see it that way," Malone said. She wasn't sure if she was arguing on behalf of Sato, her own presumed allegiance to him, or the simple principle that one injustice didn't excuse another. "He thought he was rescuing Recoletta from its illegitimate overlords, not seizing it for himself."

"That's always been his problem," Arnault said from his seat just over her shoulder. "He's got one story in his mind, and it's not the same story everyone else hears."

Six heads, Malone's included, turned to regard Arnault. He only shrugged.

Malone looked back to Macmillan. "So the underclasses took Sato's overthrow of the Council as a license to address their own grievances against the Vineyard and its whitenails."

He gave her a quick, humorless smile. "That's the funny thing about grievances, Inspector. Once you air them out, they breed and multiply. It may have started as street sweeps and factory hands against whitenails, but it came to include anyone who'd ever held an advantage over someone else. Whitenails turned on one another over generations-old grudges. The middle classes were caught at both ends."

"And now you're continuing that grand tradition," Farrah said. "Sending angry whitenails to the factory districts to finish what started there."

Cabral's face reddened. "Have you listened to a word we've said? This goes beyond whitenails and factory workers. This is about all of Recoletta."

Malone pulled a rumpled leaflet out of her coat pocket and laid it on the wobbling table. Even smeared in grime from the street, the boldface print was clear enough. The slogans variously denounced Sato as a madman, an impostor, and a public menace, and those who collaborated with him were labeled traitors and opportunists.

"You can't blame that on us," Dalton said. He sat further back in his chair as if to distance himself from any association.

"You all printed these, didn't you?" Malone asked. Cabral, Parsons, and Macmillan had looked away at first, but they were slowly beginning to examine the paper.

"So?"

"You saw them in the streets. The mob left them everywhere. They'll probably drop them all the way to the factory districts."

He pointed an accusing finger at the surface. "Are you blaming that mess on us?"

"The rioters were clearly inspired by your words. Isn't that what you wanted?"

Dalton gritted his teeth, but the other three were already looking away again, their faces darkened with recognition and chagrin. "We wanted," he said, "to tell people the truth. About

Sato. How he came to power and what he's doing to our city."

"So you did," Malone said. "And it seems people took a different message from that."

"But that's not our..." The words died in Dalton's throat with a growl of exasperation, and even he looked away.

"This isn't going to stop," Malone said, surprised at the vehemence in her own voice. "Not with Sato righting old wrongs, and not with you righting his. All you're doing is splintering your allies and creating new enemies. You've got to end this." It had been a long time since she'd been this angry about anything. It felt good.

The room fell silent for several seconds.

Finally, Parsons spoke up. "What do you want from us?"

"I need to meet your organizers. The Bricklayer, since you obviously know him. This Clothoe person who's put these resources at your disposal."

"Very well," Parsons said.

Even Dalton didn't protest.

CHAPTER 11

FIRE

Covas's soldiers struck in the morning.

Fog blanketed the outer fields, just enough to camouflage the haze of smoke. Enough of the darkness had burned off that the little tongues of flame were easily missed until it was too late.

By the time the first cry went up from the reapers three fields away, half an acre of barley was ablaze. When they returned with shovels and field hands to dig a trench, the fire had spread. At the northern horizon, the first flames appeared amongst the hay.

Only the work of every able-bodied man, woman, and youth saved Meyerston's crops.

The meeting amongst the farmers that afternoon was worse. Salazar, Callo, and the rest of the representatives stood on the porch together, much as they had days ago when they were already trying to bolster the flagging resolve of the rest of the group.

Salazar smelled their shifting commitment like smoke on the changing winds. Before, there had only been doubt and concern. Now, many of them wanted out. Salazar could see it in their eyes, hear the apologetic defiance in their voices.

"They called our bluff," Sister Brody said. "We're lucky Sato's people burned our fields and not our homes. This was a warning."

Murmurs rose. Perhaps this was right.

On the other side of the crowd, Brother Danvers added his

voice to the rising swell. "It's not worth it. If they're willing to go this far, what else will they do?"

The voices grew louder, arguing and speculating. Next to Salazar, Callo and the other representatives looked between one another, saying nothing.

Salazar stepped forward, gripping the rail. "I'll tell you," he said. "And listen well, because it's much worse than whatever you're thinking."

The spring sun hung over the square, and the murmurs died down. Salazar waited until he knew he had their attention, until he heard nothing but the crowd's slow, steady breathing.

He paced the top step of the town hall. "Sato burned our fields because he's scared. That makes him dangerous."

A few in the crowd glanced at one another and shuffled their feet. Salazar continued. "Sato would rather see Recoletta starve than compromise with us. He can barely keep his own city in line – there's no chance he'll show us mercy. He will answer any challenge, whatever the form, to his authority. He can't afford to do otherwise." He stopped pacing. "And if we show him any weakness, he will dig in and pry it open until he breaks us."

Danvers, Brody, and the rest of the doubters pursed their chapped lips.

Jack raised his arms in an expansive shrug. "Do you think that, if we step down now, Sato will forgive and forget? Remember this: he's not trying to make a deal with us. He's trying to force us to submit. Sato will never bargain with us. A bargain is a compromise, a sharing of power. And if Sato shares any of his, his fragile empire will collapse beneath him.

"He'll bear his victory like a trophy, lest any of the poor sods in his caves get the wrong idea. He'll double our quotas. Send his troops to occupy our homes. He'll divide us into work camps and use our loved ones as hostages if he believes it will keep us under his heel."

Now, they were starting to look worried. Good.

He spoke again while they were gripped by images of labor camps and executions, before they had a chance to return their thoughts to burned fields and marching troops.

"The road ahead will be long and difficult. We know this. We knew it when we chose to strike. But the choice now is not between months of hardship and a return to the status quo, but between months of hardship and years of slavery."

He looked briefly over the crowd, at their wide, fearful eyes and the grim set of their mouths.

"Philips, Vasquez, and Dormer, organize your teams and clean up that field. Widen the firebreaks around the others. We'll hold our regularly scheduled town hall meeting tonight."

CHAPTER 12

CONSEQUENCES

Perhaps against her better judgment, Malone had agreed to release Parsons to summon Clothoe and, if he was to be believed, the Bricklayer. It wasn't as though he could just pick them out of a crowd – there were certain channels, which none but a trusted associate would be allowed to pass through. It was a risk, but the other three Revisionists had agreed to stay readily enough (actually, Cabral and Macmillan had agreed to stay, and they'd silenced a grumbling Dalton). And, to her greater surprise, neither Farrah nor Arnault had objected.

Realistically, they didn't have much choice.

So Malone, Arnault, and Farrah had left the other three locked in the safe house and allowed Parsons to disappear into the night, hoping they wouldn't return to find their remaining leads gone.

But Malone remembered their uneasy silence after the mob, and she had seen the looks on their faces as she'd described Sato's latest developments. They were running out of options, too, and they knew it.

Now, she found herself in an anxious lull. There was nothing to do but wait for Parsons to surface. Sato had disappeared immediately after the Cabinet meeting three days ago, and she'd heard no sign of him since. There was news that a squad under Covas's command had set fire to one of the farming communes, but it seemed impossible to get details from anyone but Covas herself, who was nowhere to be found.

All anyone in Recoletta cared about was that Madina's trains were bringing rations to make up for the lack from the communes.

Yet beneath the uneasy wait, Malone felt the little tremors that warn of an earthquake, saw people moving around her like pieces on a game board.

She focused her restless, nervous energy on churning through the stacks of reports on her desk. She and Farrah had said almost nothing to one another all day, and so she was surprised when the other woman walked into her office with a folded square of paper and a nervous expression.

Malone set her report down and looked up.

"Sato's summoned you to the train station," she said, stopping halfway to Malone's desk.

"I didn't realize he'd returned," Malone said.

"Neither did I. But he apparently wants you over there right away."

Malone eyed the paper between Farrah's fingers. "What's this about?"

"How should I know?" Farrah bit her lip, twisting and turning the folded paper in her hands and finally surrendering it to Malone. "Take a look yourself. He just said he wants extra security for the delivery this afternoon, all right?"

"Fine," Malone said, reading the same thing in the note. She hadn't heard of riots or unrest around previous deliveries – presumably Covas's troops had seen to that – but she could understand the concern. She gathered her coat while Farrah returned to her desk, masking her own vague distress with a frenzy of activity.

Before Malone left the station, she gathered twenty of her more experienced inspectors.

"We're running security?" Inspector Wallis asked.

"That's what I'm told," Malone said. Her tone put an end to further questions.

The way to the train station was clogged. Increasingly, venturing through Recoletta was an exercise in extremes. It was either a ghost town, the winding, brick-lined tunnels abandoned and unswept, or it was plugged with the concentrated excesses of humanity.

Sato had set up a distribution system at the offices near Dominari Hall – he'd been careful to avoid the feeding-trough madness of parceling out the goods anywhere near the train station. But people came still, whether in anticipation of a riot, to see that the much-needed shipments actually did arrive, or simply because there was little else of note going on at the moment.

Her inspectors bunched around her as they navigated the thickening mass, making their way with loud shouts and sharp elbows.

Malone had gotten better at reading the mood of a crowd. There were moments, as now, when the teeming swell of humanity was so focused on a singular goal that she could have been invisible to them. Their focus made them predictable. They shoved and milled around one another, only dimly aware of each other as warm, moving obstacles.

But that could change in a heartbeat. Their bovine single-mindedness could turn feral, turning on anything and everything in their way.

So Malone kept an eye on the vacant gazes around her and an ear to the steady, discontented murmuring.

They finally reached the train station, packed full with people. Only the loading platforms next to the tracks were empty, and that was because station staff kept shooing people back, waving off reaching hands and bull-rushing any who dared approach the steps.

But something didn't look right.

"Chief," one of the inspectors shouted in her ear. "Where's all the soldiers?"

Where, indeed. Malone looked around, but the only people

she saw apart from the gathering crowd were the station staff, sweating in their bright coveralls.

"Pair up and spread out," she said, turning to her inspectors. She kept her feet wide and planted as the crowd bumped and crushed around her. "You eight, take up positions around the platforms. Everyone else, disperse and take up positions around this station. On your alert, but keep them holstered unless you've got no choice. Understood?"

Twenty heads nodded in response. As the inspectors scattered, Malone turned and shouldered her way to the nearest loading platform.

She reached the stairs, and the man patrolling the broad platform nearly shoved her back into the crowd until he saw the silver seal in her hand.

Instead, he sighed with relief and reached out to help her up. "Thank God, the cavalry's here," he said, wiping his shining brow. "Don't tell me it's just you."

"I've brought twenty of my best with me," Malone said, feeling the hollow promise of those words.

He blinked, patting down a thin, wiry thatch of hair. "You're joking," he said. "What the hell are twenty of you supposed to do?"

"Twenty-one," Malone said calmly, "and we'll do everything we can, but it would help if you could tell me what needs to happen."

"I don't even know where to begin. For previous shipments, we've had a whole battalion of soldiers to keep things in line." He shook his red, round dome. "See that track there?" He pointed, and Malone had to squint between the writhing masses to see the faint shape of a shallow channel. "Needs to be clear. 'S where the wagons roll up. We load 'em and they cart the goods off to Sato's storehouses. But good luck clearing this lot out of the way. And even if you managed that, I'd bet you my rations that they'll have the carts turned over before they clear the station."

It was a formidable problem. As for what Sato could have been thinking in pulling Covas's troops and dispatching Malone and a handful of inspectors, she could only guess. "How long before the train arrives?" she asked.

"It's almost twenty minutes overdue," the man said, pointing up and to a wide, round clock that, amazingly, still worked. "The deliveries have been pretty regular until now. Could be some real loons have overrun the tracks. Or maybe Covas's soldiers are dealing with the hold-up."

Malone opened her mouth to reply, but a new tide of emotion had started moving through the crowd. It was subtle at first – rising voices and a quickening of movement – but by the time Inspector Chilson, stationed in front of the platform at Malone's feet, looked up at her, the crowd was at full surge.

They were shouting about something, though it was impossible to tell what. They didn't seem to know where to direct their fury, either – they turned to the ceiling, the empty tracks, and one another, teeth bared. A fight broke out near the back of the crowd, but most in the surrounding mob ignored it.

"What's going on?" Malone asked the station attendant.

"How should I know? Maybe it's just other people piling in. Pushing from behind."

But Malone didn't believe it, and he didn't appear to, either.

The mob was getting rowdier, spasming with little fits of fighting and shoving. Chilson and the other seven inspectors she'd stationed around the platforms were pushing against the swell, keeping the bodies back, if just barely. She could see about half of the other twelve across the station. She motioned for them to come forward.

She was already cursing herself for splitting them up and Sato for not giving her a warning of what awaited them. If she'd only known–

Just then, shrieks rose from the back of the crowd. Somewhere, a gun went off. Not one of her inspectors', she hoped, but in the boiling mass, it was impossible to tell just what was happening.

Something slammed against the platform. A protester, either

charging at full tilt or shoved by the people behind him. And he wasn't the only one. The whole crowd seemed to be rushing the platform, and their anger was wheeling and turning in the same direction, as laboriously and unstoppably as a herd of beasts.

Chilson and the others, she saw, were fighting a redoubled effort from the men and women at the front of the crowd, dodging fists and shouting down the mob. They wouldn't last much longer.

She was dimly aware of the red-faced station attendant standing beside her and shouting into her ear, begging for direction. His hand clamped down on her shoulder, and she looked at him blankly.

Malone pointed at the other inspectors stationed around the loading platform, their shoulders just rising above the edge. "Help me get them up here," she said.

The man scuttled off – she'd be lucky if he had the presence of mind to help, but at least he had something to occupy him now – and bent down to grab Chilson's shoulder, shouting at him to retreat to the platform. It was a miracle he heard her, but he turned around allowed her to hoist him up by his outstretched arms. Without a word, he jogged further down the long platform to help the rest of their fellows up.

Malone almost laughed with relief when she saw Angelo and Wallis shove their way to the front of the platform. She reached out for Angelo while Wallis gave his partner a boost from behind.

"Saw Gupta and Klemsky back there," she shouted as she cleared the lip of the platform. "Good twenty-five feet behind us before we lost sight of 'em." It was part apology and part explanation. In that roiling throng, twenty-five feet might as well be a mile.

They'd reached down to grab Wallis when the man's eyes went wide in shock and pain. He was just short of them when he slumped forward and crumpled at the base of the platform, something seeping from the back of his uniform. A man standing behind him glared up at Malone and Angelo, his knife and the hand holding it glistening with blood.

"Shit," Angelo whispered.

The mob surged over Wallis almost as soon as he fell.

"Watch the stairs," Malone said. "Keep an eye out for the others."

Angelo nodded dumbly and rushed over to stand guard at the top of the narrow steps. Chilson and the station attendant were halfway to the end of the platform, where it ended at the mouth of the empty tunnel from which the train should have emerged. Between them, they'd pulled up most of the other inspectors, who had in turn fanned out to pull more of their brethren to safety or push back bolder members of the mob.

It was a valiant effort, but even if everyone but Wallis made it to the platform – an assumption that grew unlikelier by the second – they couldn't hold the position forever.

Feet thundered along the wooden planks toward Malone. She turned to see Velez and Hsu – two more from the crowd – jogging down the platform toward her. Martin had joined Angelo at the top of the stairs. It was almost everyone.

"They got Thomas," Velez panted, angled forward with his hands on his thighs.

Malone leaned toward them. "Any sign of Gupta or Klemsky?"

Hsu shook her head.

Malone looked out over the station. Fighting their way out the way they'd come would be almost impossible. The crowd was fast clotting into something impenetrable, and anyway, the mob's once-idle wrath had latched on to Malone and her comrades. That only left–

Two shots rang out, loud even over the roaring of the crowd. Malone looked back toward the stairs in time to see Inspector Martin, his revolver in hand, pulled off of the platform and into the mob. Angelo reached for him, but it was probably a lucky miss for her. He disappeared in a tangle of arms and legs.

"Get back!" Malone shouted.

Angelo retreated, and it was only the crowd's newfound confusion and fixation with Martin and the men and women who had pulled him down that kept them from following her.

"He fired into the air," Angelo said, her voice shaking. "He was furious over Thomas. Meant to subdue them, but he just stirred them up."

"Chief, we can't stay here," Hsu said.

The other inspectors – and a few station attendants – were already making their way toward Malone across the platform. Back where Martin had fallen, the stairs shook as members of the crowd began climbing two and three abreast, wedged tight and pulling one another back as they fought for passage on the narrow steps.

There was only one way left to flee.

"Into the tunnel," Malone shouted at her officers.

The red-faced attendant hurried over to Malone, bellowing. "You crazy? If that train shows up, we'll have nowhere to run."

"We don't have anywhere to run now," she said.

The officers were already lowering themselves over the edge and picking their way down the scaffolding. There was no noise from the depths of the tunnel, but it would have been difficult to hear anything over the roar of the crowd.

Malone knelt at the edge and climbed down herself. The beams and poles juddered as the crowd pressed against the other side of the platform and finally poured over it. She could only hope that anyone climbing up after them was of the same mind to escape.

Her feet reached the smooth stone of the tunnel, and she dropped the last couple of feet to the tracks. The inspectors ahead of her were already jogging toward the tunnel.

Malone did the same as the scaffolding above her creaked and groaned under the increasing weight of the mob.

The tunnel ahead was dark, but lights flickered and glowed to life as some of the inspectors at the front of the group stopped to light their hand lanterns. Malone kept up a quick trot as she passed into the shadow of the tunnel, feeling grit and gravel crunch underfoot. With the clamor of the crowd still blaring behind her, she didn't dare slow down.

The attendant she'd spoken with earlier caught up to her. "Tracks continue about two miles like this before they break to the surface. Got service tunnels every half mile or so, but lately they've been locking 'em to prevent some fool from sneaking onto one of the trains. Or from fleeing the city that way."

"One of you has keys, right?" Malone asked.

The motion in the darkness looked like a shrug.

The inspectors and attendants ahead had slowed down enough for Malone and the rest of the stragglers to catch up. The commotion from the station still echoed down the tunnel when they reached the door to the first service tunnel, and the attendant shook his head.

"Probably just drop us right back into the thick of it," he said. They kept jogging.

As they regrouped, Malone counted the survivors. She saw thirteen of her own inspectors. Of the seven missing, she'd seen Wallis and Martin fall, and Gupta and Klemsky had never made it to the platform. That left three others who had either perished before the others could pull them up or who had never made the climb down from the platform. In addition, they'd picked up eight uniformed station attendants.

A cold, calculating part of her mind recognized that twenty-one survivors was more than she'd had a right to expect after the catastrophe that had unfolded at the station. But that knowledge didn't lessen the sting of losing seven officers.

The noise of the mob receded to a dull roar. By the time they reached the second service corridor, the disaster felt distant enough to risk a slow trot.

"Hold up," Malone called.

The other inspectors and the station attendants turned to look at her, their faces blank but for the exhaustion of a burned-out adrenaline rush. Many of them looked grateful for the stop.

Malone walked over and tried the handle of the door. Locked. "One of you have the key?" she asked, making sure to look each of the station attendants in the eye.

A woman with a stringy ponytail pulled a key ring from her pocket. She tried a new-looking key of shiny brass, which glinted in the lamplight as she turned it. It made a half circle that ended in a metallic thunk, yet when the woman pushed on the door, Malone heard the same stubborn resistance that she'd felt.

"It's locked from the other side," the woman said.

"Let's keep going," Malone said, still too raw to feel surprised.

They continued on. They had yet to hear or feel any sign of the late train, but halfway into the tunnel, Malone didn't dare express relief just yet. The rest of the group seemed to be in the same state – they hadn't sped up from a brisk walk since leaving the last door, and they hadn't said a word, either.

When they reached the third door, the attendant tried her key again, and to no one's surprise, it stayed wedged shut.

Malone didn't realize how heavily she was breathing until she stopped to listen again for the noise of the mob. It echoed down the tunnel, sounding more distant and harmless by the minute. Thinking back, it was amazing that none of them had followed her group into the tunnel.

Perhaps even they weren't crazy enough to wander onto the tracks with a train long overdue.

"Almost through," Malone said. "Let's pick up the pace."

The rest of the group followed her lead, listless and exhausted.

The tracks sloped upward. Gray, ghostly light filtered in from somewhere up ahead. They had just left the third door around a slow bend when Malone heard a distant rumble.

She wasn't the only one. "What's that?" Hsu asked, skidding to a stop and holding her arms out as if to feel a disturbance in the air.

"Train," Angelo said.

"Can't be," Malone said. But she was already calculating the remaining distance and wondering how many of them could make the half-mile sprint uphill.

"It's not a train," the red-faced attendant said. He didn't sound relieved.

"Then what else?" Angelo said, straining to hope.

"No idea."

"Come on," Malone said, jogging again. "Hurry."

The others didn't need any goading. They dashed after her, panting and grunting in the fading dark. As they got closer, Malone thought she could feel the commotion under her feet. It didn't seem to be moving, which was a relief. But Malone was certain she heard screams and cries – not the ravings of a mob, but something else entirely – over the labored breathing of her companions. An icy splinter of fear wedged itself into her heart.

They didn't bother to stop as they passed the last door. The mouth of the tunnel was a circle of gray, backlit clouds up ahead. Aimed at the sky, it gave no clue as to what waited on the ground.

Minutes blitzed by as the mouth of the tunnel widened around them. Finally, it was a yawning, luminous portal, and the sounds of screams were unmistakable.

So was the smell. Burning fumes, fuel, and something else.

"What is that?" Angelo asked. No one dared spend the breath to answer her.

They reached the lip and topped the rising ridge of the tracks.

Hunched over, their hands on their knees while they caught their breath, they saw the train.

"Shit," Angelo muttered. "Shit, shit, shit." No one else said anything.

A few hundred feet away, the train lay on the tracks, bent into two trailing sections like a broken-backed animal. The dozen or so cars, and the grass around them, burned, belching noxious smoke into the air.

Yet movement flickered from the belly of an open compartment.

Something launched itself from one of the upright compartments. It was a someone, she realized, shrieking and flailing in the middle of a shroud of flames. The unfortunate dove into the grass, rolling wildly. But the flames burned on as the poor soul's efforts slowed and stopped.

And then Malone realized that the patches of flame in the grass were other men and women, crawling and twitching while their bodies smoldered. It was like looking into a swarm of ants – once her mind registered the first quivering movement, she saw it everywhere.

The stench, she realized, was burning flesh.

"That's... not normal fire," Chilson said, sounding as if he were about to be sick.

He was right. It clung to the dying and dead with unnatural persistence, and even where burning scraps of human and machine debris littered the tall, thick grass, the flames didn't spread. They clung to their sources and ventured no further.

Standing on a knoll rising beside the tracks were Covas's soldiers. The same ones who would've guarded the station, Malone suspected. Instead, they looked down on the scene, pointing their rifles at men and women who were already dying beneath them. More than one turned away from the massacre on the tracks, heaving into the grass. They either hadn't noticed Malone's group yet, or they didn't care.

"Did they... What did they do?" Velez asked.

"I don't know," Malone said. "But we should get back."

No one needed much convincing. They turned back toward the solemn, steepled verandas of the city.

As much as Malone hated to admit it, there was only one person she trusted to give her answers. She needed to find Roman Arnault.

CHAPTER 13

IN MOTION

Malone left the other inspectors at Callum Station and instructed them to brief their fellows, spread out, and keep order where they could. The memory of the chaos on the night of Sato's invasion was fresh enough that everyone moved quickly. Malone felt a stab of guilt at the thought of leaving the rest of the station to handle the building madness in her absence, but if Recoletta was on the verge of another city-wide cataclysm, her presence would do little to stem the changing tides.

Unless she could get answers and fight this thing at its root.

So when Malone didn't find Arnault or Farrah at the station, she headed to the safe house.

In a way, it was a relief to leave the orbit of Callum Station. Vague rumors of disaster were already spreading throughout the city, and though the particulars of the calamity differed from one story to the next, the same keening note of panic pervaded them all. Everyone had questions – about the riots at the train station, about fires outside the city, about Sato's ever-changing whereabouts – and she had no answers.

As Malone made her way through the city, she smelled trouble brewing. Near Callum Station, people had begun to clear the streets, fortifying themselves in their homes as whispers of danger percolated through the tunnels. Yet the nearer she got to the

Vineyard, the more citizens she saw boiling out of their homes, congregating and prowling like ants guarding a smashed nest.

She reached the underground entrance to the safe house and pulled out her key ring. She'd just unfastened the first lock when the remaining two clicked and the door swung open, revealing a wide-eyed Farrah.

"What the hell took you so long?" the redhead asked, standing in the doorway.

"Trouble on the other side of town," Malone said. "The train–"

"I heard," Farrah said, closing her eyes and waving a hand in the air between them.

"Has Arnault gotten here yet? I need to speak with him."

Farrah's eyes snapped open again. "He's gone."

"Gone? What do you mean?"

"I mean he left. Disappeared. Saw him at Callum Station earlier today talking with Saavedra. He vanished just before I heard about the trouble uptown."

Malone sucked a breath through her teeth and looked up and down the still-empty corridor. "Will you let me in already? We shouldn't be standing in the door like this."

"Well, don't stand on ceremony," Farrah muttered, finally stepping clear of the door.

Malone followed her into the bare entry hall. "When did you last see Arnault?"

"Probably an hour and a half ago. I came here as soon as I heard about the train."

Malone looked for any reasonable possibility or contingency that might explain his absence. All she found was the dull realization that she should have seen this coming. "If he hasn't shown up here, then he must have gone to Sato."

"Possibly," Farrah said slowly, as if testing the word.

"Where else?"

Farrah looked at a stain on the wall. "He just... It didn't seem like he was sticking his neck out only to betray us."

"Arnault picks winners," Malone said. "And he plays both sides as long as it takes for a victor to emerge." She felt downright foolish – how could she have missed this before? Understanding rose in her mind like so much noxious, billowing smoke. "Now that Sato's revealed his arsenal – that fire, Covas's army – Arnault is playing his hand."

Farrah didn't look convinced. Still, it was the most logical explanation, and there was no time to take a chance on distant contingencies.

"Sato's troops could be here any minute now," Malone said. "We need to go."

"Didn't want to leave without you, boss," Farrah said, scowling. "Besides, they wanted to talk with you first."

Before Malone could ask Farrah more, the other woman guided her into the drawing room, where two elderly matrons sat, flanked by the Revisionists. Where one was tall and wizened, the other was, as if by design, short and rotund. Yet with teacups and saucers in their hands and a patrician languor tugging at their eyelids, they looked as if they were holding court.

"Chief Malone," Farrah said, "Meet Madame Francine Attrop and Madame Lucinda Clothoe."

"A pleasure," the taller woman, the one Farrah had introduced as Attrop, said. "I've been following your work closely these past months." Her manner was too genteel for even Malone to perceive a taunt.

"I suspect I could say the same," Malone said carefully.

"I'm certain you could." Attrop smiled, showing teeth.

"You've been leading the Revisionists."

"Not precisely. That honor belongs primarily to my ally." She gestured with gracefully unfolding fingers to Clothoe, who had yet to say a word. Attrop seemed to notice Malone's confusion. "You can see why she prefers letters to speeches."

Farrah's face was still, as if none of this was news to her. All four of the Revisionists, even Dalton, were solemn in their silence.

Malone looked back to Attrop. "Then that must make you the Bricklayer."

The older woman actually blushed. "I'm afraid I never chose the name. Still, it has a certain bourgeois charm." She raised her teacup but a fraction of an inch, and Macmillan took the teapot to refill it.

Distantly, Malone supposed that she should feel insulted at having been thwarted these months by a woman who looked to be at least seventy years old. She couldn't quite muster the vexation, though.

She did, however, feel the anxiety of seconds ticking by, each likelier than the last to bring Sato's forces down on them. Yet the two women sat in their chairs as if to hide the cushions. Malone knew just enough about social niceties to recognize that no command but their own would move these two.

"Parsons must have brought you," Malone said, hoping to remind them of the purpose of their visit and the urgency behind it.

"Sato did, in his way. We'd been planning on making our introductions to you soon enough, but Sato's rashness today pushed things along faster than we had intended."

With her surprisingly knobby fingers wrapped around the teacup, however, Attrop hardly looked like a woman in a hurry.

"That's interesting," Malone said. "Because it seems as though Sato's given you exactly what you wanted."

Attrop's smile was flat, but her eyes flashed with intelligence. "What might that be, Chief Malone?"

Clothoe's beady eyes danced between them.

"A nail in his own coffin," Malone said. "You have all the proof you need of Sato's incompetence and his excess. And sufficient motivation to move your followers against him."

"Straight to the point," Attrop said. "I thought I'd like you."

"And what is it you want from me?" Malone asked.

Attrop took a slow sip of tea, and Malone marveled at the woman's claws. Along with Clothoe's, they were, perhaps, the longest, straightest fingernails Malone had ever seen.

"As much as it may surprise you, I am not entirely pleased with Sato's latest move," Attrop said. "As you gathered, I was hoping he would expose himself. However, I had hoped he would not do it so... boldly."

"You were just hoping he'd crack down on a few of your rioters," Malone said.

Malone counted it as a point in her favor when the other woman scowled. "I had hoped Sato would create a manageable disaster. But this," she said, tapping the blade of one nail against her teacup, "a burning train loaded with invading troops? In the middle of a food shortage? Even I can't control this." Occupying her chair like a throne and sipping her tea, Attrop looked much more like a frustrated chess player than an architect of overthrow.

Yet as they stayed here bandying challenges, precious minutes slipped away. Even Farrah was beginning to gnaw at a nail. In the five or so minutes they'd wasted here, they could have been clear of the block and halfway out of the Vineyard.

"What's the next step in this plan of yours?" Malone asked.

Attrop showed her a brittle smile. "That is why I came to you."

"What exactly do you expect from me?"

"Aid. Succor. In Parsons' telling, you've got as much to lose as I if we're caught." She favored the Revisionist man with an approving nod.

Hairs rose along the back of Malone's neck. Attrop's nerve was galling, but the woman had a point. "Maybe so," Malone said, "but I still don't understand what you think I can do about it."

"Are you not the chief of police? With hundreds at your disposal?"

Malone laughed humorlessly. "Maybe a hundred. If you want to count the ones who've been properly trained. Hardly an army in numbers or discipline."

"You are part of Sato's Cabinet." Attrop waved her hand at the word as if she were shooing away a bug. "Am I to believe that none of your confederates are similarly disillusioned?"

What had felt like a promising and fortuitous alliance was rapidly deteriorating into an exasperating farce. "They're all disillusioned. Thanks in no small part to your own antics behind the scenes, by the way." She glared at the old woman, willing her to take responsibility for this much, if nothing else. "But there's a wide gulf between disillusionment and willingness to take part in a second rebellion. Particularly after seeing the means Sato has at his disposal."

"What about Arnault?" Cabral asked.

Another dry laugh scratched at Malone's throat. "The man who helped Sato seize Recoletta in the first place? He's not here. We have to assume that means he's thrown in with Sato."

"Which is why we should get going," Farrah said, folding her arms.

"Come to think of it, you've got far more at your disposal than I ever did," Malone said to Attrop. "The crowd I saw marching on the factory districts must have been a few hundred at least. But you're not throwing them at Dominari Hall, are you?"

"Don't play the fool, Malone. The role hardly suits you," Attrop said coldly. "You know as well as I that you don't put that kind of power into the hands of the mob."

That was when Malone realized that Attrop and Clothoe were desperate. They weren't the kinds of people to throw themselves at her mercy based on a hunch.

"There's an option," Malone said. "But you won't like it."

"My dear, Recoletta today is full of things I dislike. Your proposal could hardly be any worse."

"The farming communes."

Attrop's smile fell, as Malone had known it would. But, to her credit, she picked it up and tried it back on like some broken, precious thing she'd dropped on the pavement. "An interesting notion, Chief Malone."

"You won't like their creaking, overheated huts. You probably won't like them. And you certainly won't like the majority of what they stand for," Malone said. "But they're the one group that's just as firmly against Sato as you are. And they're the only people who wouldn't dream of handing you over to him."

Attrop smoothed the wrinkles from her long, ruched skirt and drained her tea. "Then it seems we've no better alternative. Let's go."

"Hold on. I know where the commune is, but getting out of the city–"

Attrop held up a hand, her nails slicing through the air like knives. "Leave that to us. You can be certain we've kept a few escape routes open for contingencies such as this."

Attrop and Clothoe stood with more speed and grace than Malone would have expected from women of their age and led the way out.

Jane had not heard from Arnault or Lady Lachesse in days. She had not heard from much of anyone, in fact – Bailey and the Qadi had left her to her regular duties, and she'd had no further run-ins with Chancellor O'Brien or Father Isse. As much as she wanted to take satisfaction in keeping out of the meddling of so many mercurial and opposing groups, being suddenly cut off from them left her uneasy. They were, of course, still meddling, but now she had no perspective on the details.

And as the days crept closer to the invasion mentioned in the chancellor's letter, she found herself more and more on edge. She had to remind herself that Arnault would handle the matter. And, more importantly, that it was not her concern now.

Fredrick, on the other hand, had remained buoyant since starting his new job. He'd become a font of gossip, narrating rumors about local luminaries that even Jane knew little of and whispering about political ripples that Jane only heard echoed at work a day or two later. He'd even taken to helping out more around the apartment, picking up Jane's slack without complaint.

And he'd said nothing further about Lady Lachesse. If he noticed a change in Jane's mood or suspected anything about his new position, he certainly hadn't mentioned it.

But at the Majlis on the day of the planned troop shipment into Recoletta, Jane couldn't focus on anything else. Tension seemed to thicken the air at the Majlis, too. Even though no one said anything about the looming offensive, it felt as if everyone were awaiting something, distracting themselves with work in the meantime.

Jane kept herself distracted with a fairly routine load of paperwork – the kind of thing she could churn through without much effort or attention. Yet as the day wore on, her nerves wore thinner and thinner. When the people around her began packing up and turning in for the evening, she did a double take at the clock in disbelief that the whole day had passed with no news from Recoletta.

That the Qadi and her allies might have backpedaled on the plan seemed like too much to hope for. Unfortunately, the lack of news could mean anything. And there was no way to inquire without raising further suspicions.

A thousand wires and fibers had been drawn taut over the course of the day. Jane could feel them wind even tighter, ready to snap.

She headed home, trying to pretend as though she had no reason for anxiety or concern.

Outside of the Majlis, the streets were crowded and sultry. All of the homes and workplaces of Madina had sighed in unison, filling the streets with the heat and musk of thousands. And a day of sun had warmed the upper layer of rock and filtered underground through the ample windows, turning the tunnels into a kind of convection oven. Jane was grateful for the loose fabric of her long tunic and trousers as she squeezed through the crowd.

She'd been looking over her shoulder for days – for Lady Lachesse, for Father Isse's spies, for some other informant from the

Majlis – only to find nothing. The effort now seemed as pointless as it was exhausting, and she was glad that the enshrouding throng made it all but impossible.

So she wove through the crowd, brushing against flesh-padded fabric as she moved. But when a hand dropped to her shoulder, she surprised even herself with how fast she spun.

She surprised Roman, too, who gazed back at her with wide, alarmed eyes.

Her mind filled with questions and dread. "Roman? What are you–"

"I'll explain everything, but we need to go somewhere we can talk. Privately."

Her daily routes and routines rarely took her outside of a circuit that included the Majlis, the market, and her apartment. "The Pheasant?" she asked.

He started to say something but only shook his head.

She could only assume that, for whatever reason, he no longer believed it was safe. Impatience for answers and certainty burrowed under her flesh. "Where, then? Unless you want to come home with me, I don't know what else to suggest."

He glanced around as if he might find the answer just over the heads of passersby. "Just find us a tea shop. Whatever it is they have out here."

"Follow me." Jane pressed through the crowd, feeling Arnault at her back. She found a tea house on the next street, marked by a bright banner that rose above the throng. It looked crowded inside, but everything would be at that hour.

Jane didn't look over her shoulder but wound her way to a tiny table in the back of the shop that seemed far from the people-watching and the view of the street. Roman glanced at the crowds, the distant exit, and the walls hemming them in, but said nothing.

They sat down. The corners of Roman's eyes and the edges of his mouth were drawn tight.

"Talk," Jane said.

"It's about the train," he said.

Her stomach dropped. Somehow, she had known as much from the moment she'd seen him in the street. She pictured troops pouring into the city and another round of surprise battles in the streets. For the first time, she noticed his haggard appearance – the greasy knots in his hair, a missing button at his collar, a small rip in the cuff of his sleeve. The all-too-familiar signs of someone who'd left in a hurry. "They- they really did it? The chancellor's troops took Recoletta?"

He blinked back at her and finally uttered a dry, humorless chuckle, shaking his head. "No. Not even close. They–"

A shadow fell across the small round tabletop. Jane turned to see a rising hand and a glint of metal. Her body was still rigid with fear when the waiter placed the silver teapot on the middle of the table and set two short glasses beside it. Roman nodded his thanks, and the waiter's eyes lingered on him a moment longer before he faded back into the teahouse crowd.

Was it Roman's distinctly foreign attire or his run-down look? Maybe an unconscious faux pas? Or just an innocently curious glance?

She turned her attention back to Roman, who had also fixated on the waiter's quick glance and sudden disappearance.

Jane poured the tea, if only to busy her hands.

At the sound of the liquid trickling into his cup, Roman turned his attention back to Jane. He clasped his hands, chapped and edged with grime, on the table and seemed to think deliberately on what to say. "Sato burned it," he finally said, holding Jane's gaze. "The train and every man and woman on it."

Speechless, Jane waited for him to continue. The news was too shocking and grotesque for her to feel gratitude that the battle she'd feared had evidently been avoided.

"I told him about the invasion," Roman said. "I thought he'd rip up the train tracks. Close off the city. But he wanted to make a statement."

"How...?"

Roman ran his fingertips through the mess of his hair. "I don't know. Whatever it was, it wasn't a normal fire. He stationed troops–"

"No, how did you make it here?"

"Oh. That." His eyes fell on the full tea glass. He raised it and took a drink. "Luck and quick action. As soon as I heard what was happening, I got to the train yard. It was just a hunch. The train station fell apart in a riot – getting in or out of there was useless. But I was able to slip outside the city before the perimeter tightened. There were only a dozen cars there and a few engines to pull them, but a crowd had already gathered. One of the engineering crews was there, too, ready to get out of town before something happened to the rest of the rails." He tossed back the rest of his tea and looked back at her with a wry smile. "Not my usual travel experience. But hardly more grueling than yours, I should admit."

Jane found herself inexplicably cold. She wrapped her fingers around the base of her own still-warm glass, watching the oblivious masses around her chatter and laugh over pots of tea and piled cakes. "You came all the way here to tell me this?"

He laughed again. "No, Jane. To get you away from here."

"You what?"

"I'm sorry. I–"

"Again?" she said. "I left my home once after getting tangled up in your schemes. But I've made something for myself here." She heard her own laughter, high and feverish. "People respect me. I earn as much here in a week as I did in three back in Recoletta. And you know what? When the Qadi hired me, she didn't ask who my family was." Her voice scraped and rang against her throat. Other patrons and passersby were starting to stare at her, and she didn't care. She knew it was imprudent, but the last thing she wanted was to silently slink away as she had from Recoletta. Let them look. Let him try to pry her away. "I like it here, Roman."

He winced, though it wasn't clear if it was a response to the scene she was making, sympathy with her frustration, or the expression of some private and deeply buried emotion. "I really am sorry, Jane. But the Qadi's going to suspect a leak. That suspicion's going to turn on you."

Jane knew he was right. But she also surmised there was more to it.

"You didn't just come here to warn me," she said. "You fled, too."

"Sato's mad, Jane," he said. But for the briefest of moments, he glanced away and into his empty glass. "Of course I ran."

What began as a hunch was taking on the substance and form of certainty. "You knew what he was like from the beginning, yet you stayed. You helped him. Something changed."

"He burned hundreds of men and women alive in a train today. That changed a lot of things."

Jane believed him, but something in his hurried monotone told her there was more to it. There always was with Roman.

She was tired of guessing.

As she rose, she fished a few coins out of her pocket and left them next to the teapot.

"Where are you going?" Roman asked.

"Away from here. Away from you."

"Please, not like this. We'll be safer leaving together."

She whirled on him. "Will we really? Because it seems that almost all of my trouble has come thanks to my association with you."

He stifled a grimace. "I know. But you've got to move carefully. If the Qadi's people are watching you–"

"Then being caught with you is the last thing I'd want, isn't it?"

His mouth snapped closed in defeat. As much as she would have liked to, Jane couldn't enjoy his momentary speechlessness, tinged as it was with sorrow. So she turned away again before either of them could regret anything more.

The crowd flowed and meandered just outside the tea shop with movements that seemed strangely hypnotic. Jane wanted to dive into the stream and let it carry her away – to the false comforts of home, to the borders of the city, to some other corner where she could disappear. Anywhere but here.

As she passed out of the teahouse, the throng seemed to part around her.

No, she realized as people crowded again behind her. Not around her. Around someone moving toward her.

Two armed guards shed the crowd like a winter coat. "Jane Lin?" they said, looking at her. "Come with us, please."

"What's this about?" Jane said, trying to ask the question as though she didn't already know the answer.

"We can explain that along the way," one of the guards said, taking her arm.

Jane kept her neck rigid and forced herself not to look back toward the teahouse and Roman. Yet even as she willed the two guards to bear her forward, she saw four more slip past her out of the corners of her eyes.

Even as she considered running, the woman holding her bicep tightened her grip as if sensing Jane's intentions in the rising hairs on her arm. The other guard took hold of her just above the elbow.

The crowd seemed to break apart much more readily in the presence of Jane's captors. After half a minute, a waiting carriage loomed like an island above the stream of people. Unlike most of the conveyances in Madina, it was dark with closed, windowless walls and a top.

She could hear Roman struggling behind her by the time the carriage door swung open a few short feet away. She allowed herself to be led into it.

It was larger than it had looked from the street. While her eyes adjusted to the relative darkness, one of her captors cuffed her hands behind her. Seconds later, Roman followed her inside, subdued but furious.

For a moment, she heard only the rattle and clink of cuffs and Roman's shallow, rasping breaths.

As they began moving, a voice rose from the darkened end of the carriage. "So sorry about this unpleasantness, my dear. Try to think of it as an uncomfortable formality."

Jane knew that refined voice. And as a long-nailed hand adjusted the gas lamps in the carriage, she realized she knew the face, too.

"What are you doing here?" she asked Lady Lachesse.

The whitenail arched her chiseled eyebrows. "Really, I should ask you the same." She looked at Roman. "Consorting with the enemy. Providing aid and comfort." She cocked her head at Jane. "And I thought his regime had forced you to flee Recoletta."

"And I thought you were keeping your distance from the regime here," Jane said.

Roman's head turned toward her.

Lady Lachesse chuckled. "I hate to think I might have misled you in this. As a matter of fact, the Qadi and I have had some splendid chats of late. I did, however, need your help to hear about the ones she was having without me."

Jane felt as though the floor were rushing toward her. Her body seemed to float and bob as the carriage jostled around her. "You mean..."

"Old friends," Lady Lachesse said. "Whose company did you think was responsible for the railways running between Madina and Recoletta?" She laid a clawed hand on her chest. "I don't mean to take credit for all of them, mind you. But these are the kind of links that a person in my position will take great pains to maintain." She paused again. "I truly am sorry, Jane. I thought you'd have figured that out."

Jane could almost believe the woman meant it.

"What," Roman panted, "is going on?"

"And how nice it is to see you again, Mr Arnault. You are going to visit the Qadi and some of her present acquaintances. There are matters they wish to discuss with you, issues that concern Madina's immediate security, so you will understand if these individuals are impatient. I suggest that you answer them quickly."

"How did you find us here?" Roman asked. His voice was low and quiet.

"That is a rather long story," Lady Lachesse said. She turned over one shoulder and peered behind a curtain at her back before returning her attention to Arnault. "On the other hand, it appears as though we still have a little ways to go in this traffic. And, as Jane can tell you, I'm a soft sell when it comes to storytelling." She smiled.

"As you must have surmised, I came here after Sato's rebellion. I reconnected with the Qadi and have managed to carve a niche for myself here. Of course, I've been keeping my eye on Recoletta. I'd be a fool not to, especially after such an instructive example of how quickly things can change.

"I was pleasantly surprised, therefore, when the Qadi let slip mention of a certain young Recolettan emigrée she'd brought on as a jurist. When she told me your name, Jane, I didn't mention that I knew you, but I did suggest that such a person might make for a welcoming face in any unofficial discussions with Recoletta's representatives." She paused, smiling again. "I've known the Qadi long enough to tell when she likes an idea even if she doesn't say so."

Lady Lachesse's mysterious approach and her seeming prescience days before her introduction to Bailey and her first meeting with Arnault now made sense. She told herself she might have guessed it before were it not for the sense of frustration and displacement she'd observed in most of her fellow exiles, especially the whitenails she came across in her proceedings as a jurist.

But she felt some further explanation lurking beneath all of this. She thought back to another conversation with Lady Lachesse in another carriage. "You've done all of this – manipulating the Qadi and working through me – to get to the Library?"

Lady Lachesse laughed. "You say that as if it's a simple feat,

Jane. A gambit like this requires planning and foresight. One must predict how others will act and react. Strategy is not about making a decisive, finishing move, but rather about setting the board so that others make those moves for you."

Evening traffic was a benign murmur outside the carriage. It sounded so distant even though only a thin carriage wall separated them from bustling normalcy.

Jane looked over at Roman, who had remained silent since Lady Lachesse's story. She wanted to believe that he was working out an escape for the both of them, or perhaps waiting for the right chance to enact some already-developed plan, but it was impossible to tell what he was thinking.

"But you got the information you wanted. What do you want with us now?"

"In the matter of that ghastly incident with the train, Sato has demonstrated that he's a force to be reckoned with. As is the Library he protects." She scratched her cheek with the back of one long fingernail. "It has significantly eased my burden of convincing the Qadi and her fellows that the Library must be preserved rather than destroyed, but it has also made them eager for collateral." Her gaze swiveled directly and deliberately to Roman.

"If you think Sato will bargain with you over me, you understand him even less than I thought," Roman said. "My loss will be little more than a minor setback. He's certainly sacrificed more for lesser goals."

"Mr Arnault, that is not at all what I intended," Lady Lachesse said. "And you know that perfectly well."

Roman said nothing more, but when Jane looked over at him, his face was unnaturally pale in the lamplight. A bead of sweat left a shining snail's trail down his temple.

"And as for you," Lady Lachesse said, looking back at Jane, "I am sincerely sorry that you've gotten mixed up in this. The Qadi will, however, want to know who's been handing her secrets over to the other side."

The bumps in the road seemed to mark long, uneven seconds as Jane considered this. "If the Qadi wasn't telling you about the meetings, just how did you know that Recoletta had sent Roman? Or that I'd met with him... unofficially?"

"That," Lady Lachesse said, "will become clear once we return to the Majlis." She sat back with a finality that suggested that she'd have little more to say on the subject – or any other – for the rest of their journey.

Jane kept quiet and shifted to ease the pain in her knees as the din outside grew quiet and as the motion of the carriage grew steady over the wide, flat tiles leading to the Majlis.

The carriage finally stopped, and Jane's escorts let her and Roman out at the edge of the glass-smooth plaza just before the steps of the Majlis. The building's wide, windowed arms were already wrapped around them.

A few ambitious administrators and overworked clerks were still trickling down the steps, and they turned to stare at Jane and Roman's armed guard with unabashed curiosity. Those were not the surreptitious glances they would have received in Recoletta, and Jane felt herself look down with reflexive embarrassment.

She counted the steps as they continued upward. They reached the plinth where the yawning mouths of the Majlis waited to swallow them. Roman was still silent and withdrawn beside her, his gaze downcast and his face even paler than it had been in the carriage.

As they passed through the doors and into the Majlis, Jane relinquished the hope that he was biding his time with some elaborate ruse to escape their captors. He looked like he'd already given up.

The twisting and winding halls in the Majlis emptied out as Lady Lachesse and her guard escorted them deeper into the structure. Feeling the now-familiar rhythms of the place in the ebb and flow of its people and the shifting shape of its halls, she intuited their progress toward one of the dim, quiet lounges where she'd had tea with the Qadi on earlier occasions.

Sure enough, a robed attendant was waiting at tall, carved double doors as they approached. He swung them open as if inviting Jane and her strange assembly to yet another cordial gathering.

As expected, chairs and settees were arranged around the wide, low table. But the person who sat waiting for them was not the Qadi.

It took Jane a moment to place him, crawling split seconds that felt longer than they were. But when he smiled, his teeth as radiantly white as his cottony hair and long goatee, she knew him.

"Hello, nephew," Councilor Ruthers said to Roman.

One guard knelt discreetly behind Roman and fastened his cuffs to the chair.

The guards waited outside while Lady Lachesse followed Jane and Roman into the room. Stunned, Jane felt the older woman's hard, sharp nails on her arm as she guided her to a chair.

Roman said nothing, but in his eyes bulged with fury.

"Nothing to say after these long months," Ruthers said. "You've always preferred the silent roles. Then again, I suppose that's why the code was entrusted to me, wouldn't you say?"

"Damn you," Roman said, jerking forward and tugging at his cuffs. The chains rattled mightily, but the chair held them in place.

"Watch your language, my boy," Ruthers said, pointing a four-inch fingernail at Roman. "And your temper. Those guards are only waiting outside as a courtesy, but they'll dispatch you readily enough." He fussed with the lapels on his jacket, but Jane saw fear in his eyes and nervousness in the twitching movements of his hands.

"Then you'd better hope they're fast," Roman said. "And good shots."

Ruthers laughed, but his voice sounded high and mechanical. "Just remember, we don't actually need you alive."

"Then why bother?"

"We are still blood, Roman. And I know that even you are

not immune to a certain degree of sentimentality," Ruthers said, looking over at Jane for the first time.

Up until Sato's revolution, Councilor Augustus Ruthers had been the most powerful man in Recoletta. It was surreal to be so close to this man a second time – the first was when Roman had been instructed to assassinate him.

She'd taken Roman's gun and set Ruthers free.

Now, Jane was beginning to question the wisdom of that decision.

"You're making a mistake," Roman said, his teeth clenched.

"I'm making do," Ruthers said. "Believe me, I wouldn't have chosen these circumstances, but we're all stuck with them now. Circumstances which you helped bring into being."

"Just what did they offer you for all of this?"

Ruthers's back straightened, and he raised his chin. Even as a dethroned exile, he looked as haughty as Jane remembered. "This isn't some paltry power play. They're putting me back in charge of Recoletta after Sato is taken care of. Someone capable needs to clean up the mess Sato has made."

"How altruistic of you," Roman sneered.

Jane felt dark amusement at watching the two men argue, their complex history rising around the as-yet unclear bounds of their argument. As discreet and detached as he normally was, Roman sounded as though he were voicing opinions and objections he'd left unsaid for years.

"You can't honestly believe that Recoletta is better off with your unschooled demagogue. From what I've heard of conditions in the city, it's a mercy I was forced to leave. But you know as well as I that I can restore order and confidence in a way that your artless idealist never could. Both Recoletta and Madina will be better off for it."

"And all you had to do was offer up a secret that should have died with us," Roman said.

Ruthers's lip curled in the barest hint of a scowl. "Part of the changing circumstances. When the stakes rise, so do the wagers. Even I had to offer something to stay relevant."

"Even you should know better than to trust them with this kind of power," Roman said.

Ruthers's shoulders stiffened, and he looked away, as if the entire discussion were beneath him. "Coming from someone who put a petulant and embittered child on the throne, that's ironic, indeed."

"Well," Lady Lachesse said, consulting a pocket watch. "As delightful as it's been to witness this family reunion, Augustus and I are due for another meeting presently. One that shall, I hope, be more productive." She glared at Ruthers.

"We shall continue this later," Ruthers said with a look at Roman. Jane almost thought she'd been forgotten until she felt a guard behind her chair, prompting her to rise.

CHAPTER 14

PLANS

True to her word, Attrop had found a way out of the city and onto one of the few remaining trains waiting just outside Recoletta. Her uncanny knowledge of the routes through Recoletta's perilous and ever-shifting territories, as well as her seeming acquaintance with the many figures who prowled and guarded those areas, had brought Malone, Farrah, Clothoe, and the four Revisionists blinking into the late afternoon sunlight faster than she'd believed possible. And it was only her unassailable authority with the men and women guarding the trains that allowed the eight of them to push through the thick crowd and into a compartment while one train already pulled away in the distance.

Things had gone smoothly enough until the train had reached Meyerston, stopping long enough to let Malone's group and a few others disembark. After that, things had gotten interesting.

It hadn't taken long for Malone to find Salazar and his cohorts. They were grouped in the town hall, as before, where they were discussing their next move. They'd managed to salvage the confidence of the rest of the farmers after Sato's burning of their fields, and they'd already learned of the incident with the trains. They had seemed glad at the support that Malone's presence – and that of her whitenail counterparts – implied.

All of which had changed once the two groups actually began talking.

Both groups saw that Sato's recent extremes left him vulnerable. Recoletta wouldn't long abide a madman, and fewer of his supporters were likely to stand by him as he resorted to such excesses. But where the farmers saw a chance to push for broader reforms, the Revisionists perceived an opportunity to reinstate a more comfortable and familiar system of governance.

And as darkness overtook the village, Malone found both sides rehashing familiar arguments in the town hall.

"Madness," Attrop said. "Sato's nearly broken Recoletta while trying to reshape it. You would bend it even further."

"And you're missing the point entirely," Salazar said, gesturing over a greasy plate of chicken bones that, a few short hours ago, had been his portion of a cordial supper. "The problem wasn't what Sato wanted to change, it's how he went about it."

"The one says much about the other."

"And what about your Council's infamous corruption? How much does that say about those policies you'd return to?"

Tedium and tension left the rest of the group – Farrah, the nine other delegates from the communes, and the rest of the Revisionists – quietly fidgeting around the table. While the farmers seemed preoccupied with the wood grain of the long table between them, the Recolettans flinched at every groan and creak of the old building. As the discussion had worn on, both parties had increasingly left their arguments with their most vocal members, Madame Attrop and Benjie Salazar.

Attrop graced Salazar's remark with a casual flick of her eyes. "Don't be simple. That's merely the way things get done. Even you wouldn't be above a little inducement were you in the position to receive it."

Salazar's eyebrows lowered. "Speaking from experience, I take it. No wonder you're so eager to have your old system back." He nodded at the Revisionists. "Do your bootlickers know they're just helping you climb back over them? Or have you promised them a share of the cream, too?"

Attrop raised her chin, turning her face away from Salazar. "I could well ask the same of your little in-group. What kinds of empty promises and reassurances have you offered to keep them in line?"

Salazar was leaning over the table when Malone brought her hand down on it. Hard. "Enough," she said.

Both Salazar and Attrop looked at her with shock tinged with indignation. But she had their attention.

"We've got to come to some kind of agreement. Between the missing food shipment and the train incident, he'll have his hands full. We need to act while he's still off balance," Malone said.

Both parties glared at her, suspicious and resentful.

"As much as we appreciate the hospitality, we didn't come all the way out here to join an ill-fated farmers' revolt," Attrop said icily.

"And we're not sending our people to die just to prop up your dynasty," Salazar said.

Malone counted it as evidence of her evenhandedness, at least, that both sides seemed to mistrust her equally. "I don't care what you all decide," Malone said, "but you need to agree on something."

Attrop held up a hand, her rings and fingernails flashing in the moonlight. "I don't see why we're even discussing this. The primary issue is the governance of Recoletta, a city in which our... esteemed colleagues do not reside. What matters is what the people of Recoletta will support."

"They'll support whatever you tell them, and you know it," Salazar said. "And we'll give you the same treatment we've given Sato until you give us a fair deal."

"He's right," Malone said. "Nobody will last long in Recoletta without the support of the farmers."

"Then the Qadi and her allies will punish you soon enough,"

Attrop said. "If they'd send troops into another city, what do you think they'll do to you?"

"Whatever it might be, it won't end with us growing your food, that's for damn sure," Salazar said.

Attrop said nothing, but Malone could see her mind at work and her silent, reluctant acceptance of the facts.

"He's right," Malone said to Attrop. "You need their cooperation." She turned to Salazar. "But you're going to need Recoletta's support to deal with the Qadi's allied forces. And, like it or not, you're going to need some kind of agreement from Recoletta's leaders to get what you're asking for."

There was, at last, a long silence. The commune delegates and the Revisionists looked at the table as if reading something from its scars in the dappling patches of moonlight.

Finally, Callo spoke up, dragging a callused hand through his white hair. "I think we're missing the larger issue. Even if we reached common ground, we've still got to find a way to oust Sato."

"That should be easy enough," Salazar said. "Between the communes, we've got plenty of–"

"They're not going to march to war in a city," Callo replied. "They'll defend their homes here, but they're not going to take up arms on someone else's doorstep."

Salazar frowned, looking around the table as if he'd just been betrayed. "They wouldn't be alone. When they reach the city, the rest of Recoletta–"

"Will hide in their homes if we're lucky or shoot them in the streets if we're not," Callo interrupted. "Whatever their feelings about Sato, they're not going to welcome another invading army."

"Speaking of which," said another delegate, the woman who had brought the wine when Malone had last visited, "Sato has a proper army. And he defeated an invasion from another proper army just this morning. Even if we were to work together, we won't get anywhere trying to take Recoletta by force."

"I suppose we should just ask nicely," Salazar said.

"She's right," Callo said, glaring at Salazar. "The troops from the Hollow never stood a chance."

"Because they were foolish enough to cram themselves onto a train in the first place," Salazar said. "And they had no idea about Sato's secret weapon."

The woman shook her head. "He'll be watching any way into or out of the city. There's no way we could sneak the numbers we'd need into Recoletta without attracting his attention. And how do we know he doesn't have more surprises like that fire?"

Voices rose around the table with questions and arguments, agitated after so many hours of tense silence. The sudden outpouring found farmers and Revisionists alike questioning and asserting the efficacy of force and the threat posed by Sato's mysterious fire, all to no one in particular.

Such was the ruckus that no one heard Madame Clothoe's quiet murmur at first. But Malone saw the old woman's lips moving and raised a hand for silence. Eventually, the group grew quiet.

"Greek fire," Clothoe said. "It was Greek fire."

"What are you talking about?" Attrop asked.

"The fire Sato unleashed on the train. It's called 'Greek fire.' Or it was at one point, anyway."

"You know what that stuff is?" Salazar asked.

"Silly boy. Anyone who's read a little history knows what it is." Clothoe cackled, seemingly oblivious to the irony in the statement. "But how to make it – that's the real trick."

Salazar pressed closer. "You know how?"

"Certainly not. But I know where Sato learned."

"The Library," Attrop said.

Salazar looked to Malone.

"He did make a sudden trip to the Library just a few days ago," she said.

In that moment, Attrop and Salazar exchanged glances with one another and with Malone, sharing the thrilling communion of sudden understanding. The rest of the group, delegates and Revisionists alike, were quiet, fearful of breaking a spell they didn't quite understand.

"This is how we get him," Salazar said.

Callo sat back, looking between the three. "You can't... You don't mean to go after Sato's secrets in the Library, do you?"

"No," Salazar said, "we mean to go after the Library."

Attrop nodded. "Burn it down if we must."

Malone's muscles tensed with a strange sort of anxiety, yet she finally saw cooperation in the faces of her once-combative and disparate allies. Even Farrah was nodding, her brow wrinkled with firm purpose.

"It'll certainly get his attention," Malone said.

Jane was firmly but courteously escorted to a quiet room somewhere in the depths of the Majlis immediately after the surprise meeting with Ruthers. Roman was taken in a different direction and she tried to still her fluttering panic with several months' worth of experiences, all of which indicated that Madina was not a place of wanton cruelty or barbarism.

The reassurances almost worked.

Yet the room in which her escort left her was comfortable if featureless, and she was left almost entirely on her own. The hours passed somehow, in a seamless haze of sleep and wakefulness, anxiety and grim resignation. She counted time passing in the meals her captors left with her.

She estimated that it was mid- or late morning on the second day after her arrest when two of the Qadi's guards returned, their expressions urging her to hurry even while their voices were tight and controlled.

"Sayideh, please come with us," one of them said.

Jane gave them no cause to wait.

She was led along nearly empty hallways and past the many offices and meeting rooms of the Majlis to a carriage bay, where another pair of large but inexplicably sleek black conveyances awaited her.

So, too, did Roman.

He looked exhausted but unharmed, and Jane read in his face the same tired relief that she felt at seeing him. They said nothing, but the guards made no move to stop them as they silently drew together.

For their part, the guards stood in a tense, nervous formation, their eyes darting to the door through which Jane had come.

After a handful of agonizingly silent seconds, the Qadi swept through, trailed by Chancellor O'Brien, Father Isse, Lady Lachesse, and Augustus Ruthers.

"The decision is made, Augustus," the Qadi said.

He quickened his pace to circle around in front of her. "You can't mean to leave me out of this," he said.

"We aren't, you insufferable fool," the chancellor growled. "We're sending you straight to Recoletta."

Jane's pulse quickened, and she suddenly realized she was holding her breath. Something big had changed while she'd been locked away in the Majlis.

"You think I'm going to stand aside while you settle matters with Sato?" Ruthers asked.

"No, we think you're going to start getting Recoletta in order," the Qadi said.

"The city you lost," the chancellor said.

"I mean to be there when you catch Sato. I mean to see him dealt with," said Ruthers. He squared his shoulders in front of the others, but already he sounded less insistent, less sure of himself.

Standing next to Roman, Jane felt like a child watching adults argue, helpless and invisible. She looked up at Roman, but his face was a study in impassivity.

"Augustus," Father Isse said, his voice as smooth as silk. "I know this is personal for you. We all know that Sato robbed you of your dignity along with your position." He paused just long enough to let Ruthers cringe, the ends of his ears beginning to redden. "But the best thing you can do now to regain it is to cement your place in Recoletta. Return in triumph when Sato has fled in ignominy. The people will welcome a decisive and familiar presence."

Ruthers looked overpowered rather than convinced, but he kept his head high. "Very well. But they come with me," he said, pointing at Jane and Roman.

Jane's heart raced as the city leaders looked over at her, wondering and calculating.

"He's my family," Ruthers said before anyone could object, "and my responsibility."

It wasn't the kind of thing Jane would have imagined Ruthers saying. The others looked equally dubious.

"Not to be crass, but you've made him the subject of collective interest," Father Isse said.

"Without me, he's of no use to you," Ruthers said. "He comes with me."

The others looked between one another with stoically forbearing expressions, their mouths pressed into thin lines.

"Take Roman, then. But you've no need of her," the Qadi said, nodding at Jane.

"She and I have a history," Ruthers said. "And she'll be useful for keeping Roman in line."

Jane's blood chilled.

The Qadi didn't meet Jane's eye. She said nothing further.

Lady Lachesse looked at the chancellor and Father Isse. "We need to move. The farmers have two days' head start. There's no telling what will happen if they reach the Library first."

Father Isse nodded, his spectacles winking in the lamplight, and Chancellor O'Brien folded his arms and grunted as if the hurry had been his idea in the first place.

But when Ruthers trudged off to one carriage, the nearest two guards nudged Jane and Roman toward the same. Lady Lachesse, Father Isse, and Chancellor O'Brien hurried toward the other, their voices lowered in urgent conference.

As Jane was packed away into the back of the coach, she stole one last glance back at the door to the Majlis. The Qadi stood beneath the ornate wooden frame, silhouetted by a faint halo of light.

Once the guards had chained her and Roman to the benches in the back compartment, the door slammed shut and the carriage pulled away.

A thin haze of light filtered into their compartment from a two-foot wide grill into the main section of the carriage. Jane looked at Roman, seated across from her, his eyes averted. They were, at last, alone together, though she couldn't guess for how long.

"It's going to take days to reach Recoletta like this," she said.

He looked up as if at a sudden noise. "They're taking us to the train station. About half an hour away. Supposedly, Sato's only blocked off one railway leading to the city."

"Then we don't have much time to talk," Jane said. Still, it seemed like as much as they'd ever had for their secret soirees at the Jeweled Pheasant.

He sighed. "What do you want to know?"

"Everything. Why did Sato leave Recoletta? What's going on at the Library? And what's this secret between you and Ruthers?"

He smiled in defeat. "That's a lot of everything."

"Not my fault. There's a lot you've been keeping from me."

"That goes both ways," he said, suddenly serious again. "You never told me you'd been meeting with Lady Lachesse."

"It didn't seem relevant at the time," Jane said, scowling and looking away. She knew it only made her seem guilty, but she was too angry to face the accusation in his eyes. He, of all people, had no right.

"Jane, if you'd told me–"

"You'd have done what?" she said, snapping her gaze back to him. "You'd have seen this all coming? You'd have found a way to turn it all around to your favor?"

He tried to raise his hands in a placating gesture, but the chains stopped them just short. "I'm not saying that. I'm just saying that you don't know these people as well as you think."

"Given what's happened with Sato in Recoletta, I don't think you do, either."

He fell silent. Already, Jane realized, they were getting hopelessly sidetracked.

"Let's take turns," she said. "I didn't tell you about Lady Lachesse before. But she approached me shortly before you and I met up. Told me she was trying to make the best of her exile and needed some inside information. It made sense enough, and I couldn't risk making an enemy of her. So I told her about my meetings with Bailey and the Qadi and about my official meetings with you." She paused. "I didn't mention your name, of course."

He nodded.

"Your turn," she said. "Start with Recoletta and the Library."

And so he told her about the rumor of marching farmers, a force that had begun moving south some forty-eight hours ago, gathering strength and spreading rumors as it passed from one commune to the next. Their numbers were estimated to be in the thousands now, and they were closing on the Library.

"What do they want with it?"

He shrugged. "No one's had the chance to ask them. Sato had ignored their requests for lower quotas and better opportunities. The chancellor thinks they mean to burn it down for spite. Ruthers is afraid they're going to dig around for their own secrets."

"What do you think?" Jane asked.

"All I know is that Sato's apparently left Recoletta to see to the Library personally. Which is why we're headed to Recoletta now."

"So that Ruthers can take back his throne."

Roman nodded haltingly.

"But that's not all," Jane said. "This is also about that secret you two share."

He looked over at her slowly. "Not much of a secret now."

"Then tell me. Because I'm apparently the last person who doesn't know."

He lowered his elbows to his knees and rested his forehead in the heels of his hands. "This is a long story."

Jane glanced through the grill at the guards rocking to and fro with the motion of the carriage. "You've got twenty minutes," she told Roman.

"Fine. But keep it down." He took a moment to rub circles into his forehead before looking up. "You know that my family came to Recoletta when I was very young." His voice was low.

"Yes," she said. Lady Lachesse had told her as much in Recoletta long ago.

"There was a reason we fled our home city. And a reason we made friends so fast."

"I thought you got your start in Recoletta because of Ruthers."

"In a way," he said. "That's certainly why we came to Recoletta of all places. The connection isn't that close – he's the youngest brother of my grandfather's brother's wife. At the time, he was our best chance."

"Best chance for what?"

"Escape." Roman paused and seemed to search for his next words somewhere in the wood grain behind Jane. "There aren't many things that have survived the Catastrophe. But the Library isn't the only one that did."

In the near-silence that followed, Jane heard only the shifting of guards in the main compartment. She was certain that no one else could hear Roman's whisper.

"There is a vault," he said, his voice soft. "A place where the peoples of old locked away some of their most potent weapons. Things that even they, in all their reckless savagery, didn't trust themselves with."

"And this... has something to do with you?" Jane tried to keep the tremor out of her own voice.

"With anyone directly related to my mother. Which, at this

point, is only me. There were two keys," he said, looking down at his manacled hands and running his thumb along one metal cuff. "One hidden in numbers and the other in blood. Whoever sealed the vault wanted to make certain that only a blood relative entrusted with the proper code could open it." He snorted a brief, humorless laugh. "I'm sure it made sense for the ancients, thinking all of those bulwarks of destructive power would protect their little empires forever. Now, it just means I'm entrusted with a key I don't want."

"But you don't know the code," Jane said.

"My parents did. I refused to learn it. But they taught others – that was the price of Ruthers's aid. And the reason for the Satos' friendship." He massaged his knuckles. "Ruthers is the only other one who knows now."

"Jakkeb Sato's parents told him?"

Roman shrugged. "Most likely. But he's never mentioned it. That was a condition of my agreement to support him."

"And a reason you were comfortable seeing him replace Ruthers," Jane said.

He only nodded. The carriage rattled on through quiet streets before Jane spoke again.

"Do you know what's in the vault?"

"No," he said quickly.

Given everything else he'd said about it, Jane suspected he was telling the truth. In either case, there was no point in pressing him on the subject.

He leaned forward, reaching for her hands. The chains stopped him short. "Damn it," he said. "I wish you'd trusted me."

Jane was taken aback by the emotion in his voice and the hopelessness in his eyes. She reminded herself that she'd done what she'd needed at the time. "Coming from you," she began. But the words tasted cold and bitter, and she swallowed the rest of them. "I've learned not to give away more than I have to," she said. "And I would imagine that's something you understand, too."

He laughed bitterly. "After my parents traded our independence for the illusion of safety? I'd say so. But I'd thought..." He sighed, rubbing his knuckles again and looking at the toes of his scuffed boots. "I'd hoped you were different."

Jane winced. "Circumstances change, Roman. People change."

He looked again at the manacles on his wrists. "I wish that were true."

CHAPTER 15

CONFRONTATIONS

Malone, the farmers, and the Revisionists reached the Library at sundown after almost three days of travel. They had begun with almost a hundred from Meyerston, but their group had snowballed as they'd continued south and east past other communes. Malone had stopped trying to count around Woodsey, but she estimated that they must have nearly a thousand. Word had it that more were gathering in their wake.

It was a larger, clumsier approach than Malone had planned, but the revolutionary enthusiasm proved contagious. By the end of it, they'd sequestered a train stopped outside Shepherd's Hollow to carry their swelling number the rest of the way to the Library. As busy as the routes between the cities had become, and as busy as the spies from the cities had gotten, such bold maneuvers hadn't remained hidden for long – a small advance force had staked out the Library and revealed that Sato had beaten them by a day.

The faces of the men and women around her were flushed with exhaustion and exhilaration. She only hoped that their momentum would carry them forward even as they hunkered down for what could be a wearyingly long or a violently short stay.

And, looking at the curling rows of razor wire that stretched between their encampment and the Library, she feared the stay might be longer than her cohorts had expected.

The dome of the Library rose against the darkening sky, much as she'd remembered it. Sato's soldiers crawled across the hill and between the barricades of rubble and ruin that lay along the path to the Library. They were making their presence conspicuous, she suspected, but they'd kept their distance.

The multitude with Malone was large enough to present a danger even to several squads of armed troops. And Malone could only hope they'd positioned themselves far enough away to be safe from Sato's Greek fire.

Farrah approached from the edge of the crowd, her swift, decisive stride distinct even in the growing darkness. But she still hadn't grown accustomed to the outdoors – she hunched her shoulders and lowered her head like a cat doused in water.

"More of the same all the way around," Farrah said, drawing close. A musk of sweat and smoke hung around her, the odor of days of travel. Malone suspected that she smelled the same. "Guards, barricades, razor wire. Looked like a few spots had even been dug up."

"Land mines?" Malone asked.

"Probably."

"There's got to be someplace where the defenses are a little thinner," Malone said.

Farrah shrugged. "There's a narrower passage off to the east. Still guarded and fortified, mind you, but if I were going to send a small group in under the cover of darkness, that's where I'd do it. Of course," she said, looking toward the broad, trap-strewn field ahead of them, "if you sent a larger group – say, a few hundred – this would be the place to do it. It'd be messy, but there's no way Sato's traps or his troops could stop them all. Enough would get through."

Farrah was right, but something in Malone's gut tightened. She'd seen enough massacres lately that the thought of another turned her stomach. "We'll find another way," Malone said.

Farrah nodded, her features and her posture relaxing.

Other footsteps, heavy but no less quick, pounded toward her. Malone turned to see Salazar hurrying toward her, another man she'd seen a handful of times trailing just behind him.

"Trains approaching from the northwest," he said. "They'll be here any minute now."

"Any idea whose?" Farrah asked.

"They all look the same from here," he said.

The three looked at one another. They wouldn't have to wait long to find out.

"Farrah, round up Attrop and Clothoe and meet me on that ridge," Malone said, pointing to a rise half a mile away that sheltered their camp from the train tracks. "Salazar, get a few of your people to keep a lookout, but don't cause a stir. We'll check it out together."

Malone trudged up the hill, choosing her steps carefully in the gathering dark. The slope was rugged and uneven, but the night was clear enough that Malone could see her destination as a lip rising just below a field of brightening stars. Only the low hum of conversation rose from the plain behind her. Malone had been adamant that they avoid campfires and anything else that could make their position easy to target from a distance, and to her great surprise, Salazar had communicated her request and his farmers had complied.

She reached the top and savored the cool breeze that swept the crest, the wide vista stretching all around her, and the dull ache in her legs. The endless expanse, with everything laid bare, haunted and enchanted her. She looked below and beyond her hill to where tracks stretched away from the main rail line and to a makeshift depot. Sato had ordered it built to facilitate travel to and from the Library.

Whoever Salazar's scout had seen in the distance was just pulling in amidst shuddering black iron and groans of steam.

"Who's it look like?" Farrah asked, climbing up behind Malone. Attrop and Clothoe followed behind her, two heaving, gasping presences.

"We'll find out soon," Malone said.

More footsteps crunched up the hill. "Now, we're going to be stuck with Sato on one side of us and these people on the other," Salazar said. "All we need is a small group to slip past the Library's defenses. He may expect something, but he won't know when or where."

Malone heard the scowl in Farrah's voice. "I'm sure the troops on that train days ago thought the same thing about fifteen minutes before they were roasted alive."

"Sato snuck an entire army into Recoletta under the Council's nose," Attrop said. "We won't get him by surprise."

"Someone's yet to explain how we are supposed to get him," Salazar said.

"Look," Malone said, pointing down toward the train. It was almost half a mile away, but shadows of movement stretched and spread around it. They moved with oiled precision, and she heard nothing more than the distant roll of train car doors.

"Seems like a lot of them," Farrah said. At least a dozen cars were strung along behind the engine, and they all appeared to be shedding personnel. The farmers still outnumbered the newcomers, but if these were armed and trained soldiers – as Malone was beginning to expect – their numbers would be a poor advantage.

"Reinforcements from Recoletta?" Salazar asked.

"If they were, they wouldn't be moving so quietly," Attrop said. "This is someone else. A force from one of the neighboring cities, most likely."

"The same neighbors who sent a trainload of troops to Recoletta before you people left?"

Attrop gave a low, quiet laugh. "You're learning, dear boy."

A throaty sigh came from Salazar's direction. "What I want to know is whether they're friend or foe to us."

"That probably depends," said Attrop.

"Then we need to move camp. Pack up our people and get

some distance before they find us," he said.

"We'll do no such thing. The five of us need to lie low until we've figured out how we'll get to Sato. That these newcomers might stumble upon the camp is simply a risk we'll have to take."

"Like hell we will," Salazar said, his voice rising. He turned and pointed back down the hill. "They're less than a mile away. Those are my people. My responsibility. They–"

"They knew the risks when they came along," Attrop said. "And now, you need to decide whether your priority is stopping Sato or protecting them."

Salazar fell silent. Malone could feel him fuming, but Attrop was right, and he knew it. No one else said anything for several moments.

"I'll go," Malone finally said. "It would help us get to Sato if we at least knew what they were up to."

"Good luck to you, then," Attrop said.

Malone looked at the older woman and the contours of her arched eyebrows and dismissive frown. "You're coming with me," she said.

"I beg your pardon?"

"If these are representatives from other cities, you're more likely to recognize them."

"I admire your pluck, but the field down there is crawling with soldiers. If they hear us–"

"Then you'd better be quiet," Malone said. "Farrah, keep an eye on things here. Hopefully, this won't take long."

They set off down the hill, cleaving to a line of trees that tumbled down toward the train tracks. For all her protestations, Attrop proved silent and nimble. The woman had shed her skirts and ruffles for spare corduroy trousers from Meyerston when the march had begun, and she moved easily enough in them. They were down the hill and crouching in the foliage some two hundred feet from the train in less than twenty minutes.

Men and women in gray uniforms had filed out of the cars

to bind together as disparate parts of some collective organism. Several rows of the straight-backed figures formed a layer of tissue around the train while others raked the grass like probing fingers. So far, they'd ignored the copse where Malone hid with Attrop. In any case the thicket seemed deep enough to give them room to retreat if the soldiers ventured closer.

Then, as if at some silent, invisible command, the patrols returned to the train. A signal spread from the sentries to the troops and on toward the middle car of the train like an impulse jumping synapses. At last, the door of a middle carriage opened, and out stepped three figures, backlit from within the compartment.

Attrop raised her head, bracing herself against a slender tree trunk. "I don't believe it," she said.

"What?"

"It's her," Attrop said between clenched teeth. "Lachesse."

The three figures had moved away from the glare in the carriage, and Malone could make them out more clearly now: a slender, bald, dark-skinned man in a fitted black cassock; a bearded man who wore a finer version of the gray uniform the troops wore; and a woman about Attrop's age, sturdy and substantial in her wide skirts.

Malone looked to her side and saw murder in Attrop's eyes. "Control it," she muttered.

Lachesse and the two other figures standing in the pool of light exchanged whispers and retreated back to the train compartment as decisively as they'd left it. Malone shot Attrop a hard glare, and the older woman followed her deeper into the woods. They stopped behind a thick screen of trees, well out of earshot of the train.

"You know these people?" Malone asked.

"I know the woman. A whitenail from the old days."

"Does that change things?"

"You mean can we trust her? Absolutely not." Attrop directed her icy stare at the undergrowth, and Malone wondered whether she could trust the woman's embittered assessment.

"What does she want?" Malone asked.

Attrop shook her head. "Sato. A seat on a reconstituted Council. A night's diversion. Could be any, all, or none of the above."

Malone thought back to the two men. "Did you recognize the others?"

"The leaders of other cities. The Hollow and Underlake, most likely. Lachesse has been busy making useful friends." She looked slowly back at Malone.

"Yet this Lachesse isn't with us."

"No. But her useful friends could be."

"To get to Sato, you mean," Malone said.

Attrop nodded.

"They'd never cooperate with the farmers."

The older woman gave her a slow shrug. "It's like I said before. How badly do you want to stop Sato? You may not be able to save everyone."

The words struck Malone like a hammer blow. As much as she hated to admit it, there was a cruel logic to the idea. And yet she couldn't help but wonder how much of Attrop's suggestion came from days of simmering in silence alongside the farmers, of looking for an escape from the unsuitable alliance they presented.

Besides, there was a simpler, cleaner option. If the city leaders had come with a trainload of troops, it was because they already had a plan. One that did not involve the thousand farmers.

Unless they had come to resolve both threats – Sato and the communes – at once.

Too late, Malone realized that she couldn't allow Attrop to reach the train.

"Over here," the older woman called, rising to her feet. "In the forest." A thunder of shouts and running feet answered Attrop's cries, and she held her empty hands over her head. "I'd raise my arms if I were you," she said. "They sound nervous."

Malone mirrored the other woman's posture, scowling and

cursing herself for setting her own trap. Fifteen seconds later, soldiers crashed through the foliage, their weapons pointed at Malone and Attrop.

"Don't move!" one soldier said. In a classic example of overkill, he and half of the squadron kept their weapons trained on Malone and Attrop while the other half either patted them down for weapons, bound their wrists, or stood by and observed the process.

And then they were marched back toward the train, through a parting cluster of soldiers. The door to the middle carriage was already open by the time they arrived. They received a final pat-down before they were ushered inside.

The two men and the woman who had stepped out of the train minutes ago were seated around a low, carved table, a teapot and curving glasses between them. The men eyed Malone, but the woman's eyes flew directly to Attrop.

"I was wondering when I'd see you again," Lachesse, the woman, said. "How obliging of you to join us."

"And I'm glad you finally returned," Attrop said.

Malone felt the barb even without understanding the nature of their bitter history. Yet Lachesse deflected it with a cool smile. "Manners, Francine," she said to Attrop. "You haven't introduced us to your new friend."

"Malone, this is Lady Myra Lachesse, formerly of Recoletta. Myra, this is Chief Liesl Malone."

"And this is Chancellor O'Brien and Father Isse," Lachesse said, motioning to the two men. "And now comes the moment when we ask what you two are doing here."

Malone didn't like allowing Attrop to do all of the talking, but she felt the barrel of a rifle in her side when she opened her mouth to speak.

"We're here to stop Sato," Attrop said.

"It's the thought that counts," Lachesse said after a pause. "I'm afraid your presence here is superfluous. Then again, you knew that when you called the soldiers, didn't you?"

With a flash of frustration, Malone knew where the discussion was headed, just as she knew that she was powerless to stop it. "You can't–" she began, only to feel a sharp blow between her shoulder blades. She fell to her knees, coughing, while Attrop continued unruffled.

"Sato's only half of your problem. I can give you the farmers. They're camped out here. Not far away," Attrop said.

There was a long silence around the table as Lachesse and the two men looked at one another. "You presume to give us what we can take ourselves?" said the bearded man, Chancellor O'Brien.

"You can mow down the camp without my help if that's what you're suggesting," Attrop said, sneering at the man. "You'll only succeed in crippling the workforce. One you'll need if you're to avoid exacerbating the food crisis in Recoletta."

"What exactly are you offering?" Father Isse asked, his hands folded in his lap.

"Their leader. The firebrand who's kept them united. Eliminate him, and the rest of the resistance will fall."

"She's wrong," Malone said, pulling herself to her feet again. "Almost a thousand farmers have come. The strike is bigger than any one person now. Taking action against them will only galvanize them."

The three seated figures looked again at one another in silent conference.

"You think destroying one man will break the rebellion?" Father Isse asked Attrop.

"That's why you've come to the Library in the first place, isn't it? To destroy one man? Besides, for every one who's come with us," Attrop said, "three have stayed in the communes. I've traveled with these people for days. They will not be so hard to convince."

Malone could see Attrop's logic working on them, deepening their thoughtful frowns.

"Let me bring him to you," Attrop said. "I can convince him to come without a fight."

"And what do you expect in return for your kind assistance?" Father Isse asked.

Attrop glared at Lachesse. "Whatever you've promised her."

Lachesse arched one contemptuous eyebrow but said nothing.

"Bring him here, then," Isse said, nodding at the door.

Attrop left, but not without a dubious glance over her shoulder. There had been no promise in Isse's tone, but she had little choice but to trust her new bedfellows now.

"You're making a mistake," Malone said when she was sure Attrop was out of earshot.

"That's what someone in your position always says," Lachesse said, inscrutable and sipping her tea.

"You really trust her?" Malone asked.

"Of course not. But I trust her motives. Ambition is always predictable."

"Her ambitions won't end here. You're setting her up right beside you."

"There will be enough to go around once Recoletta's back in order," Lachesse said. "Besides, I could use a little help running the Library."

Malone laughed. "Is that what you think she wants? She and Clothoe came to burn it."

Lachesse's face turned a shade paler.

"Besides, you're gambling on Attrop's assessment," Malone said. "If she's wrong about the farmers, you'll only harden them against you."

"As if they aren't already set against us," the chancellor said.

"Right now, they want a deal," Malone said. "But if you shoot them like dogs, they'll go on the offensive. And you're surrounded by them."

The notion wrinkled brows and tightened mouths.

"So you'd have us gamble on your assessment instead," Lachesse said.

"It's the least risky of the two," Malone said. "You need them."

The three leaders said nothing more, and Malone kept quiet, hoping her logic was working on them in the silence. Sooner than she would have liked, quick footsteps plodded through the wet grass outside. Attrop climbed the stairs into the carriage, followed by Salazar, who grimaced as he looked at the three seated figures.

Then he looked at Malone and her cuffed hands, and his pupils narrowed to pinpricks.

"So this is the fierce firebrand," Lachesse said. "Pleased to make your acquaintance."

Salazar turned back to the older woman. "I hear you lot have a plan. One that requires the farmers' assistance," he said. Malone heard little conviction in his voice.

"That is one way of putting it," said Lachesse.

"Another is that you're about to trade problems with Sato for problems with the folk harvesting your food," he said.

Lachesse smiled, but the corner of her mouth twitched.

"And you've brought, what, a couple hundred soldiers?" he asked. "They won't get you any closer to the Library. Whole perimeter's sown with mines and strung with razor wire."

"Are you volunteering to march your own fellows through the barricades?" Father Isse asked.

"We've hung back for a reason," Salazar said. "Just giving you a little friendly advice."

"How kind of you," O'Brien said.

In the pause that followed, Malone read smug satisfaction and a strange sense of irony. "You've already sent a force to breach the Library," she said.

"There's no time to waste, and we've the cover of night on our side," O'Brien said.

"Are you crazy?" Malone asked. "You saw what Sato did the last time you sent soldiers to his gates."

"It's a risky operation, but the chancellor's soldiers are the best," Father Isse said. "Besides, Sato wouldn't dare try that tactic here. He won't risk destroying the Library."

"A few months ago, you would have said the same thing about Recoletta," Malone said.

Her comment drew sober expressions from the group around the table, but neither Lachesse nor the city leaders said anything.

Finally, Chancellor O'Brien sat forward, scowling behind folded hands. "No sense delaying this further," he said. Two soldiers approached Salazar, grabbing his arms.

"Wait!" Malone said. "Just listen."

The soldiers looked at the chancellor, who held up a hand.

"You don't need to do this now," Malone said. "If your soldiers get through to Sato, you can deal with Salazar then. In the meantime, there's no reason to get rid of someone who could be useful."

The chancellor's beard bristled with a scowl. Yet Father Isse gave the faintest of grins. "She speaks wisely."

Attrop looked from the seated group back to Malone. "This is foolishness. She's stalling you so that she can escape with him."

"Francine, don't get overwrought. Even the good Chief Malone can't possibly evade a hundred of the chancellor's finest, much less with a friend in tow," Lachesse said as Attrop fumed.

"I'm inclined to agree," said Isse.

"Fine," said O'Brien. "We'll wait until–"

Someone was approaching the train car at a swift trot. Murmurs rose from the troops stationed outside the door, low and ominous. The man who clomped his way into the compartment was panting, his breaths as ragged as the torn and frayed edges of his uniform.

The three conspirators around the table drew back, their eyes wide with apprehension.

"Report," Chancellor O'Brien said.

"We were unable to break through to the Library, sir," the man said. His eyes were red, filled with the horror and humiliation of defeat. "We took fire as we pushed toward the building. We returned shots and suppressed most of their attacks. But when we reached the wall of the building, we... they..." He cleared his throat. "They poured something onto us. Like liquid fire. Threw capsules of the stuff behind us to block our retreat. It clung to whatever it touched – stone, metal, everything." He fell silent for a moment, his mouth opening and closing wordlessly. "Most of the troops were bunched up around the building, taking cover by the wall. Got covered in it. Barely a dozen of us made it back."

The chancellor leaned forward, gripping the arms of his chair. "Out of the original force of ninety, only a dozen of you survived?"

"Fourteen precisely, sir." The soldier looked down.

"What about the Library?" Lachesse asked. "Did it take damage?"

"Hard to say, madam. A corner of the wall was hit with that fire. Most of the stuff hit the ground. But it was still blazing when I lost sight of it."

"Brick and stone," Chancellor O'Brien said, looking at Lachesse. "Even Sato's fire can't breach it." He didn't sound convinced.

"That's not the point," she said, rubbing the back of one long thumbnail. "It's a message. He'll let this place go up in flames before he surrenders it."

"Perhaps we should adjust our priorities," O'Brien said.

Lachesse looked at him sharply. "The only thing we're changing is our approach. Malone was right. You can't breach Sato's defenses through sheer force."

"We could with heavy munitions," said O'Brien.

"Don't be absurd. You'll make a mess of the Library. Nothing more."

"I suppose you have a better idea?"

"I do," Malone said. Attrop, Salazar, the soldiers, and the trio at the table looked at her, their faces betraying various shades of anger, hope, and curiosity.

"Please share," Father Isse said.

"Sato's going to notice a big crowd," Malone said, remembering Farrah's earlier suggestion. "But we found a smaller approach off to the east. A squadron of soldiers wouldn't make it, but one or two people might."

"Only to be surrounded by Sato's forces in the Library," Chancellor O'Brien said, frowning.

"Which might not be a problem if Sato has reason to trust them," Father Isse said. "Do I understand you correctly, Chief Malone?"

Attrop shook her head. "You've been absent from Recoletta for days," she said. "Sato's as likely to execute you on sight."

Malone had considered this. It remained a strong possibility. "Perhaps not. If I bring him someone he's more interested in." She turned to Salazar, who looked back and gave her a faint nod.

"Preposterous," Chancellor O'Brien said. "You could bring anyone to Sato and call the poor sap any name you'd like."

"Are you volunteering?" Salazar asked.

The chancellor stiffened in his chair, looking away from the younger man.

"Sato's met all sorts," Malone said. "He brought all sorts with him to Recoletta. It won't take much to prove that this man's a farmer. Especially not when he sent me to deal with them in the first place."

"Sato will see what he wants to believe," Lachesse said, nodding. "He always has, anyway."

"And he's going to believe that his absentee chief of police has just sauntered into the Library, escorting the one man he wants executed?" O'Brien jabbed a finger at Malone and Salazar, his face turning red.

Father Isse smiled placidly. "It's certainly more likely than his absentee chief of police staking her life as part of an elaborate ruse."

Attrop made a swiping motion with one splayed, thick-fingered hand. "The bigger problem is getting Malone inside. None of this will matter if Sato's guards shoot her from the rooftops, and let's be honest, that's the likeliest outcome of this farce."

"That's why we'll need a distraction," Salazar said. "One my farmers can provide."

The gathering turned their attention to him.

"We're almost a thousand strong. That's plenty to spread around the western perimeter and keep Sato's guards busy. Especially if we light a few torches and make some noise."

"You'll have to do more than that to hold their attention," Lachesse said, her eyes narrowed to slits. "This will be costly for your people."

Salazar rolled his shoulders back, setting his mouth in a grim frown. "We've paid costs already. You give us your guarantee of a fair deal, and we'll do our part to get rid of Sato."

"You'd sacrifice your own people to solve a problem between the cities?" Attrop asked, her arms crossed.

"This problem is bigger than the cities," Salazar said. "I thought I'd made that clear."

Father Isse tented his fingers. "Say we accept your help. How do you know we'll keep our word?"

"You can't afford not to. When word gets round you threw a thousand of us at Sato's barricades only to betray us, you'll have an even bigger problem on your hands." Salazar looked at the assembled group, his eyes bright and angry. "You act as if we'll disappear if you ignore us long enough. But even if you deny us, betray us, how long will you have before another group of us bands together and rises up? A year? Five years? One way or another, it'll happen. You just have to decide what it's going to cost you." He glared at Attrop. "And how much you care about stopping Sato in the meantime."

After a long silence, Father Isse spoke up. "Then it seems we are decided. The remainder of the chancellor's forces can keep Sato's guards busy here, on the northern end."

Chancellor O'Brien only furrowed his brow.

Salazar nodded. "I'll need to speak with my people. Tell them the plan."

"Then there's no time to lose. Hurry, while darkness is on our side," Father Isse said.

Attrop looked from Salazar to Father Isse. "You can't mean to let him just walk out of here."

"I must if we mean to confront Sato."

"This is foolish. Nothing stops him from melting back into his group and disappearing."

Father Isse shared a long look with Salazar. "Nothing but the promise of stopping Sato. And the threat of the status quo." He looked back over at Attrop before she could speak again. "And you shall nevertheless have your promised reward."

Attrop said nothing further, and Malone left with Salazar before anyone else could object.

They made their way back up the hill. Malone didn't dare check over her shoulder until they were halfway up the rise, and when she did, she was surprised to see the chancellor's soldiers still clustered around the train.

Salazar hadn't said a word since they'd left the train. Malone cleared her throat. "I'm sorry for dragging you into this," she said. "And for volunteering you without–"

"What's the difference?" he said. "Way I see it, they wanted to kill me, and so will Sato. At least this way, we've got a fighting chance. Let's leave it at that."

Malone nodded and did exactly that.

Farrah was waiting for them when they reached the top of the hill. "What the hell happened down there? We were talking about sending a larger group after you, and then we saw fires by the Library..."

"Long story," Malone said, noticing Dalton, Cabral, and Macmillan hovering nearby, along with a small knot of farmers. "Where's Clothoe?"

"Sleeping," Dalton said. "The march took it out of her. Is something–"

"Have someone keep an eye on them," Malone said, pointing to the three Revisionists. She turned to Farrah. "We need to talk."

"I'll round up the rest of the leaders," Salazar said, trotting down the hill towards camp. The waiting farmers surrounded the three baffled Revisionists and gently, but firmly, guided them down the hill after Salazar.

Farrah gripped Malone's arm. "What's going on? And what is that?" she asked, pointing toward the Library.

Malone looked and saw a faint orange glow and a thread of flame running up one corner of the building. "That's what we're up against. What Salazar's farmers are going to have to draw away from us."

"From you and Salazar? While you do what, exactly?"

"We're going into the Library. After Sato."

Farrah blinked. "That's insane."

Malone hoped that Salazar's conference with his associates would save her from having the same conversation yet again. "It's our only option," she said.

"Not much of one," Farrah said.

For a long time, neither of them said anything. Malone watched the fire that still burned at the distant corner of the building and tried not to think about what she was about to do. Behind her, the camp murmured and rustled.

"Are you prepared for this?" Farrah asked.

Malone shrugged. "It can't be that much worse than infiltrating smugglers' nests. Or crossing Bricklayer territory." It felt odd now, using that name. Even those memories from the last couple of weeks had begun to feel distant.

"That's not what I mean. If you do this, you're going to have to kill Sato."

That was what Malone had avoided contemplating. And yet as Farrah said it, the realization crept up on her with a prickling of cold sweat. She had served Sato for over six months. She'd marched into Recoletta with him, and since then, she'd kept order in his name. He would have succeeded without her, but her presence at his side had given him legitimacy. The Municipal Police had been known as honest brokers before his revolution, and as one of the most senior surviving inspectors, she'd held the organization together.

And she'd done it without asking Sato too many questions, because Recoletta had needed a leader and so had she. At the time, anyone had seemed like an improvement over the openly corrupt Ruthers.

Killing Sato now meant that the last six months had been a crime in which she was complicit.

Malone almost told Farrah that, yes, she had considered and made peace with the idea, or that she was not convinced it would be necessary, but she worried that hearing the fragile lie from her own lips would shatter what resolve remained to her.

So she said nothing and waited for Salazar to return.

The moon had achieved a few arduous inches by the time Salazar trotted back up the hill. Malone turned back toward the camp, where shadows scurried amidst the low hum of hurried activity.

"No sense waiting around. They'll be in place by the time we get to the east side of the building," he said, jerking his head toward the bustle below.

"Let's go," Malone said.

"Wait." Farrah took a step forward. "Should I come with you? Might help your story if Sato sees two of us..."

Malone could hear both the hesitance and the sincerity of Farrah's offer. "Stay here," she said. "Sato will either believe me or he won't. In the meantime, I need you to keep an eye on the Revisionists. Attrop's defected, and I don't know about Clothoe or the others. Just see that the farmers get their due when this is finished."

"You got it," Farrah said, looking into the wet grass. "Just be careful."

Malone turned down the hill with Salazar, cutting through the camp. The farmers were busy organizing themselves into squads and passing around torches, barrels of pitch, and other cobbled-together flammables. They took no notice of the pair, which was just as well for Malone. She and Salazar passed through the camp and into the debris field beyond without once exchanging words with anyone.

The Library loomed a mile away, an ominous fixed point as they made their slow circle. With its wild, broken angles and knotty humps and tufts of earth rising around it, it looked almost like a watchful, wounded beast. It seemed worthwhile to keep to a conservative distance and the cover of ancient, overgrown rubble until they were ready to make their approach.

"There," Salazar said. "Farrah's eastern approach is just beyond that broken wall." He pointed to a cleft in the darkness. He'd been quiet since descending from the hill, but Malone recognized the nervous edge in his voice from a hundred abrupt, pre-raid chitchats in the old days.

They reached the wall and its sheltered nook in ten minutes. Malone looked back in the direction of the camp to the horizon smoldering. She could just hear the din of the farmers' assault on the perimeter.

"It's started," Salazar said. "You ready for this?" His forehead glistened in the moonlight.

"I should be asking you," Malone said.

"Well, don't. I might just change my mind."

They turned toward the Library, skulking through the shadows.

The approach Farrah had mentioned was indeed narrow, which perhaps explained the broad passages between the sparsely strung razor wire and the few and well-spaced mounds of dirt that marked land mines. Moving carefully but steadily, Malone estimated they'd be able to make it to one shadowed wall of the Library in another ten or fifteen minutes.

"Let's go," Malone said.

Salazar hesitated, peering at the faintly silvered landscape ahead. "Remind me why we aren't just approaching with a white flag."

"Because I wouldn't count on anyone seeing it," Malone said. "Not at this time of night and especially not after the soldiers' earlier incursion. But Sato's troops will know me up close. I just don't want to give them any bright ideas about disarming me."

Salazar grunted and grumbled but said nothing, following her down the approach.

They settled into a comfortable rhythm, ducking under wires and taking careful, exaggerated steps over suspicious patches of earth. Proceeding behind Malone, Salazar was careful to follow her every step, and his movements were just as quiet as hers. She took strange comfort in knowing that death would be swift and sudden if they made a mistake. And such an error was more likely to come from her miscalculation than his clumsiness.

By the time she looked up from the winding, treacherous path to judge their progress, they were halfway to the Library. Flames still singed the distant horizon, and though the noise from the Library had grown louder, it was clear enough that it was focused on other sides of the building.

However, she and Salazar were getting close enough that any guards stationed at their end would be able to spot them without too much difficulty. Malone concentrated on pressing forward, keeping low.

She saw barricades built against the Library wall as she peeled through the last layers of Sato's defenses. She stopped, holding a hand out behind her for Salazar to do likewise.

Yet as she looked around, she saw no movement and no colors beyond the dimmed neutrals of brick and stone. Most of the firing seemed to be coming from the roof, anyway.

Malone turned back to Salazar. "Let's go," she whispered.

He pulled himself out of a painful-looking crouch. "Shouldn't you have a gun to my head or something?"

"Plenty of time for that later." Malone looked back at the Library just in time to see a shadow crawling to the nearby corner. "Hurry!" she hissed to Salazar.

They scurried over open ground and behind the barricade just as voices reached them from around the corner. Malone heard the steady deliberate footsteps of a patrol approaching.

"Still nothing over here," a man said. "They're all throwing themselves against the wires on the other sides."

"Then this ought to be quick," came another voice, a woman's.

They moved quickly, like two people ready to be done with their task. Malone took stock of their cover – it was little more than a low, broken wall that zigzagged around them on three sides. It should be just enough as long as the two weren't thorough.

Malone crouched on all fours, pressed against the barricade and facing the direction of the approaching patrol. She felt a sudden tug at her ankle and turned her head to see Salazar, pointing frantically at something.

She looked. Halfway down the wall was a window nestled at ground level. The rest had been boarded up or buried in rubble or bricked over. But there, just a few dozen yards away, was the telltale shimmer of glass.

Salazar tugged at her trouser leg again, as if she'd somehow failed to notice.

Malone shook her head as emphatically as she dared. She held up a finger and pointed in the direction of the guards, who were just about to draw level with them on the other side of the barrier.

"...don't understand the point," said the man.

"They've got numbers," the woman said. "They think they'll make it through if they push hard enough."

"So will they?"

There was a long silence. "We're here to make sure they don't." Even as Malone heard the woman's words, she heard the dull resignation behind them.

Malone had turned and was following Salazar now, creeping from one jagged section of wall to the next. The window grew ever closer.

"But what if they do?" the male guard asked.

"Enough," the woman said. "If you want to know so badly, go ask Sato yourself."

That silenced the argument, and Malone had only the sound of their footsteps to follow as they marched through the gravel.

"Stop," said the man. "What's that?"

"What's what?" the woman asked, turning to some point behind Malone.

"There. Tracks."

Malone felt a curse form behind her lips.

"Ours?" the woman asked.

"Don't think so. Look at the shape of that boot."

"Shit."

Malone felt as though the other woman might have been speaking for her. She turned back to Salazar just in time to see him kneeling, his arm wound back.

Before she could stop him, he hurled something toward the far end of the barricade. It clacked against the stone.

"There!" the woman said. She and her partner hurried back past Malone and toward the sound of the disturbance.

As soon as their backs were turned, Salazar crawled toward the window, beckoning Malone with one arm. She had no choice but to follow.

Salazar wedged his fingers under the pane and slid it open. Malone glanced in the direction of the two guards, but they were still nothing more than indistinct blobs in the darkness, moving steadily away. Salazar slid in through the window, and Malone followed him.

She found herself on a tile floor next to a balcony. Lights shone from further down the hall, but there was no sign of activity nearby. Malone checked that the area around them was clear before easing the window shut behind her.

"Which way?" Salazar asked.

"Around and up," Malone said. It was a hunch, but it felt right. They found the stairs and made their way upwards. Voices and lamplight spilled down the steps.

Malone took a deep breath. "Here's where I put a gun to your back," she said.

Salazar stopped and held his hands out behind him, saying

nothing as Malone fastened cuffs around his wrists. The snapping, clinking metal sounded impossibly loud.

She grabbed the back of his collar and eased him forward. "Time to see if this works."

He half-turned back to face her. "Thank you," he whispered.

She stopped. "For what?"

"For giving us a chance. Fighting for us."

Something squeezed the breath out of Malone's throat. "Come on." Her voice was a warm rasp.

Two of Sato's guards found them as they reached the top landing.

"Stay back! What are you doing here?" cried a young man, clean-shaven and ruddy-cheeked. He already had a bayonet raised and pointed at Malone.

"Put that gun away, soldier," Malone said, mustering as much authority as she could. "I'm still your chief of police."

The young man and his companion lowered their guns, chins trembling. "I'm so sorry, Chief," said one. "I–"

Just then, more soldiers spread into the hall from the adjacent rooms. From among them came a voice as hard as iron. "What's going on in here?"

The troops parted around General Covas, whose eyes were hollow but alert.

Malone hadn't expected to see Covas, but it meant that their plan of drawing Sato's attention away from Recoletta had worked even better than she and the farmers had thought. Perhaps too well, depending on the extent of Covas's loyalties to Sato. But the general had always been difficult to read, and her apparent exhaustion did not make matters any easier.

Malone stepped forward, gripping Salazar even tighter. "I'm bringing him in to Sato."

Covas's face registered a shifting spectrum of emotions – surprise, anger, mistrust – each delayed by microseconds. "How did you get in?" she finally asked.

"The hard way. Let me see Sato."

Covas's brows lowered over tired eyes. "He's not expecting you."

"He'll want to see me. And he'll want to see my guest, Salazar."

The other woman's eyes kindled with recognition, and she looked at Malone's quarry. "Salazar..."

"This could all be over soon," Malone said, watching Covas's expression. She thought she saw hope. Relief.

Resignation.

"This way," Covas said. She led Malone and Salazar down the hall while the soldiers behind them murmured and looked on.

Salazar said nothing as they marched down the hall, but Malone saw the hairs and gooseflesh rise along the back of his neck.

"I'm surprised Sato brought you out here," Malone said.

Covas shot her a sharp look. "What's that supposed to mean?"

"Means he's left Recoletta unprotected."

Covas turned her shoulder to Malone. "He has his priorities." Her tone was carefully neutral.

"Priorities that mean leaving the city he fought for undefended?"

"Take it up with him yourself. I'm just trying to get us out of here in one piece," Covas said, stopping in front of wide double doors. They were already open.

Sato stood at a window, his profile lit up by the fires burning outside. Malone risked a glance through the nearest window and saw the ruined field in front of the Library alive with flames and running, raging, convulsing bodies.

Sato only slowly peeled his attention away from the scene to glare at Malone. "Where have you been?"

"Busy with the task you gave me among the farmers." She looked him in the eye and forced herself not to blink or flinch.

He did not look at her captive. "Then you must forgive my concern at your sudden and unexplained absence," Sato said. "You left us rather short-handed in Recoletta."

Malone swallowed. "An opportunity presented itself. One of the commune representatives surfaced. I thought it would be a chance to learn what they were up to, but by the time I realized what was going on, we were on the move. I had to wait for a chance to act."

"And so you marched down here with a thousand farmers and gave me no warning?"

Malone angled her head at the fire-bright window. "Forgive me. I thought a thousand farmers marching was a warning."

He uttered a short, grunting laugh.

"Allow me to present Salazar. Of Meyerston." Malone couldn't see Salazar's face, but the back of his neck was fever-hot and drenched with sweat.

Sato's eyes lighted, but he frowned. "I ordered you to kill him, not to bring him here."

The muscles in the back of Salazar's neck twitched under Malone's hand, but he didn't react otherwise. "A battlefield martyr does you no good," she said. "Not like a runaway. Or a traitor."

Sato was still and silent for several seconds. Finally, the corners of his mouth spasmed upwards. "Well done, Chief."

She saw approval, complacency, and trust in that smile. The doubts that she'd pushed to the back of her mind raced to the front, and she wondered whether she could go through with this. She released her grip on the back of Salazar's collar as Sato's gaze swiveled from her to some point behind her.

"You may go, Covas," Sato said.

Malone heard the door snick shut behind her. Muted footsteps receded down the hall, and then all behind her was quiet. Only she, Sato, and Salazar remained.

She was conscious of their isolation not as an absence, but as a presence in and of itself. The air seemed tangibly thick all of a sudden, and every movement – from the twitching of Salazar's bound hands to the smooth, reptilian jerks of Sato's head as he looked from her to Salazar and back to the scene outside – sent ripples and vibrations through the room. It felt as if the air had congealed around her right hand, freezing it at her side. Even if she could reach toward her gun, it seemed as though the movement would be impossible to hide.

Sato grinned. "Don't look so anxious. Those farmers will wear themselves out on the barricades eventually," he said. "As the troops on the other side already did. When that happens, I can send a smaller force to lob a few barrels of spreading fire into their camp to clear the rest of them out. And then, of course, we'll put your prize to good use." He nodded at Salazar.

"And then back to Recoletta?"

"Yes. Back to Recoletta and peace at last." He looked back at her, smiling, and she felt her resolve flutter and waver all over again. It was an enticing promise. "We'll still have the other cities to deal with, but they'll be more cautious now. I'm beginning to doubt that Arnault has been entirely productive on that front, but perhaps we can put your skills to good use again. You've certainly proven full of surprises."

"I assure you, everything I've done has been for–"

He waved a hand. "I'm not talking about your loyalties. I know you're committed to Recoletta. It's your resolve I was worried about."

Hairs rose along the back of her neck. "My what?"

"Your will. Your determination. Your ability to do what's necessary even when it's unpleasant." He looked to Salazar. "You just needed time and incentive."

Malone's revolver was raised and pointed at Sato before she realized she'd even drawn it.

He looked up, and he had just enough time to register the gun in her hand and wrinkle his brow in confusion before she fired.

There was a crack, and one corner of Sato's head erupted. He fell to the carpet, still.

Salazar turned to look at her, his body tensed. Slowly, he let out a great, shuddering sigh.

The door burst open behind Malone. Covas and four of her soldiers rushed in, their pistols drawn. They looked from Malone and Salazar to the prone body on the floor.

Malone raised her hands – not in surrender but rather in placation. Salazar slowly turned next to her, seemingly afraid to do anything too quickly.

"Give me one reason not to lay you down next to him," Covas said.

"The only reason you had to kill me is dead," Malone said. "You're not going to order your troops to burn this place down. Not when you can lay your arms down and walk out of here in one piece."

Covas's lip twitched. "That a fact."

"Just like you said. This was only ever about Sato."

Malone watched as Covas slowly lowered her weapon. Her men did the same.

Sato's blood spilled into a widening pool on the floor. Outside, the fires burned on.

Jane was separated from Roman for the train ride to Recoletta. When the train finally rolled to a stop in a wrecked station, she was dragged out to follow Ruthers's honor guard along the outskirts of the Vineyard to Dominari Hall. Recoletta seemed strange and unfamiliar, though perhaps not as much as she'd expected. In her absence, her imagination had constructed impossible new landscapes from the rumors and fables she'd heard of Recoletta's famine, chaos, and ruin. In the end, all she saw was a tired and half-deserted city.

The trip was brief but tense. Most of Sato's troops were rumored to have followed him to the Library, and those that remained were spread thin around the city. The civilians seemed to have taken shelter in their homes.

Once in Dominari Hall, she and Roman were separated again, and she was locked away in a small office that had been cleared of all but a few chairs and a desk that must have been too heavy to move. It worried her, but she realized that what frightened her most was being tucked away with no clue as to what plans were being made, what outcomes discussed.

Roman's fate, at least in the near term, seemed clear. Ruthers would secure him somewhere to keep him safe and out of trouble until they could travel to the vault. Despite the older man's previous threat, Jane didn't think he'd run the risk of killing Roman until he'd gotten what he needed.

Her future, however, was uncertain. At any rate, she was beyond hoping for reciprocal mercy from Ruthers.

Several quiet hours blended together and brought no change – no interrogations, no guards, not even the sound of stray footsteps outside her door. Jane began to think she'd been forgotten, that Ruthers and Roman had moved on to the vault and simply left her there.

When the door to her room finally opened, the last person she expected to see was Freddie.

She blinked, saying nothing, certain that he'd somehow been brought to join her as a captive. But he opened the door wider and motioned for her to follow him out.

"What on earth are you doing here?" she asked, following.

"Nice to see you, too," he said. "Now hurry up before we both get stuck in here."

She followed him into a hall and around a corner. There were no guards to be seen, but she didn't dare speak until Freddie had led them into a narrow servants' corridor and sighed more dramatically than was strictly necessary.

"Should be safe enough here for us to catch our breath," he said.

"What are you talking about? And how did you get here?"

He sighed again, as if she were being impossibly stupid. "Please. I heard the newsroom rumors about two Recolettan prisoners before you'd even left town."

"But that doesn't explain–"

Fredrick rolled his eyes. "Just back the way we came. Except I hopped a train this time." He leaned in. "I told you that was faster."

"And no one stopped you on the way in?"

"The point is to avoid Ruthers's men, not to ask them for a proper welcome," Fredrick said.

"I know! I just..." She took a deep breath. "I'm happy to see you."

"Likewise. But consider this me returning the favor from all those months ago. In the future, we'll both try to avoid these situations."

"Fine," Jane said, at last feeling the first warm stirrings of relief.

"Now, let's get out of here. Should be able to head back this way," he said, turning deeper into the servants' corridor.

But as she lingered there, she felt the walls of the corridor suddenly tight around her. From where she stood, the torchlit corridor seemed to terminate in a dead end. "Where are we going?" Jane asked.

"I told you, back this way. It was mostly clear when–"

"No, I mean when we get out of Dominari Hall. Where can we go? Back to Madina? To our old apartments here?"

"We can worry about that when we've gotten away from this place," he said, irritation creeping into his voice.

Her objections caught in her throat, and she followed him further down the hall, swallowing her misgivings.

They turned a corner and came to a door. Fredrick nudged it open and peered out, cursing.

"What is it?" Jane asked, already guessing.

"Guards. They weren't there before." As if it made any difference now.

"So what now?"

"Uh, back. The way we came." He scratched his head. "There's a flight of stairs from this tunnel, but they only lead further down."

In other words, deeper into Dominari Hall.

They scurried through the corridor and back to the hallway where Freddie had first appeared, and when he peeked through the door and stiffened, Jane knew what he saw.

"More guards," he said. "And from the looks of things, they've found your room."

"The stairs, then," Jane said, already turning back to the tunnel.

Fredrick winced. "But that'll only take us–"

"We've got no choice."

They headed back to the middle of the corridor, where a wide set of stairs led to the lower levels and main offices of Dominari Hall.

The next floor down seemed quiet. The torchlit corridor continued on in both directions, but Jane saw a door only a dozen feet to her left, and she turned towards it.

"Wait," Fredrick said, his hand on her shoulder. "Let me take a look first."

It didn't seem to matter which of them did it, but she was too tired to argue, and so she stepped back. He eased the door open and looked around. "Looks clear," he said. "I'm going to see–"

A noise like thunder sounded from within the room. It was so loud and so unexpected that Jane at first didn't know what to make of it.

But Fredrick's knees buckled and he fell forward, and she understood.

Instinctively, she ducked. Voices shouted from the other end of the room. It was too dark for her to see where they were coming from, but they sounded like they were still a dozen yards away.

She looked at the motionless body in the doorway that her brain only dimly registered as Fredrick. She fled.

Jane ran back to the stairwell and took the steps two and three at a time. She had no thought of where she was going, just somewhere away from Fredrick and their attackers.

She turned into another corridor on a lower level and stopped long enough to catch her breath. Voices echoed down to her from two floors up, muffled and distorted.

Jane took a deep, shuddering breath and tried to focus on escape.

There was another door at the end of this corridor, not far. She reached it with quick, soft steps and put her ear to it. Silence.

She hesitated, but only a moment. The noises two floors up had shifted from arguing voices to pounding feet.

She cracked the door and peered into a hall much like the one she'd left. It looked deserted. There was nothing to do but go.

Jane turned into the hall and eased the door shut behind her. The space felt too wide and too open, and a feeling of vulnerability prickled at her from all sides. She moved forward in an awkward, halting manner, caught between competing urges to run and to crouch and hide. But gaslights bounced off of clean, white tiles, casting no shadows.

A set of double doors huddled in a nearby alcove. Jane had turned the knob before she could stop herself, and so she froze, gripping the polished brass and waiting for someone to descend on her.

But no one did. When she finally worked up the nerve to ease the door open, she found nothing but a dark and empty office on the other side.

She took a deep breath and vowed to be more careful.

Jane continued on to another set of doors. This time, she noticed a keyhole, yawning and lined with brass. With a final glance down the hall, she knelt and peered inside.

The keyhole gave her a surprisingly clear view of the room beyond. Like the last, it was mostly dark – only a few scattered radiance stones showed her the outline of chairs and a long, rectangular meeting table. She was sorely tempted to seek safety inside, but she didn't need a place to hide. She needed a way out.

Jane looked down the hall, which turned a sharp corner four doors away. It was certainly no worse than any other option.

She continued onward with only the briefest glances at the doors she passed.

Just as she was about to turn the corner, she heard a cough. Looking to her left, she noticed light spilling from beneath the final door. With a silent gasp, she flew around the adjacent corner and waited, listening.

She heard nothing else. She wondered if she'd imagined the noise.

After several seconds of waiting, her curiosity got the better of her. Perhaps it was unnecessary, but a part of her wanted to know it was nothing. Peace of mind suddenly felt like a precious commodity.

Jane shimmied back along the wall and knelt in front of the door, gazing through the keyhole.

The room was empty – no desk, no chairs, no carpet – except for a man.

Roman sat on the floor, his legs crossed and his wrists manacled together. He raised his head and looked up, not quite at her but close enough to pretend.

Something – bitter anger or bitter relief – warmed behind her eyes. She shook with a sudden, unexpected sob and raised her hand to the doorknob.

And stopped. And watched.

Roman's hair hung about his shoulders, loose and unkempt. Behind it was a purpling eye, and beneath it a jacket ripped at the shoulders.

She had no key for the door, no pick for his manacles, and nothing for the small army that encircled them both. He was still trapped, and she was just as alone.

Jane heard a small ruckus from further down the hall, back in the direction of the servants' corridor she'd left. She hurried back around the corner, her steps swift and silent.

The hall emptied into a lobby of sorts, a spacious rectangular room paneled with painted wood and portraits of long-dead councilors. It sprouted broad hallways in front of and behind her and two narrower halls on either side. She took a left into one of the small hallways and away from the curve of her own.

She was beginning to realize that Dominari Hall was bigger than she'd thought. She missed the familiar, labyrinthine corridors of the Majlis. At least there she'd had the benefit of a disguise.

As she turned into yet another paneled hallway, she realized she had little idea of where she was going and no clue as to whether it led out of or deeper into Dominari Hall.

The other notion that struck her was the stark absence of guards. It felt almost as if the place were deserted.

That meant two things, she realized. First, she stood a better chance of escape than she'd thought. Second, if Ruthers's forces were limited, they were likelier than not to have clustered near the exits and the main thoroughfares.

It at least gave her a place to start.

Jane crept back towards a wider corridor and realized that she could hear the moderately distant sounds of activity through the walls – the low murmurs of conversation, the muffled clatter of feet. She followed the sounds.

A few more halls and a flight of stairs later, she found herself outside a winged gallery lined with fluted columns. It certainly seemed like a way out.

No sooner had she gotten a good look at the place than she heard footsteps echoing toward her. She retreated back around a corner and into an alcove and waited.

Eventually, the melody of distorted voices joined the slow cadence of footsteps. Jane waited and listened, and as the patrol drew nearer to the end of the gallery, their shadows growing and solidifying on the wall opposite Jane, the voices resolved into fragments of a conversation.

"...doing here," one voice muttered.

"Orders of the chancellor himself," said another. "I don't question those."

The two men's voices were thick with the brogue of the Hollow, but Jane had heard enough of the accent by now to discern their conversation well enough.

"I'm not questioning the orders, just the intent," said the first man. "What does the chancellor – or either of the other two, for that matter – want with this Ruthers character?"

"Someone to clean this place up," the other man said, his shadow flickering against the wall. "You saw it on the way in."

"And I also saw how few of us the chancellor sent. Barely enough to hold this place."

"Because there's no one to hold it from. That Sato character ran and hid in the Library. Besides," the second man said as both turned the corner. "Our friend here. What's his name."

"Ruthers."

Jane circled behind the marble pedestal as the two guards drew nearer.

"Ruthers didn't want this to look like some foreign invasion. Not after Sato's foreign invasion."

"Speaking of the man, where is he? Ruthers, I mean."

"Holding court somewhere on the top floor. A few of his old cronies wanted to congratulate him on getting his old job back and see if they could get theirs. That's what I heard, anyway," said the second man.

"And I'll bet you he's handing those jobs out like candy, if only to make sure that he's got enough support to keep his." The first speaker paused as two sets of footsteps passed Jane's position. "Which brings me back to my first question."

"When's dinner?"

"No. Why do our chiefs care one way or the other about this guy?"

"Let's just finish the round. Right now, all I've got room to think about is dinner."

Jane listened to their footsteps recede down the hall and around another corner before daring a peek from her hiding place. When she saw the way was clear, she hurried back to the gallery.

An idea was forming in her mind. Not quite a plan, but the outlines of one. She only hoped it would take shape while there was still time to act.

She scuttled along through the wings of the gallery, and by the time she emerged on the other side, the sounds of a gathering were clear enough. Something down the main hall and off of yet another tributary corridor. It was easy enough to avoid.

There was open space up ahead. A wide lobby with a grand stairwell if she was even half lucky. As a lifelong city dweller, she could feel the subtle changes in the shape of a space in the drafts on her skin.

But there were voices, and they were headed toward her.

She ducked into a room on her right – she didn't have time to check it first.

Jane found herself enveloped in darkness. She backed away from the door and into a closet as the voices drew closer, passed outside the door, and moved on. Only when they faded to a distant echo did she feel herself breathe again.

Jane stepped out of the closet and took stock of her surroundings. The faint light of radiance stones showed her an office that had been commandeered for haphazard storage – crates were clustered in one corner of the room, and jackets, belts, and other fragments of uniforms had been strewn across a long desk.

As she moved toward the door, something gleamed atop one of the gray jackets. She looked again and saw a gun.

It was a revolver, dull chrome with dark wood stocks. It felt heavy in her hands, yet the weight was somehow familiar.

She took it and tucked it away, not yet certain what she could even use it for but feeling that it would be foolish to pass it up.

Jane left her hiding spot and moved back toward the lobby. Just as she'd hoped, the wide arms of a grand staircase opened around her as if in greeting. She took the steps two at a time and almost cried with relief when a wide, carpeted hallway – one she recognized from her last and only visit to Dominari Hall – stretched out before her.

She was so close to escape. She had to will herself to keep from breaking into a sprint. If there were guards anywhere, they were bound to be here.

Sure enough, she heard more footsteps approaching the bend

in the hall, and she ducked through an open doorway.

The sound faded more quickly than she'd expected, and it was only then that she stopped to take stock of her surroundings.

The office was larger than the last few she'd been in, with a soaring ceiling, lush carpets, and curtained windows that looked out onto a small atrium. The gas lamps were turned up, and, more concerning, a leather briefcase sat open next to the desk.

There was another doorway at the far end of the office. A more inconspicuous exit, perhaps. She eased the door behind her closed and hurried towards it.

She reached the door only to find herself face to face with Councilor Augustus Ruthers.

He smiled.

"You have an uncanny way of showing up at the most interesting times," he said.

Jane backed away, tingling with fear, confusion, and a bizarre sense of déjà vu.

"I'm afraid you won't get out that way," he said, tilting his head back at the door behind him. "Though I am curious to hear how you got this far."

Jane knew whitenails well enough to hold her tongue until he'd gestured at her with one long-nailed hand.

"Carefully," she said.

He laughed, his lined face strangely fierce. "You've proven most surprising. You can't imagine my shock when I learned that you'd wormed your way into the Qadi's confidences." He sauntered over to the desk. "You may as well sit."

She did.

"Then again," he said, "you managed to do the same with my nephew."

"Nephew," Jane said, feeling something begin to boil inside her. "You mean the man you've betrayed and imprisoned here."

Ruthers scowled. "He was the one who betrayed me for Sato. You should remember that much."

"He'd never use anyone the way you're using him now," Jane said.

"My, but you put such trust in that man."

"Not nearly as much as you've put in the Qadi and her allies," Jane said. The growing sense that she had nothing much to lose filled her with unusual boldness.

"My allies," Ruthers said.

"For now. How does this work out for you, anyway? Is Recoletta supposed to welcome you back?"

"Actually, yes," Ruthers said. "You'd be surprised at how much people crave familiarity after something like Sato's mess."

"And what's to stop another Sato from rising up against you? Your allies in Madina and elsewhere won't keep fighting your battles."

"You think I don't know that?" he snapped. "This," he said, spreading his hands and gesturing at the office, "this is a balancing act. And one that's never more than a step or two from collapse. People like you, your parents – you think position is somehow a protection. A source of safety and comfort. That couldn't be further from the truth." Ruthers scowled, his face showing lines carved by years of slow but persistent pressures.

Just as quickly, his expression shifted again to that look of well-bred authority that all of Recoletta had known for years. "But once you're here, there's nowhere else to go," he said.

"But you have a plan. The vault," said Jane.

He nodded. "Sato and I are the last two people who know the code."

"Once it's open, you'll have outlived your usefulness," Jane said.

His smile flattened. "You should start worrying about yourself, Miss Lin."

Jane looked at her hands, two empty and useless appendages in her lap. "What's going to happen to Roman and me?"

"That's a matter of some debate. The Qadi's fond of you, but

O'Brien would just as soon not take any chances. Roman will last at least as long as I need in order to access the vault. And you will last as least as long as needed to keep Roman under control. I'm afraid I can't guarantee more than that, even considering your previous mercies."

She remembered that moment in another room not far from here, a gun in her hand but mercy in her heart. She had let Ruthers go, thinking that it would free both Roman and herself from haunting guilt and not realizing that it would imprison them both in other ways.

The revolver shifted in her robes and nudged her hip, as if reminding her of its presence.

She realized, too, that she hadn't heard any noise in the hall since stepping into the room. It seemed suddenly curious that Ruthers hadn't summoned any guards.

Ruthers had read the emotion flickering across her face. Misread it, it seemed. He leaned forward, interlacing his fingers. "Understand that it's nothing personal. Merely the way of things. That's what separates my class from yours, you know. It's not intelligence or diligence, as many of my peers have often suggested. It's the ability to recognize what must be done and to do it, no matter the cost."

Jane understood. Over what felt like an eternity, she reached into her robes and grabbed the revolver, wrapping her fingers around the textured stocks. She raised it, feeling the strange balance of the thing in her hand.

Yet Ruthers did nothing. He watched her with polite, even indulgent, amusement. "What is it you hope to accomplish this time?"

Jane thumbed the hammer back.

Ruthers chuckled.

"What's in the vault?" she asked. The question surprised even her, but the currency of information was familiar to her now.

"Does it matter?"

It did not. She fired.

Pressing her finger on the trigger took more effort than she'd expected yet not as much as she felt it should, given the consequences. Yet even as she squeezed the trigger, dragging the microseconds into an arduous procession, Ruthers waited patiently.

It was only as the bullet lodged beneath his sternum that she saw other emotions bloom from his dry confidence – doubt, surprise, and horror.

Distantly, Jane knew that it had all happened in a matter of seconds, that the slow unraveling was a trick of the mind to assign order to chaos. The bullet had found its mark before there was a chance to consider the consequence of the choice.

Ruthers slumped forward in his chair with a strangled groan. He stirred, bringing his hand to his chest. It came away red, and he laughed.

Jane looked at the revolver, torn between impulses to hide it and to fire it again. The first inklings of doubt had begun to creep into her mind. She barred the door against them, focusing on the red between Ruthers's teeth as he looked up at her, on the blue veins popping out from his old man's hands, on the minute asymmetries of his pharaoh's beard.

Anything to keep from thinking about what she'd just done and whether she should have done it.

He looked then from his hand back to her. He smiled as if he saw her doubt like nakedness.

"You wanted to know about the vault," he said, coughing. "Let me tell you a story."

A part of Jane knew that she shouldn't listen. And yet another part of her craved anything to distract her from the doubt already festering in her conscience. Besides, there was nowhere to go, and she had never turned down an opportunity to listen in on good information.

"Two, eleven, one-oh-one. The first three primes of one, two, and three digits. There once was a young lady who made a terrible choice to destroy a secret, only to become the last person who knew it. The code is two-one-one-one-zero-one. Absurdly simple, isn't it?" He coughed. "It had to be memorable. Whoever built the vault was, no doubt, counting on the other safeguards to bar it off. Or maybe they wanted it to be found, the way you want someone to find your deepest, darkest secrets to save you the trouble of guarding them. It's easier letting these things into the open, isn't it? Easier to let go of these veneers of civility. There's a catharsis in letting it go, a relief in letting it pass to someone else." His eyelids fluttered and his voice faded.

He laughed, blood bubbling between his lips. "Well, Jane. Now you know. And what are you going to do with that? How badly do you want to take that knowledge out of the world?" He grinned, his teeth like little pearls etched in blood.

Just then, Bailey and a guard burst into the room. "Augustus, what's going on in here? We heard–"

They stopped, and Ruthers looked away from Jane and over her shoulder at the newcomers. His face was milk-pale, and his eyes rolled with the first signs of delirium.

As the others pounded into the room and toward the desk, Ruthers looked back at Jane and smiled again, and she hoped fiercely that he would die before the others reached him. To her surprise, she realized that, if she had another ready shot and another frozen capsule of time, she'd shoot him again.

Bailey and the guard knelt by Ruthers's side, feeling his wattled, sweat-slicked neck for a pulse, pressing Bailey's jacket into a useless bunch against his wound. Ruthers only winced.

He looked at Jane one last time, but whatever he'd begun to say was no more than a garbled death rattle.

Bailey and the guard looked back at her, and Jane felt as though they could see that dark core of her secret the same way Ruthers saw her guilt.

The guard spoke first. "She–"

"Yes," Bailey said.

"Sir, he's dead. That means Sato–"

"Is the last one who knows the code. Run."

The guard was on his feet and out the door, not sparing a glance back at the prone body.

Bailey looked back at Jane. "Do you have any idea what you've done?"

But her eyes were fixed on Ruthers's as she made sure they didn't open again.

"This changes everything," Bailey said.

ACKNOWLEDGMENTS

As a new author, I told myself that getting my first book published was the real test. If I could just get one out the door, it would all be downhill from there. How wrong I was. *Cities and Thrones* was a challenge and a joy to write, full of false starts and leaps of faith. I'd like to thank the family, friends, and colleagues who helped me celebrate the good and work through the bad.

First of all, thanks to agent extraordinaire Jennie Goloboy as well as Dawn Frederick and Laura Zats of Red Sofa Literary. Jennie's calm, seasoned advice and her help with the business side of writing have been invaluable.

It was a pleasure to work with Angry Robot again on this book and to feel their enthusiasm for it. I count myself fortunate to have found a publisher full of passionate people willing to take risks, and my special thanks go out to editor Phil Jourdan for his insightful feedback, Caroline Lambe and Penny Reeve for all things publicity, and Mike Underwood for all things, period. I'm grateful as well to Marc Gascoigne and Lee Harris for inviting me to join Team Robot a year and a half ago.

One of the joys of becoming a writer is meeting and befriending others with the same passion. I've met so many wonderful people over the past year, and in particular I'd like to thank Tex Thompson for her sassy good sense and eleventh-hour advice; Wes Chu,

Craig Cormick, and Anne Lyle for reaching out to a newbie; and Dan Bensen, Paul Krueger, Dan Koboldt, and Jamie Wyman for their support and friendship.

I couldn't have finished *Cities and Thrones* without the thoughtful criticism of my regular critique group, which includes Jacqui Talbot, Michael Robertson, Bill Stiteler, and Joy Johnson. I'm blessed to have had them with me since *The Buried Life*.

Thank you also to the wonderful team at Obsidian Entertainment. I'm lucky to have two of the best gigs in the world, and doubly so to be surrounded by such talented and hardworking people.

Most importantly, thank you to my family for their love, encouragement, and patience. Thank you to Richard and Jackie Lytle, Pravinchandra and Sonal Patel, Julie Lytle, Ryan and Sydney Thompson, and Hiren Patel most of all.

ABOUT THE AUTHOR

Carrie Patel was born and raised in Houston, Texas, in the USA. An avid traveller, she studied abroad in Granada, Spain, and Buenos Aires, Argentina. She completed her bachelor's and master's degrees at Texas A&M University and worked in transfer pricing at Ernst & Young for two years.

She now works as a narrative designer at Obsidian Entertainment in Irvine, California, where the only season is Always Perfect.

electronicinkblog.com • twitter.com/carrie_patel